ALSO BY MARY KAY ANDREWS

The Newcomer

Hello, Summer

The High Tide Club

The Beach House Cookbook

The Weekenders

Beach Town

Save the Date

Christmas Bliss

Ladies' Night

Spring Fever

Summer Rental

The Fixer Upper

Deep Dish

Savannah Breeze

Blue Christmas

Hissy Fit

Little Bitty Lies

Savannah Blues

Sunset Beach

Mary Kay Andrews

St. Martin's Paperbacks

This is a work of fiction. All of the characters, organizations, and events portrayed in this novel are either products of the author's imagination or are used fictitiously.

Published in the United States by St. Martin's Paperbacks, an imprint of St. Martin's Publishing Group

SUNSET BEACH

For information, address St. Martin's Publishing Group, 120 Broadway, New York, NY 10271.

www.stmartins.com

Library of Congress Catalog Card Number: 2019003126

ISBN: 978-1-250-12612-2

Our books may be purchased in bulk for promotional, educational, or business use. Please contact your local bookseller or the Macmillan Corporate and Premium Sales Department at 1-800-221-7945, ext. 5442, or by email at MacmillanSpecialMarkets@macmillan.com.

Printed in the United States of America

St. Martin's Griffin edition / April 2020
St. Martin's Paperbacks edition 2021

10 9 8 7 6 5 4 3 2 1

Dedicated with thanks and love to Meghan Walker,
on the tenth anniversary of a great working partnership,
with thanks for helping advance my evil plot
for total global domination.

Acknowledgments

Writing *Sunset Beach* literally took me home to my roots and the Gulf beaches of St. Petersburg, Florida. The Sunset Beach of this novel is a highly fictionalized version of the real community of Sunset Beach, but my affection for those same beaches and their residents is real and enduring. I owe a debt of thanks to all who helped with the research for this book, especially Andrew Payne, whose innocent answer to a nosy question several years ago sparked the idea for this book. Huge thanks go out to my friends Phil Secrest and Melissa Post for their invaluable help and advice. Lawyer types who patiently answered questions include Joe Bayliss, David Eicholz, Beth Fleishman, Jean Higham, and Howard Spiva. Retired St. Petersburg Police Detective Ralph Pflieger and retired Atlanta Police Homicide Captain G. M. Lloyd helped with the cop stuff. Thanks to C. J. Case for giving me a glimpse into the world of kiteboarding, and for connecting me to kiteboarding pros India Stephenson and Claire Lutz. Marianne Bushman gave physical therapy advice for rehabbing a blown-out kiteboarding knee, and Diane Kaufman offered insight into hotel back-of-house operations. Jay and Linda Mastry, of Mastry's Bar and Grill in downtown St. Petersburg, assisted in a fun trip down memory lane. I'm also grateful for Judy Trew and Danielle Thompson, who purchased naming honors with their generous donations to the American Heart Association at the Southern Coast Heart Ball.

As always, I'm eternally thankful for the skills and enthusiasm of my entire publishing team: literary agent Stuart Krichevsky at SKLA; marketing guru Meghan Walker of Tandem Literary; and of course, my publishers at St. Martin's Press: Sally Richardson and Jennifer Enderlin. *Sunset Beach* marks my tenth book with this dynamic duo, and I'll forever be grateful for that long-ago meeting at the Flatiron Building. Many thanks and love go out to the whole St. Martin's team— especially Jessica Zimmerman, Tracey Guest, Erica Martirano, Brant Janeway, and art director Michael Storrings for always giving me the perfect book cover.

It goes without saying, but I'll say it anyway that I'm nothing without the love and support of my family: my husband, Tom; daughter, Katie; son-in-law Mark; Andrew, and the grandest grandkids ever, Molly and Griffin.

1

Sunset Beach, April 2018

Drue turned the key in the ignition and the white Bronco's engine gave a dispirited cough, and then nothing.

"Come on, OJ," Drue muttered, trying again. This time the engine turned over. She gave it some gas and the motor roared to life.

"Thanks, babe." She gave the cracked vinyl dashboard an encouraging pat, then shifted into reverse and eased her foot onto the accelerator. The motor gave a strangled wheeze and cut off again. Now every single indicator on the control panel began blinking red.

She tried again, but the third time was not the charm. The engine caught briefly, the Bronco's battered chassis shuddered, then fell still.

"Noooooo," she moaned.

She glanced down at her watch. She now had fifteen minutes to get downtown to work. "No way," she muttered.

Back when life was good, when she was living in Fort Lauderdale, she would have taken an Uber or called a friend for a lift when the 1995 Bronco she'd bought off Craigslist was having what Drue thought of as PMS. But she hadn't exactly had time to make friends since moving back to Florida's west coast, and she no longer had a viable credit card for Uber, or even viable credit, for that matter.

Drue had a vague memory of seeing city buses lumbering past on nearby Gulf Boulevard. She pulled her phone from her backpack, found the transit authority website and schedule, and determined that with any luck, she just might catch a bus that might get her to the downtown St. Petersburg offices of Campbell, Coxe and Kramner in the next thirty minutes. Which would make her late for her first day of work.

She started walking. It was barely eight-thirty, and only April, but the temperature already hovered in the mid-eighties, and within two blocks of leaving her house, her cotton tank top was damp with perspiration and her right knee was throbbing.

Shit. She should have gone back to the house and put on the tight elastic brace the surgeon had given her. In fact, she should have been wearing it anyway, even if she hadn't had to walk five blocks. But the damn thing was so hot. The elastic chafed her skin and gave her a rash, so she left it at home more times than she wore it.

Drue gritted her teeth against the pain and kept walking. She was on Gulf Boulevard now, the busy north–south thoroughfare that threaded through all the tiny beach towns before eventually making a sharp right turn at Treasure Island Causeway, heading east toward downtown St. Pete. A clutch of giggling teenage girls, spring breakers, probably, dressed in bikini tops and microscopic neon-bright shorts with the waistbands rolled down to their navels, approached on the sidewalk, headed in the opposite direction, and made an elaborate show of sidestepping her.

She heard a quavery voice behind her.

"Excuse me, darling." She turned her head to see an elderly man, his bony bare chest glistening with sweat, power past, pumping small dumbbells in each hand.

She squinted and saw, just half a block ahead, the shaded bus shelter. Thank God. She wasn't sure if she could walk much farther. Half a block, though. That, she could do. She picked up the pace, trying to ignore the red-hot stabbing pain in her knee.

Briiiing, briiinnng, a bike's bell and then a booming woman's voice: "On your left!"

She stumbled over her flip-flop and toppled onto the grassy verge just in time to avoid being mowed down by a white-haired octogenarian wearing wraparound sunglasses and a Tampa Bay Rays sun visor furiously pedaling past on an adult tricycle.

"Hey!" Drue yelled after her. "Get on the bike path."

"Up yours," the woman called, turning around briefly to flip her the bird.

As she struggled to her feet, she saw, almost in slow motion, the city bus passing her by. She winced in pain, but also at the ad emblazoned along the side of the bus.

SLIP AND FALL? GIVE BRICE A CALL! The ad was accompanied by a five-foot-tall airbrush-enhanced color portrait of W. Brice Campbell, arms crossed defiantly, his chiseled chin jutting pugnaciously, a stance Drue knew all too well.

The bus slowed momentarily at the bus stop. The air brakes whooshed. "Stay there," Drue muttered. "Stay right there." She broke into her current version of a run, a lopsided, sorry, limping affair.

A young Hispanic woman stepped off the bus, turned, and waved goodbye to the driver.

"Hey," Drue yelled breathlessly, closing the gap, now maybe only three bus-lengths away. She waved her arms over her head. "Hey!"

The woman turned and gave the stranger a hesitant smile. "Hey."

The bus's brakes whooshed again and it started to move.

"Tell him to stop," Drue cried. "Tell him to wait."

But it was too late. The bus picked up speed. It moved on. The woman stood by the bus shelter. She was dressed in a gray and white uniform smock, her name, Sonia, embroidered above her left breast.

"Sorry," she said softly, as Drue approached, limping badly. "Are you okay?"

Drue grasped the back of the bench as she tried to regain her breath. The bench was painted blue and white, with the Campbell, Coxe and Kramner signature logo superimposed across Brice Campbell's visage. HAVE A WRECK? WE'LL GET YOUR CHECK!

"No," Drue managed, as she collapsed onto the bench. She

jumped up immediately, gingerly extracting a half-inch wood splinter protruding from her right butt cheek. "No. Definitely. Not. Okay." She looked down at the screen-printed face of Brice W. Campbell. Her new boss. Her long-lost father, and as always, a major pain in the ass.

A job in his law firm had been the very last thing Drue had wanted from her long-estranged father. But what choice did she have? That five-second midair kiteboard collision three months earlier, and her mother's subsequent death, only reinforced the fact that she no longer had any reason to stay in Fort Lauderdale.

Drue had been adrift, self-medicating with tequila and Advil and wallowing in self-pity on the day of her mother's funeral. As she was leaving the memorial service, with the bronze urn containing Sherri's remains tucked under her arm, she'd been shocked to spot a well-dressed businessman standing uneasily at the back of the church.

At first, she wasn't even absolutely sure it was really him. His hair was longer, touching the collar of his open-neck shirt, and flecked with silver. He was tanned and slim, and in his expensive tailored blazer and sockless Gucci loafers looked distinctly out of place in the former fast-food restaurant turned Fortress for All Faiths Chapel of Prayer.

She approached him warily. "Dad?"

"Hi," he'd said softly, giving her an awkward hug.

She'd endured the embrace with what she thought was admirable forbearance.

"What are you doing here?"

He shifted from one foot to the other. "Why wouldn't I be here?"

"I mean, how did you know? That Mom died? I didn't even put an obituary in the paper until today."

"Sherri called me. To tell me she was sick. And I asked the hospice people to let me know . . . when it happened." He glanced around the church, which was nearly empty now. "Look, can we go somewhere else to talk about this?"

"Like where?" Drue wasn't about to let him off that easy. Twenty years ago, he'd shipped his sullen teenage daughter across Florida, from St. Pete back here to Lauderdale, choosing peace with his second wife and her obnoxious sons over loyalty to his only daughter. He'd dutifully sent the birthday cards and child support checks right up until her eighteenth birthday, but she hadn't laid eyes on him since that boiling hot summer afternoon so long ago. She wasn't about to let him waltz in here today and play the grieving dad and ex-spouse.

"I thought maybe we could go to lunch somewhere." His blue-gray eyes took in her frumpy black dress, the only remotely funeral-ready dress she owned, and the too-large black pumps, which she'd appropriated from Sherri's closet.

"Why?"

He let out a long, aggravated sigh. "Why? Because your mom is gone and I'm now your only living relative. And because there are some business matters we need to discuss. Okay? Can you just cut me some slack and go to lunch? Or do you really need to keep busting my balls for the rest of my life?"

She shrugged. "I guess I could do lunch. Where do you want to go?"

"I heard there's a bistro on Las Olas that has great mussels."

"Taverna." Why was she not surprised that he'd chosen the most exclusive, expensive restaurant in town?

Outside, in the parking lot, Brice pointed a key fob at a black Mercedes sedan and clicked it. Drue went to the backseat and opened the door.

He stood by the driver's side, looking puzzled. "You're getting in the backseat?"

"No," Drue said, carefully stretching the seat belt across the bronze urn. "Mom is."

When the waitress brought their drinks Drue knocked back half her margarita in one gulp.

Brice sipped his martini and rearranged the silverware on the tabletop.

"Can I ask you something without your getting pissed at me?"

"Maybe."

He pointed at her right leg, with the knee ensconced in the hideous brace.

"What happened there?"

"I had a kiteboarding accident. Right after Mom got diagnosed."

"So you're still into that? Guess it wasn't a phase after all, huh?"

Kiteboarding had been a major source of friction between Drue and Brice and her stepmother. Joan had objected to the cost of her board and kite (although it was money Drue earned from working at a surf shop), her kiteboarding friends (an admittedly motley-looking crew) and, especially, her obsession with the sport—to the detriment of her already mediocre grades.

Drue chewed the inside of her cheek. "Definitely not a phase. How is Joan, by the way?"

He picked the olive from his drink, chewed, and smiled bitterly. "Let's see. She soaked me for a waterfront house, a new car and attorney's fees to keep both Kyler and Kayson out of prison. Last I heard she'd moved up the marital food chain and married an orthopedic surgeon. So, I'd say she's doing great."

"So you two split up? Sorry to hear that."

He sipped his martini. "No, you're not."

"That's true. She never liked me, and the feeling was mutual."

He started to say something, stopped, shook his head and took another sip of his martini.

"You said you had some business to discuss with me?" Drue prompted.

"That's right." He reached into the inside pocket of his blazer and brought out a key ring with a tacky pink plastic flamingo fob. Two keys dangled from the ring. He slid the key ring across the table toward his daughter.

"What's this?"

"It's the key to Coquina Cottage."

"Nonni and Papi's house? The old place on Sunset Beach? I thought Mom sold it after Nonni died."

"She almost did, but in the end, she decided to keep it. I think maybe she thought one day the two of you would move back and live there. Anyway, it's yours now."

Drue picked up the key ring and turned it over and over. "You're serious? For real? Like, I own Papi's cottage?"

"You do," Brice said. "Before you get too excited, though, I should warn you it's in pretty rough shape. The last tenant lived there for six or seven years, and he was kind of a hoarder. He always paid his rent on time and never had any complaints about the place, so I sort of let things slide. It wasn't until last year, after the hurricane damaged the roof and the old guy moved out, that we realized how bad things had gotten."

Drue's eyes filled with unexpected tears. "Mom never said a word. All those years, she drove crappy secondhand cars and we lived in shithole apartments. She could have sold that place—it's right on the Gulf, right? I bet it was worth a lot of money. I can't believe she hung on to Papi's house."

"Your mom was never the sentimental type, as you know, but I think she regarded the cottage as her legacy to you. It was the one thing of value in her life. Well, that and her daughter."

Not trusting herself to speak, Drue could only stare down at the keys.

"What are your plans now?" Brice asked.

"I don't know," she admitted. "Things are kind of up in the air right now."

"Sherri said you've been waitressing at a bar?"

"That's right."

His raised eyebrow spoke volumes.

"And . . . no romantic ties keeping you here in Fort Lauderdale?"

She scowled. Since Trey, her faithless boyfriend, had been

a no-show at the funeral, she'd already relegated him to ex-boyfriend status. "Are you deliberately gloating over the fact that I'm thirty-six and have a shitty job and no life?"

He raised his hands in surrender. "I was going to offer you a job, but obviously that's a deeply offensive move on my part."

"A job? Doing what?"

"Working at the law firm. We've affiliated with half a dozen boutique personal injury firms in the Southeast in the past year. Business is crazy good. Another firm in town just poached my most senior intake associate. I'm really shorthanded."

"No thanks," Drue said firmly. "I have no interest in moving back to St. Pete and zero interest in the law."

"You mean, zero interest in working for me."

Her eyes met his. "That too. Sorry. I mean, I appreciate the offer. And your coming over for Mom's funeral. And letting me know about the cottage. Thanks. I really mean it." She looked down at her watch. "Can you get the check now? I've got to work tonight."

He let out a long sigh. "You're as goddamn stubborn as she was. More, even."

"I'll take that as a compliment," Drue said.

2

It was her first night back at work since the surgery, and it was also two-dollar well drink night at Bozo's on the Beach. As luck would have it, the first person she saw as she was clocking in was Rick, the assistant night manager.

Prick, as most of the servers called him behind his back, was all of twenty-five years old and the owner's nephew, and roundly despised by the entire Bozo's staff, right down to the youngest high school busboy. He was just over five feet two, with a weirdly long over-muscled torso, rounded shoulders and short legs, which gave him the appearance of an orangutan in cargo shorts.

"Hey," he said, giving her a curt nod. "I see you're back."

"I am," she said, smiling brightly. "Thanks for letting me take a shift. I was going stir crazy sitting at home on the sofa."

He looked her up and down and frowned, noting the form-fitting orange tank top with the bar's clown logo and the ripped and faded jeans she wore instead of the hated mandatory Bozo's booty shorts. "You're out of uniform."

"Yeah," she said. "The thing is, I have to wear this big ugly knee brace, and it looks super freaky with the shorts. I'm wearing the top and I swear, nobody will even notice."

"That's not the point," he snapped. "It's a uniform because I want all the girls to look alike—hot. Those jeans don't look hot. They look ghetto." He ducked into the closet-size office, came out with a pair of the microscopic white knit shorts and tossed them to her. "Here. You can change before you go on shift."

Kaitlin, the lead bartender, came bustling into the kitchen. "Welcome back, girlfriend," she said, giving Drue a high five. "Now get your ass out there. Courtney's back in rehab and Shanelle called in pissed off, so we're short two girls tonight and the natives are restless."

Drue hustled out of the kitchen in her wake, turning to look over her shoulder at Rick. "Sorry. Duty calls."

Old-school rap music blared from the wall-mounted speakers and the Thirsty Thursday crowd was, as Kaitlin had warned, loud and demanding. The sprawling room was packed, the noise level ear-splitting.

"What's going on?" Drue asked, placing her lips beside Kaitlin's ear.

"Do you have to ask? Look around."

Drue estimated the average age in the room at 19.2 years. College kids, sunburned, buzzed and looking for fun in the Florida sun. She knew what that meant. Crappy tips and plenty of customers who thought dine and dash was an intramural sport. "Spring break? Already? It isn't even Easter yet."

"It comes earlier and earlier every year," Kaitlin said. "Hey, how'd you manage to ditch the crotch cutters tonight? Every time I come to work wearing normal pants Prick orders me to go home and change."

"He was about to make me change when you saved the day," Drue said. "I think the little perv gets off looking at camel toes."

"Ya think?" Kaitlin crossed her eyes and stuck out her tongue. "By the way, how's the knee?"

"Hurts like a mother," Drue said.

Kaitlin glanced around and lowered her voice. "I've got Percocet in my purse, if you want. My boyfriend had dental surgery and he saved 'em for me."

"I'd love a Percocet, but anything with codeine makes me puke. Advil's all I can take."

"Poor you," Kaitlyn said. "You're on station three, by the way."

"Got it." Drue headed out to her station, six four-tops and four six-tops.

The next two hours were a blur. She took orders, delivered drinks and dodged drunken gropes. At one point she fought her way through the crowd to the bathroom, locked herself in a stall, dropped her jeans and unfastened the brace. Her knee was red and swollen to the size of a cantaloupe. "Not good," she whispered.

She heard the bathroom door swing open with a bang. "Drue!" Prick's voice echoed in the tile-floored room. "Get out here, goddamnit! Your tables are backed up."

"Can I just pee in privacy?" she called, flushing the toilet.

"I'm not paying you to pee. Now get your ass out here and get to work."

"Hey!" screamed a petite blonde in an oversize sorority jersey, pelting Drue in the face with a soggy wadded-up paper napkin. "Hey! I mean, could we *finally* get some service over here?"

The napkin bounced off her forehead and onto the floor. Drue froze in her tracks as the blonde and her college pals around the table giggled and guffawed.

"What can I get you?" she asked.

"Um, well, a new attitude would be nice," the blonde shot back, tossing her hair over her shoulder. "I mean, don't y'all work for tips?"

Drue felt the blood rise in her cheeks. "What would you like?" she repeated.

The blonde pointed at the stacked-up empties on the tabletop. "So, I need two of these, and—"

"Could I see some ID, please?" Drue asked.

"What?"

"ID. Like a driver's license."

The girl pouted. "You're kidding, right?"

"Not at all."

"Oh, for God's sake," the girl exclaimed. "Look, I didn't bring a purse tonight, right? So I don't actually have my ID on me."

"How were you planning on paying for your drinks?" Drue asked.

The blonde gave an arch smile and turned toward the balding salesman sitting next to her. She flung an arm over his shoulder. "Oh, no worries. My new friend Sammy here is buying tonight. Right, Sammy?"

"Right," the salesman replied. "But, uh, it's Stanley. Not Sammy." He flipped a platinum Amex card onto the table. "Bring the lady whatever she wants."

"Sorry," Drue said. "But I can't serve her alcohol without a valid ID."

The girl half-rose from her seat, until her face was inches away from Drue's. "Look," she said, her voice soft. Her breath stank of rum and fruit juice. Her face was flushed, her eyes were glazed. "Don't be such a bitch. I need two of those strawberry thingies. Okay? Stanley's gonna take good care of you, you understand?"

Drue moved two inches backward. "I understand perfectly. And you need to understand that I still can't serve you alcohol. We both know you and your girlfriends here are underage."

The girl's face twisted in rage. "What the hell do you care? Are you a fucking cop?" Her high-pitched voice rose to a shriek. Heads turned, their eyes glued to the unfolding drama at table six. "Now go get my drink, bitch!"

Drue started to say something, but before she could respond, she felt a hand tighten on her upper arm.

It was Prick. "In my office. Now."

He turned to the table. "Sorry for the misunderstanding. I'll send somebody over with a round for the table. On the house."

They didn't make it all the way to the office. He turned to her just inside the doors to the kitchen. "What the hell?" he yelled. "You come in here tonight with a shitty attitude, out of uniform, but I cut you some slack because I feel sorry for you. Then you limp around out there like some kinda lame-ass zombie and spend half the night hiding out in the bathroom. Your job here is to smile and sling drinks, not get in a fight with the paying customers."

"I had to pee. One time. I was off the floor for five minutes. And that blond chick threw a napkin at me!" Drue protested. "Called me a bitch. And she was totally underage."

"I don't give a shit," Prick said, hands on his hips. "Go ahead and clock out. You're gone."

"You're firing me?"

"Damn straight."

"I'll go," she said, her voice steely. "But don't even think about trying to stiff me for my share of the tip-out tonight. With this crowd it should be at least two hundred bucks. And I'm not leaving here until I get my money."

"Fat chance," he said, sneering.

She ripped off her apron and tossed it in his face. "Two hundred dollars," she repeated. "In cash. Tonight." On a whim she pulled her cell phone from the pocket of her jeans and held it up for him to see. "Or I call the state beverage control board and text them photos of all the shit-faced underage Barbies in here tonight. And tomorrow night your spring break bonanza comes to a screeching halt."

Out in the parking lot, Drue smoothed the crumpled-up wads of bills on the front seat of the Bronco. The total came to exactly two hundred. She closed her eyes and rested her head on the steering wheel. The sobs came from deep down in her chest, wracking, choking, gasping, uncontrollable sobs. After what seemed like a long time, she sat back up, pulled the Bozo's tank top over her head, wiped her eyes and blew her nose on it. Then she tossed it out the window onto the parking lot pavement and drove home in her sports bra, which was more than a lot of women wore in Fort Lauderdale that time of year.

When she got home she sat alone in the dark for a long time in Sherri's nearly bare condo. Her mother had sold the furnished condo at the onset of her diagnosis to help pay her medical expenses, but the new owners, snowbirds from Michigan, had allowed the two women to stay on until the end of the month, which was fast approaching.

She'd donated all Sherri's personal effects to charity, and her own belongings were packed up too, awaiting the now-aborted move to Trey's place. Drue stretched out on the sofa, swallowed three Advil, and eventually drifted off to a troubled sleep.

She was skimming along the surface of the water, the sun at her back, her red-and-white-striped kite high in the air, her boots firmly planted on the board beneath her feet. When the moment came, she bent her knees, leaned back on her heels and suddenly, gloriously, she was aloft. She felt the familiar rush of adrenaline, heard her own heart pounding, the blood humming in her veins. In midair she looked around and then down, saw the bright blue curve of the ocean meeting sugary sand, tiny specks she knew to be people, toy-size cars in the parking lot.

Time and life stood still and she was flying—soaring past seagulls and pelicans and jet airplanes and billowing clouds. The wind was perfect and the kite kept her aloft, the longest hang-time ever. She closed her eyes, and then, in a split second, it happened. An arrow, a lightning bolt, a bullet, a knife blade, slashed at her right knee.

And then she was falling, endlessly spiraling down and down. She worked her feet out of the boots, feeling the board fall away. Frantically she thumbed the quick-release button on her harness again and again as the surface of the water grew nearer. She heard the splash of her body hitting the water, felt the impact on her chest and back and knees, the still-inflated kite dragging her face-first through the water, filling her eyes and nose and mouth and lungs with the burning salt water. Her body was broken and she was drowning . . .

Drue woke up, gasping for air, her body slick with sweat. She clawed at a clammy sheet that seemed to be dragging her back down beneath the surface of the water. "No, no, no," she heard herself whimper.

Freed of the sheet, she pushed herself up to a sitting position on the sofa, her chest heaving, pulse pounding. She fumbled around on the coffee table, found her phone, thumbed the home button. It was 2:15 A.M. There would be no more sleep tonight. She could never resume sleeping after the dream descended upon her in the night, which it did regularly.

She walked stiff-legged to the kitchen, found the bag of frozen peas in the freezer, and limped back to the sofa, where she extended her right knee and applied the makeshift ice pack.

She reached for the phone, scrolling through the list of contacts until she found his number, which he'd insisted on typing into it.

"No." Drue shook her head. She shoved the phone under the sofa cushion. Ten minutes later, she sighed and dug the phone out from its hiding place.

She tapped the text message into the phone. *Hey Dad. About that job?*

3

"This is a terrible idea," Drue muttered, as she approached the green stucco bungalow housing the law offices of Campbell, Coxe and Kramner. Several other homes on the quiet, tree-shaded street had also been converted to commercial space. She'd spotted a dentist's office, a title search company and three other law firms as she walked down the block from the bus stop, searching for the address Brice Campbell had texted her.

Their Friday-morning conversation had been brief. "You changed your mind!" Brice said when he called. "I mean, I'm glad, but frankly, I'm surprised."

"Me too," Drue told him. "Change of circumstances. So, when would you want me to start?"

"The sooner the better," Brice said. "As I said, we're short-handed and about to roll out a new ad campaign. Could you start Monday?"

"Why not? Uh, what about the cottage? Is it okay for me to go ahead and move in? I mean, you did say it's mine."

He hesitated. "It's yours, free and clear, but I don't think you want to stay there right away. I did tell you it's a wreck. But I guess you could stay with me until you've gotten the place cleaned up."

"Yeah, maybe." *Never gonna happen*, Drue told herself. "But tell me about the job, okay?"

"Sure. We'll start you off as an intake clerk on the Justice Line. We can discuss salary when you get into town, but I assure you, it'll be much more than you've been making waitressing. We have to be competitive to get the best kind of employees. You'll have full medical and dental benefits, of course."

"That sounds great," she managed. "So . . . I'll see you Monday. And, uh, what time should I show up?"

"The office opens at nine, but don't you want to maybe get together over the weekend?"

"No thanks," she said firmly. "I'm not sure how long it'll take me to wrap things up here in Lauderdale. I haven't even started packing yet."

"Okay, well, if you're sure." Brice sounded disappointed. "Call me when you get into town, okay?"

"Will do."

Of course Drue hadn't called him. Physically and emotionally exhausted from the ordeal of leaving her old life behind, she'd finally rolled into St. Petersburg on Sunday shortly before midnight and checked into a cheap beach motel she estimated was only a block or so away from the cottage.

Her plan had been to wake up early, check out her new home, then report for work. But things didn't go as planned. They seldom did in Drue Campbell's life.

She stood on the sidewalk in front of the law office, fighting the instinct to run. Dread gnawed at the pit of her stomach. Why had she agreed to move back here? To the scene of the crime, as it were. And to work for the very man who was the architect of so much of her unhappy childhood?

Because, she thought. Because there is nothing left for you, back there in Fort Lauderdale. At least here you have a house. Papi's house, she reminded herself. And a job.

She took a deep breath and pushed open the front door to the law office. A pale-faced young man with round tortoiseshell glasses resting on cherubic pink cheeks sat at a large reception desk. He was dressed in a lime-green dress shirt and a skinny purple tie. He wore a headset and was typing on a computer terminal. He nodded at the visitor and held up one finger, signaling he'd be right with her. Drue nodded back.

The reception area had been carved out of the former living room. Thick Oriental carpets covered the gleaming hardwood floors and stiff formal draperies framed the picture windows that overlooked the street. There was a handsome fireplace and glass-front bookshelves full of obsolete leather-bound law journals. A pair of navy leather armchairs flanked the fireplace and a matching leather sofa was placed against the adjacent wall. A framed generic color photograph of a Florida sunset hung over the mantel.

"Hi," the young man said, turning to her. "Can I help you?"

"Hope so. I'm Drue Campbell. My father is expecting me."

"The new girl!" he squealed, clapping his fingertips together. "Thank God!" He stood and extended a hand. "Welcome! I'm Geoff. Spelled with a *G,* not a *J.* It's so nice to meet you."

"Okay," Drue said slowly. "Good to meet you too."

"Listen," he said. "Brice is in with a client right now, but he asked me to take you back to Wendy, the office manager, since she'll be doing your new-employee orientation."

She followed him through a doorway and down a short corridor until he paused in front of an open door. He poked his head inside. "Hi, Wendy, I have our new employee here." He gently pushed her into the room. "This is Drue."

The office manager sat at a contemporary glass-topped desk. She lowered a pair of Chanel reading glasses onto her nose and looked up, her pale eyes appraising Drue with a hint of amusement. She was very tan and wore a chic blush-pink sleeveless sheath dress with a string of rose quartz beads looped around her neck.

Drue returned her gaze with an uncertain smile of her own. There was something eerily familiar about this woman.

Before either could speak, Brice burst through the door of his adjacent office.

"Oh good, you're here," he said, beaming at Drue. He stood behind the glass desk, one hand placed lightly on his manager's bare shoulder.

"Drue, you remember my wife, Wendy, right?"

She gawked, trying to make sense of the surreal scene in front of her. Drue knew that name, but the rest of the package was different. This Wendy was slender and petite, not pudgy and awkward. The orthodontia and mall bangs were gone. The frizzy long strawberry-blond hair was now short and sleek and a shimmering red. The sharp chin and high, rounded cheekbones were the same, but the lips were plumper. It was the nose that had thrown her off. This nose was definitely not factory equipment.

"Wendy Lockhart?" She blurted out the name, glancing at her father for confirmation. "Wait. You *married* Wendy Lockhart?"

"That's right," Brice said. "It'll be three years on the twenty-eighth."

"Twenty-seventh, you shameless cradle robber," Wendy cooed. She gave Drue a mirthless smile. "So that makes me your stepmother. Isn't that hilarious?"

"Hysterical," Drue mumbled, sinking onto the wing chair facing the desk. "Mind-blowing."

What's the worst that could happen? she'd asked herself, the previous night on that long, mind-numbing drive across Alligator Alley from Lauderdale to St. Pete. And now she had the answer to that rhetorical question. This. Right here. The prospect of having Wendy Lockhart, her junior high best friend/worst frenemy as both stepmother and supervisor. *This* was absolutely the worst that could happen.

"I didn't even know you'd remarried," she finally managed, when her brain began to thaw.

"It was a very *intimate* ceremony," Wendy said, casually

flaunting the motherlode of an engagement ring on her left hand. "Just a few friends and close family."

Drue chewed the inside of her cheek and wondered if this office had a trapdoor, or maybe a fire escape.

"How did you two, uh, reconnect?" she asked.

"Reconnect?" Brice frowned. "I handled some legal work for Wendy, but I didn't actually ask her out until after she'd gotten her settlement." He winked. "Don't share that with the Bar Association ethics committee, okay?"

"He didn't remember me at all," Wendy assured her. "I mean, it was *so* long ago. And when I hired him, I was Wendy Harrison, which was my ex-husband's name."

"We were in eighth grade," Drue said, her voice cracking in disbelief. "You spent the night at our house nearly every Friday night of eighth grade. We'd tape *Sabrina the Teenage Witch* and watch it together on Friday nights. How could he not remember you?"

Wendy laughed and waved away Drue's insistence. "Same old Drue. Still wildly exaggerating things. It wasn't *every* Friday night. I spent the night maybe twice, three times tops. Your dad wasn't even around that much back then, the way I remember it."

Drue's memories were distinctly different. She and Wendy had been nearly inseparable in the eighth grade, bonding initially over their shared misery at being the new girls in school, their friendship deepening over painful problems at home.

"Whatever," she said now.

"Right," Wendy said briskly, consulting her Rolex. "I was actually expecting you earlier, so we're already behind with your training schedule."

"My car wouldn't start this morning," Drue said, instantly feeling both lame and defensive.

"I'll let you two girls get to the training room," Brice said. "Why don't we meet up and have lunch together at your break? I'll get Geoff to make a reservation."

"Can't," Wendy said. "We need her on those phones tomorrow. Which means she's got the whole legal training module to get through, which is six hours, and then there's the employee handbook. And she's still got to run over to Medical Associates for her drug test."

"Drug test?" Drue asked. "Are you seriously telling me I have to pee in a cup before I can work here?"

"Surely we can skip that for Drue," Brice said. "I mean, she's family."

"Sweetie?" Wendy said, raising one eyebrow. "You know it's office policy. How will the rest of the staff feel if they find out we made an exception for your daughter?"

"Oh. Right." He glanced at Drue. "The drug test won't be a problem, will it?"

"No," Drue said, her lips tight. Unlike many of her friends in and out of kiteboarding, she'd never really developed an appreciation for pills or weed. But the drug test itself wasn't the issue here. The issue was that her father was once again siding with his wife, instead of her. The last time it had been Joan. Now it was Wendy.

Suddenly, she was fifteen years old again. Pissed off and pissed on. Literally.

~

The training room was a cramped space with a conference table, a desk, complete with desktop computer and phone setup, and a whiteboard that took up one entire wall.

"Okay," Wendy said, gesturing for her to sit at the table. She plunked a thick loose-leaf binder onto the surface in front of Drue. "Policies and procedures. Basic best legal practices. Company policy." She consulted her watch again. "Read it, digest it, memorize it."

Drue opened the cover and scanned the first typewritten page.

"What kind of sandwich do you want?" Wendy said. "I mean, you're not a vegan, right?"

"Huh?"

"Sandwich. For lunch," Wendy said, rolling her eyes. "You can have a fifteen-minute break. I'll have Geoff order something in for you. I'm sorry, Drue, I know Brice means well, but things will go much smoother here for all of us if you're treated exactly the same as your coworkers."

"Right. Turkey on rye. Tomato, no lettuce, mustard, not mayo. Unsweet tea." She turned back to the page, willing Wendy to disappear, which she finally did, after drilling Drue on the importance of discretion and nondisclosure in all things regarding the firm's clients.

After three straight hours of reading and note-taking, the type began to swim around the page. Drue stood, walked around the room, then sat and did some stretches.

Wendy walked into the room with a white paper sack and a Styrofoam cup.

"What are you doing?"

"Stretching my knee," Drue said, feeling guilty for slacking off. She eyed the bag hungrily. She hadn't eaten since leaving Lauderdale the previous day.

Wendy placed the bag on the table and pointed at Drue's knee. "I was wondering about the brace. What happened?"

"Sports injury," Drue said. She opened the bag, took out a sandwich wrapped in waxed paper, took a bite and nearly spat it out.

She pried the sandwich apart and glanced over at her supervisor. "Mayonnaise."

Wendy shrugged. "That place never gets orders right. I keep meaning to tell Geoff to find a new deli."

Drue lifted the top layer of bread and set it aside. Using a single leaf of lettuce she managed to scrape most of the mayonnaise aside. She ate four bites, then set it aside in disgust. Mayonnaise taint.

"What kind of a sports injury?" Wendy asked.

"Torn ACL, torn meniscus, torn medial collateral."

Wendy regarded her with disbelief. "You don't look like a runner."

"I'm not. I hate running."

"So, what then? How did you hurt your knee? Jesus, Drue, why are you so angry and hostile? Your dad and I are just trying to help you."

Drue wiped her hands with a paper napkin. "I hurt my knee kiteboarding. Right before my mom got sick. Some quack at an emergency room at Delray Beach sewed me up, and I'm pretty sure he botched it. So now, I can't do the one thing I was good at, the one thing I loved. And, oh yeah, I'm essentially an orphan because my mom is dead and my dad doesn't actually consider me real family, hence the not letting me know about that 'intimate wedding' to you."

She turned a level gaze at Wendy.

"You and I were best friends a long time ago, whether or not you choose to admit that. Now you're married to my dad, who happens to be, what, thirty-five years older than you? Swell. Good luck with that, because he's such *awesome* husband material. I know he cheated on my mom, and I'm guessing he cheated on Joan too. I don't know and I don't care. But don't expect me to throw you a lingerie shower, m'kay?"

Wendy's face turned pale. She brushed imaginary crumbs from the front of her dress. "Look," she said, her voice dangerously calm. "First off, he's only thirty-two years older than me. And since we're being so brutally frank right now, let me just go on the record as saying I was against Brice offering you a job here, but he absolutely insisted on hiring you out of some sense of misplaced obligation. You've got, what, two years of community college? You can't even keep a job waiting tables at some shitty beach bar. You've clearly got anger management issues, and it's a total conflict of interest to have you working for this law firm. As for my marriage to Brice, let me point out that you know absolutely nothing about your father. He's the finest, kindest man I've ever known, but you'll never figure that out, because you're thirty-six years old and still whining about being from a broken home."

Drue stuffed the sandwich remains in the paper bag. "Are we done here? If so, I think I need to get back to my training manual."

"Oh, we're more than done," Wendy said. She looked at her watch. "When you're finished with the manual, go out to the reception area. We're so shorthanded I can't spare anybody to train you on the phone the way I'd planned, but Geoff can show you how everything works. He's got a copy of your phone script too. And they're expecting you at Medical Associates on Fourth Street no later than five. No test, no job."

"I'll be there."

4

~~~

Drue was walking out the office door for her drug testing appointment when the black Mercedes zoomed up to the curb and Brice leaned out the open passenger window.

"How'd it go today?" he asked.

"Okay. I'm just headed over to the testing lab."

"Good," he said. "Hey, did Wendy tell you about happy hour tonight?"

"No."

He laughed. "She's so focused, probably slipped her mind. Anyway, Monday nights we have staff happy hour at Sharky's. This is perfect timing. You can meet your coworkers outside the office, let your hair down a little."

Drue was instantly wary. "It's been a really long day for me, Dad. I was gonna go check out of the motel and start moving stuff into the cottage—which I haven't even seen yet. If it's okay with you, I'll take a rain check."

"Hey," he said earnestly. "It's gonna be a little awkward, at first anyway. You're the boss's daughter, and the office manager's stepdaughter."

She cringed at the stepdaughter description, but kept quiet.

"If you want to get off on the right foot, get yourself over to Sharky's tonight, six o'clock."

"I don't even know where that is," Drue protested, making one last stab at bowing out. She hated everything about happy hour. Hated the mindless boozing, the forced camaraderie, the vision of over-served guys pawing every woman in sight, and shit-faced girls facedown in their own vomit by the end of the evening.

"You don't remember Sharky's?" Her father was incredulous. "It's that big bar just down the beach from the cottage. You can't miss the place. There's a giant fiberglass shark head out in the parking lot."

"Oh, that place."

Sharky's had been a Sunset Beach landmark for decades. She'd been fascinated with the place as a young teen. Music blared out of their deck-mounted speakers, from eight in the morning 'til 3:00 A.M. It was a something-for-everyone kind of swim-up beach bar, with sprawling decks, sand volleyball courts and rows of roped-off lounge chairs pointing toward the Gulf.

"Just come to happy hour," Brice said. "And that's an order from the boss."

As he drove away she noticed her father's vanity license tag: ISUE-4U.

~

Back at the motel, Drue picked through the meager offerings in her suitcase until she found her designated "casual date" outfit, which consisted of white skinny jeans and a black halter top with large white buttons down the back. She peered into the steam-clouded bathroom mirror, trying to evaluate her appearance. She pulled her dark shoulder-length hair into a high ponytail, brushed on some mascara, and after careful consideration, added lipstick and a pair of gold palm-frond earrings.

Okay, she told herself. Not "trying too hard" but also not "currently living in a van down by the river." She stuck her cell phone, motel key card, driver's license and some folded bills in her back pocket and set out walking along the beach, her best flip-flops hooked over her thumb.

She hadn't realized how nervous she was until she was standing at the water's edge, looking up at the orange traffic cones that demarcated Sharky's beach zone. The palms of her hands were damp and she felt a trickle of perspiration slide down the side of her face and between her breasts.

For a moment, she was transported back to middle school, to that horrible first day in her new school when she stood in the cafeteria, looked around and realized she was the only girl wearing bib overalls in a high-waist acid-washed-jeans world.

"Chill out," she muttered to herself now. "It's just happy hour. You *own* happy hour, damnit."

Brice must have been waiting for her, because he walked out to meet her the moment she stepped onto the deck. He was dressed in sharply pressed golf shorts, and a polo shirt with an embroidered yacht club logo.

"Hey!" he said, looking genuinely pleased to see her. "I was afraid you weren't coming."

"Sorry. It's a long bus ride out here," she said.

"Why didn't you say something? I could have given you a ride home."

"I've got a car, it just didn't choose to start this morning. It's fine now, though." This was a bald-faced lie, but she couldn't risk the hideous proposition of having to ride to work in the morning with Brice and Wendy.

"Okay, but let me know if it acts up again." He pressed a drink into her hand. "Here. Tonight's drink special. The Kinky Dolphin."

She could see the layers of viscous blue and green liquors through the sides of the plastic cup. "What's in this?"

"You used to work in a bar, so you tell me."

Drue rolled her eyes, then discarded the paper umbrella skewering a maraschino cherry and orange slice garnish. She took a gulp of the Kinky Dolphin and immediately wished she hadn't. It was both mouth-puckeringly sour and sickeningly sweet. "Mmm. If I had to guess I'd say antifreeze and Ty-D-Bol."

He held up his own bottle of beer in a salute. "Come on. I want you to meet the rest of the Campbell, Coxe and Kramner gang. We're at a table inside."

She followed him under the tin-roofed porch toward a table around which a dozen people were gathered, trying to quell a growing sense of unease.

"Hey guys," Brice announced, standing at the head of the

table. "Quiet down, okay? I want you to meet my daughter, Drue. I'm thrilled to announce that she's joined the Campbell, Coxe and Kramner team." He gestured around the table. "Drue, meet the team."

The music and hum of chatter from the growing happy hour crowd made it hard to hear as one by one, the "team" introduced themselves. There were Deanna and Priscilla and Sylvia in accounting; the two paralegals, Marianne and a woman whose name she didn't catch; Geoff, the receptionist; and at the end of the table, two men, one a bespectacled ginger who said his name was Ben and . . .

"I'm sorry, what was that name?" Drue shouted, leaning in to hear.

"It's Jonah. With a *J*," the other guy said. He was what she and her girlfriends back in Lauderdale liked to call "frat-tastic," meaning he was your typical entitled white college grad. Tousled dark hair with a high forehead, square jaw and full lips, he was a Ralph Lauren ad come to life. Totally hot, if you liked that type.

Ben, who was tall and gangly, stood up and pumped her hand. "What are you drinking?"

Before she could reply, Brice gestured at the server, a busty brunette dressed in a midriff-baring tee and shorts. "Bianca, can you bring my daughter another Kinky Dolphin?"

"No, no, no," Drue said quickly.

"Okay, what do you want?" Brice said expansively. "Everything's on me tonight. You want something to eat? They've got wings, burgers, grouper sandwiches . . ."

Her stomach growled at the mention of food.

"Maybe just some nachos? And an iced tea?"

"Iced tea?" Jonah scoffed. "Brice, I can't believe your daughter is a liquor lightweight. Definitely not a chip off the old block."

"You don't want a drink?" Brice asked. "Doesn't have to be the special."

"Well, maybe just a margarita, no salt," Drue said, relenting. She took the only vacant seat and looked around at the gathering. With the exception of the boss, she realized, everybody at the table looked to be under the age of forty.

Brice, she reflected, had always liked 'em young.

"Where's Wendy tonight?" she asked, turning to her father.

"Oh, she never comes to happy hour. Being the office manager and all, she worries that it'll make people inhibited. This is supposed to be a team-building kind of event."

"Team building." Drue turned the phrase over in her mind. Before she could ask any more questions, though, her food and drink arrived.

The nachos were just gummy processed cheese melted over mildly stale corn chips, scattered with a representational amount of pickled jalapeños, chopped tomatoes and cubes of avocado, but she had to restrain herself from gobbling them down all at once.

Instead she sipped her drink and nibbled at the chips and nodded and listened to the conversations swirling around her.

"I didn't even know Brice had a daughter," Ben said, taking a swig of his beer. "Did you know anything about a daughter, Jonah?"

"Nope," his pal said. "You live around here, Drue?"

"I do now," she said.

"Where'd you grow up?" Jonah asked.

"I was born here in St. Pete, but I guess you'd say I grew up in Fort Lauderdale."

"Cool," Ben said. "I still haven't even been over to the east coast yet."

"So, what, you're taking Stephanie's old job?" Jonah asked.

"That's what they tell me."

His hazel eyes lazily flicked up and down, checking her out.

She returned his gaze, thinking, Dude, I've been checked out by way better than you.

"That's awesome," Ben said. "You'll be in our pod."

"Pod?" She turned toward him.

"Yeah, that's what they call our group. We do phone intake, speak to potential clients, assess their situation, and if it seems they have a likely case, we work up their info and forward them on to Brice, his paralegal, or sometimes, refer them to one of the firms we partner with. I also do some of the firm's basic IT work."

"Okay," Drue said.

"It's not rocket science," Jonah said. "But you'll need a working knowledge of Florida law. You ever done this kind of work before? I mean, you did grow up with Brice as your dad, right?"

Drue took a long gulp of the margarita, enjoying the momentary brain freeze.

"No," she said succinctly. "My mom and I moved to Fort Lauderdale after they split up. So there hasn't been a lot of 'contact' until just recently."

Wanting to short-circuit this line of intrusive questioning, Drue raised her cup in the direction of the hovering waitress. "I'll have another of these," she called.

While she waited for her drink she watched Brice at the other end of the table. He seemed to know everybody in the place, as a string of people stopped by to greet and talk to him.

"Your old man never met a stranger," she remembered Sherri telling her when she was a teenager. "It's the secret to his success. People meet him once and leave convinced he's their new best friend. Especially the women, and the younger and prettier the better," she'd added bitterly.

An older man approached the table. Brice stood, slapped him on the back and pulled a chair from a vacant nearby table so he could join the group. He wore baggy black dad jeans and a black short-sleeved shirt whose buttons gapped over his considerable paunch. The remaining strands of his hair had been carefully arrayed and sprayed over his head, and his sagging jowls and dewlaps reminded Drue of the Nestlé Quik bloodhound.

"Jimmy Zee's in the house," Jonah drawled.

"Who's he?" Drue asked.

"He's our investigator," Ben said.

"You mean, like a detective?"

"You catch on fast," Jonah said. "Jimmy Zee and your dad go back a long ways. He's a retired St. Pete police detective. Zee and Brice used to be partners, back in the day, before Brice started law school at Stetson."

"Oh yeah," she said slowly. "I remember him. Jimmy Zee. He and his wife used to hang out at our house, when I was little."

"Hard to believe the old man was ever a cop," Ben said. "I'd have guessed he was born a lawyer."

Unbidden images tugged at Drue's memory. Of her father, arriving home at the end of his shift, carefully unbuckling his holster, stashing his service weapon in a box kept on the top shelf of the bedroom closet. She remembered Sherri, every Sunday night, with the ironing board set up in the living room, starching and ironing a week's worth of her father's white uniform shirts, while smoking and watching the soap operas she'd taped. Some days, if he was in a good mood, Brice would prop Drue up on a phone book in the driver's seat of his green-and-white cruiser, turn on the blue flashers and siren, and she would laugh and clap her hands, because those were the days she was Daddy's girl.

She watched as the two men bent their heads together, deep in conversation.

"Where'd you go to school?" Jonah asked.

"On the east coast," she said, annoyed. She'd already noticed his flashy gold UF college ring.

"I meant, what school?" he persisted.

"Miami," she said. She hadn't actually said UNIVERSITY of Miami, right? If he jumped to the wrong conclusion, that wasn't her fault.

"Miami. Cool. Mark Richt is kicking ass and taking names down there. You a Hurricanes fan?"

"Not at all. I detest football," she said, trying desperately to shut him down. Why had she lied like that? Why not say Miami Dade College? There was nothing wrong with it. Nothing wrong with her.

She sucked down the last of her margarita and started to stand. "I gotta go. Tomorrow's a school day, right?"

"You just got here," Ben said, looking dismayed.

Brice had spotted her. He came around the table, put a hand

on her shoulder. "You're not leaving already. The party just got started."

"Actually, I am," Drue said. "I've gotta get an early start in the morning. Don't want to get off on the wrong foot with the office manager."

Brice frowned at her lame joke. Before he could say anything, his cell phone rang. He pulled it from his pocket, took a few steps away from the table, and a moment later was back.

"Speaking of. That was the boss," he said cheerfully. "I've been summoned home."

He motioned the server over. "You've already run my Amex. Keep the tab running for this motley crew."

Brice clapped his hands to get the group's attention. "Gotta go, guys, but don't stop the party on my account."

"Booty call," Ben yelled, and the others at the table took up the refrain, banging beer bottles on the tabletop. "Booty call. Booty call. Brice has got a booty call."

The boss grinned widely, and gently pushed his daughter back down to her chair.

"Stay, okay? The night's young." He turned to Ben and then Jonah. "I'm appointing you two characters as her wingmen. Make sure she's taken care of, right?"

"We got this," Ben said, shooting Brice a thumbs-up.

"Shot time!" yelled somebody at the end of the table.

"Yeah," one of the accounting girls echoed. "Shots for everybody!"

Their server materialized, taking orders as they were shouted out.

"Jägerbomb!"

"Buttery Nipple!"

"Mind Eraser!"

"Redheaded Slut!" Ben yelled.

"Angel's Tit!" Jonah called. He pointed at Drue. "What's your pleasure?"

"Lights-out," Drue said.

"Huh?" Ben looked puzzled. "That's one I've never heard of. And I've tasted every shot ever invented." He held up his phone and tapped an icon. "Look. I've even got a Shots Spreadsheet."

"It's not a drink, it's a statement," Drue said. "Sorry to be such a wet blanket, but I've gotta head out."

"No way," Ben said. "You heard the man. You gotta at least stay for a round of shots."

"This is so ridiculous," Drue said, shaking her head. "I've never understood why they call it 'happy hour.' More like 'amateur hour,' if you ask me."

Jonah groaned. "Spare us the lecture about how immature we are. Can't you just let go and join the party? Have a little fun? I never would have thought any kid of Brice's would be such a tight-ass."

"Shows how little you know me," Drue shot back. She drained her margarita. "Okay, I'll play if you'll play. How about you order me a shot, and I'll order one for you."

"Deal." Jonah turned to the server. He gave it some thought. "Can you make a Crouching Tiger?"

The girl shrugged. "I guess." She looked at Drue. "How about you?"

Drue smiled. She'd mixed a Crouching Tiger or two during her bartending days. Tequila and lychee juice. An obnoxious combination, in her opinion. But if he wanted to go that route, she could do him one better.

"Bring my friend here a Prairie Fire."

"Does he still want the, uh, Angel's Tit?" she asked.

"Doesn't everybody?" Ben said, smirking. She could tell he was fairly wasted.

Their server nodded and just before she turned to head back to the bar, shot Drue a secret, congratulatory smile.

Their server had some skills. When she came back she expertly unloaded the correct glass in front of each member of the team. She hadn't written anything down, Drue noticed. She was just that good.

When she reached the end of the table she slid the bright red shot glass in front of Drue. "Crouching Tiger for you."

"Redheaded Slut for the redhead," she said, placing Ben's glass in front of him.

"And for the gentleman, an Angel's Tit *and* a Prairie Fire."

Drue reached for her drink. She'd get this over with and get out of here before things got too intense. She knew she was buzzed and was already regretting that margarita.

Jonah stayed her hand with his. "Not yet. This is team-building night, remember? And Marianne, as the most senior member of the CCK precision-drinking team, gives the signal."

"Hey, Marianne. Waiting on you."

Marianne, who had short, white-blond hair and the angular body of a runner, stood up.

"On my count. One. Two. Three. Drink up, assholes!" she screamed.

Every member of the team, including Drue, raised their glasses and downed their drinks.

She grimaced. If Jonah wanted to give her liquor poisoning, he'd made a good start of it. Her head was swimming.

He'd downed the creamy confection he'd ordered for himself in one gulp. Now he wiped his mouth, smirked and reached for the amber-colored shot.

He tossed it back and his eyes widened. He gagged, then forcefully swallowed. His eyes were watering. Thirty seconds passed, and then he picked up Drue's empty margarita glass and spat out his drink.

"What the fuck?" he croaked. "What . . ."

"Oh. You want to know what's in a Prairie Fire?" she asked sweetly, sliding a glass of water his way.

Jonah drank the water. "Hot tequila? Who does that?"

"I didn't invent it. I just ordered it. So yeah, hot tequila *and* Tabasco. You're lucky I didn't ask her to garnish it with a ghost pepper."

Drue reached into her pocket, pulled out a five-dollar bill and pressed it into their server's palm. "Thanks, girl." Then she turned to Jonah and Ben and stood, swaying a little as she did so. "Good to meet you both. I'm heading for home now."

Ben jumped from his chair. "Let me give you a ride home. You probably don't need to be driving."

"Uh, dude. You don't need to be driving either," Drue said. She pointed at Jonah. "And neither do you. But it's cool. I walked here. And I can walk home."

"You seriously walked here?" Jonah asked. "From where?"

She turned and had to grasp the back of her chair to keep her balance. "Just down there," she said, jerking her thumb to the north.

"Should have known. You're the boss's daughter. He has a house on the beach. You have a house on the beach. No biggie."

She leaned down until her face was only inches from Jonah's and whispered, "My dad has nothing to do with where I live, okay? You're such an asshole, by the way."

He leaned away from her and stood. "You're wasted, by the way." He looked over at Ben. "We can't let her walk home like this. You want to drive her? If not, I can. I Lyfted here, and I can just have the driver drop her off."

"Hey!" Drue protested. "I'm right here. Stop talking about me. I told you, I'm fine. I don't need a ride. And I don't need an escort."

"I can drive all three of us," Ben said. And then his face fell. "Damn. I just remembered. It's such a nice night, I rode over on the Vespa."

"A Vespa?" Drue whooped. "Hell yeah! I changed my mind. Let's go for a ride."

"Can't," Ben said. "I only have one helmet."

"Don't be such a rule-follower," Drue exclaimed. "It's only a couple blocks." She tugged at Ben's arm. "Come on."

"Not a good plan," Jonah advised. "This is the boss's daughter.

Remember? What if she falls off and sustains a head injury? Who ya gonna call?"

"Campbell, Coxe and Kramner," Drue sang, mimicking the firm's catchy jingle, which was sung to the tune of "Maxwell's Silver Hammer." "Had a fall? Give Brice a call!"

"Enough said," Ben agreed. "You want me to walk her home with you? I mean, she says it's only a couple blocks."

"Not necessary," Jonah said. "I'll walk her, make sure she gets home okay, and then I'll call for a Lyft from there. I'll text you if there's a problem, otherwise, I'll see you tomorrow."

5

"Y ou really don't have to do this," Drue said, as they trudged along the beach. "I'm perfectly capable of walking home all by myself."

"Sure you are," Jonah said, rolling his eyes. "Which motel did you say you're staying at?"

"Behind the 'at,'" Drue said, giggling at her own joke. "Don't they teach you guys grammar up there in Gainesville?"

"Which motel?" he repeated.

"Mmm, it's one of those, right up there," she said, pointing at a cluster of small motels just beyond the dunes. They were fifties throwback tourist courts, each painted in a different Easter egg pastel—coral, turquoise and yellow.

"Okay. Can you be any more specific?"

"It's the Sea . . . something, I think."

"The Sea Breeze?" he asked, pointing at a C-shaped complex built around a glowing turquoise swimming pool.

"That's the one!" She playfully punched his arm. "I take it back. You're not such a dummy after all."

As they started toward the dune line, Drue stumbled and toppled backward onto the soft sand.

"Whoops!"

Jonah grabbed her arm to help her up, but instead, she pulled him down beside her.

"Hey!" He started to protest, but on an impulse, she shut him up with a kiss. Which he returned, in a chaste, closed-mouth sort of way.

He pulled away after a moment. "What's this about?"

She wasn't sure. But he was a good kisser, that she did know. And in the dark, she decided to just let the tequila do the talking. She wrapped her arms around his neck, leaned in and kissed him again.

His response was definitely more enthusiastic the second time. He parted her lips with his tongue and ran his hands up her bare back. She shivered at the touch of his warm hands, and pressed herself closer to him.

"Oh man," he said, sitting up after a few moments. "This is a terrible idea." He put his head in his hands.

"What?"

"This," he said, indicating her prone position on the sand. "You're the boss's daughter."

Drue grabbed the collar of his stupid preppy polo shirt and pulled him down beside her. "Shut up," she murmured in his ear.

She slid her hands up the back of his shirt and he slowly eased a knee between her legs. He nuzzled her ear, ran his tongue down her jawline, and her neck, and her shoulder, and at the same time, his hands were working their way from her back and under the front of her halter top.

Drue couldn't remember the last time she'd had sex. She and Trey hadn't been getting along all that well in the months leading up to her mother's illness. And after her mother's diagnosis, she'd spent every free moment she had with Sherri, ignoring Trey's pointed comments about *his* needs.

After the kiteboarding accident, sex had been the last thing on her mind. Not anymore, though.

And apparently, Jonah was rapidly overcoming his initial apprehension. He was fumbling for the zipper on her jeans.

"Let's take this somewhere with less sand," Drue said, kissing him again, and momentarily forgetting herself.

"You sure?"

"Positive," she said.

"You're the boss." He stood and helped her to her feet.

"Damn straight," Drue told him, taking his hand and leading him toward the motel.

"You sure this is the right room?" he asked, as they stood in front of a door looking out at the pool.

She whipped the key card from the back pocket of her jeans, slid it into the slot and tried the door handle, which didn't move.

Drue frowned and took a step backward. "I could swear this was my room. I know it faces the pool."

"May I?" He took the plastic card, wiped it on the front of his shirt and inserted it into the slot, easily pushing the door open.

"Hey. How'd you do that?"

He smiled. "I've got the magic touch."

She pulled him into the room and turned the dead-bolt lock. "We'll see about that."

Moonlight shone in through the room's sheer drapes. Drue dropped her shoes on the floor, unzipped and discarded her jeans, and pulled her top over her head, letting it drop onto the floor. She collapsed naked onto the bed, leaning back against the headboard.

He shrugged and pulled off his polo shirt, dropping it on top of the clothes she'd so readily discarded.

He had a nice body, Drue decided, not as wiry and lean as Trey, who spent all his spare time surfing or kiteboarding, but muscular and toned.

Jonah glanced at the noisy window air conditioner, which barely cooled the room. "Doesn't it get hot in here?" he asked, kicking off his loafers and unzipping his shorts, letting them fall to the floor.

"Not as hot as it's gonna get." She held out her arms, and he smiled and joined her on the bed.

She awoke with a start, her heart racing. Her head throbbed and her mouth tasted like a sewer. She was startled to hear the sound of soft snoring. Slowly, she turned her head. Sunlight seeped through the window and now she saw, sprawled facedown beside her, a sleeping, naked man. She glanced down and realized that she was also naked.

"What the . . ." She started to sit up, but a jagged lightning strike of pain threatened to split her skull in half.

Drue sank back down onto her pillow. Slowly, the previous evening's events came back to her. "Come to happy hour," her father had said. "Meet the team," he'd said. "Drink up," he'd urged. She was pretty sure Brice hadn't meant for her to get shit-faced and literally take one for the team.

"Oh God," she muttered, as she vaguely remembered how easily she'd shed her inhibitions once she'd willingly guzzled the equivalent of half a bottle of tequila. She looked down at Jonah's sleeping form. Just how drunk had he been?

She groped around on the floor beside the bed until she found her cell phone, thumbing the home button to bring it back to life, and gasping when she saw the time. Eight o'clock! She had to be showered, dressed and at work, in downtown St. Pete, which was thirty minutes away, in an hour.

Her stomach roiled and she ran for the bathroom, reaching the toilet in the nick of time. She kicked the door shut, knelt and retched until she felt she might have barfed up her own toenails.

"Oh God." She sank onto the edge of the bathtub. "What the hell did I do?" she whispered.

Drue shook Jonah's shoulder. She'd taken a hasty shower and gotten dressed. "Wake up."

He didn't move. She shook him harder, and slowly, he turned his head. His eyes opened slowly. "Huh?" Spittle left a narrow trail from his mouth to his chin.

"Wake up! You've gotta get out of here. I have to get to work."

He groaned and rolled onto his back. "What time is it?"

"It's eight-thirty. I've got to leave. It's my second day of work and I can't be late."

He shot straight up, looked down, blushed and covered himself with the sheet. "Eight-thirty? Why didn't you wake me earlier?"

"Because I had to get showered and dressed. Now you've got to get out of here right now."

His eyes were bloodshot and his hair tousled and he looked as thoroughly hungover as Drue still felt. "Okay, okay, I'm going." He found his briefs on the floor and put them on.

Of course, she thought, they were Ralph Lauren underpants.

"Shit." He looked up at her. "I can't go to work like this." He held up the shirt and shorts he'd worn the previous night. "Everybody will know I didn't go home last night. And I don't even have my car here. I took Lyft last night."

She was digging around in the tiny closet for a pair of shoes, any pair of shoes. Finally she found a pair of Gap navy espadrilles she hadn't worn in years.

"So?"

He pulled on his shorts. "So, everybody saw me leaving Sharky's with you last night. It doesn't take a rocket scientist to figure out I must have spent the night with you."

She sank down onto the bed. "Oh God."

He turned puppy dog eyes toward her. "I told you this was a bad idea."

"Shut up," she snapped, shoving her feet into the shoes, which were, predictably, too tight.

"Look, you're right. It was a bad idea. The worst idea ever." She narrowed her eyes. "So here's what we're going to do. I'm leaving here right now to go to work. You're leaving too. Call in sick or dead or whatever you want. But if you ever, ever breathe a word about last night to anybody, I will hurt you. Do you understand?"

"It's not my proudest moment either, you know," he said. He reached into his pocket and found his phone and billfold. "Look. Can you at least give me a ride up to Gulf Boulevard? It'll be easier to call a Lyft from there."

"Oh hell no," she said. "Brice and Wendy live three miles down the beach. What if they're passing by on the way to work and see me dropping you off? No way. You can either call for a ride from here or walk up there on your own."

"Okay," he said finally. "I'm going."

"Yes. You are." She poked him in the chest for emphasis. "And remember. This never happened. And it will never happen again."

Drue sat very still in the driver's seat of the Bronco. "Please, OJ," she whispered. "Please in the name of all that's holy, please start."

She turned the key in the ignition and gently pumped the accelerator. "Please start. Please start. Please start."

The motor caught! She gave it a little more gas, nodding in encouragement. "Attaway, baby. Attaway."

As she pulled out of the motel parking lot she glanced to the left and spotted Jonah, head down, shirt untucked, slinking toward the motel's coffee shop, phone in hand. The walk of shame. She knew it well.

6

~~~

Drue slipped into the bullpen at 9:55 on Friday. She went directly to her cubicle, donned the sweater she kept draped across the back of her chair and reached for her headset, congratulating herself on three days of avoiding eye contact with Jonah Kelleher. If she was careful, she could make today four days in a row.

Ben, whose cubicle was closest to hers, was on a call, his fingers racing across his computer's keyboard as he listened. He nodded at her, then glanced meaningfully up at the clock on the wall of the bullpen.

Drue shrugged and sat down. Now Ben jerked his head toward the bullpen door. *Incoming,* he mouthed.

She heard the distinctive click of Wendy's spike-heeled Louboutins on the wood floor as her tormentor approached.

Quickly, she powered up her computer and switched on her phone, praying that the next call into the firm's twenty-four-hour-a-day phone bank would be routed to her.

"Drue?" Wendy had wasted no time in hunting her down. Her voice was low and sultry. Jonah swore that Wendy's résumé included a stint doing phone sex. Now her pronounced Southern drawl drew out the vowels to three syllables.

Drue glanced up. "Hi. What's up?"

"We need to talk," Wendy said. Her voice frowned, even if her forehead, freshly Botoxed, could not. "You're an hour late . . . again. I can't cut you slack just because you're the boss's daughter, you know—"

The phone icon miraculously flashed yellow on Drue's computer screen.

"Can't talk right now," she said, pointing at the screen. "Got a call."

Without waiting, she launched into the scripted greeting she'd easily memorized.

"Campbell, Coxe and Kramner," she said crisply. "You've reached the Justice Line. This is Drue. How can I help?"

Wendy didn't budge.

Drue's caller was a white male. Early twenties, she guessed.

"Yeah, uh, look here. I got hurt, pretty bad, actually, got hit by a taxi, you know? And I saw your television commercial this morning, and, uh, my leg is hurting pretty bad—"

"Sir?" Drue broke in. "Can we back up for a moment? I'm going to need your name and address, date of birth, all that information?"

She'd pulled up the firm's questionnaire on her desktop computer, filling in the blanks and then working down the rest of the list of questions.

He said his name was Martin Sommers. "But you just call me Marty, okay?"

"When, exactly, did this accident occur?"

"I guess it's been a couple weeks. I kinda lost track of time."

The call was a loser, she already knew. Another time, without Wendy the Step-Witch breathing down her neck, she would have cut this potential client loose without another thought. He couldn't tell her when his accident had occurred, and if he'd been hit by one of the local independent cab companies, whose insurance companies were notoriously shady, they'd have no case. But Wendy didn't need to know that. For now, she just needed to get Wendy off her back. The way to do that was to keep Marty Sommers talking.

"I see," Drue said, nodding her head encouragingly. "Head-on collision? What were your injuries?"

"Well, uh, I banged up my knee, busted my lip. Smashed the hell out of my cell phone. And it was only a year old, ya know? If nothing else, that taxi company needs to buy me a new phone . . ."

Wendy showed no sign of retreating to her office, so Drue kept going, winging it. She clicked *yes* on the boxes of the referral form, the one that would be forwarded to the big man himself, if enough *yes*es were checked. In reality, the box she'd just checked should have been a *no*. A *hell, no.*

"Oh wow." Drue clucked her tongue sympathetically. "I'm

so sorry, Mr. Sommers. That sounds incredibly painful. And the emergency room noted all those injuries on your discharge forms?"

"Call me Marty, okay? Now, what was that you asked about the hospital?"

She repeated herself, speaking even more slowly this time. "When you were released from the emergency room, were your injuries noted on the discharge papers? Did you keep those documents?"

"Oh yeah. That piece of paper they give me? See, I don't think anybody wrote that on anything. Like I told the nurse there, I just needed something for the pain. Like, a prescription for Oxy? My knee was swole up something awful."

"Do you think you can find your discharge papers, Marty? It's kind of important."

Wendy made a show of tapping her shoe. *Tap. Tap. Tap.* She poked Drue's shoulder with a long pink acrylic nail, then twirled her forefinger in the air, the signal that Drue should wrap up this call.

"Oh my gosh!" Drue's eyes widened in feigned horror. "Shattered pelvis? Broken clavicle? Concussion? Have you regained vision in that eye yet?"

"Nobody said nothin' about a shattered pelvis," Marty said. "And I can see pretty good. My head does still hurt, though. Like I said, I really think some Oxy would help a lot. I mighta thrown the emergency room paper away. They treated me like I was some kinda drug addict or something."

"Very disturbing," Drue said, clicking all the *yes* boxes

on the intake form. "And you've been out of work for how long?"

"Well, I'm actually not working right at the moment. See, my tools got stolen outta my truck a couple months ago . . ."

Wendy, finally sensing that Drue had a live one on the line, sighed loudly.

"Come see me when you're done with this call," she hissed, turning and walking rapidly toward her office, her hips, encased in a short, ultra-tight skirt, swaying gently.

Drue glanced over and saw Ben appreciatively following the office manager's retreat.

Marty was still talking. "So, that television commercial I seen, it says Brice can get me a check. Like, when can he come see me?"

"See you?" Drue's mind was already racing toward her inevitable confrontation with Wendy.

"That's what I said," he said, sounding peeved. "That cab come out of nowhere, right when I was leaving the club. I coulda been killed."

Drue sighed. "Which club was that?"

Marty coughed delicately. "It was one of those clubs in Tampa, over there on Dale Mabry. I can't think of the name of it right now. Kinda over near McDill?"

"A strip club? You were leaving a strip club?"

"Gentleman's club," he corrected.

"I see," Drue said. "And the police were called at the time you were hit by the cab, is that correct?"

"Huh? No way. I mean, we didn't think the cops needed to get involved." He lowered his voice. "My friend, he mighta had some weed on him. Strictly for medical reasons. He gets seizures sometimes, you understand."

Drue looked at the big whiteboard at the front of the room. It had a hand-scrawled scoreboard, listing each of the cube rats, calls taken and cases signed for the week and month to date. She was already dead last.

"I do understand," she told Marty. "You don't know the date of your accident. Don't have any kind of hospital records, and the police were not called at the time because you and your friend were holding. You're not currently employed, and the only thing that's broken is your iPhone. Is that about the size of it?"

"Hey now," Marty said. "You can't talk to me like that. I'm gonna need you to go get Brice on the line now."

"Hold please," Drue said, as she terminated the call.

She sat back in her chair and let out a strangled-sounding sigh. Ben looked over. "Bad morning?"

"The worst. My car wouldn't start. Again."

"You should have called me," Ben said. "I could have given you a ride in."

"All the way from Sunset Beach? That's, like, twenty minutes out of your way. And I was already running late as it was. But thanks anyway."

She pushed back from her desk and stood up. "Enough stalling. Wendy needs to yell at me."

Ben stood too. "But first, coffee."

"Good thinking," Drue said.

~

She really should have called Ben Fentress for a ride this morning, she thought, following him toward the break room.

But she had a long-standing aversion to asking anybody, especially a man, for favors. Raised by a single mom, she'd had it drummed into her head from an early age that the only person she could count on was herself.

Ben Fentress was skinny, with long arms and legs that never seemed to move in any kind of coordinated fashion. He owned an impressive array of concert T-shirts for obscure eighties grunge bands, and from the first day she'd shown up at work at the law firm, Ben had gone out of his way to be kind to her. He was a true Boy Scout. No, an Eagle Scout, probably.

He was younger than Drue, only twenty-nine. Over sandwiches at the coffee shop across the street from the law office, on her second day of work, he'd told her all about himself.

"I'm your typical data bro," he'd said, munching on the potato chips he'd filched from her plate. "Undergrad degree from Colorado State. I started work on my master's, but then I ran out of money. And motivation too, if you want the truth."

"St. Pete's a long way from Colorado," Drue said. "How did you end up here?"

A bright pink flush crept over his freckled face. "Followed my girlfriend. She had a job with Honeywell. Three weeks after I got here, she dumped me for some dude she met at her gym."

"You didn't want to go back to Colorado after that?"

"No," he said succinctly. "It took moving to Florida before I figured out I don't really like winter. I don't ski. Don't snowboard either."

"I loved snowboarding," Drue said dreamily. Then, she asked, "Are you interested in the law?"

"I'm not *un*-interested in it. And besides, Brice Campbell isn't just a good lawyer, he's a genius at business. I can learn a lot from him. And I'm getting paid at the same time. It's not a bad gig."

Drue rolled her eyes. "Just what I always dreamed of becoming. A cubicle monkey." She leaned forward. "So, if you're not interested in becoming a lawyer, what *are* you doing working here?"

Ben's smile was enigmatic. "I'm working on something. A side hustle, I guess you'd call it. You ever play video games?"

"My ex-boyfriend was big into *Call of Duty*, but I don't really see the point," Drue said.

"Ex? Why'd you break up?"

"Lots of reasons. Including too much *Call of Duty*."

When they got to the break room they found Jonah already standing in front of the coffeemaker. He nodded a greeting, then reached into his pocket and brought out one of his special coffee pods. He slotted it into the machine, poured in a beaker of water and stood, waiting, his back to the counter.

"Hey y'all," he said, looking over Drue's and Ben's shoulders. "If the dragon lady sees all three of us in here with the phones unattended, she'll ream us a new one."

"I'm already on her shit list for being late," Drue said. "So I'm not too worried."

"Yeah, what's she gonna do? Fire her stepdaughter?" Jonah taunted.

Drue felt herself flush. "I'm *not* her stepdaughter."

"Let's see now. Wendy is married to Brice Campbell. Brice Campbell is your daddy. Doesn't that make Wendy your stepmother? Or is there some technicality that I'm overlooking here?"

"Wicked stepmother," Ben corrected. "World's biggest cliché."

"Just brew your stupid coffee and get out of our way, okay?" Drue snapped. She went to the refrigerator, got out the container of half-and-half and found her mug in the cabinet while Ben unwrapped a granola bar, which he managed to wolf down in two bites.

Drue watched Jonah watching the coffeepot, silently loathing him.

She loathed his looks: his unruly, sun-bleached hair, his wide-spaced hazel eyes, his rangy, athletic build. She loathed his casually expensive-looking clothes and the perfectly polished penny loafers he wore, sockless, as if to show the world he could get away with that kind of thing. She loathed the class ring he wore on his right hand, she loathed his alma mater, the University of Florida, loathed that he'd finished college and law school, and was only working here because he was killing time, waiting to take his bar exam again.

Most of all she loathed the fact that Jonah Kelleher was aware that she hated him and didn't give a rat's ass.

Jonah took his obnoxious orange and blue mug and flashed Drue a mocking smile. "Guess I'll head back to the salt mines. Coffee machine is all yours, gorgeous."

~

Wendy had turned her chair toward the wall of windows in her office, her back to the doorway, where Drue now stood. She was on the phone, her voice low, strained. "You're sure? Maybe we should get a second opinion?"

Princess, Wendy's French bulldog, poked her snout from under her mistress's desk and eyed Drue suspiciously. "Grrrrrr."

The desk chair spun around. "What?" Wendy demanded when she saw who her visitor was. "Hang on a sec," she said, speaking into the phone before placing it facedown on her desktop.

"You said we needed to talk," Drue said, her face and affect deliberately flat.

"Not now, for God's sake. Can't you see I'm busy?"

"Okay. It's just, the phones are pretty busy. This is the first time I've been able to get away from my cubicle."

Wendy gave a long, martyred sigh. "Okay fine. I'll come right to the point. You need to get to work on time, Drue. You know perfectly well we started running the new ad campaign last night, which means all the lines were jammed, last night and this morning. As I explained during your training, we run a small, tight ship here. Everybody has a job to do and nobody else has time to do yours. If you want to work here, you have to pull your own weight."

"I understand that. But my car wouldn't start—"

Wendy held up her hand, palm out. "I don't care. Your car is not my problem. I don't care if you have to walk to work. Just get here on time. Or we'll find somebody else who can. Understood?"

"Perfectly. Are we done?"

Princess crawled out from beneath the desk and jumped onto Wendy's lap. She placed her front paws on the lip of the desk and stared at Drue, her tiny body quivering like a tuning fork, snout lifted, her teeth bared, ears pricked.

Wendy kissed the top of the dog's head and Princess instantly calmed, her pronounced underbite curling into what Drue would swear was a smile.

"Sweet girl," Wendy murmured, her chin resting atop the dog's head. "Mommy's bestest, sweetest girl." She looked up at Drue and picked up the phone again. "Okay. Yes, I need to take this call. We're done here. For now."

Drue nodded.

"One more thing," Wendy called. "Your dad wanted me to ask if you have dinner plans tonight."

"Sorry," Drue said, shrugging. "I'm moving into the cottage. Can't make it."

7

~~~~~~~

Drue drove the short three blocks to Coquina Cottage Friday night after checking out of the Sea Breeze motel. The last time she'd been here she was fifteen. It was the summer before Papi died. She cringed now at the memory. She'd been a horrible teenager: angry, rebellious, full of pent-up hormonal rage at the world in general and her family—especially her father and her stepmother Joan.

Poor Nonni. Her darling grandmother had been heartbroken at the change in her only grandchild that summer. The sweet, fun-loving child who'd spent two weeks at Coquina Cottage every summer since she was old enough to walk had turned into a selfish, sullen shrew.

She had the address, of course—409 Pine Street. But after such a long absence, the street, the houses, virtually everything was unrecognizable. Papi's cottage—for that's how she would always think of it—had been the middle house in a row of five humble wood-frame homes. The Harrells, a family with three rambunctious red-haired boys, had lived in the white house to the left of the Sanchezes, and the Maroulises, a retired pharmacist from Tarpon Springs and his wife, lived in the pale green house to the right.

Those summer weeks had been idyllic for a tomboy like Drue. She spent long sunny days swimming, bodysurfing and skateboarding with Brian, Charley and Davy Harrell, and evenings fishing and crabbing from the Johns Pass Bridge with Papi. In those days, she was rarely indoors.

Now, on the lot where George and Helen Maroulis had tended their basil, tomato and banana pepper plants, there was a boxy, towering gray concrete three-level contemporary house so large it completely blotted out the view of the Gulf behind it.

And the Harrells' home had somehow morphed into a pink stucco faux-Mediterranean villa, with terra-cotta roof tiles and a turret that looked straight out of the Alhambra.

But there, crouching on the sand, dwarfed in between the pair of magnificent mansions, was Papi's humble place, easily distinguished from its splendid neighbors by its complete lack of splendor—and the blue tarp covering the roof.

Everything about the cottage, from the peeling blue paint on the cedar shingles to the dust-covered windows, seemed sad, saggy and forlorn. It was a far cry from the tidy, trim home on which her grandparents lavished love and attention.

Papi was so proud of this cottage. After tobacco imports from Cuba were embargoed in 1962, shuttering most of the cigar factories in Tampa, including the one he'd worked in most of his adult life, Alberto Sanchez had operated a small neighborhood grocery store in Ybor City. Somehow, he'd managed to save enough money to begin building this small summer cottage, and eventually, when their only daughter, Sherri, married and left home, Papi and Nonni, whose given name was Anna, retired and moved full-time to Sunset Beach.

A blast from the car directly behind hers, a gleaming white convertible, let her know she was blocking the narrow road. How long had she been stopped there, just staring at the house?

She gave an apologetic wave and pulled the Bronco into the rutted sand driveway.

Drue picked up the key chain her father had given her and looked wistfully at the cottage.

She thought of that last summer, more than twenty years ago, when Brice had pulled into the driveway and beeped his horn, impatient to load her onto the Greyhound bus back to her mother in Fort Lauderdale, and out of his and Joan's hair. Papi had stowed her suitcase in the back of Brice's BMW, and at the last minute, Nonni had tucked something into the pocket of her shorts and whispered in her ear, "This is for you. Come back whenever. You call, and Papi and I will come get you." It wasn't until she'd climbed into the front seat of her father's car that she'd thought to examine her grandmother's gift. It was a fifty-dollar bill, wrapped around the key to the cottage.

But she hadn't come back. Until now.

Brice had warned her not to expect much.

"We had the same tenant for the last seven years. I hired

some guys to haul out the crap he left behind, but I just haven't had time to really take a look at what needs to be done."

Of course, Wendy had to put her oar in the water. "I walked through it. It'll need a hundred thousand dollars' worth of work to make it livable. Frankly, if I were you, I'd sell the house to one of these rich gay couples and walk away." Drue had stared Wendy down with what Joan had termed her "dead-eye." "I am not selling Papi's house."

The front door had been painted red for as long as Drue could remember. Somebody, the hoarder, maybe, had slapped a coat of school-bus-yellow paint on it. She easily flecked a chip of the paint with a fingernail, revealing the red beneath. "Repaint front door" would be among the first items on her to-do list for the cottage.

The door hardware was shiny brass, obviously new and cheap-looking. She fit the key into it, turned the handle and pushed. The door was stuck, the old wood swollen and warped. She pushed harder, leaning into it with her shoulder. The rusted hinges squealed and the door gave way.

It wasn't until she'd stepped over the threshold that she realized she'd been holding her breath.

Once she'd exhaled, and inhaled, she wished she hadn't. The air inside was hot and fetid, ripe with the dank smell of mildew and the lingering stench of cigarette smoke.

She was standing in the living room. The wooden floors, which Nonni had mopped and polished weekly with her home-made lemon-wax mix, were now covered with garish green wall-to-wall shag carpet coated with a fine dust of plaster from the peeling walls. She walked slowly through the wide arched opening into the dining room. Like the rest of the house the room was bare of furniture. The doors of the corner cabinets Papi had built to house Nonni's wedding china gaped open, their glass panes coated with a thick yellow sludge of nicotine.

Clamping one hand over her nose, she rushed to a front window, pushing and tugging at the swollen wooden window sash until she'd managed to shove it upward a scant six inches. There were no screens, of course, but those would have to come later. She worked her way around the living and dining rooms, desperate for fresh air. Some of the windows had been painted shut, but she managed to open two of the four picture windows in the front room, and one in the dining room.

Drue followed the abbreviated hallway toward the two bedrooms, which were separated by the cottage's only bathroom. She poked her head into the bath, breathing through her mouth in anticipation of whatever horrors she would find there.

At least, she thought gloomily, the Hermit Hoarder hadn't been able to do too much permanent damage here. The black-and-white penny tile floor was filthy, but the tiles were all intact. The ballerina-pink toilet and matching pink sink and bathtub were still standing, though coated with what looked like decades of grime.

The chrome towel bars and toilet paper holders had been wrenched from the walls, and a lone, nearly empty roll of toilet paper stood atop the toilet tank.

"Bleach," Drue muttered. "Gonna need a lot of bleach."

Swallowing hard, she stepped into the bathtub and wrenched

the aluminum sash of the window there upward, letting in a welcome rush of fresh air.

Drue tiptoed into the larger of the two bedrooms. By current real estate standards Nonni's room was tiny, hardly the stuff of a real master bedroom suite. The carpet here was a purple red, the walls painted to match. In Nonni's day, the walls and carpet were baby blue. The picture window opposite the wall where Nonni and Papi's bed had been was covered with venetian blinds, giving the room the overall effect of a burgundy cave. Without another thought, she went to the window and yanked the blinds free of the wall, flooding the room in welcome sunlight. This window had been painted shut too.

She stood in the center of the room, waiting to see if she could sense her grandparents' presence here. On the right side of where her grandparents' bed had been, she imagined the mahogany nightstand, with its ever-present box of tissues, Nonni's Avon hand cream and, always, her white-leather-covered missalette. She glanced over the door frame and was jolted, and then reassured, by the presence of the hand-carved wooden crucifix. It was still there!

Reluctantly, she moved on to the second bedroom, her bedroom, Nonni always called it. She'd furnished Drue's room with a frilly white-canopied bed and a fussy French provincial dresser and nightstand, which Drue had adored until she turned fourteen and decided she hated everything, including this room.

In the intervening years someone had painted Drue's room mud brown. Two walls were covered with crudely constructed sagging wooden bookshelves still loaded down with rows of paperback books. Obviously this had been the hoarder's den. The double window, which had been adorned with ruffled, white dotted-swiss curtains during Drue's youth, was now covered with a beige woolen blanket, which had been nailed to the wall. Maybe the tenant had been a vampire?

At least this window had screens. After opening the sash, Drue stood at the picture window, which now left the room flooded with light. Outside, she could see what was left of the narrow patch of lawn Papi had seeded and weeded and babied. The tangerine tree she'd climbed to pick fruit to eat out of hand (and to use as ammunition in the never-ending rotten-fruit wars with the Harrell boys) was still there, stunted now and nearly leafless. But beyond it stood the fringe of Australian pines, and beyond that, the dunes. Just barely visible was a sliver of turquoise ocean.

She sucked in her breath. It had never occurred to her until this moment that her grandparents had given her the room with the best view of the water. In fact, they had always lavished her with the best of everything they had to give. She put a hand to the grimy glass. Even now, Nonni and Papi were looking out for her.

Her cell phone rang. She extracted it from the pocket of her jeans and reluctantly answered.

"Hey Dad."

"How's the house?"

She walked back toward the front door, mouth-breathing as she went. She stood outside on the abbreviated front porch, gulping in the clean air.

"Pretty grim."

"Sorry about that, but you're young. Probably nothing a little elbow grease can't fix."

Staring around the corner of the living room, she saw a mound of plaster shards she'd overlooked earlier. Glancing up, she saw the source of the problem. A huge brown water stain blossomed over the ceiling, where the raw lath was exposed.

"Yeah, elbow grease and a new roof," she muttered.

"I meant to ask, what are you doing for furniture?"

"I dunno," she admitted. "My old garage apartment came furnished. All I brought was my clothes, my kiteboard rig, some books and my coffeemaker."

"Pretty much what I figured," Brice said. "After we talked earlier, it occurred to me that we've been paying rent at a self-storage place out in Pinellas Park ever since we redecorated our house. I know there's some of your grandparents' stuff left from after Nonni died, and of course, the stuff from my 'bachelor pad' that Wendy made me get rid of. I don't remember what all's there, but you're welcome to it, if you want."

Drue ground her back molars. It was on the tip of her tongue to tell him she didn't need Wendy's rejects, but she forced herself to reconsider. The reality was, she needed those hand-me-downs. Spite could wait.

"Uh, thanks. That'd help a lot."

"I'll text you the address, unit number and key code for the gate, but you'll need to come by here to pick up the keys. Anything else?"

"I've got to get the cottage cleaned. It's been closed up for so long it's like a mildew buffet. The first thing I need to do is pry the windows open so I can breathe, but I don't even have a screwdriver."

"Yeah, I guess it would be pretty bad, what with the hurricane damage to the roof. Tell you what. Alberto's shed is still there. We never gave any of the tenants access to it. Maybe his tools and stuff are there. The keys are on that ring I gave you. Okay, well, Wendy and I are about to leave for dinner at the yacht club, but I'll put the storage unit key in our mailbox for you. Unless you want to join us?"

She looked down at her shredded jeans, tank top and flip-flops, thankful for an excuse to decline.

"Better not," she said. "I've got a lot of carpet to rip out tonight."

8

Papi's toolshed was a peak-roofed wooden building he'd built in the side yard of Coquina Cottage.

As far as she could tell, the shed was just as he'd left it. She pictured him here now, puttering away at the workbench that ran along the back of the shed, his bald head bent over his project, the transistor radio blaring his favorite talk radio station. He'd be chewing one of the cigars Nonni banned him from smoking in the house, humming as he worked, or talking back to the radio host, dropping the occasional cuss word in Spanish.

Everything was in order, although coated in dust, cobwebs and what looked like an entire village of dead bugs. A pegboard held his saws, chisels, hammers, vises and screwdrivers. He'd used old wooden cigar boxes with tiny knobs screwed to each to construct drawers for a homemade cubby holding a wide assortment of nails, screws, bolts and washers. The power tools were neatly arranged on the wooden shelves beside the bench. An old nail barrel held scraps of lumber. She inhaled deeply. The shed smelled of cigar smoke, WD-40 and sawdust. It smelled like Papi.

She gathered hammers, screwdrivers, pry bars and a box cutter and loaded up the leather tool belt that hung from a nail near the door.

Back in the house, she used the pry bar to remove a wooden broomstick that had been jammed inside the aluminum sliding-door track in the living room, and with what felt like herculean effort, managed to shove the door open, allowing for a welcome rush of fresh air. She stood in the doorway, looking out past the now-rotting deck toward the beach. It had gotten dark while she worked, but she could hear the waves lapping at the shore and that was enough for now. She had work to do.

She dragged a box fan in from the shed, set it up near the open front door and got busy. For the next two hours she pried and cut and cursed and sweated and ripped at the filthy carpet, bagging it up and ferrying it out to the trash in the wheelbar-row she'd found inside the shed.

It was a clean sweep, she thought elatedly, sitting on an up-ended mop bucket to survey her work and eat her dinner—a convenience store sub sandwich, bag of chips and quart of red Powerade. She swallowed three Advil and was considering her next move when her cell phone rang.

She was surprised to notice the time—after 10:00 P.M.

"I thought you were coming by to get the key to the storage place," Brice said. "We just got back from dinner, and the key's still here."

"I got busy ripping out all the old carpet, and I lost track of time," Drue said. "Anyway, I can't put furniture in here until I get it cleaned. This house is like a toxic waste dump."

"Okay, well, maybe tomorrow," Brice said. "Call me and let me know your plan."

At midnight, she carried in her suitcase and the few boxes of belongings she'd brought from Fort Lauderdale and set them down in the clean but barren living room.

She washed up and brushed her teeth, then went out to the living room and unearthed her sleeping bag from one of the boxes, unrolling it on the floor in front of the open sliding-glass doors.

Every bone in her body ached, and the wooden floor beneath her was unforgiving, but she propped her head on a pillow improvised from a rolled-up sweatshirt and sighed a deep sigh of contentment. She closed her eyes and listened to the hypnotic whoosh of waves washing up on the beach. She was home.

She felt a toe, gently prodding her in the ribs. "Hey, lazybones!"

Drue's eyes blinked open. Sunlight streamed in through the open sliding-glass door. Her father looked down at her, clearly amused.

She sat up, yawned and stretched. "What time is it?"

"Ten o'clock."

"Seriously?" She grabbed her phone and saw that it was. "Oh my God. I haven't slept this late in months."

She stood up and headed for the bathroom. When she came out, dressed in a faded T-shirt and jeans, he handed her a Styrofoam cup of coffee and a white bakery bag.

"Thanks," she said, taking a gulp. "How'd you get in here, anyway?"

Brice turned and pointed toward the front door. "It was standing wide open when I got here. You might want to lock it in the future. Sunset Beach isn't like it was when your grandparents were alive. There's actual crime now."

Drue opened the bag and lifted out a sugary pastry. She took a bite and smiled despite herself. "Apple fritter from Publix? I can't believe you remembered."

"I remember more than you give me credit for," he replied evenly.

Brice changed the subject. "I saw all the trash bags piled at the curb," he said, looking around the living room. "You must have worked your tail off last night. Okay if I look around?"

"Help yourself," she said, still chewing.

His footfalls echoed in the empty rooms as he took the brief tour. "The bathroom doesn't look too bad," he commented, sitting down on the upturned bucket and taking a sip of his own coffee.

"You should have seen it when I got here," she said, shuddering at the memory. She squared her shoulders and finished off the fritter. "I want to get the carpet pulled up in the bedrooms today, and then tackle the kitchen."

Brice pointed up at the patch of exposed lath and plaster in the water-stained ceiling. "I'm thinking you are going to have to replace the roof."

"I can't think about that right now," Drue said. "Definitely not in my budget."

He started to say something, but a faint chirping noise emanated from his phone. He looked down at the incoming text message. "Wish I could hang around and help, but we're meeting some out-of-town friends for brunch."

He handed her a small envelope. "That's the key to the storage shed. Take all or as much as you need."

At noon, Drue changed into a tankini and walked out onto the deck. She could feel the heat of the sand beneath the rubber soles of her flip-flops as she made her way along the dune path to the beach. She dropped her towel and shoes and waded through the shallow water until it was up to her neck. The Gulf was warmer than she'd remembered. She floated on her back and forced herself to just breathe, letting the gentle waves pull her back toward the shore before paddling back out and washing ashore a dozen times.

For a moment, she wondered when the last time was that she'd actually felt the balm of salt water on her skin. And then she remembered. It was the day of the accident.

Hundreds of people were scattered across the beach today, huddling under umbrellas or stretched out on blankets and chairs. Music drifted through the air as she sat on the hard-packed wet sand, her legs stretched out in front of her.

Drue guessed that an hour passed before she walked back to the house. Papi had rigged up an outdoor shower stall on the side of the shed, enclosing it with wooden shutters he'd found on somebody's trash pile. She struggled out of the swimsuit, slinging it over the top of the stall, then stood under the showerhead and let the shockingly cold water sluice over her body. She dried off, then wrapped the towel around her body and went back to work.

The kitchen had been Nonni's kingdom. She'd painted the walls a soft, buttery yellow, and the wooden cabinets, hand-built by Papi, were white enamel, with chrome knobs and pulls.

The Formica countertops were yellow with mica flecks, and the linoleum tile floor was a green and white checkerboard pattern.

Now, of course, everything was coated in years of grease and dirt. She opened every cupboard and drawer and scrubbed them inside and out, sweeping away the dried corpses of a village of cockroaches.

Grease spatters flecked the walls and the boxy old white range. She used an entire bottle of spray cleaner and two rolls of paper towels to scrape off the accumulated layers of grunge.

The unmistakable roar of a motorcycle engine pierced the afternoon quiet. She ran to the front window and peered out in time to see her father dismount from a gleaming red Harley-Davidson. "What the . . . ?"

Drue met him in the driveway.

"Nice bike."

Brice pulled off his helmet and tucked it under his arm. "This was my birthday present."

"Wendy bought you a Hawg for your birthday? Is she the beneficiary on your life insurance?"

He ran his fingers through his hair. "For your information,

Wendy hates the Harley. This was my present to myself. For outliving all the other bastards."

"Never would have pegged you as a biker," Drue said.

"There's a lot you don't know about me," Brice said. He unzipped a hard-shelled saddlebag on the back of the bike and lifted out a six-pack of beer, which he handed to her.

"That stands to reason, since you haven't been a part of my life since I was fifteen," she shot back.

"Christ!" Brice exploded. "Did you ever stop and ask yourself why that was?"

Drue shrugged. "You and Joan made it pretty clear at the time that you wanted me out of your hair. So I got out. I moved back to Lauderdale. And that was that. Birthday and Christmas cards, sure, but let's not forget that until the day you showed up out of the blue for Mom's funeral, you pretty much ghosted me."

"Did your mom ever mention I never once missed a child support payment? And that every year, without a court order, I upped the payment because I thought that was fair?"

"No."

"Did she tell you about all the times I offered to buy you a plane ticket to St. Pete?"

"She told me, but what was the point? You could have come to Lauderdale to visit me, but you never did."

"I was working," Brice said. "Building a law practice."

"So you could take Kayson and Kyler skiing in Breckenridge, and buy Joan a boob job," Drue said.

"You can't resist taking cheap shots at me, can you?" he asked.

"Not when you make it so incredibly easy."

She walked into the kitchen and stashed the beer in the fridge.

He turned to look at her. "So, do you want some help or would you prefer to keep laying your guilt trip on me? Your call."

Drue sighed. Bickering with Brice would get her nowhere. He was never going to understand her feelings of abandonment, so maybe it was time for her to let it go. "Okay, sure. I could use some help."

By five o'clock, they'd managed to pull up all the carpet in both bedrooms and haul it out to the trash.

"It's beer-thirty," Brice announced, reaching into the fridge. He popped the bottle cap on the countertop and handed her an ice-cold bottle.

She took a long swig, burped and wiped her mouth with the back of her hand.

"God, that tastes good. And I don't even really like beer," Drue said. "Thanks. I was beginning to get pretty overwhelmed."

Brice took a long swig from his own bottle. "I should have hired a cleaning crew to come in before you moved in. So that's on me."

She shrugged and looked around the kitchen; the linoleum floor was still damp from her degreasing effort and the chipped Formica countertops newly shone. "I still can't really believe the place is mine. I think of all the Saturday mornings right here in this kitchen, with Nonni fixing pancakes, and Papi making his Cuban coffee . . ."

"I remember Alberto's coffee. It was like drinking mud," Brice said. A faraway expression came over his face as he looked around.

"You know, your mom and I lived here for a while."

"Really? When was that?"

"Mid-seventies. After I got back from Vietnam. I was on the police force, and Sherri was working for a real estate outfit. Alberto hadn't retired yet and they were just using this as a weekend place, so he rented it to us for peanuts. It was all we could afford."

He sighed. "We had some good times in this place."

Before Drue could ask him when things had changed, a faint chirping noise began emanating from his jeans. "Uh-oh." He pulled out his cell phone. "I gotta get home and get showered. Promised Wendy I'd take her out to dinner tonight."

"Dinner last night, brunch earlier, dinner out tonight? Does she know how to cook?"

"That's not fair," Brice said, his amiable mood gone. "Why all the hostility toward Wendy?"

"Ask her."

"It seems to me that you're the one with the attitude," Brice said. "She's gone out of her way to be nice to you."

"Riiiighhhht," Drue said, swabbing at the sink with a sponge to avoid meeting the hurt look on his face. "Just forget I said anything. Bad joke."

He drained the rest of his beer and threw the bottle into the trash. "Drue? If you and Wendy are going to continue to work together, you two need to call a truce with this bullshit. Whatever happened all those years ago, it's all in the past. Time to get over yourself and move on."

She set her half-finished beer on the countertop. "Great advice in theory. Maybe you should suggest the same thing to her."

He sighed and threw his hands in the air. "I give up. I'll see you Monday."

9

After Brice left, she resumed cleaning. A late-afternoon squall brought heavy rain and a welcome drop in the temperature. When she went into the kitchen she noticed a puddle of water on her newly cleaned floor.

Drue looked up at the ceiling. A large wet blotch the size of a dinner plate had formed in the plaster, and as she stared at it, another drop of water fell on her forehead.

Another roof leak! She sighed heavily and walked into the narrow hallway, reaching up for the cord that dangled from the ceiling and yanking, hard, until the pull-down attic stairs unfolded with a loud squeak from rust and disuse. She went back to the kitchen and fetched the heavy flashlight she'd unearthed from Papi's shed, switching it on to make sure that the new batteries she'd installed were working.

As she climbed the ladder she felt a growing sense of dread.

She'd never liked dark places. She'd never lived in any other place in Florida that even had an attic. Or a basement. The attic at Coquina Cottage she knew only from her grandfather's occasional forays, when he'd climb up to set and retrieve rat traps, prompted only by Nonni's insistence that she'd heard ominous scratching sounds in the kitchen coming from overhead.

"Okay, rats," she called loudly, right before she reached the top rung of the ladder. "I'm coming up, so you better get gone."

She listened carefully, ready to beat a hasty retreat at the first suspicious squeak. But all she heard was the steady, ominous drip of water coming from the roof. She popped her head through the attic floor and swung the flashlight in a wide arc. The attic was almost unbearably hot, and dank-smelling.

The first thing the flashlight revealed was a faded blue plastic child's wading pool. "What the hell?" she muttered. But when she looked overhead, she realized the pool's purpose. Somebody, maybe the last tenant, had decided to utilize the pool as a catch basin for earlier roof leaks. The pool held maybe a half-inch of murky brown water, and another pool of rain had begun to puddle on the rough wooden floor an inch away. A new leak. And a new headache for the new homeowner.

Drue pulled herself up to a standing position, wincing at the strain on her knee. She played the flashlight over the roof, spotting at least three slow drips of rain. She tugged the wading pool over a few inches, and was rewarded with the sound of raindrops splashing into the pool. Problem solved. For now. Until there was another heavy rain, or at the end of summer, the potential for a hurricane.

Aside from the wading pool, the attic was mostly empty. There was an old sewing machine base that she remembered from her childhood, and a funny split-level metal dollhouse that she'd never seen before, along with several outdated suitcases that looked like they'd last been used in the sixties. Pushed up under the roof gables was a row of worn wooden crates, some still bearing faded fruit labels. She lifted the lid of one of the crates, revealing a cache of old books, their covers faded and spotted with what looked suspiciously like roach eggs. She closed the lid with a shudder and moved on to the next crate, which was filled with stacks of tiny, carefully folded baby clothes in shades of pale pink and yellow. They were too old to have been Drue's, and anyway, Sherri had never been the type for keepsakes, so these must have been Sherri's own baby things, lovingly tucked away by Nonni.

Shoved into the crawl space behind the fruit boxes was a cardboard banker's box with SHERRI'S PAPERS written in red Magic Marker, in her mother's familiar scrawl. As Drue pulled it toward her, the sides collapsed under the weight of its contents.

Packets of rubber-banded canceled checks, old bills marked "paid" and two file folders spilled onto the rough-hewn attic floorboards. The first folder had IMPORTANT PAPERS written on the tab.

Drue smiled as she leafed through the miscellany of Sherri's life: an unframed high school "Certificate of Achievement" for stenography, and fastened together with a paper clip, faded photocopies of Sherri Ann Sanchez's birth certificate, her first Florida driver's license, both Drue's grandparents' death certificates, copies of Sherri's Social Security card, Drue's parents' marriage certificate, and at the bottom of the stack of papers, their divorce decree, dated November 27, 1988.

Drue ran her finger over the black-and-white print, marveling that the official dissolution of a family could not only be reduced to a single page, but that it would end up here—in the attic of her grandparents' house, along with a handful of other documents that her mother had deemed important but not important enough to keep close by.

The second folder contained a dozen or so yellowed newspaper clippings from the *St. Petersburg Times,* all of them apparently about the mysterious disappearance of an attractive local woman whom the press had dubbed "missing local beauty." Drue's interest was piqued by the fact that the missing woman, twenty-six-year-old Colleen Boardman Hicks, had vanished after shopping and dining at a local department store, Maas Brothers, which had once stood only a few blocks from the present-day law offices of Campbell, Coxe and Kramner.

She carefully set both folders near the attic stairs so she wouldn't forget to take them when she went back downstairs.

The third crate had a label scrawled in Sherri's familiar handwriting. BRICE'S CRAP. Drue laughed out loud. The box was full of books and papers. Law books, loose-leaf notebooks and half a dozen composition books, all bearing the name Brice Campbell on the inside covers. She rifled idly through the contents of the crate, stopping when she found a thick black binder. A typed adhesive label on the front had faded, but the type was still legible.

COLLEEN BOARDMAN HICKS—Missing Persons. 8-20-76.

This had to be the same "missing local beauty" whose disappearance had been chronicled in the old newspaper clippings.

Drue leafed through the three-inch-thick binder. There were page after page of typed police reports, handwritten notes and carbon copies of more reports. A pocket on the inside back cover of the binder held yellowing black-and-white photographs.

She stared down at the binder. She knew virtually nothing about police procedures, but the book she was holding looked a lot like official police business. But what was it doing here, in her grandparents' attic?

When she heard a faint scrabbling sound coming from the far end of the attic, she tucked the folders and the binder under her arm and scrambled down the ladder as fast as she could go.

Downstairs, she typed "Colleen Boardman Hicks" into her phone's search bar. The screen filled with dozens of citations.

She clicked on the most recent article, published six months earlier in the *Tampa Bay Times.*

FORTY-YEAR-OLD MYSTERY REMAINS UNSOLVED. She skimmed the article, which confirmed that Colleen Hicks had never been found.

Colleen Boardman Hicks was a vivacious blond 26-year-old newlywed. She had a loving husband, successful career, and strong local ties. Then, one evening in 1976, after a day of shopping and dinner with a friend, she vanished, seemingly into thin air.

Now, more than forty years later, officials say they are no closer to solving the puzzle of the bay area's most enduring mystery than they were on the day she was discovered missing.

In fact, Ralph Pflieger, a now-retired St. Petersburg Police detective who was involved with the Colleen Hicks investigation in the late 1970s, says the case has gotten murkier with the passing of time.

"For a while there, every five years or so, me or one of the other detectives would pick it up again, chase down some leads, talk to some potential witnesses. But we never really got anywhere. And then, not long after I retired, when I asked about the Hicks case file, a buddy of mine said it had gone missing," Pflieger said.

"I couldn't believe it. Back then, we didn't have computers. All our work was typed or handwritten. The interviews, the evidence logs, the detective's notes, all of that, years and years of investigative work, was in that file. And it's gone just as sure as Colleen Hicks is gone."

Drue looked down at the dusty black binder sitting on the floor beside her. Was *this* the missing file?

10

~~~~~

"Drue?" Wendy stood beside her cubicle, looking uncharacteristically frazzled. Her Hermès scarf was haphazardly knotted around her shoulders and her eyeliner was smudged. "I need you out in reception. Right now."

Drue finished the referral form she'd been working on. "Why?"

"Because I'm your supervisor and I asked you, that's why," Wendy snapped, turning on her heel. "And bring your headset."

Drue gave a martyr's sigh and trailed Wendy out to the reception area.

"You're covering reception today. It shouldn't be that busy. Brice is OOO, so he doesn't have any appointments until this afternoon."

"OOO?"

"Out of office," Wendy said.

"So, where's Geoff?"

"He called in sick. Impacted wisdom tooth."

"Why me?" Drue asked. "Why not Jonah? Or Ben? Or Marianne or one of the other paralegals? Or the girls in accounting?"

"Because I asked you," Wendy said. "The others are busy." For the first time she stopped to take in Drue's outfit, which today consisted of her usual skinny jeans and a navy-blue-and-white-striped T-shirt.

"Don't you own any dresses? Or something that even vaguely resembles what a grown woman wears in a professional setting?" Wendy asked.

"I've got a dress I wear for funerals," Drue said defensively. "And why do you care what I wear? I never interact with any of our clients in person. I'm stuck in the bullpen all day. So I wear what's comfortable. Is that a problem for you?"

Wendy rolled her eyes. "I just think you should take a little more pride in your appearance. You're a cute girl, Drue, or you would be if you'd ever put on some makeup and fix your hair."

Drue sat at the reception desk. "I'm not auditioning for *The Bachelorette*, you know. And since I've never heard you take issue with anything the guys wear to work, I consider your remarks about my personal appearance to be sexual discrimination. Possibly harassment too."

"Whatever. Just sit here, okay? You can still take whatever calls are routed to you, and use Geoff's desktop. If we get any walk-ins, just run through the intake forms, same as you do on the Justice Line. Sign for any package deliveries. Got it?"

"I guess."

"You can call me if there's anything urgent, but things should be fairly quiet," Wendy said.

~

The morning was largely a bust. The Justice Line was humming, but none of the calls yielded a single signed-up case. Drue sighed. The week was shaping up to be a big fat zero. She ate lunch at her desk: a peanut butter and jelly sandwich, carrot sticks and a bag of green grapes.

The office door chimed softly and a burly African-American woman marched directly up to the reception desk. She was dressed in mauve-colored cotton scrubs. Her graying hair was cut close to the scalp. A young girl of eight or nine peeped out from behind her bulk. She wore pink eyeglasses held together with what looked like a paper clip, pink shorts and a T-shirt that featured a sequined pastel porpoise.

"I'm here to see Brice Campbell," the woman announced in an overly loud voice.

Drue gave the visitor her best smile. "I'm afraid Mr. Campbell is in court this morning."

"Yeah, uh-huh," the woman said, wagging a finger in Drue's face. "That's what that woman on the phone been telling me for weeks now. He's all the time in court. I have called and left messages, and nobody ever calls me back. So I'm here right now, and I'm not leaving until I see that man." She planted her feet on the plush carpet and crossed meaty arms over her bosom. The little girl gripped the fabric of the woman's pants tightly in one hand, and twirled one of the dozen pink-rubber-banded cornrows that cascaded to her shoulders.

"Uh, okay." Drue picked up a pen. "Could you tell me your name and what case this is in reference to?"

"My name is Yvonne Howington. *H-O-W-I-N-G-T-O-N.* You got that? What this is in reference to is how my baby girl, Jazmin Mayes, ended up dead and stuffed in a laundry cart at the Gulf Vista Resort. This is in reference to how, thanks to Brice Campbell, ain't nobody ever been arrested for killing my baby girl. Been nearly two years now. It's in reference to how he messed up and let those hotel people get away with paying me hardly anything. That's what this is in reference to."

She looked down at the child and gently removed her hand from her hair. "Stop that fiddling now, Aliyah. You gonna mess up that pretty hairdo."

Yvonne Howington gestured at the child. "Aliyah, she's got asthma. Needs two different inhalers and two different kinds of pills. You know what one of those inhalers costs? A hundred and fifty dollars. And if she gets a cold, or an ear infection, which she does all the time, that's another visit to the emergency room, and antibiotics and I don't know what all."

"Oh, wow," Drue said, for lack of anything better to say. "That's terrible."

Aliyah looked up and gave her a shy smile. "Hello." When she stepped from behind the woman who Drue presumed was her grandmother, Drue noticed she had what looked like an iPad with a cover plastered in childish stickers.

"Hi," Drue said. "I wish I had an iPad like yours. What do you like to do on yours?"

"I like to read, and sometimes I draw or watch videos." Aliyah ducked her head and looked away.

"Her mama bought her that for Christmas, but I can't afford to let her download all those books and movies she wants. This girl reads all the time," Yvonne said. "She likes those YouTube videos too. But she needs new glasses. How I'm gonna pay for glasses and medicine and all of that? With a hundred thirty-five thousand dollars but it's in a trust for her 'til she turns eighteen? Money I can't touch, even though I'm raising her? How I'm gonna keep my job and look after her and see she keeps out of trouble in that bad neighborhood we live in? Tell me that."

"I . . . I don't know," Drue said. She picked up her pen again. "Honest. Mr. Campbell really is in court today. But I can take down your name and let him know you'd like to see him and I'm sure his assistant can get you an appointment—"

"Listen to me!" the woman thundered. "Me and Aliyah, we are staying right here in this office until that man comes out here and does right by me. A hundred and fifty thousand dollars? Minus Brice Campbell's lawyer fees? That's what those hotel people say my baby girl's life was worth? That's a joke! But ain't nobody laughing."

She turned and herded her grandchild toward the sitting area, heaving herself down onto the sofa with a grunt. Aliyah sat down too and waited expectantly while her grandmother pawed through the contents of a backpack, handing the girl a juice box and a container of animal crackers. After the child was settled, she plucked a book of crossword puzzles from the backpack and attacked it with a pencil.

Drue picked up her headset and plugged it into the back of the phone.

"Oh hi, Wendy," she said softly. "There's a, uh, client here who would like to see Mr. Campbell."

"I *told* you, Brice is out of office today," Wendy said. "And he doesn't see walk-ins. You know that. Just tell her to call and make an appointment."

Yvonne Howington was staring at her, listening in.

"I suggested that, but she's pretty adamant about seeing Mr. Campbell."

"Who is it?" Wendy asked.

Drue swiveled the desk chair around so that her back was to the sitting area. "It's Ms. Howington," she whispered. "She says her daughter was murdered? At the Gulf Vista? And she's got her granddaughter with her."

"Her again? Jesus H.," Wendy said. "That woman does not give up. Brice has explained the settlement to her numerous times, but she just doesn't want to hear it."

"Maybe you could come out and talk to her? She's pretty worked up."

"No, I can't come out there. I'm busy. Do whatever you need to do, but get rid of her. We don't need a disgruntled client out there scaring off new business."

"What if she doesn't want to leave?" Drue was starting to feel nervous. She hadn't signed up to be the law firm's bouncer.

"Speak to her firmly. Suggest that she leave, or otherwise you'll call the cops. And then do that."

"Call the cops? On a woman whose daughter has been murdered? A grandmother?"

"Handle it!" Wendy snapped. The phone went dead.

Drue swiveled the chair back around. Her fingers raced over the computer keyboard, accessing the firm's case management database. She typed in the name Jazmin Mayes and waited for the files to download.

She glanced up at Ms. Howington, who was glaring at her again. "I'm on hold with Mr. Campbell's assistant," she lied.

"I don't wanna talk to that heifer," Ms. Howington said, waving away the suggestion. "Mr. Campbell is the one promised me we'd get four million, five million easy from those hotel people. Now I want him to look me in the face and have him tell me how I'm supposed to raise Jazmin's daughter with that little bit of money I can't even touch."

As she read the file Drue kept glancing up at the little girl, who sat placidly looking at her iPad.

Drue arrowed down the intake report, condensing the facts in her mind as she read. Yvonne Howington had called the Justice Line for the first time eighteen months earlier, on October 30. She was forty-six, single and lived in a neighborhood on the city's south side. She'd listed a sister, Francine Meeks, as her emergency contact, and according to the form, Yvonne had viewed one of the firm's television commercials, which is where she'd seen the firm's distinctive 777-7777 Justice Line phone number.

On the line where the form asked "Relationship to Injured Party" someone had typed MOTHER.

Drue glanced up at Ms. Howington, who was penciling something into her crossword book. Aliyah, finished with her juice, was folding the plastic straw into segments, and her iPad lay closed in her lap.

The reception desk's bottom drawer yielded a stack of white printer paper. In the top drawer she found red, blue and yellow highlighter pens, and pads of the neon-colored self-stick tabs used to designate where clients signed documents. She took the tabs, paper and markers over to the girl, squatting down beside her.

"Hey," she said, smiling. "Looks like you finished your book. Do you like to draw?"

The girl's face lit up. "Yeah, I like to draw."

"Yes, ma'am," Yvonne Howington corrected, not looking up from her book. "We say 'yes, ma'am' when we are talking to grown-ups."

"Yes, ma'am," Aliyah said.

Drue handed her a few sheets of paper and put the stickies and markers on the carpet beside her. "I'm sorry we don't have any crayons, but I think markers are way cooler, don't you?"

"Yes, ma'am," she agreed.

"What do you say to the lady?" Yvonne asked, nodding her head at Drue in a reluctant show of gratitude.

"Thank you!" Aliyah said. She seized a marker and began drawing.

Jazmin Mayes, according to the intake sheet, had been twenty-four years old at the time of what the form called "the incident" on September 15, 2016, which had occurred at the Gulf Vista Hotel and Resort on Gulf Boulevard on Sunset Beach.

Drue shivered involuntarily. The Gulf Vista was a gated oceanfront resort development maybe half a mile from her own cottage. She passed the beach side of the property every day during her early morning beach walk, skirting the rows of turquoise-cushioned beach chaises and canvas-topped cabanas. She'd even tried once, but only once, to get a better look at the sprawling property by ignoring all the private property signs and walking up to the fence separating the beach from the pool deck, only to be turned away by a security guard who'd asked to see her resort key.

She skimmed through all the mundane questions Justice Line clerks asked of prospective clients—time of day, weather, exact location, including address and nearest intersection, and details of what the injured party was doing at the location of the incident—until she got to the meat of the form, known as the narrative.

"My daughter, Jazmin Mayes, worked at the hotel as a housekeeper," Yvonne Howington had written. She'd skipped many of the questions on the form, typing in question marks, or "don't know."

Finally, she got down to brass tacks.

IN YOUR OWN WORDS, PLEASE DESCRIBE WHAT HAPPENED.

Yvonne's response was succinct, bone-chilling and heart-breaking.

> Jazmin gets off work at 11 o'clock on Sunday nights, but that night she didn't come home, like she told me she was going to. The police say she was killed some-time after midnight. Another housekeeper called hotel security after she went to the laundry and found Jaz-min's body wrapped up in sheets in a laundry cart. The guard was the one that called the police. The police told me she'd been strangled. The police came to my door

at eight o'clock that morning. There were two of them, a man and a lady, who said they were detectives. That's when they told me my daughter was dead. They didn't say nothing about how it happened, not at first. They just asked me a whole lot of questions about Jazmin, and who her friends were at work, and how long she'd been working at the hotel, and whether or not anybody had been bothering her.

Yvonne Howington slapped the crossword book shut. "Look here. Did that assistant say when Mr. Campbell will be back?"

It was nearly two o'clock. Brice's office hours could best be described as erratic. Although she hadn't seen it yet, Drue knew he had an office at home. If he was working on a big case and didn't want the distractions of the office, he often decided to work alone, at home.

"Mr. Campbell's assistant told me he probably won't be back in the office today," Drue said. "I really think it would be better if you made an appointment to see him. I can have his assistant call you to set up a time."

"That assistant is just stalling me. I been trying to get to see Brice Campbell ever since she called to tell me about the check I was going to be getting. He promised me four, maybe five million dollars. And I get nothing? That ain't right. He knows it and I know it, and you'd know it too, if you knew what I know."

Drue swallowed hard. The desktop phone buzzed. She picked up her headset.

"Tell me she's gone." It was Wendy.

"Afraid not."

"I'm coming out there and we'll get this taken care of right now." Wendy disconnected.

A moment later, the door from the back office swung open and Wendy marched right up to their visitor.

"Ms. Howington?" Wendy's voice was pitched. "I'm Mr. Campbell's office manager, Wendy. I know we've met before. And we've talked on the phone. The thing is, Ms. Howington, Brice won't be back to the office this afternoon. If you'd called to ask about an appointment I could have saved you all the trouble of coming down here today."

"I been calling about an appointment and getting nothing but the runaround," Yvonne said, her own voice rising. "So I come down here today, and I brought Jazmin's girl with me."

She touched the child's shoulder. "Stand up, Aliyah."

The child scrambled to her feet and ducked her head, self-conscious and shy under Wendy's none-too-friendly gaze.

"I want you to look at this girl, Miss Wendy. You look at her and tell me her mama's life was only worth one hundred and fifty thousand dollars."

Wendy let out a long, martyred sigh. "Ms. Howington, we've been over this before. Brice and I and everybody here at the firm are deeply sorry for your loss. Truly, we are. And as Brice told you himself, he did everything he could to hold the hotel responsible for what happened to Jazmin. He had hoped to be able to prove wrongful death, which would have resulted in a much larger settlement from the hotel's insurer. But the fact is, because the incident happened while she was on duty, it became a workers' compensation claim. And workers' comp claims in Florida are, by law, capped at a hundred and fifty thousand, which was the amount of your settlement, before legal fees."

Yvonne Howington struggled to her feet. "No, ma'am," she said, her voice hoarse with anger. "Like I told *you* and anybody who would listen, Jazmin got off work at eleven o'clock that night. She didn't never work later than that, because I had to get to work, myself, in the morning."

"That's not what her supervisor said," Wendy replied. "He said she got to work almost one hour late that day, and then begged him to give her an extra shift to make up the time. Our investigator saw her time card, which verifies that account. And we looked at the security videos, which showed Jazmin, in her housekeeping uniform, after her shift should have ended at eleven, entering a room on the first floor with her passkey, then leaving the room around one-thirty."

"Those hotel people lie like rugs," Yvonne said. "All of 'em ain't nothing but a pack of liars. And criminals." She started to say something further, then stopped.

"Aliyah, there's a water fountain out there in the hallway. Why don't you go get a drink, and then go in the bathroom. Can you do that by yourself?"

She leaned down and her voice softened. "Make sure you wash your hands after, and don't you talk to nobody. You just go in that bathroom and do your business and come right back here."

Wendy hesitated, then took a plastic card from the lanyard she wore around her neck. "Here. This is the key to our private bathroom. You hold that up to the round pad on the door, and the light will flash green, and it'll unlock and let you in. Can you do that?"

"Yeah, I can do that," Aliyah said.

"You mean 'yes, ma'am,'" Yvonne put in.

Yvonne walked to the door, held it open and watched as the girl scampered out to the hallway.

Then she turned to Wendy and Drue. "I didn't want to say anything in front of Aliyah, but there was bad stuff going on at that hotel. One of the bosses, he was always coming around, Jazmin said, grabbing at her and touching her. She never said his name, just that he was a married white man, and he was old enough to be her daddy!"

"You told us that before, but the investigator couldn't find anybody who could corroborate that," Wendy said. "So it was her word against hotel management."

Yvonne's dark eyes flashed angrily. "And everybody knows a white man's word is always worth more than what some trashy little colored girl says, right?"

"I didn't say that," Wendy said. "I don't think that way. Neither does Brice."

The office door opened and Brice Campbell strode inside, his briefcase tucked under one arm. His face was sunburned, and he was dressed in jeans and an untucked dress shirt.

"What's going on?" He looked from Wendy to Drue, and started to say something else, but stopped when he caught sight of Yvonne Howington. He wrinkled his brow, clearly trying to place the face.

"Oh hi . . . uh, Ms. . . ."

"Yvonne Howington," the client said, looking him up and down. "You don't remember me, do you?"

"I know your face," he said, untroubled by her glare. "Wrongful death suit. Your daughter, isn't that right? One of the beach hotels?"

Yvonne Howington's clenched fists rested on her hips. "Her name was Jazmin. Jazmin Mayes. It shoulda been a wrongful death suit. Would have been, but nobody cares about another dead black girl."

Brice looked stricken. "The Gulf Vista. Of course." He glanced at Wendy. "You explained to Ms. Howington about the workers' comp statutory limits?"

"I tried," Wendy said.

Brice touched Yvonne's elbow. "I'm sorry. The matter is out of my hands. The hotel can prove that your daughter was on the clock when she was killed. The law says—"

She shook him off. "Don't you tell me what the law says," she said, her voice hoarse. "I know what's going on here. You took some kind of payoff from the insurance company, didn't you? What'd they pay you?"

Wendy bristled. "Now just a minute. You can't come in here and accuse my husband of unethical behavior."

"Oh, he's your husband? That explains a whole lot," Yvonne shot back. "All of y'all are just a bunch of thieves. But let me tell you, you haven't heard the last from me. I'mma get me another lawyer."

"You do that," Wendy said.

Drue saw the door open a crack. Aliyah pressed her face to the opening, her dark eyes wide at the grown-up argument winding down inside. She opened the door and crept silently back into the office, picking up a marker and returning to her art project.

Brice waved a hand. "All right, let's all just cool down now. Ms. Howington, I'm sorry you think you weren't properly represented. You're of course free to retain any attorney you like. And as you know, our fee structure was explained to you from the outset. You signed a document to that effect."

Yvonne grabbed her pocketbook and backpack. "Bunch of crooks," she muttered. She put her hand on the little girl's shoulder. "Come on, child." She yanked the door open and led the girl outside.

Wendy watched the two depart, a sour expression on her face. "I *told* Drue to get rid of her an hour ago. Next time she shows up, I'm calling the police."

Brice placed an arm around his wife's shoulder. "She's upset. Just let it go."

"Easy for you to say. She didn't call you a heartless bitch," Wendy retorted. "When the final papers for her settlement arrive, I'm having them messengered over to her house. I don't want potential clients to be subjected to her harangues."

"Good idea," he agreed. He looked over at Drue. "You've been promoted to receptionist?"

Through the reception room window Drue watched as Yvonne Howington loaded Aliyah into the back of an ancient rust-bucket Plymouth that was parked at the curb. The car's engine belched and backfired. Plumes of black smoke streamed from the tailpipe as she backed out of the parking space. The little girl was turned around in her seat, gazing toward the law office.

"I feel terrible for that lady," Drue murmured. She turned to Brice. "That doesn't seem fair. The girl was murdered on their property, and the hotel only pays one hundred and fifty thousand?"

"Blame the insurance lobby," Brice said mildly. "They're the ones that convinced the state legislature to cap workers' comp benefits."

"You have no idea how complicated these cases are, or how hard it is to prove wrongful death," Wendy said, her voice terse. "This firm wasted tens of thousands of dollars investigating that woman's claim. What we'll recover is a pittance of what we spent. You can go on back to the bullpen now, Drue. I'll cover the phones for the rest of the day."

Drue walked over to the seating area and picked up the abandoned art supplies. She scooped up the markers and looked down at the top piece of paper. The little girl had drawn an undersea tableau featuring a mermaid with long, flowing yellow highlighter hair, a grinning crab and a jolly yellow flounder. On the bottom, she'd signed her name in the tiniest letters possible. *Aliyah.*

When she got back to her cubicle, Drue pinned the drawing to the wall above her computer screen.

11

Okay, team, listen up." Wendy stood at the head of the long table in the law firm's windowless conference room. She wore a sleeveless, form-fitting white dress and sling-back nude stilettos that, Drue thought, must be excruciatingly uncomfortable.

"Today is day one of our new elder abuse ad campaign. Last night, during *Wheel of Fortune*, we started airing the new commercials. Those will be on heavy rotation for the next six weeks. We'll supplement with radio commercials, and of course, print and social media, with a heavy emphasis on Facebook advertising. We've also bought three billboards, one over near the Bay Pines VA hospital, the other on I-75, north of the first Tampa exit, and the third on U.S. 19 in Clearwater.

"Last night's shift experienced a huge volume of calls spurred by the new campaign, and I'm expecting the same today,"

Wendy went on. "We know from our market research in Arizona, California and, of course, Florida that juries are more and more willing to award huge settlements for these nursing home cases, which also means insurance companies are being pressured to settle quickly, and out of court. So I'm giving all of you a new case quota. We want to see three confirmed 'viable' cases from every member of the team this week. And for every prospective client who does go ahead and sign with us, that team member will be entered into a drawing for a one-hundred-dollar Visa gift card!"

"Awesome!" exclaimed Ben, who was, as usual, sitting beside Drue.

"Okay, then," Wendy made a sweeping motion, "everybody get out there now. I want to hear those Justice Line phones ring!"

"Good morning." Her first caller, Drue thought, sounded surprisingly articulate. "I believe I might have an excellent case against the assisted living facility where my mother has been living for the past two years."

Drue went down the questionnaire, filling in the potential client's information, her excitement mounting. She had a referral!

"It's probably financial abuse more than anything," the woman said. "You see, my late father was meticulous in his financial planning. Mother has a set amount of money in her bank account, and up until now that's been more than sufficient. But lately, we've noticed that her spending habits have gone through the roof. It's only May, and she's already run through all her money for the year."

"Okay," Drue said. "Do you believe she's being coerced, or somehow blackmailed by one of the employees? Is it embezzlement? Or possibly identity fraud?"

"Nothing like that," the woman said. "It's the damned Home Shopping Network. I've asked, I've put it in writing, I've even gone to the director of the home himself, but they refuse to do anything about it."

"About what?"

"The Home Shopping Network! I want it blocked. Or disabled. Or something. Her entire suite is full of Capodimonte porcelain shepherdesses and sets of nonstick copper cookware. Cookware! She didn't cook when she had a kitchen. And don't get me started on the electronic toothbrushes that arrive every month like clockwork. Mother wears dentures! Now they're shipping the stuff to my house. My garage is full of this crap. It has to stop!"

Drue looked at the other cube rats, all of them busily typing away.

"I guess I don't understand how that constitutes abuse. Or neglect," she said, choosing her words carefully. "Maybe you could just have a talk with your mom? Explain that her spending has gotten out of hand? Take away her credit card? Or, I don't know, remove the television?"

"I took Mother's credit card away and she called her attorney and directed him to have me written out of her will," the caller said. "And did you just say take her television away? You have no idea what you're suggesting," the woman said. "That television is her best friend. Her only friend. I just want them to *block* the damned HSN."

Drue took a deep breath. "All right. Well, I've got your information, and I'll, uh, forward that to the appropriate associates."

She disconnected, switched her phone to Off and headed for the break room.

Jonah was standing with his back to the counter, sipping from his mug of coffee. He spotted her before she could slink silently away. They were the only ones in the room.

"How's it going?" he asked. "Sign up any cases yet?"

"Not really. You?"

"I've got one really solid prospect. The caller claims his grandfather's nursing home was negligent because they allowed the old guy to have unsupervised visits with his wife," Jonah said.

"I know I'm going to regret asking this, but how is that negligent?"

Jonah sniggered. "It turns out the granddad is quite wealthy, eighty-two and frail, and the wife, it turns out, isn't legally his wife at all, but a twenty-eight-year-old 'masseuse' whose brother is a maintenance worker at the home. Seems the maintenance worker struck up a friendship with the patient, who expressed his, ah, longing for female companionship. Apparently some money changed hands and a date was arranged."

"I'm guessing the date did not include scripture readings?" Drue asked.

"You are correct," Jonah said. "And to make sure the patient and his bogus wife were afforded privacy, the maintenance worker stood guard outside the room. Eventually things got a little rowdy, and the patient actually fell out of bed and fractured his hip."

"You're making that up," Drue said, struggling to maintain a straight face.

"If I'm lying, I'm dying," he pledged. "Got to love an octogenarian horndog, right?"

Drue went to the refrigerator, got a bottle of water, uncapped it and took a swig.

"That's a good case, right?" she asked.

"It's a no-brainer. The maintenance worker has a criminal record, which the nursing home should have known about, the masseuse works for an escort service, and, get this, now Granddaddy has an STD. Brice is absolutely gonna love it."

"All I've got is a woman who wants us to sue the nursing home because they won't cut off her mom's access to Home Shopping Network," Drue said glumly.

"Weak sauce," he said, sounding sympathetic.

Drue was trying hard to cling to her childish and unreasonable loathing for Jonah, but the fact that he was so annoyingly funny made it hard for her to maintain her grudge.

Over coffee earlier in the week, Ben had confided that Jonah had interned summers during law school at Campbell, Coxe and Kramner and was still at the firm because he'd failed his first try at the Florida bar exam. Jonah, she realized, had institutional memory.

"Hey," she said, trying to sound casual. "You know anything about the Jazmin Mayes case?"

He ripped open two sugar packets and dumped the contents

into his mug. "That's the girl whose body was found stuffed into a dryer at the hotel on Sunset Beach? Like, two years ago?"

"It was actually a laundry cart, but yeah."

"I know Brice thought it was a slam dunk for criminal negligence and/or wrongful death. Why do you ask?"

"Her mom, Yvonne Howington, came into the office this week. She was raising hell, because we settled it as a workers' comp case. She as much as accused my dad of taking a payoff from the hotel's insurance company."

Jonah snorted. "That's how it is with some of these clients. They don't want to hear the bad news, so they blame it on the messenger. Assume the worst, accuse the firm of bribery, bad faith, the works."

"But this girl was murdered. Strangled to death. It's so horrible. I can't believe the best we could do was get a workers' comp settlement," Drue said.

"Why do you care?" He sipped his coffee.

"Because," she said, sputtering. "It's not right. Jazmin Mayes left behind a six-year-old daughter with serious medical issues. So now the grandmother's a single mom, dealing with that stuff. And we settle it for chump change?"

"You're right, it sucks, but it's the law."

"I don't care what you say. Something's seriously wrong if that's the best Brice could do. The grandmother swears her daughter was being harassed at work, and that she was not on the clock that night. She never worked past eleven."

"Don't know what to tell you," Jonah said. "I'm sure Jimmy Zee looked at it from every angle. The guy's slick."

"And a little girl lost her mom," Drue said. "I just lost my mom too. Maybe I'm just overly sensitive about this stuff right now."

Jonah nodded. "I gotta get back to my cube. Gotta make my granny quota. One down, two to go."

"One down, two to go," Drue mimicked. She needed to get back to her own cube, but her heart wasn't in it. She kept thinking about that Aliyah with her shy smile and her Band-Aid-rigged eyeglasses. Who was working the Justice Line for her?

12

~~~~~

Drue's phone lit up and she eagerly stabbed at the button on her console. It was Friday and she still hadn't booked a single nursing home case referral. In fact, she hadn't had anything close to a solid case lead in the two weeks since she'd started work.

"You've reached the Justice Line at Campbell, Cox and Kramner. This is Drue speaking."

The caller was a youngish-sounding woman. "Hi. I wanna talk to somebody about how I fell in the 7-Eleven and broke my tailbone, and I got doctor bills and so I went over there to tell them they needed to give me some financial help, and the store manager called the cops on me."

"Okay," Drue said slowly, wishing she'd let the call roll over to the off-site phone center.

"First, what's your name?"

The woman on the other end of the line paused. "Why do you need my name?"

Drue inhaled and exhaled. "If you're going to be a client of the law firm, and we file legal action on your behalf, we need your name. And your address, and all your other personal information."

"Oh. I got ya. Sure. It's Vyckylynn. With *y*'s instead of *i*'s."

"I've never seen a name spelled like that," Drue said as she typed.

"Yeah. My mom always liked to be unique. You want my real last name?"

"That'd be best," Drue said.

"Okay. It's Young. Spelled the usual way."

"Okay, Vyckylynn. Why don't you tell me about your accident?"

"I already told you. I was at the 7-Eleven in Pinellas Park, well, me and my boyfriend were there, and he'd already left, and I was about to leave, and I slipped and fell, like, really hard on my ass. I, like, passed out. And when I came to, they were putting me in the ambulance. They took a bunch of X-rays and did some tests, and finally just said I broke my tailbone, which I coulda told them my ownself. I was bruised all up and down. Had some cuts, too, from all the broken glass. My boyfriend took a bunch of pictures on his phone. I can send 'em to you."

"Maybe later," Drue said. "Let's go back to the part about the broken glass. How did that happen?"

"He dropped the bottle of Smirnoff Ice, when the lady at the counter started chasing him, and it busted all over the floor, and that's when I slipped and hurt myself."

"Who's 'he'?"

"My boyfriend. Glenn. I already told you that part."

Drue was having a bad feeling about this call.

"Why was the clerk chasing your boyfriend?"

"I don't know. I guess she thought he was trying to steal something."

"Was he? Trying to steal the Smirnoff Ice?"

"Why are you asking me all these questions? I seen a billboard, right across the street from that 7-Eleven, it said, 'Slip and fall? Give Brice a call,' so that's what I'm doing."

Drue felt a tap on her shoulder. She looked up. Ben and Jonah were standing by her cubicle. "It's quitting time," Ben said. "We're headed over to the Chattaway. Wanna come?"

"Hello?" Vyckylynn said. "Are you even listening to me?"

"I am," Drue assured her. "But one of my colleagues has an important matter to discuss. Can you hold for a moment?"

She took off her headset and rotated her shoulders. "Sorry. I need to finish this call. You guys go on without me."

Ben's face fell. "We can wait a few minutes." He looked over at Jonah. "Right?"

Jonah shrugged. "Why not. Is the call legit?"

She rolled her eyes. "Her boyfriend got caught trying to shoplift a bottle of Smirnoff Ice at a convenience store, and he dropped it when the clerk chased him, at which point she slipped and fell and broke her tailbone."

Ben snickered. "Go ahead and disconnect. This one's bogus."

But Jonah leaned over the cubicle to read what she'd typed on the intake form. "Hang on. A slip-and-fall at a franchised store could be golden. They all carry major liability insurance."

Jonah looked at Drue. "You need any coaching? I can walk you through it."

"I think I can handle this," Drue said.

"Suit yourself," Jonah said. "If you get done anytime soon, you know where we'll be."

He started to walk away, then came back. "Okay, I know you don't want to hear it, but ask her if either she or the boyfriend were in any way detained or arrested. Find out if the store filed charges against them. If they didn't, you're golden."

"I got this," Drue said, turning back to her phone.

"Hi. Vyckylynn? Are you still there?"

"I got no place else to go," the caller said, smacking her gum loudly.

"Were the police called? Were either of you arrested and charged?"

Click. Her caller had disconnected.

The office was deserted. She'd watched while the rest of the staff drifted out of the building, headed off for their weekend plans. Her own weekend plans consisted of ordering takeout pizza and using her first paycheck to start painting the cottage.

Somewhere outside, a car backfired and an image flashed in her mind: of Yvonne Howington, and her Plymouth, and the face of Aliyah, as she peeked from the backseat of her grandmother's rusted car. It had been a busy week, but every time she'd looked up she'd seen the child's mermaid drawing pinned to her cubicle wall and she thought about Aliyah's mother, Jazmin.

Drue logged back on to her computer and toggled around the firm's database, looking for the Jazmin Mayes file. She pulled up the file and looked guiltily around the empty room.

Wendy had left shortly after five, and she hadn't seen Brice at all that day, which wasn't an unusual occurrence.

Drue had signed a nondisclosure agreement her first day of work, and she'd had the words "client confidentiality" drilled into her brain every day since. As far as she knew, there wasn't an official policy forbidding her from removing files from the office, but she could assume such an action wouldn't meet Wendy's approval.

She pushed the Print button and stood nervously over the printer, snatching up each page as it slid onto the paper tray and shoving it into her backpack.

While she waited for the documents, she thought again of all the unanswered questions surrounding Jazmin Mayes's murder. Why had she agreed to work a later shift, knowing she needed to get home in time for her mother to leave for her own job? Who was the supervisor who Jazmin told Yvonne was sexually harassing her? Had she reported the harassment to management? And if so, what, if anything, had been done?

The printer clicked off and Drue leafed through the stack of sheets she'd accumulated. Less than three dozen pages? Was that all the life of a twenty-four-year-old mother amounted to?

She was unlocking OJ in the law firm's parking lot when her phone dinged. The text was from Ben.

Still here. U coming?

Can't. She typed the word rapidly, then reconsidered. Why not go grab a burger with a couple friends from work? She did consider Ben her friend, and if she had to put up with know-it-all Jonah, so what? She didn't feel like going home to Coquina Cottage and eating another solitary pizza by herself. God help her but she wanted to be part of the team. She x'd out the previous message and retyped, *On way.*

Ben and Jonah were seated at a table outside the wood-framed building, in the shade of one of the dozens of palm trees planted around the Chattaway's deck area in old claw-foot bathtubs.

"I'm telling you right now," Jonah said, leaning across the table. "We had our best recruiting year ever. We've got defense, we've got offense, this is going to be the year of the Gator."

"Gross," Drue said, pulling up a chair alongside Ben's. "Football, again? Don't you guys ever think of anything else?"

Jonah waved to their server, who arrived tableside with a menu and order pad.

"There is nothing else besides football," Ben said, raising his glass and clinking it against his friend's. "And gaming. And women. What took you so long? We were about to give up on you."

"Tell you in a minute. I'm starved." She opened the menu. "What's good here?"

"Get the Chattaburger and onion rings," Jonah advised, taking the menu and handing it back to the waitress.

Drue frowned.

"What? Oh, I get it, you're a hippie east coast girl and you don't eat meat, right?"

He knew precisely how to get under her skin.

"No, asshole. I just don't feel like a burger tonight, okay? Is it all right with you if I order my own food, or do you need to tell me how to do that too?"

She hadn't eaten red meat in ages, but suddenly would have killed for a rare, juicy, greasy burger. Drue looked up at the server. "I'll have a grouper sandwich. And a side salad." She glared at Jonah. "And a glass of iced tea. Okay?"

"You were about to tell us what took you so long," Ben prompted.

"I got strung along with my 7-Eleven caller," Drue admitted with a sigh. "I really thought I might have my first referral of the week. Right up until I asked her the question about an arrest. Which is when I heard crickets."

"Just as well," Ben advised. "Brice hates slip-and-falls."

"Then why do we have billboards and ads for them on the side of every bus in town?" Drue asked.

"Visibility," Jonah said.

"Too many of those clients are hoaxers," Ben explained. "Even if we get a settlement, it's nickels and dimes, because their injuries are rarely all that serious."

"Just remember, in the land of personal injury, the badder the injury, the better the case," Jonah added.

"So a wrongful death suit should be the best kind of case, right?" she asked.

"You'd think so," Ben said. "But the very best cases are severe, catastrophic injuries, especially if our client loses a body part, like an eye or a hand."

"Or a leg," Jonah chimed in. "There are actuarial tables that tell you just how much lost limbs are worth."

"Botched circumcision cases are the real gold standard," Ben added.

"Don't tell me any more," Drue pleaded. "It's too depressing."

"Like three years ago, Brice had a case where a utility truck hit our client's car, and she was almost decapitated," Ben said cheerfully.

"Oh my God!" Drue pressed her hands over her ears. "No more!"

"No, it's okay. She lived. It took three years of investigating and negotiating, but I think that was like an eight-million-dollar settlement," Ben said.

"It was six million," Jonah corrected.

"Whatever, all I know is when the dust settled, he and Wendy got brand-new his-and-hers S-class Mercedes," Ben said.

Drue's food arrived but her appetite had, not surprisingly, departed. She picked at her grouper sandwich and chewed slowly.

"Speaking of cases," she said, trying to sound casual. "I'm interested in the Jazmin Mayes case."

Ben raised an eyebrow. "Why?"

"Because a young mom was murdered. Strangled and beaten, at a hotel less than a mile from where I live. I pass the Gulf Vista every day. I can't believe that even happened. It's been two years, and still no arrest? It bugs me that my dad settled that case for next to nothing."

"Yeah, it's sad, but Brice can only try the case he's been given," Ben said.

"Like I told you before, it's a workers' comp case," Jonah said, sounding annoyed.

Drue shook her head. "Have you ever met her mother? I have. I was working the reception desk when she came in last week. And Ms. Howington, that's the mother, was adamant that Jazmin was killed after she clocked out. Not during. She didn't work the overnight shift, because she needed to take care of her daughter so her mom could get to work early in the morning. You guys, she was only six when her mom was murdered. Her grandmother is raising her and working as a nurse's aide at some hospital, and they can't even afford to get the kid decent eyeglasses because the settlement will be in a trust for Aliyah until she's eighteen."

She took a deep breath and stabbed at her salad. "It's not right. It isn't."

Jonah and Ben exchanged a knowing look.

"You can't get caught up in this stuff, Drue," Ben said, his face earnest. "Everybody who calls, everybody who walks in the door, they all have a sob story."

"Or they think they do," Jonah agreed.

13

After two weeks of camping out in her sleeping bag in the living room of the cottage, Drue was ready to start feathering her nest.

By seven o'clock Saturday morning, she was unlocking her father's storage unit. The hinges on the sheet metal door groaned as she pulled it open and flipped the light switch.

"Score," she whispered as she waded inside. The first things she hauled out to the Bronco were a queen-size mattress, box spring and bed frame. Sweating and cursing, she managed to shove them into the cargo area of the SUV. She returned to the unit and dug out a nightstand and two drawers from a dresser that she recognized as being Nonni's, which completed her first load.

Drue dragged the furniture, piece by piece, into the cottage, dumping everything in the bedroom, before returning to the storage facility for her next load.

Three loads later, she'd barely made a dent in the contents of her father's storage shed. She'd easily passed up the heavier, more opulent pieces in the shed, a black leather U-shaped sectional, an Asian-inspired teak entertainment center that took up six feet of wall space, and a commanding onyx-lacquered four-poster king-size bedroom suite. She reluctantly gave Wendy credit for banishing Brice's fugly man cave furnishings to storage.

Instead she'd settled for whatever could be dragged and shoved into the obliging OJ: a three-piece rattan settee and matching armchair that had been Nonni's pride and joy, along with a boomerang-shaped Formica-topped coffee and matching end table. She'd found a pair of lamps, with their kitschy bullfighter-ceramic bases, and strapped them into the front seat, along with the settee cushions.

For the last load she took a rickety card table and folding chairs. She remembered how Papi would set the furniture up in the living room for his Saturday-night poker games, and how Nonni would fuss about all the cigar smoke and beer bottles, but still spend the entire day before the game fixing sandwiches and cookies for the big event.

In the years after her parents' divorce, as she and her mother had moved to and from crappy apartments and rental houses in her youth, Drue had been mostly indifferent to her surroundings. Sherri wasn't a nester, and neither was she. As long as their home had beds, a sofa and a television—and later on, a place to store her kiteboarding gear—she'd been, if not exactly content, not exactly unhappy either.

Now, though, Drue felt an absurd sense of satisfaction in "setting up housekeeping," as Nonni would have put it.

In a far corner of the storage unit she'd found some dusty cardboard cartons labeled KITCHEN STUFF in Sherri's handwriting, and upon lifting the box flaps had been delighted to discover an assortment of battered pots and pans, silverware, utensils, and odds and ends of glass and china.

Every night of the previous week she'd spent coating the interior of the cottage with white paint—it had taken three coats to cover the previous tenant's color scheme.

Late Saturday afternoon, after she'd moved all the furniture into place, she was sore and exhausted, but not too tired to make a Target run, picking out towels and bed linens, including a white and coral seashell-patterned quilt for her new bedroom, along with a shower curtain and a set of white cotton curtains for her bedroom window.

Right before sunset, when she could work no longer, Drue shed her shoes at the edge of the dune, then picked her way through the sea oats, following the well-worn footpath until she reached the fringe of deep green Australian pines. It was nearly eight, but the sand was still warm. She sank down into the shade of the towering trees, leaned back on her elbows and stretched out her aching legs.

The sun was only inches from the horizon, the sky glowing in fiery reds and oranges. A slight breeze rippled the fronds of the sea oats. The Gulf was calm tonight and the turquoise surface of the water rolled in lazy layers onto the shore.

Looking down the beach, she saw plenty of people prolonging their day by the water. Kids splashed in the surf, family groups unloaded picnics from coolers and couples strolled along the sand, stopping to embrace or take selfies.

She was struck by how many of those couples were same-sex, mostly men. Sunset Beach had definitely changed over the years, and it wasn't just the appearance of mega-mansions.

Athletes were out too now, speed walking, running, riding bikes, lured back to the beach by the moderating temperatures. As she watched, a tall, particularly buff male specimen wearing only neon-green shorts, whom she'd noticed several times in the previous week, made another sprint past. He stopped at the water's edge, bent double, hands on his waist. Even from here she could see his bare torso slick with sweat. He had the muscled calves and lean, toned physique of a runner, and his hair was cropped so close he looked nearly bald.

He straightened and turned, staring in her direction. She gave a curt nod and looked away, not wanting him to think she was ogling him. Although she was.

Drue sipped from the bottle of beer Brice had left her in the refrigerator, and savored her hard-won sense of accomplishment.

Back at the cottage, she stayed up 'til one, making up the bed, hanging the drapes and styling the bathroom. Then, she'd propped the box fan in the window and fallen into a dead sleep.

She allowed herself the supreme luxury of a lazy Sunday morning, marked only by a trip to Publix to buy groceries. Now that she had a real kitchen, she'd vowed, no more convenience store sub sandwiches or roller dogs.

After she got home from the grocery store, unloaded groceries and fixed herself a pitcher of iced coffee, it was after two. The beach was lined with hundreds of people who'd set up colorful umbrellas and beach chairs. Children splashed in the surf. She heard strains of music, and watched as the bald runner she'd seen over the previous week paused again at the water's edge to catch his breath and drink from the metal flask he wore at his waist. She wondered idly if he lived nearby.

Papi's shed had yielded an ancient folding beach lounger, the kind with woven plastic webbing. She went back inside, changed into a bikini, tucked the Jazmin Mayes file in her beach bag and set the chair up in the shadows of the Australian pines.

After a moment's hesitation, she walked down to the water's edge, letting her toes sink into the soft sand, feeling the turquoise waves lapping at her ankles.

Drue set off walking to the south, stopping occasionally to tilt her face toward the sun, enjoying the sensation of sweat prickling her neck and shoulders and back.

She still couldn't get used to the inactivity of her new life, of sitting all day in an overly chilled cubicle, talking on the phone, typing, reading and assessing deadly dull legal documents. Her past life seemed like a dream now. Had she ever really spent her days skimming over the water on her board, living for those brief moments when her kite filled with air, taking her aloft? Even on the worst nights, when she was tending bar and fending off drunken good ol' boys at Bozo's, it had been worth it, because she knew that the next morning, weather permitting, she'd wake up and head for the beach.

When she reached the rocky breakwater barely half a mile down the beach she was abruptly reminded of just why her life had taken such a dramatic turn. Her knee ached and she was already out of breath. Two months earlier, she would have happily scrambled over the rocks and kept going. Instead, she turned and started trudging back toward the cottage.

Her thoughts turned again to Jazmin Mayes.

She didn't look up from her pondering until she was only a few yards from the cottage. Her lounge chair was now nearly obscured by the deepening shadows of the pines. Which was why she was startled to realize that someone was sitting in her chair.

"Oh!" He jumped up as she approached. "Sorry, I, uh, well, sorry."

It was the shirtless jogger she'd been watching for the past week. He clutched his water bottle in his left hand and a damp shirt in his right.

"That's okay," Drue said, laughing. "Don't look so guilty. You must live around here. I see you running past here almost every day."

"Down there," he said, pointing in the direction she'd just come from. "I've got a condo at Land's End."

"Nice," she said.

"How about you?" he asked.

She turned toward the dune line. "That's my place. Up there."

"Really?" He looked surprised. "You're the new tenant? What happened to Leonard?"

"Leonard?"

"The previous tenant. He's lived there for, I don't know, since before I bought my place, and I've been at Land's End for seven years. Nice old guy."

"I figured it must have been a guy. He had some seriously questionable decorating taste. I'm actually not a tenant. I own the place." She stuck out her hand. "Drue Campbell. First-time homeowner."

"Corey Wagner. Random beach jogger and chair usurper." He shook her hand. "Welcome to Sunset Beach."

"Hey," she said impulsively. "Wanna come up and have a drink on the deck?"

"I'm not really dressed for cocktails," he said.

She grabbed her beach bag. "Me neither. C'mon up."

By the time they walked onto the deck, he'd donned his shirt, unlaced his running shoes and left them at the edge of the dune line.

"I do that too," Drue said approvingly. "I love the beach, but I can't stand tracking sand in the house."

"I'm compulsive about it," Corey confessed. "Glad to know I'm not alone."

He followed her up the stairs to the deck.

"Careful where you walk. Most of these boards are pretty rotten."

"Yeah, Leonard wasn't much of a handyman," Corey said. "And I gathered, from what he said, he was renting the place for such a bargain, he didn't feel like he could ask the landlord to spend money to fix the place up."

Drue pushed the sliding door aside and walked into the kitchen with her new friend right behind.

"Wow," he said, pausing in the doorway. "What all did you do? This place never looked this good while Leonard was living here."

"A lot of white paint, a lot of Pine-Sol and a lot of trips to the Dumpster at that construction site up the block. Don't tell the owners, okay?"

She went to the refrigerator and got out a beer. He shook his head and grinned sheepishly. "I actually don't drink. Anymore."

"Oh. Okay. Want a water?"

"Brought my own," he said, brandishing his stainless steel bottle.

She put the beer back and poured herself a glass of white wine.

"I don't have any real deck furniture yet," she said, stepping back onto the deck, "so these will have to do." She pointed at the pair of folding lawn chairs she'd found in the shed.

He unfolded both chairs and they sat, facing the beach.

"So, Drue Campbell, pardon my nosiness, but what do you do that you can afford to own a swell cottage like this, right on the Gulf?"

"I inherited it," she said. "After my mom died. It had been my grandparents'."

"Lucky you," Corey said. "But I can't believe you didn't want to live here yourself all these years, instead of renting it out."

"It's complicated. My parents split up when I was about five years old, and I moved with my mom over to the east coast. After Nonni, that's my grandmother, died, I just assumed my mom sold the cottage. But she didn't. I guess my father agreed to manage the house for her, and he's the one who rented it to your friend Leonard. That last hurricane did a number on the roof, hence that attractive blue tarp it's sporting. And that's when Leonard moved out."

"And you moved in," he said. "From where?"

"Lauderdale. After my mom died, I was sort of at loose ends, so when my father offered me a job at his firm, there was really no reason not to move back here. I had a free place to stay, and a job, so why not?"

"I've always admired this house," Corey admitted. "This past year or so, since Leonard moved out and the place was vacant, I had this far-fetched fantasy about buying it myself and fixing it up."

"Sorry to spoil your fantasy, but I don't see selling it. Even after Mom and I moved to Lauderdale, I'd come back every summer and spend a couple weeks here with my grandparents. It's a special place to me."

14

Drue had done enough talking about herself. "What about you? Tell me the Corey Wagner story. I bet you do something at a gym. Like, maybe a trainer or something?"

"I'm pretty boring. I'm only a trainer in the sense that I'm my own best client," he said. "My day job is as a physical therapist. I'm in training to do an Iron Man triathlon, which is why you see me running so often."

"Do you work at a hospital or a clinic or something?"

"I'm in a practice with a couple other therapists. We specialize in sports injuries."

"Single?" She was mentally crossing her fingers. This man was seriously hunky. He had a great body and brilliant blue eyes and a genuine smile. What was not to like?

"I am single," he said. "How about you?"

"Same," she said.

He pointed at her knee. "Torn meniscus? ACL?"

"Both. Plus the usual," she said.

"That sucks. Can I ask how you injured yourself?"

"Kiteboarding," she said. "Midair collision with a guy I didn't even see coming."

He bent over, then looked up. "May I?"

His finger traced the thick white scar. It extended six inches above and six inches below her knee, zigzagging around the kneecap. "Wow. Who was your surgeon?"

"Just some guy they referred me to at the emergency room. Ezra Cline? He's in Delray Beach."

Corey placed a hand on either side of her knee. "Was he in his eighties or something?"

"Yeah, as a matter of fact he was. Why?"

"'Cause this is some old-school technique here. It's pretty swollen right now. Does that happen a lot?"

"After I walk, yeah. It's so stupid. I only went down to the breakwater and back, but it's killing me right now."

"We should ice it. Do you have an ice pack or a dish towel or something I can use?"

"Hanging on the hook by the sink," she said. "The fridge doesn't have an ice maker, but there's a plastic bin of cubes in the freezer."

He disappeared into the kitchen, emerging with a make-shift ice pack, which he pressed to her knee.

"Extend your leg for me, please," he said, kneeling on the deck and placing his hands on either side of the joint.

"Bend it.

"Now flex your foot.

"Do you ever feel the joint popping, or hear clicking when you walk?"

"Sometimes."

He sighed and took his seat again. "What kind of post-op instructions did the surgeon give you? Did you do physical therapy?"

"He just said I should take it easy and gave me the name of a physical therapist I should call. Which I didn't do."

"Why not?"

"No insurance," she said, shrugging. "I'm still paying for the surgery, which my father assures me the doctor screwed up, based on the look of the incision."

"How's your mobility?" he asked. "I did notice, when you were walking up, that you seemed to be favoring your good leg. Didn't they give you a brace or anything?"

"My mobility isn't great. It really hurts going down stairs. And yeah, he gave me a brace, but it's too hot and itchy to wear this time of year. Anyway, I couldn't tell that it was doing me much good. So I mostly don't wear it."

He shook his head. "How old are you?"

"Thirty-six. How about you?"

"I'm thirty-eight. But let's talk about you. I'm guessing you must have been a pretty good athlete before your accident. Have you started back with any kind of physical activity?"

"I walk on the beach some," she said, feeling instantly defensive. "But it's hard, you know. I work in an office all day, come home, walk on the beach a little, and by then I'm kind of wiped out."

"I get that," he said, smiling. "That ACL of yours is still

pretty loose. You need to start working on it, or it's only gonna get worse. You mind if I give you some advice?"

"As long as it's free," Drue said.

"First of all, walking on sand, which isn't the most stable surface, isn't doing you any favors. Now, if you had a bike, that's way better exercise for your knee."

"I don't have a bike, but I guess I could buy a used one, once I catch up a little on my bills," she said.

"Here's another idea—get yourself to a pool. You can do exercises, walking, pedaling, like that, without putting any weight on the knee. The passive resistance of the water is great for injuries like yours."

"Again, I don't have a pool," she said. "And a gym membership definitely isn't in the cards for me anytime soon."

"No friends with a pool at their complex?"

"I've only just moved here recently," Drue said. "My father and his, uh, child bride have a pool, but I don't see me inviting myself over there for water aerobics."

"Tell you what," he said. "We've got a pool in my condo complex. This time of year especially, it's mostly deserted, because all the snowbirds are back up north. If you want, I can get you a key card, and you can use our pool. We can set a time, and I'll meet you out there and show you some simple exercises you can do."

"Really?" Drue was taken aback. "That's so nice of you. I mean, we just met."

"It's no big deal," Corey said. "I'm sorry Leonard moved. I mean, he was one interesting old guy, but I'm glad to meet his replacement. You're not into, uh, nude sunbathing, are you?"

She felt herself blushing. "No. Why?"

"That's actually how I first met him. I was running down the beach, and I looked up here, and there was this old man, stretched out, stark naked on a towel. I ran up because I thought maybe he'd passed out or had a heart attack or something. Turns out he was just really into nudity. He'd move his chair down onto the beach in the afternoons, after the deck was in the shade. People were all the time calling the cops on him. He eventually got tired of the hassle, so he made himself a loincloth out of some washcloths. I asked him once why he didn't just get a Speedo or something, and he told me . . ." Corey started to laugh. His chest rose and fell, and he tried to speak but couldn't, he was laughing so hard.

"He told me . . ." Corey was wheezing, tears running down his face. "He didn't even wear underwear, because he liked to air out his undercarriage. Swear to God, that's what he called it. His undercarriage."

15

After her guest departed, Drue wandered into the kitchen to consider her dinner prospects. In the end, she settled on her default comfort food menu: a bowl of ramen noodles topped with a poached egg and a dollop of her favorite, Cholula Hot Sauce.

She unloaded her backpack onto the card table—a yellow legal pad and some pens she'd swiped from the office, and the documents from the Jazmin Mayes file—and eagerly leafed through the docs, choosing to do a closer read of the questionnaire, transcribed by a CCK intake clerk whose name she didn't recognize.

Not much information there that she didn't already have, she thought, setting it aside and picking up what turned out to be a preliminary report by J. Zilowicz, or, as everyone at the law firm called him, Jimmy Zee.

She slurped noodles and jotted notes as she read about the short life and hard times of Jazmin Mayes, as seen through the lens of the investigator.

> Victim (Jazmin Mayes) (age 24) is only child of Yvonne Howington, age 46, of 1372 Hibiscus Way South, St. Petersburg. Father not in picture. No adult criminal record, although mother states daughter got in trouble for fighting in school. Juvenile records not available. However, Ms. Howington volunteered her daughter had two misdemeanor shoplifting arrests, and during second arrest was found to be in possession of less than an ounce of marijuana. Victim was transferred to diversionary high school (Bayside High) but dropped out at age 17 after becoming pregnant. Following birth of daughter, victim re-enrolled in school and earned GED.
>
> Mother states father of victim's child was killed in motorcycle accident shortly after birth of the child. She also says daughter quit using any drugs during pregnancy and was taking business classes at University of South Florida. USF registrar's office confirms.
>
> Subject hired as housekeeper at Gulf Vista Hotel and Resort on 1-12-16. Hotel personnel records produced in discovery indicate Ms. Mayes worked 2–11 p.m. shift, generally Tuesday–Saturday, but occasionally picked up additional shifts. Hotel requires mandatory drug testing and personnel records indicate there were no positive drug tests during her employment.

Mother states victim and victim's child (Aliyah, 6) lived with her. Mother has no knowledge of whether daughter had boyfriends, but states daughter sometimes "stayed out partying" all night with friends on nights off. Does not know friends' names, other than Neesa.

On night of 9-15-16, victim clocked in at Gulf Vista Hotel and Resort at 2:45 p.m., nearly an hour late for her shift. Supervisor H. K. Byars stated subject claimed her car broke down on way to work, which was why she was late. Byars also claims victim requested to be allowed to work additional shift, 11 p.m. to 7 a.m., which he agreed to because another housekeeper had called in sick.

However, Ms. Howington insists that her daughter would not have asked to work until 7 a.m., because she was due home to take over child care responsibilities so that Ms. Howington could leave for her own job as nurse's aide at Palms of Pasadena Hospital.

Ms. Howington states that the last communication she had from her daughter came at 2:15 p.m. 9-15-16, when daughter called to say her car had overheated and she was forced to take cab to get to work. The vehicle, a 2001 Kia, was subsequently towed to Bayside Towing. According to police inventory, nothing of interest recovered from vehicle.

At 7:30 a.m., 9-16-16, Pinellas County Sheriff's Investigators S. C. Shumate and R. D. Hernandez arrived at Ms. Howington's home to notify her of daughter's death.

She turned the page and found herself staring down at a copy of the coroner's report and skimmed it quickly, trying to push aside the grisly details, phrases like "ligature strangulation" and "cuts and contusions to face and upper torso consistent with defensive wounds."

Drue picked up the bowl of ramen and drank the last bit of salty broth. She looked down at the report she'd just read. Set down in black and white like this, Jazmin Mayes's death might not seem too traumatic. She'd been an unwed teen mother, onetime shoplifter and a high school dropout. But from the looks of things, Jazmin had turned her life around, getting a GED and a steady job, even enrolling in college.

Probably, she'd been trying to make a better life for her own little girl, Aliyah, who loved to read and color pictures of mermaids. Her life had been irrevocably altered. Drue turned the page and found another report written by Jimmy Zee.

Interview with H. K. Byars, former Gulf Vista housekeeping supervisor, 11-25-16, interview took place at Superior Tire Company in Largo, where he is now employed as a salesman. Mr. Byars stated Jazmin Mayes was a generally reliable employee, although she had been late to work two or three times due to transportation issues. On night of incident, stated he warned her that she would be placed on probation if she was late to work again. Hotel was at full occupancy that night because of large convention of Shriners, and housekeeping was backed up because of late checkouts and because several banquet rooms were not vacated until past 10 p.m.

Victim was assigned to cleaning banquet rooms and guest rooms in north wing of hotel, which is separated from main building of hotel by covered walkway. Wing consists of three stories of guest rooms, 20 rooms on each floor.

Interesting, Drue thought, that Jazmin Mayes's former supervisor no longer worked at the hotel. But maybe not too surprising. Having worked at bars and restaurants off and on for most of her adult life, she knew firsthand that most hospitality-related jobs in Florida had high rates of turnover.

She turned the page and found another of Zee's reports.

Interview with Brian Shelnutt, Gulf Vista Security Chief, 2-10-17. Took place at Gulf Vista Hotel and Resort, where he is still employed.

Shelnutt states that security cameras were located in all hallways of guest wing, lobby, elevators and hotel kitchen and parking areas. Gulf Vista is a gated resort, with two full-time security guards manning entrance to resort property from Gulf Boulevard. Guests use hotel room key cards to enter and exit parking lot. Employee parking located on lower level of three-story parking deck on north side of hotel. This area has separate key-card entry and employees are restricted from using guest parking.

Subject states that he viewed all relevant camera footage of 9-15-16 and 9-16-16, at direction of investigators from Pinellas Sheriff's Office. States he no longer

has access to video footage but he states his best recol-
lection is of seeing video of victim using key card to
enter room on first floor of north wing at approximately
11:00 p.m. Victim seen pushing large housekeeping
cart and vacuum cleaner into guest room and exiting at
1:30 a.m. Next seen pushing cart on service elevator and
ground floor walkway to hotel laundry room. Access to
area is limited to employees with master key card.

Shelnutt states exterior video camera footage showed
several other housekeepers and engineering employees
entering and exiting laundry room before and during
time victim was in room, but no video showed her exiting the room, which did not have operational interior
video cameras at time of incident.

Why not have cameras inside a large commercial laundry
room? Drue wondered. She noted that Zee's report specified
"operational" video cameras. She made a note to herself to see if
any other documents in the file referred to video cameras. She
turned the page to read more.

At approximately 4:45 a.m. on 9-16-16 Shelnutt states
he received a phone call at home from security guard
Eli Greene, telling him that the body of a housekeeping
employee had been discovered in rolling laundry ham-
per in laundry room. Shelnutt said Greene was called to
laundry room by another housekeeper, Lutrisha Smallwood, who was in room, loading used guest linens into
washer, when she uncovered body of an African-American

woman, later identified as Jazmin Mayes. Shelnutt says he advised Greene to call 911 and seal off area, which he subsequently did, until arrival of Treasure Island Police Department officers. Shelnutt said he called hotel manager at home to alert him of the incident, then drove directly to the hotel, arriving at 5:45 a.m, where he was met by deputies. He states police did not allow him to enter the crime scene, but he was shown a photo of the victim, who he was able to identify as hotel employee Jazmin Mayes. Shelnutt called Byars at home, and Byars subsequently met with officers to share next-of-kin notification.

Asked about victim's claim of sexual harassment, Shelnutt stated quite strongly that to his knowledge Jazmin Mayes never complained of harassment to him or any other hotel management.

Zee's next interview was with Lutrisha Smallwood, who'd discovered her coworker's body.

Met with Lutrisha Smallwood, 25, on 5-17-17, at Publix in Treasure Island, where she is now employed in bakery as apprentice cake decorator. Subject states that on 9-16-16, she entered laundry room at resort at approximately 4:30 a.m. No one else was in room. She stated that she was annoyed to find cart full of soiled linens that should have been washed, folded and dried by someone on previous shift. Cart was located in back of room, some distance from bank of washers and dryers. She said she pushed cart, which is on casters, toward washing machines, noting that it was unusually heavy. When she unloaded first armful of sheets and towels she said she encountered a sheet with bloodstains, that seemed to be wrapped around a large object. Upon moving sheet she said she saw a woman's foot. She fled area and called security on hotel-issued radio. At that point, she said, Eli Greene met her in hallway outside laundry room, and instructed her to wait for police in the hotel security office, which she did. Subject said she had known victim for only a few months, and had limited contact with her since they usually worked on different shifts at hotel. Subject said victim had never complained to her about harassment from any employees at hotel, and said she had never experienced harassment at hotel. She also stated that she believed victim's closest friend at hotel, a woman named Neesa, was fired in weeks following victim's death. Has no knowledge of Neesa's last name or current whereabouts. On checking personnel records, appears woman she referred to is Neesa Vincent, who was a housekeeper until she was discharged by hotel management on 9-27-16. Reason given for discharge was chronic absenteeism. Phone number for Neesa Vincent in hotel records no longer connected. Visited Bay Pines Trailer Park on 5-20-17, man living in trailer listed as subject's address states he was Neesa Vincent's boyfriend, but she moved out not long after losing job. He has no knowledge of her current whereabouts.

Drue closed the folder and rubbed her eyes. There were more documents, but they could wait. She'd been sitting and reading for what seemed like hours. She walked over to the sliding-glass doors and stepped out onto the deck. She stared up at the sky. The moon was only a crescent tonight. A faint breeze stirred the sea oats at the edge of the dunes closest to the house. She would have loved to have taken a walk on the beach this time of night, but her knee was still swollen and she'd been so absorbed in reading the Jazmin Mayes file she hadn't noticed how late it had gotten. After nine, and tomorrow was a school day.

"Hey!" a man's soft voice called from the beach. She walked over and saw Corey, her new friend. He'd changed into walking shorts and a white tee and was holding a package in his hand. "I brought you something. But I can come back another time if I'm disturbing you."

"No, no," Drue replied. "Come on up. I was just getting ready to turn off the lights and head to bed."

His footsteps shook the weathered deck boards. When he grew closer, she saw he was holding a roll of some kind of tape.

"This is K-tape," he said. "Kinesiology tape. We use it in the clinic to stabilize joints. I've always got rolls of it in my car and at the condo. Tools of the trade. I thought, if you want, I could show you how to tape your knee. The knee brace would be better, but I get that it's hot and unwieldy."

"Oh yeah," Drue said, gesturing for him to come into the house. "I've used K-tape before, when I banged up my shoulder." She slapped her forehead. "Why didn't I think of that?"

"If you'd gone to a therapist, they would have suggested it,"

Corey said. He pointed to the kitchen chair she'd just vacated. "Want to sit down and I'll show you how it's done?"

He knelt on the floor before her. His fingers were long and tapered and cool on her skin as he smoothed the tape in strips around her ruined knee. She wondered if this was his way of coming on to her. And what she would do if he actually *was* coming on to her.

But the moment passed. He stood and smiled. "And that's how it's done." He produced a business card from the pocket of his navy shorts. "Here. I put my cell phone number on it. Seriously now, call me if you want to take me up on my offer for a bike ride or to go swimming. You need to start working that knee right away."

She picked up the roll of tape and walked him out onto the dunes, watching him disappear in the moonlight.

16

~~~

After an uneventful Monday, on Tuesday Drue rushed into the bullpen at exactly 9:55 A.M. She donned her sweater and headset and sat at her desk for a minute, trying to catch her breath.

Her phone dinged. An incoming text from Ben, whose cubicle was right next to hers.

Car trouble again?

She looked over the divider. He was on the phone, listening but not typing, and looked up at her.

She nodded, sat back down and replied.

Literally driving me crazy. Every other day, OJ refuses to start. I had to LYFT to work.

"Hey." Ben stood looking over the divider, his headset around his neck. "Want me to take a look? I'm pretty good with cars."

Her eyes lit up. "Really? I took it to a mechanic last week, but he says I need a new starter, and I just don't have the money for something like that."

"Replacing a starter's a piece of cake. I can pick one up at a wrecking yard."

"Not to rush you or anything, but when can you do it?" Drue asked.

"I just need to get to the wrecking yard and pull one, then it's like an hour or so. I could probably get it done on Saturday."

"And I will owe you big-time," Drue said. The phone on her desk lit up, so she sat down and went back to work bringing justice to the people.

17

Brice's office door was ajar. Drue knocked lightly, then pushed it open the rest of the way.

Her father was leaning back in his desk chair, chatting with the firm's in-house investigator, Jimmy Zilowicz.

"Oh, sorry. Didn't realize you were busy," she said, starting to back out.

"Come on in," Brice said expansively. "Zee and I were just shooting the shit." He gestured at his guest. "You two have met, right?"

Zee lumbered to his feet. "Have we met? I was at the hospital the night this kid was born." He took the hand Drue extended, drawing her closer for a hug.

"You remember your uncle Zee, don't ya?" he asked, releasing her.

"Hell, Zee, she was just a little kid when her mom and I

split up and they moved away. You're not all that memorable," Brice joked.

"I remember you and my dad taking me for doughnuts, and letting me ride in the front seat of your police cruiser, and letting me turn on the lights and sirens," Drue said haltingly. "And I remember you making me promise not to tell my mom."

"Yeah, seems like I was always on Sherri's shit list," Zee said. "For good cause, of course. Hey, I've been meaning to tell you, I'm sorry about your mom. We all had a lot of good times together, back in the day." He brightened a moment. "But I'm tickled you've joined the firm."

"Thank you," Drue said.

"I'll let you two get down to business," Zee said. He hitched up his black trousers and nodded at his former partner before leaving.

Brice stood up too. "I'm glad you came by. Wendy's got her book club tonight, so I'm batching it. How about you let me buy you dinner? There's a little place over on Central Avenue I like, we can get a pizza and split it, if that's okay with you," Brice said. "Parking's tight over there, but it's only a couple blocks."

"Okay," Drue said. They met at the lobby door a few minutes later, and she followed him out onto the street.

He glanced over at his daughter. "Will your knee be okay? If we walk?"

"Should be. I met a physical therapist on the beach this weekend. He taped up my knee for stabilization, and it already feels better." She had to quicken her step to catch up with him. One thing she had to say for Brice, he in no way seemed like a man in his late sixties. His belly was flat, his face relatively unlined and he had an enviable level of energy. She wondered if he and Wendy did couples Botox sessions.

The place was called D'Italia, and Brice was treated as a minor celebrity. A server brought two martinis as soon as they were seated. "The usual, right?" asked the server, a trim Hispanic kid with a soul patch and nose ring.

Drue pushed her martini across the table to her father. "Could I have a glass of chardonnay, please?" she asked.

"Oh sure, whatever," the waiter said, nodding.

"What's the usual?"

"Pizza Bianca D'Italia," Brice said. "You'll love it. They do a great one here."

She would have liked to order from a menu, but before she could request one, their server was headed back toward the kitchen.

"So," Brice said, "Wendy tells me you're, uh, struggling on the phones."

"Let's not talk about it, okay?" Drue said.

"If you're not happy in your job, that's something I need to know about," Brice said.

"I'm fine. Really. It's a steep learning curve, but I'll get it."

"You're a bright girl. I've always said that." Brice gave her an indulgent smile. "My brains and your mom's temperament."

When the pizza arrived, steaming and fragrant, Brice took the pizza wheel, lifted a gooey slice and plopped it onto her plate. She looked down at it, sniffed and pointed. "Are those anchovies? Tell me they're not anchovies."

"Of course they're anchovies," Brice said. "What kind of pizza bianca comes without anchovies?"

"The only kind I'll eat," Drue said pointedly.

Brice's face fell. "I wish you'd told me that before I ordered."

"You didn't give me a chance," she said.

Brice rolled his eyes and summoned the server again. "Bring this lady a menu, please," he said.

Drue held up her empty glass. "And another one of these."

"How are things coming along at the cottage?" Brice asked, as dinner was winding down.

"The cottage is good," Drue said, trying to force herself to relax. She didn't understand her constant need to challenge or confront her father. "Thanks for giving me all that furniture from your storage unit."

"I hope you took a lot of that old stuff that was originally your grandparents'. I was holding on to it for Sherri, but I think she probably forgot it was here."

"Yeah, Mom wasn't much into interior design," Drue agreed. "Most of the pieces I took I remembered from when Nonni and Papi were alive. I got a bunch of boxes of kitchen stuff too, which will really come in handy."

"I'm glad," Brice said. "I should just donate the rest of that crap in the unit to charity for a tax deduction. No way Wendy's ever gonna let any of it back in the house."

Drue allowed herself a wicked smile. "Can't say I blame her. That was some seriously bat-cave-looking furniture you had going there."

"From my BW days," Brice agreed. "'Before Wendy.'"

"Hey Dad," Drue said suddenly. "Who was Colleen Boardman Hicks?"

"Who?" Brice took a gulp of his martini.

"Colleen Boardman Hicks. I found some old newspaper clippings Mom had apparently saved about her disappearance from way back in 1976."

For some reason, she deliberately avoided mention of the case binder she'd also discovered.

Brice repeated the name aloud, slowly. "Wow, I haven't thought about her in a long, long time."

"Why would Mom have saved those old newspaper stories?" Drue asked. "Was she a friend of hers? Did you guys know her?"

Her father helped himself to another slice of pizza. "I knew Colleen from high school, but I don't think your mother ever met her."

"Weird. She disappeared while you were still on the police force, right? Was that a case you worked on?"

"Me? No. I was never a detective. Just a lowly street cop."

"Whatever happened with the case? Did she ever turn up?"

"Not that I know of," Brice said.

He checked his watch. "You want another glass of wine? If not, I should probably be getting home to look after Princess."

"I'm done," she said, then hesitated. "Speaking of cold cases, Jazmin Mayes?"

Brice's expansive mood darkened. "Christ! That again. If you're going to get emotionally attached to every hard-luck story that comes down the pike, maybe you better cut your losses now and find another line of work."

"Emotionally attached? Is it wrong to feel empathy for somebody who's obviously been injured—or killed—through no fault of their own?"

"You can feel empathy without wasting their time, and ours," her father said. "I told you before, Zee spent way more time looking at that case than he should have. I feel badly for the grandmother, and the child, which is why I cut my fee. But it comes down to the fact that we just didn't have a case. That one was a money loser. And I can't afford to lose money if I'm going to stay in business. I've got a staff to pay—including you—overhead, benefits and a pension to fund. If you stay with the firm, and I hope you will, you'll learn that every day cases are coming across the transom. Some are winners and some are losers. Jazmin Mayes, unfortunately, was a loser."

He drummed his fingertips on the tabletop. "I know you don't believe me, but we did all we could for Yvonne and Aliyah."

Drue sipped her wine. "What if I could prove Jazmin wasn't on the clock at Gulf Vista when she was killed? Would you take another look at the case?"

"That girl was savagely murdered—strangled and beaten," Brice said sharply. "Her killer is still at large. You're not a trained investigator. So you stay the hell away from Gulf Vista. You hear me?"

"Okay, sure. I'll be a good little cube rat and answer the phone and do what I'm told," Drue said. "Because you're the one who signs my paycheck."

"Let's go," Brice said abruptly. He was looking around for the waiter and their check.

"Where are you parked?" he asked.

"At the cottage." She dreaded asking, but also dreaded the long bus ride back out to the beach. "Think you could give me a ride home? OJ's still on the fritz."

"On one condition," he said. "No more shoptalk."

18

December 1975

The green and white patrol car pulled into the Dreamland motel on Thirty-fourth Street North at 10:45 P.M.

The Dreamland was one of the thousands of motels, built during the post–World War II tourist boom in Florida, that had seen better days. Half the letters on the neon sign out front were burned out, and the colorful neon pixie who'd once sprinkled dream dust among stars and a crescent moon was barely recognizable due to peeling paint and broken tubing. The palm trees lining the curb were dead or dying.

Officer Brice Campbell parked his car outside Unit 12 and waited. The dispatch code had come in first as a noise complaint, and then as a "family disturbance." Two minutes later another patrol car pulled alongside Campbell's. The officer, Jimmy Zilowicz, was Brice's beat partner. He opened the passenger door and slid inside.

"What have we got?" Zee asked.

"Some kind of argument going on. Glass breaking. A woman crying. The folks in the room next door called the front office to complain. The manager knocked on the door to tell them to quiet down and a male inside told him to get lost."

Zee was older than Brice Campbell, in his mid-thirties. He wore his dark hair as long as department code would allow, and his compact, stocky frame was a testament to the time he spent in the weight room.

"Which is where we come in," Brice added. He looked around at the single-story stretch of rooms. "You been here before?"

"You mean on business?" Zee asked, his grin sly.

"You keep that shit up, Frannie is going to leave your ass," Brice said. "Yeah, I mean business. I've had two calls over here in the last six months. One domestic, one auto breaking and entering."

"Place is kind of sad, but it's not as bad as some of these other fleabags I've been to," Zee said. "You ready?"

The officers got out of the car, jamming their nightsticks into their belt loops, each letting their fingertips graze the handles of their holstered Smith & Wessons.

"Hang on," Zee said. He fetched the heavy Maglite flash he'd stowed under the seat of his cruiser.

As they approached the door of Unit 12 they heard the sound of a woman's hysterical sobs.

They stood to the side of the door and Brice knocked. "Police!" he called loudly.

Nothing.

Zee banged at the door with the Maglite. "Come on in there, open up."

The door opened an inch, the chain lock engaged. A man, early-thirties with thinning brown hair and a pink flushed face, glared out at them. His white dress shirt was unbuttoned to the waist. "What do you want?"

"Somebody called in about a disturbance coming from this room," Brice said.

"We didn't call the cops. Must be a mistake."

"Sir?" Brice said, trying to sound firm. "We just heard a woman crying when we arrived here. Your neighbors in the next room seem to think there's been some kind of a fight."

"They need to mind their own fuckin' business," the man said, shouting now, as he looked toward the right and the left. "We don't need the cops. There's no disturbance. So leave us alone."

"We need to come into this room and talk to that woman," Zee said. "Now."

The man turned away from the door. "Tell these cops you're fine."

The woman continued to sob.

"Goddamnit, Colleen, cut it out."

"I'm sorry," the woman cried. "I'm okay. You can go."

"She's upset, that's all," the man assured the officers. "We had an argument. She's fine. End of story."

Brice stared at the man. "You need to let us into this room. Now step aside and unchain this door or things are gonna get real ugly real fast. Is that what you want?"

The man unchained the lock and swung the door inward. "Fine, asshole. Come on in."

The room had been wrecked. A wooden chair was broken and splintered, a framed picture had been smashed into pieces, clothes littered the floor. A nearly empty bottle of Johnnie Walker stood on the dresser. The woman was crouched on the left side of the bed, which was unmade. Her back was pressed against the head-board, her knees curled beneath her, with the bedsheet pulled up to her bare chest. Her hands covered the side of her face.

Her companion stood at the foot of the bed, his fists balled, chin jutting out. He wore light blue boxer shorts and black socks.

"Put your pants on, dipshit," Zee said.

Brice approached the woman. He touched her lightly on the shoulder. "Ma'am? Could you look at me, ma'am?"

The woman turned a tearful face.

"Son of a bitch," Brice whispered, staring.

He hadn't seen her since when? Colleen Boardman ran with the popular crowd at Boca Ciega High School. Her parents had a waterfront house, she drove a cute blue VW Bug. Back then she was brunette and freckle-faced, with a pert, upturned nose and great tits. She'd been a cheerleader and class officer. Brice's parents hadn't been poor, and he wasn't dumb, but he'd run with the greaser crowd back in the day. Skipped school at every opportunity, drank and smoked dope and generally raised hell. Half the guys he hung around with in high school had been drafted and sent to Vietnam. Brice had gone too, and made it back home, but too many others hadn't.

Colleen Boardman's lip was split and bloody.

Her eyes widened with recognition. "Brice Carter?"

"Campbell."

He jerked his head in the direction of the dipshit, who was scowling at his partner as Zee searched his pant pockets for a weapon.

"Did he do this to you?"

Her gray-blue eyes welled with tears. She started to say something.

"Shut up, Colleen," the man snapped. "You don't have to talk to them."

Zee shoved the guy backward onto an armchair. "Not another word outta you."

Brice lowered himself onto the edge of the bed. "Did he hit you?"

She nodded.

"Ask the bitch what she did to deserve it," the man called.

Zee threw the pants in the guy's face. "That's it. Get dressed. You're going to jail."

"For what? We had an argument. Maybe I had a little too much to drink. Things got a little out of hand. Didn't you and your wife ever get in a fight?"

Brice got up and walked over to the chair, staring down at the guy's bald spot. "I never hit my wife. Did you ever hit your wife, Zee?"

"Nah," the other cop said. "I'd never hit my wife. In fact, only pussies hit women."

"Get him out of here, would you, Officer?" Brice said. "Call for a wagon to haul his ass to jail."

"For what?" the guy protested. "A bloody lip? You don't even know what she was up to here. Why don't you ask her that?"

"You're going to jail for aggravated assault, for starters," Zee said, gripping the man's forearm and forcing him to his feet. He took the handcuffs from his belt and clipped them over the man's wrists.

"No," Colleen Boardman whispered. "Don't take him to jail. He didn't mean it."

"What?" Brice sat down on the edge of the bed again, lowering his voice, so the other two couldn't hear what was being said.

"Colleen, this guy is bad news. He hit you once, he'll keep on hitting you. I've seen it before."

"It was a misunderstanding, that's all," she said, avoiding his gaze.

"You're saying you don't want to press charges?" His voice was incredulous.

"I'm fine. Really. Allen only gets like this when he drinks."

"If you press charges, we'll testify in court about how he hurt you. He could do real time. You could at least get a restraining order, to keep him away. So he can't do it again."

She shook her head violently. "No. Can you just, I don't know, maybe get him to leave now?"

"Are you sure?" Brice glanced over his shoulder at the husband. Zee gave him a questioning look.

"Cut him loose," Brice said.

"See? I told you. No big deal," the man said, smirking.

When he'd unlocked the cuffs, Zee gave the husband another shove, in the direction of the door. "Get out," he said. "And don't go anywhere near her, you hear me? If you lay a hand on her again? If we get another domestic call about you? I promise, things won't end like this next time."

Brice was still looking at Colleen. "Officer, maybe you could give him a police escort, say, to a friend's house, where he can cool off for a few days."

"That's a really good idea," Zee said, opening the motel

room door and pushing the man outside. "Come on, dipshit. Let's take a ride."

"Thanks," Colleen said, when her husband was gone. Through the cheap rayon drapes they saw the headlights of a car, backing out, and then the blue lights of Zilowicz's unit following, and then both cars merged onto traffic on Ninth Street.

"You should have let us lock him up," Brice said, staying by the window. "So, what now?"

She shrugged and the sheet slipped just a bit, for only a second, affording a glimpse of the top of her creamy breasts. She pointed at the empty scotch bottle. "I wish I had some of that. I could use a little liquid courage, you know?"

They found an empty booth near the back at Mastry's, an old-school dive bar downtown on Central Avenue.

Colleen waved her hand at the plumes of cigarette smoke wafting from the next table. "I can't believe people still come in here. All this smoke is so gross. You know, I used to sneak in here when we were in high school."

Brice pretended to look shocked. "You? Miss Susie Sorority? Underage drinking?"

She sipped her Manhattan. "I wasn't quite the Goody Two-shoes everybody thought I was back then."

"Could have fooled me," Brice said. He sat back in the booth. "How'd you end up with that loser from the motel?"

"The usual story," she said. "We met when I was in college,

he was cute and sweet. He had a nice car and came from a nice family." She twisted her lips in a bitter smile. "Not so sweet now, huh?"

"Has he done this before? Hit you? Beat you up?"

She was drawing loops with the condensation from their drinks. Dipping a pink-tipped finger into the beaded-up water, drawing circles and whorls. He'd waited in his patrol cruiser, outside the motel room, while she showered and changed. Her hair fell past her shoulders, shiny and blonder than he remembered from high school. She'd applied a heavy layer of makeup to the bruises.

"I don't want to talk about him."

"What do you want to talk about?" He sipped his Pabst Blue Ribbon.

"Let's talk about you. You said you're married? Do I know her? Is she nice?"

"Her name's Sherri. She grew up in Tampa. Yeah, she's great. Got a hell of a temper, though. Cubans, you know? We're actually living in her parents' house out at Sunset Beach, trying to save up to buy a place of our own."

"Sunset Beach. Where all the old hippies end up. You know," she added, tilting her head, "I never would have guessed somebody like you would become a cop."

"And I never would have figured you for the kind of nice wholesome girl who'd get married and let some asshole beat the crap out of you."

"People change," she said. "You got drafted, right? Never went to college?"

"I went to Vietnam. Made it back home. I've been taking

night classes at the junior college. I'm thinking maybe I'll go to law school."

She raised an eyebrow. "I'm impressed."

"Why do you stay married to him?" Brice asked.

"I thought we weren't going to talk about him."

"No. You said you didn't want to talk about him. I never agreed to not talk about him. What's the douchebag's name, by the way?"

"Why do you want to know?"

"So I can check for priors against him when I get back to the station."

"You won't find anything," she said. "Allen is a model citizen."

"What's his last name?"

"Hicks."

"And what does Allen Hicks do for a living?"

"He's in commercial insurance," Colleen said.

"What about you? Do you work?"

"Nothing too exciting. I'm a dental hygienist."

He nodded. "You want another drink?"

She glanced at the neon Schlitz clock on the wall. "It's pretty late. Won't your wife wonder where you are?"

"I'll tell her I had a domestic call, right before I was about to get off shift, and I had to deal with it. All of which is true."

"Why not?" she said, looking around. "For old times' sake."

19

M s. Howington?"

"Yes," the older woman said impatiently. "Whatever you're selling, I can't afford."

It was Thursday afternoon. The office was empty. Everyone else was on lunch break, but she kept her voice low anyway to avoid being overheard. "This is Drue Campbell. From Campbell, Coxe and Kramner?"

Yvonne Howington gave an exasperated sigh. "Honey, I don't wanna be rude, but I got nothing to say to you people."

"I'm so sorry about everything that's happened to you, Ms. Howington, and that's why I'm calling. I was wondering if I could come talk to you."

"What for?"

The question took Drue by surprise. She'd just assumed that Jazmin Mayes's mother would welcome her assistance.

"I want to help," Drue said. "I think the way your case was settled is wrong. And I thought maybe, well, if I could help you prove that Jazmin wasn't working that night, my father could renegotiate with the insurance company."

"I ain't got time for this," the woman said. "And what good will it do anyway?"

"It might not do any good at all," Drue heard herself say. "But I'd like to try, if you'd just let me come out and talk to you."

"I don't know," Yvonne said. "Every time I get myself all worked up over this thing, I just get slapped in the face. I'm home from work right now, because Aliyah's been sick."

"I could come after I get off work," Drue said eagerly. "Would six o'clock be all right?"

"Be fine," Yvonne said.

The Lyft driver gave Drue a dubious look over her shoulder. "Hon? You sure this is where you wanted me to take you?"

They were in a neighborhood full of boarded-up abandoned homes and shabby duplexes. Yvonne Howington's home was a single-story yellow stucco bunker bedecked with stout burglar bars. The yard was weed-choked with a single huge jacaranda tree, whose arching branches with purple blossoms nearly brushed the ground.

Drue looked at the address she'd typed into the Lyft app. "Yes, this is it."

"Okay," the driver said. "But I'm not sure this is a real safe neighborhood."

She nodded toward a group of teenagers loitering on the corner, passing around a joint.

"I'll keep that in mind," Drue said, climbing out of the backseat.

A set of frazzled exposed wires were the only sign of a doorbell. Drue was about to knock when she heard a dead bolt being slid open. The door opened three inches and Yvonne Howington peered out from behind a chain lock.

"Shh," she said, opening the door and nodding toward a sofa where Aliyah was curled up under a pink blanket, dozing. "She had a bad night. Come on in the kitchen."

A window air-conditioning unit blasted cold air into the living room, but the tiny kitchen was oppressively hot. A standing fan directed warm air at the dinette set where Yvonne directed her to sit.

"Okay," she said, folding her hands on the table. "What do you want to know? I already talked to two other lawyers and ain't none of them say they can do anything about what happened to my baby girl. Say their hands are tied."

Looking at Yvonne Howington, Drue was struck by how beaten down she seemed. Her skin, coated in a fine sheen of perspiration, had an unhealthy ashy cast, there were large bags under her eyes and her mouth was bracketed by sagging cheeks. Only forty-eight, she looked twenty years older.

"Tell me everything you know about the night Jazmin was killed," Drue said.

Yvonne gave Drue a curious look. "Does your daddy know you're here?"

"No," Drue said. "In fact, he told me to stay completely away from this case."

Yvonne got up and went to the refrigerator, reached in and pulled out a can of orange Shasta. "You want something to drink?"

"Maybe just a glass of water," Drue said.

Yvonne poured tap water into a glass and cracked three ice cubes into it. "Water's better for you, but I got to have my orange soda," she said, returning back to the table.

"Okay. So the day it happened. Jazmin called to tell me her car broke down on the way to work, guess that was around two-fifteen. She was supposed to be at the hotel at two. She left the car and called a cab to get there. And that's the last time I talked to her."

Yvonne grasped her soda can with both hands. "I fussed at her, told her she needed to save up and get her a good reliable car, and she just told me, 'Mama, don't worry about me. I got plans, and pretty soon me and Aliyah are gonna have a new car and a house of our own.'"

"What do you think she meant by that?" Drue asked, scribbling notes.

"Don't know. That girl was always dreaming big dreams."

"She didn't have a boyfriend? Maybe someone to help her out financially?" Drue asked.

"She was going out with somebody, but she wouldn't tell me his name or anything else. Said it was too early. But she'd get herself all fixed up on her night off, when they were going to meet. And she didn't come home 'til way late those nights."

"No idea who he was?" Drue asked, intrigued.

"No."

"Okay, let's go back to that night, September fifteenth. You said before that Jazmin complained about some man at work bothering her. What did she mean by that?"

"She said this man came around when she was by herself. Like, if she was cleaning a room, he'd come in there and close the door, and say things to her."

"What kind of things?"

Yvonne took a swig of soda and looked away. "At first she said he just told her how nice she looked that day. She said it made her feel funny. And then he started saying, well, sex stuff to her. Things he wanted to do to her. Or have her do to him."

"Did she ever report that to management?"

"She said she told one of the bosses," Yvonne said.

"Which boss? In housekeeping, or personnel, somebody like that?"

Yvonne scrunched up her face as she thought. "Maybe personnel? Doesn't matter, because whoever it was told her she should quit dressing so sexy at work. Sexy! She wore jeans and a top the hotel gave all the housekeepers. You tell me what's sexy about that."

"Any idea when she complained?"

"I can't remember. It's all a jumble in my mind now."

"What about her friends at work? Did Jazmin tell them about this man bothering her?"

"The only friend I met was Neesa," Yvonne said. "I don't know what Jazmin told her."

"That's Neesa Vincent?"

"Mmm-hmm. She come to Jazmin's funeral and brought me real nice flowers."

"I've read our investigator's notes about the case. He was never able to contact Neesa. Did you know that the hotel fired her? Shortly after Jazmin's murder?"

"No. I didn't know that happened to her."

"Any chance you know how to reach her?" Drue asked hopefully.

"No." Yvonne shook her head sadly. "That's been two years."

"When was the last time you talked to the police about Jazmin's case?"

"Oh, I talk to Rae pretty regular. She calls to check in, let me know if there's anything new going on."

"Rae?"

"That's Rae Hernandez. With the police. I talked to her after I left your daddy's office last week. She thinks I got a bad deal with those hotel people. And your daddy," Yvonne added pointedly.

"Have there been any new developments in the case?"

Yvonne sighed and mopped at her face with a paper towel. "I think they looked at a guest who stayed in a room Jaz cleaned that night. But Rae, last week, said it wasn't him."

"Grandmama?"

Both women looked up. Aliyah stood in the kitchen doorway, her blanket wrapped around her neck like a muffler. Her pink nightie was too short, revealing a pair of long, toothpick-like legs.

"I'm hungry, Grandmama," the child said. Her dark eyes registered a glimmer of recognition when she saw Drue.

"You're the lady who gave me markers," she said, offering the same shy smile.

"Hi, Aliyah," Drue said. "I'm sorry you've been sick." She reached into her backpack and brought out a Little Mermaid coloring book and glitter markers she'd bought at Target.

"These are for you."

A huge smile lit up the girl's face. "Oooh." She pressed the art supplies to her chest.

"What do we say to Miss Drue?" Yvonne prompted.

"Thank you."

Yvonne opened her arms wide and enveloped her granddaughter in a hug. "This girl here was real brave today. Let the doctor give her a shot and a breathing treatment."

"Can I have some soup? And some Goldfish?" Aliyah asked.

"You sure can. Grandmama's gonna fix you your supper right now," Yvonne said, rising.

Drue stood too. "Thanks for talking to me. I appreciate your time."

"I'll walk you out," Yvonne said, leading her through the living room. She looked out the window at the group of young men standing across the street.

"I don't see no car out there," she said.

Drue took out her phone and swiped over to the Lyft app. "I used a ride service to get here."

She held up the phone. "See? A car will be here in five minutes."

"Huh," Yvonne said. She motioned toward the street. "You best stay right inside here until that car gets here. Them thugs over there, ain't no telling what they might do if they see a girl like you standing alone outside."

Drue had a thought. "Did any of those guys ever bother her?"

"They wadn't living here when Jazmin got killed," Yvonne said. "There was a nice young family living over there, but they moved away. That's how it is here. All the nice people move off. That's what Jazmin wanted, for her and for me and Aliyah. She wanted something better."

20

After the driver dropped her off at the cottage, Drue went inside, stripped and put on a bathing suit. She called Corey.

"Hey, I was wondering if it would be okay if I came down and used the pool at your complex," she said, as soon as he answered.

"Oh hi, Drue. I'm headed home right now, and I was actually planning on swimming laps tonight, so yeah, perfect timing. Meet you there in twenty minutes?"

As soon as she waded into the pool, Drue felt her tensions begin to melt away. She floated on her back and closed her eyes, willing herself to relax. She heard a splash from the far end of the pool, and watched while Corey swam toward her.

"Water feels great, right?" he said, emerging at the shallow end where she was clinging to the side of the pool.

"It feels amazing," she said. "I can't even tell you how much I've missed this."

"Feel like doing some stretches?"

For thirty minutes he patiently put her through a routine of exercises designed to strengthen her still-mending knee. "Stop if it starts to really hurt," he instructed. "You don't want to do too much too fast."

Finally, she waved the white flag. "Okay, I think that's probably enough," she admitted.

"I've gotta get my laps in, but if you want, just hang around and do some really easy pedaling like I showed you," he said.

She watched appreciatively as he glided back and forth through the water, his eyes covered with swim goggles, his Lycra suit molded to his body. This could, Drue reflected, come under the category of soft-core porn.

They sat on the edge of the pool, their legs dangling in the water, while Corey took glugs from an evil-looking plastic gallon jug of something he called "go-juice."

"What all is in it?" she asked.

He held the jug out. "Just the usual. Protein powder, electrolytes, powdered kelp, vitamins, apple cider vinegar . . ."

She made a gagging sound and pushed the jug away.

"How was your week?" he asked, sliding back into the pool and doing scissor kicks.

"Boring. Frustrating."

"How so?"

"I feel like I'm doing what you're doing. Treading water. I'm useless at this job. I mean, I suck, big-time. And I can't quit because I need the money."

"It'll get better," he said.

"No, so far it's only gotten worse. I've got some weird oppositional thing going on with my father. I'm thirty-six years old, and as soon as he tells me I shouldn't do something—I go right out and do it anyway. It's nuts!"

"What? You drove without a seatbelt? Had unprotected sex?"

She blushed, thinking about her one-night stand with Jonah. "Worse. There's a case the firm handled. It involved the murder of this young girl—she was only twenty-four, a single mom with a little kid. She was murdered two years ago, right down the street here, at Gulf Vista."

"A maid, right? I remember hearing about it on the news."

"Right. Her mother hired the firm to sue the hotel for criminal negligence."

"Did they ever catch the killer?"

"No. The hotel management said Jazmin was at work when she was killed, which meant they could settle it as a workmen's comp case. And the state of Florida limits workers' comp claims to a hundred and fifty thousand dollars. Even if you're murdered! By the time our firm took its cut of the payout, Jazmin's mom, who, by the way, is only forty-eight, and is raising her granddaughter by herself, came away with peanuts."

"That's terrible," Corey said.

"I think so too. I was working the reception desk when Yvonne Howington, that's the mother's name, came in with the little girl. Aliyah. Yvonne was raising hell about the settlement, and finally, after our bitchy office manager, who happens to be married to my father, instructed me to tell her to scram, my dad showed up. He told her he'd done all the firm could. So, see ya, bye."

"Sounds like he did do all he could for her," Corey said.

"No." Drue shook her head adamantly. "Yvonne swears Jazmin wasn't working when she was killed. And she was being sexually harassed by a manager, which the hotel denies."

Drue went on to describe the time line of Jazmin Mayes's murder and what she'd learned from her visit with the grand-mother the previous day.

"I think it's great that you care so much about this case," Corey said. "But I have to ask, what is it you think you can do? You're an intake worker, as you said, not a detective."

"I *have* to do something," Drue said. "Ever since I moved back here I've felt so hollow inside, and I don't know if it's because I've lost kiteboarding—probably for good—or my mom, or what. And oh man, can you believe I just mentioned losing her and a damn sport in the same breath?"

"Yeah, I can. I don't know what I'd do if I couldn't run or swim, all the things that are such a huge part of my life." He reached out and touched her arm. "Hey, don't be so hard on yourself."

"When I went to see Yvonne Howington? Really listened to her as she talked about her daughter? It's the first time I've really felt excited about something in, like, forever. I want to help her. And Aliyah."

"How?" Corey lifted himself out of the pool and began toweling off.

"To start, I need to check out Gulf Vista, walk around, see the layout, including the laundry room where she was killed, and the back service areas."

"Isn't it a gated resort?" Corey asked. "I know you can't access the pool and patio areas from the beach, unless you have a key card."

"I think I have a plan." She glanced over at him. "Want to run a mission with me?"

He looked alarmed. "Is it something illegal?"

"I wouldn't say it's illegal. Per se." She shrugged. "Never mind. I'll go by myself." She slid her feet into her flip-flops and began gathering her belongings.

He swatted her with the end of his towel. "Now you've got me hooked."

The germ of the idea was planted in her mind as she rode past Gulf Vista the night she'd visited Yvonne Howington. She'd spotted the resort's marquee. WELCOME PHELAN-KSIONSYK WEDDING. HAPPY EVER AFTER!

"How are you at lying?" she asked Corey.

"Terrible. I'm basically an honest person."

"Okay. Let me put it this way. How good of an actor are you?"

Now he grinned, his white teeth flashing against his model-perfect tan. "I'm a normal gay man. Of course I'm a great actor."

Drue fell silent.

"Hey," Corey said. "You knew I was gay, right?"

"No," she said, trying to cover her mortification. "Which makes you an even more terrific actor. And you're just right for the role I have in mind."

They pulled up to the gate at the Gulf Vista in Corey's gleaming black BMW convertible. A security guard approached the car, dressed in a close imitation of a Royal Bahamian police officer's uniform, correct down to the white Bermuda shorts, red sash and pith helmet. "Hi," Corey said, leaning out the window. He pointed to Drue, who was dressed in a striped navy sundress and pearl earrings. "My fiancée and I are getting married this fall, and we're considering having the wedding here, so we'd like to take a look around, if that's all right."

"Have you spoken to Danielle Thompson, in our events office?" the guard asked.

"Oh no, it's a little early for that," Corey said. "We thought we'd just have a drink in the bar and walk around and get the feel of the place. I mean, we haven't even set the date yet."

"Miss Thompson is the one who speaks to all our brides," the guard replied.

"She's not a bride yet," Corey said, giving the guard a conspiratorial wink.

A car pulled in behind them and the guard looked over

his shoulder. He reached into his pocket and produced a white guest pass. "Name?"

"Sanchez," Drue said quickly. Just as well she didn't give her real name here.

He scrawled the name on the pass and handed it to Corey. "Keep that displayed on your dashboard and park in one of the visitor slots near the lobby. That's only for tonight, though."

"You were brilliant," Drue said, as she stepped out of the BMW. "Understated but persuasive."

"I played Second Elf from the Left in our kindergarten production of *Santa's Secret Workshop,*" Corey said modestly. "My parents said I killed."

"This is some spread, huh?" Drue said, as they surveyed their surroundings. The low-slung white stucco architecture of the main building was nearly obscured by lush tropical landscaping. Huge tree ferns and palms intertwined above a red tile walkway that led to the glass-enclosed three-story atrium. A white-uniformed doorman silently opened the doors as they approached. "Welcome to Gulf Vista," he murmured.

The lobby was dominated by a huge marble fountain, where water gurgled softly and bright orange koi flitted among shining copper pennies.

"Very impressive," Corey said, as they walked through the lobby. "I wouldn't mind getting married here."

"Any prospects?" Drue asked.

"Not lately. Where do you want to start our mission?"

"Let's just walk around, get the lay of the land," Drue said.

They moved through the lobby and out through another set of large glass doors to a jungle-like garden with more winding red tile walkways. Irregularly spaced uplights cast the area in moody shadows. "They must spend a fortune on all this landscaping," Corey observed.

"It's kind of creepy if you ask me," Drue said. "I keep expecting a coconut to fall on my head or a spider monkey to spring out at me from one of those palm trees."

Eventually the walkway led them to a sprawling patio and pool area.

"That's more like it," Drue said. It was dusk now, and the kidney-shaped pool seemed to beckon in the waning light. There was a thatched-roof tiki bar, where a bartender in a Hawaiian shirt with a hibiscus tucked behind her ear wielded a silver cocktail shaker. Strings of café lights crisscrossed above the pool, lending a festive atmosphere. Guests lolled on chaises and chairs around the pool, sipping drinks. Beyond, there was another line of perfectly spaced royal palms, and beyond that, they heard the distant sound of waves washing ashore on the beach.

Drue pointed at a three-story wing to the north. "That's the wing where Jazmin was working the night she was killed," she said. "Zee's report said the hotel's security cameras showed her rolling her cleaning cart from that wing to the laundry room, which was where her body was found."

"What now?"

She grabbed his hand. "Let's take an innocent stroll that way."

"What if we get stopped?"

"Who's going to stop us?" she scoffed. "We're young and beautiful and in love."

They approached a set of double glass doors leading to a small lobby in the north wing, and Drue's hopes were dashed.

"Damn," she said, pointing at the key card slot. She tried the doors, but as expected, they were locked. Drue looked around, hoping a guest would appear with a key, allowing them to tag right along, but nobody was around. She glanced upward and saw a small video camera pointed in their direction.

"The laundry room should be around here somewhere," she mused, moving away from the doors and out of camera range. She pointed at a narrower, concrete walkway that led toward the back of the wing. A discreet sign tucked into a mass of ferns proclaimed: SERVICE AREA. TEAM MEMBERS ONLY.

"I love a company that refers to employees as 'team members,'" Drue said, following the walkway toward the rear of the building. When Corey didn't reply, she turned to see him still standing in front of the guest wing.

"Come on," she called. "Let's check it out."

"Is that wise?" he asked, joining her reluctantly.

"If one of the 'team members' comes along, they're not going to *shoot* us," Drue said impatiently. "We'll say we got lost. It's not like it's the hotel vault we're trying to break into. It's only a laundry room."

"I bet they have some really high-thread-count sheets and towels here, though. Probably Egyptian cotton," Corey said.

As they progressed around the building the impressive landscaping gave way to cracked concrete and weedy-looking pine straw. The sidewalk ended abruptly in front of a set of solid-looking steel doors with a key card reader.

"Damn it," Drue fumed. She looked up at the security camera pointed toward them, and pivoted quickly in the opposite direction with Corey following closely this time. A few yards away, she stopped and peered around the branches of a bedraggled-looking hibiscus. The grass beneath it was beaten down and littered with cigarette butts.

"Looks like we found the team's smoking lounge," she told Corey.

"But did you find any clues to who could have killed the girl?" he asked.

Her shoulders slumped. "No. If I could just get inside . . ."

"Forget it," he advised. "I want to buy my fiancée a drink at the tiki bar."

21

"Hi, handsome. What'll you have?" The bartender batted her eyelashes at Corey and completely ignored Drue.

"Just an unsweet iced tea," Corey said.

"Got it." She turned to go.

"And I'll have a margarita, no salt," Drue called after her.

She studied Corey. "So you really don't drink at all?"

"No. I figured out not long ago that I make poor choices when I do, so now I don't."

"Um, yeah," she muttered. "Poor choices. Big-time."

The server brought their drinks and set a bowl of popcorn in front of them. Drue noticed that she had a lanyard around her neck with a key card dangling from it.

"That's what I need, damn it," she whispered to Corey.

"What? Fake eyelashes?"

"No," she said, nodding at the server, who was now measuring rum into a blender. "One of those lanyards. With the keys to the kingdom."

The bartender scooped ice into the blender and added chunks of pineapple. As she did so, Drue noticed a server at the far end of the bar move behind the first woman. "Okay, bye," their bartender said. "Are you working tomorrow?"

"No," the other woman said. "I'm off 'til Tuesday." She lifted a hatch in the bar top, and just before exiting, hung her own lanyard on a nearby peg.

"I need to get my hands on that key card," Drue said.

Corey gave her the side-eye. "And just how do you propose to get it?"

She crammed a handful of popcorn in her mouth and eyed the lanyard, so temptingly near but just out of arm's reach.

"Steal it."

He pushed his bar stool away and stared at her in mock horror. "Who *are* you?"

"Just a girl with a shady past," Drue said. "But don't worry, I haven't stolen anything in years and years."

"Why not?"

She shrugged. "The thrill is gone, I guess. My shrink, at the time, said I was only doing it to get my father's attention. And to further alienate my stepmother."

Corey drained half his iced-tea glass. He propped his elbow on the bar and rested his chin on his knuckles. "And was his theory correct?"

"She, not he. Yeah, she was partly right."

"Dare I ask what kinds of things you stole?"

Drue thought back. "Let's see. There was my stepbrother's

weed. Money out of my dad's wallet. My stepmother's pearl earrings. Her sterling silver Tiffany cigarette lighter. And her cigarettes. My dad's booze. And my stepmother's birth control pills. Also her sleeping pills. But not all at the same time. Sometime I'd go weeks and months without stealing anything."

Corey gave an uneasy chuckle. "If you had authority issues I get why you'd steal liquor and drugs and money and jewelry. But why take the poor woman's birth control?"

"The therapist said I was trying to gaslight her. Make her think she was losing her mind. Which I one hundred percent was doing. Like, the jewelry, after she'd searched the house and my dad yelled at her for losing it, I'd put it back, weeks later."

He shuddered. "Jesus. What a horrible, demented kid you must have been."

"Agreed," Drue said. "But Joan and her kids treated me much, much worse. They made my life a living hell, so I lashed out. In the end, she won. And I lost."

The bartender came by with a pitcher of iced tea and refilled Corey's empty glass. "How's my margarita coming?" Drue asked.

"Oh yeah. I'll get right on that," the bartender said.

"What was the deciding battle in your family feud?" Corey asked.

"Halloween, when I was fifteen. This one Friday night, my best friend was spending the night, as usual, and Joan and Dad were away for the weekend. We decided we really, really wanted to go to Fright Fest, at Disney World. And I knew where Joan hid the keys to her Cadillac. So we went."

"You're telling me that two fifteen-year-old girls loaded up in a stolen Caddy and drove two and a half hours to Orlando?"

"At night. And we'd been drinking. And we would have gotten away with it, if some asshole hadn't sideswiped the Caddy in the parking lot and ripped the right rearview mirror completely off the car."

"Ouch." Corey winced. "So you got caught and, what, put in permanent time-out?"

Drue's smile was brittle. "Something like that. My friend's father was this uptight, asshole preacher who made a big stink when my father called to tell him what we'd done. She told *her* father that I'd *forced* her to go with me. Which was a lie. She drove because my feet couldn't even reach the gas pedal. Annnnnd, after that, she never spoke to me again. Totally ghosted me. When the school year was up, my dad put me on a Greyhound bus and shipped me back to Fort Lauderdale to live with my mom."

"That's some story," he said.

"It gets worse," Drue said. "Dad and Joan divorced, but now Dad is married to my former friend—who is my boss at the law firm and who's made it her mission to make my life a living hell."

"And I thought my family was screwed up." Corey hopped off the bar stool. "Hey, I've had about a gallon of iced tea. I'm gonna go find the men's room."

"Okay. I'll be right here."

~

"Let's go," Drue said, when Corey returned to the bar. "I've already settled the tab."

She walked briskly away from the pool area. "Where to now?" he asked, glancing at his watch. "Hate to say it, but I can't hang out here much longer. I've got a five-mile bike ride to get in tonight."

"Laundry room," she said.

"How are you going to get in?"

She turned and dangled the key-card lanyard before his eyes.

"Do I want to know how you managed to snag that?"

"I accidentally spilled that whole big bowl of popcorn on the floor. The bartender was super annoyed that she had to come around from behind the bar and sweep it all up. While she was tidying, the lanyard somehow fell off that hook and into my bag."

"You're the kind of girl my mama tried to warn me about," Corey said, shaking his head.

"She never did bring my drink, so I figured this was a fair trade."

When they arrived at the service area, Corey grabbed her arm just as she was about to slide the key through the laundry room door's reader. "What if somebody comes along and catches us?"

"They won't," she assured him, pushing the door open.

The room was large, with walls of stainless steel industrial washers and dryers, and intensely hot. A stainless steel folding table ran against one wall, and shelving held jugs of bleach and laundry detergent. A wheeled canvas cart was pulled up in front of one of the machines, and Drue shuddered.

"They found that poor girl's body shoved into a cart like that one," she told Corey, her voice hushed. "It could even be the same cart."

"Thanks for that visual. This place gives me the creeps," Corey said. "What are you looking for, anyway?"

Drue walked around the room, looking down at the floor and up at the ceiling. She pointed at a spot above the doorway, where a metal bracket was bolted to the wall and wires sprouted from the plasterboard. "Our firm's investigator said there wasn't a working video camera in this room when Jazmin was killed. But it looks like maybe there was one here at some point."

"Let's just go, okay?" Corey said, his hand on the doorknob.

She took out her phone and snapped a few quick shots of the room, zooming in on the area where a wall-mounted camera might have been, and then pulled the door open again.

"God," Corey breathed, when they were well away. "It must have been a hundred and ten degrees in there. How do the housekeepers stand working in there without air-conditioning?"

Drue turned to look at him. "Good point. If I were in there doing laundry, where there's no air-conditioning? I'd leave the door open, to at least get some fresh air. Maybe Jazmin left it open that night, and that's how her attacker got in."

"If that's so, the killer could have been anybody," Corey said. "Even a guest."

As they were walking away they heard a rumble of wheels on the concrete walkway. A housekeeper in a white uniform smock was trundling a huge canvas laundry cart toward them, her body nearly dwarfed by the piles of rumpled linens.

"Busted," Corey whispered. "Almost."

But Drue wasn't listening. She was walking toward the housekeeper, a friendly smile pasted on her face. When she got close enough to speak, she noticed the housekeeper's name tag. LUTRISHA. Wasn't that the name of one of the employees Zee had interviewed?

"Excuse me," Drue said. "Could I speak to you for a couple minutes?"

The woman was young, in her mid-twenties, Drue guessed, with short reddish-purple hair and sallow skin ravished with angry red acne.

"What about?" she said, instantly wary.

"Weren't you working here when Jazmin Mayes, one of the other housekeepers, was killed a couple years ago?"

"Yeah."

"Did you know Jazmin?"

"Not that well," Lutrisha said. She paused. "I was the one who found her body."

"Ohhh. Right." That was why her name had struck a chord, Drue thought. "But I thought you left and took a job someplace else. Publix?"

"How do you know so much?" Lustrisha asked.

"I work for the law firm that Jazmin's mother hired after she was killed," Drue said. "I think you talked to our investigator not long after it happened."

"I can't talk to you," Lutrisha said, glancing around. "I gotta get back to work."

"What time do you get off?"

"Not for another hour."

"Could I meet you somewhere, so we could talk? I just live a few blocks away."

"I can't get involved," the girl said. "I'm sorry for her kid and all, but this has got nothing to do with me." She started to push the cart away, but Drue stayed right beside her.

"You know, they still haven't caught Jazmin's killer."

"Yeah, so I heard."

"Did you know that Jazmin's mother is raising her daughter? Yvonne only got a settlement of one hundred thirty-five thousand dollars, because the hotel claimed Jazmin was working when she was killed. And all the money is tied up in a trust for Aliyah, so it can't be touched 'til she's eighteen."

The girl stopped in front of the laundry room doors, fumbling for her key card, which she wore on a cord around her wrist. "That's all?" She looked shocked.

"Aliyah has severe asthma," Drue said, unabashedly laying it on thick. "Her medical bills are horrendous."

Lutrisha had the key card poised to swipe. She sighed. "Where do you want to meet? I can't take long. I been working all day and I'm beat."

"How about that coffee shop on Gulf Boulevard? Right next to the Thunderbird?" Drue asked. "At eight-thirty?"

The girl nodded. "I'll be there."

22

Lutrisha Smallwood's name was a cruel joke. She was tall and bean-pole thin, with light blue eyes that narrowed as she blew a plume of vapor from her e-cigarette. She'd been leaning up against the outside of the coffee shop, vaping, when Drue pedaled up on the beach bike she'd bought on Craigslist.

The girl smiled crookedly as Drue approached. "Did you get your license yanked for too many DUIs?"

"No. My car's out of commission." Drue gestured toward the coffee shop. "Do you want to go in and talk?"

"Waiting on you," Lutrisha said, following her inside.

"You know," Lutrisha said, staring down at her mug of coffee. "Right after that thing with Jazmin, the hotel manager called all of us in housekeeping into a meeting. He said Jazmin's mom hired some hotshot lawyer who was gonna sue the hotel for, like, ten million dollars. And if she won the case, the hotel would have to close up and all of us would lose our jobs."

"That's not true. It never got as far as a lawsuit. And besides, even if she'd filed suit and won, the hotel's insurance company would pay the claim—not the hotel."

"So you say." Lutrisha looked around the coffee shop, which was mostly empty. The only employee was busy wiping down the marble counter. "I can't afford to lose this job. I tried working at Publix, but they wouldn't give me full-time hours. I got a kid of my own. That's why I came back to work at the hotel. Plus, most of the folks there, they're not so bad."

"What about the ones who are bad?" Drue asked.

"Most of 'em left."

"Like H. K. Byars and Mr. Shelnutt?"

"Shelnutt still works there."

Drue stared at the girl, trying to figure out how much she knew and what she was willing to share. She had a poker face.

"You told our investigator you didn't know Jazmin all that well. Was that true?"

Lutrisha nibbled at her cuticle. "I don't need to get dragged back into this mess. I knew her from work, okay? We both had little kids, so it wasn't like we were going to go out clubbing together every night."

"Got it," Drue said. "Did Jazmin ever mention to you that somebody at the hotel was bothering her? Maybe sexually harassing her?"

"Where'd you hear that?"

"She told her mother that a white, older man, who was married, was coming on to her. The hotel says they never received any complaints of harassment from Jazmin."

"Huh. Her too?"

"Was somebody bothering you?" Drue asked.

"He tried." Lutrisha smiled grimly. "Started brushing up against me in the hallways, trying to corner me in the service elevator, putting his hands where they don't belong. The second time he did it, I sprayed him in the face with Windex. After that, the son of a bitch steered way clear of me."

"Just curious. Didn't you tell our firm's investigator, right afterwards, that you didn't know anything about sexual harassment at the hotel?"

"Yeah. But that's 'cuz the dude made me nervous. And I didn't want to get in trouble."

"Can you tell me who bothered you?"

"Larry Boone. He used to be head of engineering at Gulf Vista."

"Used to be? Did he get demoted?"

"He left. Maybe two, three weeks after Jazmin was killed."

"Do you know where he went?"

She shook her head. "No idea. People were still in shock about Jazmin, so I don't think anybody was too upset that Scary Larry was gone."

Lutrisha pulled her phone from her purse. "I gotta go pretty soon. My sister is watching my little boy and she gets real pissy if I'm late."

"Just a few more minutes, please," Drue said. "Do you want

something to eat? I saw they had some cookies and stuff behind the counter."

"Ugh. Sugar. No thanks. What else do you need to know?"

"Back at the hotel, my friend and I went into the laundry room. I noticed there were some brackets on the wall that look like maybe there used to be a camera up there. Was there a security camera there when Jazmin was killed?"

"I don't know," Lutrisha said. "None of us like working in there. It's hot as hell, and where it is, like at the back of the hotel, it's creepy."

"Did housekeepers ever leave the door open when they were working, to get some air?"

"Yeah. All the time."

"So anybody could get in there, if they knew where it was?"

"Why would anybody want to?"

"One more question. Jazmin's mom said she'd been seeing somebody. A man. Did she ever say anything about that to you?"

"Yeah. I knew she had a new boyfriend."

"How?"

"A couple times, she was going out with this guy right after work, and she didn't want to have to go home to get ready, because she knew her mom would ask a lot of questions. So she asked me to kind of be the lookout for her, while she showered and changed in one of the guest rooms. If the bosses ever found that out, we'd both have been fired."

Drue felt a tiny fizz of excitement. "Do you know who the guy was?"

"I know he used to work at Gulf Vista. I think he was a desk clerk maybe."

"You don't know his name?"

Lutrisha scrunched up her face. "Maybe Jorge?"

"Why didn't she want her mom to know about this guy?"

"Probably because he wasn't black. He's from one of those countries in Central America. Ecuador, Guatemala? I get those places mixed up. Jazmin said her mom wouldn't like him, which is funny, because who knew black people were just as racist as white people. Right?"

"Do you know where this Jorge lives? Or where he worked after he left Gulf Vista?"

"She said it was at another hotel on the beach."

Lutrisha's chair scraped the concrete floor as she pushed away from the table. "Okay, sorry, but I really do have to go."

"I understand. And thanks so much for your time, Lutrisha. You've been a big help. Hey, do you know whatever happened to Jazmin's friend Neesa?"

"Her?" Lutrisha rolled her eyes. "She could be anywhere. They said she was fired because she was late all the time, which kind of surprised me."

"Why?"

"Word was, Neesa had some kind of thing going on with the head of housekeeping. Herman Byars."

"What kind of thing?"

"One guess. I gotta go now."

23

On Friday, she was congratulating herself on making it through another week without any serious incidents.

Her celebration was short-lived. Shortly after eleven, she sensed a shadow over her shoulder.

"Drue?" Wendy brandished a handful of papers.

"What do you need?" Drue responded.

Wendy jerked her head in the direction of her office. "Let's do this somewhere quieter."

As she trailed behind Wendy's cloud of Miss Dior perfume, Drue experienced the same inescapable sense of doom she'd once felt on her numerous trips to the principal's office in high school.

She already knew what was coming. The "you're not living up to your abilities," the "you need to try harder" and, worst of all, the dreaded "we are very disappointed."

"Close the door, please," Wendy said, not looking up from the document she was reading.

She absentmindedly reached in a cut-glass jar on her desk and tossed a biscuit to Princess, who was lounging on an orange Hermès blanket on the only other chair in the room.

Drue stood glowering down at the French bulldog, who kept right on chewing and ignoring her.

"You can sit," Wendy said, looking up.

"Where?"

"Oh for God's sake," Wendy snapped. "Here, Princess. Come here to Mommy."

The dog hopped down and trotted over to her mistress.

"Move that blanket, please," Wendy said, before Drue could seat herself. "She's very sensitive, and it confuses her when she smells other people's scents on her things."

Drue folded the blanket and dropped it to the floor.

"What did you need to see me about?" she asked, wanting to endure as little time as possible in what she considered the Chilean chamber of torture.

"This," Wendy said, tapping a computer printout on her desktop. "I've been looking at your leads sheet, and frankly, I'm appalled. Do you realize you've been here for four weeks and the only case you've referred is this?"

"Yes," Drue said eagerly. "You're talking about the client from Sunshine Inn—the extended-stay motel on U.S. 19?"

"Bedbugs?" Wendy said shrilly. "Three weeks and all you have to show is a bedbug case?"

"It's legit, I swear," Drue said. "The poor man just moved

down here from Pennsylvania to take a job at a hair salon. He was staying at the motel while he looked for an apartment, but after three nights he had to check out because the place was crawling with bedbugs. They just chewed him alive! He went to one of those doc-in-the-box medical clinics and they sent him to the emergency room. I've seen his discharge papers. He had to have cortisone shots and they prescribed him some expensive ointments for the infection."

"Stop!" Wendy began scratching at her arms. "Just what do you think this firm is going to be able to recover in damages in a case like this? The cost of a tube of Neosporin?"

"No," Drue said. "The client hasn't been able to work since he got here. The salon took one look at the scabs on his arms and hands and withdrew the job offer. He was so desperate to work he went to one of those Kwik-Kut franchise hair salons, but the first time he shampooed a client's hair, he had a horrendous allergic reaction to the chemicals because of his infection. The man can't work, Wendy. I really think Dad could help him."

"We are not wasting our time on a bullshit bedbug case," Wendy said, taking the report, balling it up and throwing it into her trash basket.

She leaned back in her chair and Princess hopped up and began licking her chin.

"I told Brice this wasn't a good idea, but of course, he has such a soft heart, what could I do?"

"You're firing me?" Drue was incredulous.

"I wish. But Brice won't hear of it. You must have really laid a guilt trip on him when he came over there to move you into that cottage. He was really upset when he got home."

"If you're not firing me, why are we having this talk?" Drue asked, knowing she wasn't going to like the answer.

"Because I need you to get with the program," Wendy said. "You have the most dismal numbers of anybody—either here or in the offsite call center. Drastic measures are called for."

Drue waited.

"Starting now, you're in retraining. I want you to take your headset and plug into Jonah's console. He's our top producer, so my hope is that you can learn something from his technique."

"You're kidding," Drue said. "I know what I'm doing, Wendy. It's just that the calls I'm getting have all been dead ends. This is unbelievably unfair."

"No," Wendy snapped. "What's unbelievably unfair is that although I run this office, your father has overruled me and continues to allow dead weight to bring down the rest of the Campbell, Coxe and Kramner team."

"Dead weight?" Drue jumped up from the chair.

Wendy looked up expectantly, stroking the dog's ears and smiling her fake smile.

"You can torture me all you like, but I'm not going to give you the satisfaction of quitting," Drue said, her voice low. As she walked out of the office she made sure to deliberately step on the Hermès blanket with both feet.

"What's this?" Jonah said, as she wheeled her chair over to his cubicle, her headset resting around her neck.

"Retraining," Drue said. "Wendy wants me to listen to the way you handle calls, because you're so awesome at it."

He nodded. "Listen, Grasshopper, and Mr. Miyagi will share the wisdom of the ages."

His console lit up.

"Just answer the damn phone," Drue said.

24

Saturday morning, Drue poured herself a mug of coffee and sat down at the card table in the kitchen. She had a new package of index cards and a box of black felt-tip pens, and some file folders, and felt a surge of excitement. School supplies! At one time, back in elementary school, she'd loved school. Loved the smell of chalk and schoolbooks and the thrill of opening a notebook for the first time, laboriously printing her name in block letters on the inside cover.

She began jotting down what she'd learned so far about the employees at the Gulf Vista and about Jazmin Mayes and her coworkers, starting a new index card for each set of facts. It was an idea she'd picked up from reading the dog-eared paperback Sue Grafton detective novels that had been left behind by Leonard, the cottage's most recent tenant.

Drue scribbled every detail of her conversations with Lutrisha and Yvonne Howington.

An hour had passed and she'd worked her way through half a packet of cards when she heard insistent knocking at the front door.

"Good morning!" Ben Fentress stood on her doorstep. He held out a cardboard beer box with what looked like some kind of auto part inside. "Did somebody here order a starter for a 1995 Ford Bronco?"

Jonah Kelleher stepped out from behind his coworker, holding up a six-pack of craft beer. "And some emergency beverages?"

"Oh," Drue said, taken aback.

"You forgot I was coming to work on your car today, didn't you?" Ben said.

"It kinda slipped my mind, but I'm so glad it didn't slip yours," Drue said, tugging at the hem of the shrunken T-shirt she'd thrown on first thing that morning, trying to cover the exposed skin of her abdomen above her gym shorts. She gazed past Ben at Jonah. "What are you doing here?"

Jonah's face flushed. "Ben asked me to give him a hand."

Both men wore grease-stained T-shirts and jeans. "We had to take a starter out of a wrecked car at the junkyard. It's kind of a two-man job," Ben said.

"Right," Drue said hastily. "Do you want to come in?"

"Nope," Ben said. "We just need your car keys, so we can get started."

~

Drue typed the name Larry Boone into the search bar of her phone and waited. Thirty-two entries appeared. She sighed. If she was going to track down the man who'd harassed Lutrisha Smallwood, and possibly Jazmin, she really needed a laptop computer. That would go on her wish list, right after a new roof for the cottage.

She went back to the search engine and redefined her search, narrowing the location to St. Petersburg, Florida, and this time netting only five names.

One by one, she discarded the possibilities until she came to a Larry Boone who'd been named employee of the month at a local hardware store in 2018.

The citation was from a newspaper in Brooksville, a small town about an hour north of St. Pete. The story was accompanied by a photo of the man. This Larry Boone was white, balding, with a generous paunch and a dark eighties-porn-star mustache.

Drue gazed down at the tiny photo. Could this be Scary Larry?

She cursed herself for not asking Lutrisha Smallwood for her phone number. Then she pulled out a new index card and jotted down what little information she had from the article. Now what? Should she just call and ask for Larry Boone? What if he came to the phone? What would she say?

Before she could further ponder her line of questioning, she heard the front door opening.

"Drue?"

It was Jonah.

He had his head stuck inside the door. His hands and face

were smeared with grease, and sweat dripped from his hair. "Hey, can I use the bathroom?"

"Come on in," she said. He followed her through the living room and she gestured toward the bathroom. "Wait right here," she said. A moment later she was back with a roll of paper towels.

"Thanks," he said, wiping his hands on a wadded-up towel.

"I'm in the kitchen if you need me," she told him.

Jonah appeared in the kitchen doorway a few minutes later. "This house is really awesome. It reminds me of my aunt and uncle's house at Rehoboth Beach."

She looked up from her notecards, trying not to act annoyed at the interruption. She reminded herself that he and Ben were doing her a huge favor.

"Rehoboth Beach?"

"In Delaware. My rich uncle was a lawyer in D.C. They had a house down the shore, as they called it, and they'd invite my family for a week every summer. My sisters and I looked forward to that all year round. For that one week, we thought we were rich too."

"I stayed here with my grandparents for two weeks every summer for as long as I can remember," Drue said softly. "Even after my mom and I moved over to Lauderdale, I'd come back here to Sunset Beach every year." She looked around the kitchen, at the toast crumbs on the yellow Formica countertop, and the faded daisy-print valance over the sink window. "I still can't quite believe that they're gone and it's really mine now."

"It's cool that everything's so original. Especially all the wood walls. It's solid, you know? My crappy little garage apartment in town is all Sheetrock. I hate Sheetrock. You bump up against a wall and it's instantly gouged."

Drue felt herself thawing despite her own stern resolve to keep her distance from him.

"So, did you grow up in Florida? I assumed you did, since you went to UF."

"For law school," he said. "I'm originally from Seneca, South Carolina. I got my undergrad degree there."

"Where? Clemson? South Carolina?"

"I wish," he said, flashing a lopsided grin. "No, I went to a dinky community college so I could live at home. I've got twin sisters who were only a year younger than me, so paying tuition for three was a stretch for my parents."

"How's it going with the car?" Drue asked. "Do you think the new starter is going to do the trick?"

"We're almost there," Jonah said. "Ben went to pick up some lunch for all of us."

"What? No. I was going to buy lunch," Drue said.

"Too late." He paused, looking hopeful. "Is it okay if I look around?"

"There's not much to see," Drue said, leading him into the hallway. "You've seen my pink bathroom," she said, gesturing toward the open door.

"My aunt's bathroom had a mint-green toilet, sink and tub," Jonah said.

Her bedroom door was open. She was secretly thankful she'd made her bed. "Master bedroom," she said.

"Man," he said, stepping inside to look out the window. "What an incredible view. If I lived here, I'd never miss a sunset."

"I try not to," Drue said, deliberately herding him out of the room. Having him just steps from her bed gave off way too intimate a vibe for her.

Drue opened the next door. "Guest bedroom," she said. "Right now it's storage for my kiteboard gear and other random crap. Eventually, I hope to use it as an office."

"Do you do a lot of kiteboarding?" he asked, running his hand down her favorite Naish board.

"It was pretty much my life, right up until I screwed up my knee," she said. "From the time I got my first board in my teens, it's all I thought about. I dropped out of college to go pro, even had a few endorsement deals, but shit happens, ya know?"

"You must miss it, right?" he asked.

"I still dream about it sometimes," she admitted. "Hitting kickers, that's a trick, and doing rails. I miss the adrenaline, being really good at something." She shrugged. "Anyway, most women peak at this sport in their twenties. So my competitive days are gone."

She pointedly closed the door on the room and her past.

He followed her back to the living room. "This room reminds me of one of those old movies," Jonah said, running his hand over the curved back of the rattan settee.

"This was all the original furniture my grandparents had in here," she said. "After my grandmother died, Dad put it all in storage because he was renting the house out."

"I can't even imagine what a house like this would rent for now," he said.

"I don't think the rent was very high. The same tenant, some old dude named Leonard, lived here for cheap because Dad didn't want to spend a lot of money on maintenance. When I moved in, it was a dump."

"You could have fooled me," Jonah said.

"Fresh paint and sweat equity," Drue said.

"How old is this place?" he asked.

"Late 1950s?" she guessed. "My grandfather built it himself, with scrap lumber and stuff he scrounged from construction sites around Ybor City. According to my mom, it took him years to finish building it, because he paid cash for everything."

"So, you're part Cuban?"

"On my mom's side."

"I wondered where you got your olive skin and dark hair." He touched a lock of hair that had come unfastened from her ponytail.

Drue felt a tiny spark travel down her spine. Her face flushed beet red. The front door opened then, and Ben stepped inside.

"Lunch is here," he announced. "Burgers for everybody."

"I'll get the table cleared off and we can eat here," Drue said, shoving her scribbled index cards into a file folder.

"What are you working on?" Ben asked, opening the bag and distributing foil-wrapped burgers. He glanced down at the folder and the scattered pages of notes.

"Nothing," she said hastily.

"You brought a case home, didn't you?" Jonah said, his tone teasing.

"Yeah," she admitted. "I know you guys warned me not to, but it's that criminal negligence case against the Gulf Vista. The housekeeper who was beaten and strangled. Jazmin Mayes."

Ben's eyes widened. "Oh shit. You're going rogue? That's a terrible idea."

"I gotta agree with Ben," Jonah said. "It's been two years. Zee looked at that case backwards and forwards. There's nothing there."

"Yes, there is," Drue insisted. "I know there is. I've read the case file. I've talked to the mother again. I've even been to the hotel and checked out the laundry room where Jazmin was killed."

Ben sipped his beer. "When was this?"

"Thursday night. I went over there with . . . a friend. And I talked to another housekeeper. Jazmin told her mother that a white guy, another hotel employee, was sexually harassing her. She complained to somebody in management, but obviously nobody did anything. This other housekeeper told me she was harassed too. And she gave me the guy's name. Not long after Jazmin was killed, this guy mysteriously quit the hotel. Or got fired, the girl didn't say." She got up and filled a glass with ice cubes and water and drank it rapidly.

"And get this. It's the same girl who discovered Jazmin's body."

"Did Zee talk to this person?" Ben asked.

"Yes, but at that point she was scared to tell him everything she knew. She didn't want to make waves. After the grandmother hired Dad to file suit, the hotel management called a staff meeting to tell the employees that if the hotel had to settle a multimillion-dollar lawsuit, the hotel would have to close up and all the employees would lose their jobs."

"Real subtle way to make sure people kept their mouths shut," Jonah said.

"Still doesn't mean the firm has a legit action against Gulf Vista," Ben said, wiping his hands on a paper napkin. "The girl was on the clock. Like it or not, it's a workers' comp case."

Jonah shrugged. "The man has a point, Drue."

Ben pushed his chair away from the table. "You don't have a case. But you do have, I believe, a car that will start. Want to see?"

"More than anything," Drue said.

Ben slid behind the steering wheel. With a ridiculously dramatic flourish, he stuck the key in the ignition and turned.

The Bronco's engine roared to life.

"Hallelujah!" Drue exulted. "OJ has come back from the dead!"

Ben gave it some gas and the motor, miraculously, did not cut off. He got out of the car and Drue impulsively threw her arms around his neck and kissed his cheek.

"My hero!"

Ben looked at Jonah, who shrugged. "Looks like our work here is done, Batman." He picked up his toolbox and headed for Ben's car.

"Wait," Drue said. "I need to pay you for the starter. And lunch."

"Forget it," Ben said. "I'll let you take me to dinner one night instead."

"Just name the night," Drue said, following him to his Honda.

25

March 1976

The two women turned heads as they walked into Mastry's Bar, and not just because they were in their work uniforms—white polyester dresses, white hose, white shoes. Both Colleen Boardman Hicks and Vera Cochran were stunners, Colleen with her blond hair, deep tan and short skirt, and Vera with her luscious curves and Cupid's bow smile.

The lunchtime crowd at Mastry's was almost exclusively male: some retirees, the geezers who showed up when the bar opened at nine for their breakfast beers; office workers, in dress shirts and ties; cops; mailmen; and a smattering of tourists who'd wandered in off Central Avenue in search of a cold beer and a spring training ball game on the television.

Colleen pointed to a booth at the far wall, and they slid in on opposite sides of the table.

"How did you even find this place?" Vera asked, looking around the dimly lit room.

"Somebody told me they have the best burgers in town," Colleen said.

"I hope our patients won't complain when we come back smelling like the inside of a carton of Salems," Vera said, waving her hand at the smoke cloud that enveloped the room.

"Don't be such a prisspot," Colleen said.

The waitress arrived at the table to take their order.

"I'll have a cheeseburger, medium, with pickles and mustard. No onions. Do you, uh, have Mateus?" Colleen asked.

"You're gonna drink wine? In the middle of the day?" Vera looked shocked.

"Not today she's not," the redhead said. "We don't serve wine. You want something else? Beer? Maybe a Bloody Mary?"

"Never mind," Colleen said. "You've got Tab, right?"

"Yeah."

"Okay, then just a cheeseburger and a Tab. Remember, no onions."

"Got it."

"And I'll have a plain burger and a Fresca," Vera said.

"You girls want fries or no?"

"Yes," Vera said.

"No thanks," Colleen said.

The server brought their soft drinks, and the two women sat back and looked around. The walls of the bar were covered with dozens of stuffed and mounted game fish, predominantly tarpon, and old autographed black-and-white photos of baseball players, mostly St. Louis Cardinals, who frequented the bar during spring training games at nearby Al Lang Field.

"Any plans for the weekend?" Colleen asked. She'd spotted the two men at the end of the bar, but was trying not to glance their way.

"Nothing special," Vera reported. "My sister talked me into babysitting for her two brats. What about you?"

Colleen rolled her eyes. "Dinner party at the in-laws'. It's Rosemary's birthday. Not my idea of fun."

"What have you got against Allen's family?"

"They *hate* me," Colleen said. "Everybody thinks Dr. Hicks is so great, you know, because he's this beloved doctor, big in Rotary and at the yacht club, but believe me, he is such a phony." She lowered her voice. "It's an open secret at Bayfront that he's screwed half the nurses working there."

"You're kidding!" Vera said breathlessly.

"It's the truth. Of course, I guess you can't blame him, because most of the time Rosemary is zonked out of her gourd."

"She drinks?"

Colleen looked around, then lowered her voice. "She likes vodka, because she thinks you can't smell it on her breath. And diet pills even though she's a size four. One guess where she gets the pills."

The server set their plates on the table. "Here you go."

"Thanks so much," Colleen said, flashing her brilliant smile. She picked up her knife and cut the cheeseburger into quarters.

Vera watched, then did the same. "I get why you don't like them, but what do his parents have against you?"

"Where do I start?" Colleen asked. "They don't approve of

the fact that I bleach my hair. They think I dress trashy. They don't like me working as a dental hygienist. But mostly they hate the fact that I'm not the girl they had all picked out for their baby boy Allen."

"Really?" Vera dabbed a french fry in the puddle of ketchup on her plate. "Did they actually have somebody else in mind?"

"Oh yes," Colleen said. "Morton's partner's oldest daughter, Suzanne. Miss Perfect. Miss Debutante. Miss Sun Goddess beauty queen."

"And then you had to show up and make Allen fall in love with you, and spoil everything," Vera said, giggling.

"Yeah. Something like that." Colleen stood up and slung her shoulder bag strap over her arm. "I've gotta find the bathroom. Be right back."

She walked slowly toward the back of the room, as though she had no idea where the ladies' room was, although, of course, she'd used it when she'd been here three months ago. And she'd used it four more times, each time she'd come back to Mastry's.

He was watching her. His partner was watching too. They'd turned halfway around on the bar stools, waiting for her to pass by.

Should she speak, or wait to see if he would?

His partner, the shorter, older one, reached out, brushing her arm with his fingertips.

"Look here, Officer Campbell," he said. "Isn't this our damsel in distress from the Dreamland?"

"I believe you're right," Brice said, a slow smile spreading across his face.

She stopped, blushed, looked away. "Oh hi."

"Everything okay at home now?" the partner asked, his eyes stern.

"Just fine, thanks," Colleen said, feeling the blush creep down her neck and across her chest. "It was a misunderstanding. Really." She could feel Vera watching her, wondering why she was talking to these two cops.

She gestured toward the corner, where the ladies' room was located. "Okay. Good to see you. Gotta go now."

Colleen forced herself to walk slowly, until she'd entered the bathroom. She pushed the stall door open, locked it and sank down onto the toilet. Her pulse was racing, her nerves jangling. She was breathing so fast she thought she might hyperventilate.

"Oh God," she whispered. "Oh God." She fingered the tiny gold cross she wore on a fine chain around her neck, absentmindedly turning it over and over between her fingers as she rocked back and forth.

Brice, she'd noticed, was no longer wearing a wedding ring. Was that a good sign?

Finally she stood up, adjusted her hose, smoothed the skirt of her uniform. She stood in front of the sink, washed her hands and reapplied her lipstick.

"Everything okay?" Vera asked, when she got back to the booth.

Colleen grimaced. "Swell. Aunt Minnie just showed up."

"Yuck." Vera craned her neck to see the two officers, who were standing now, putting money on the bar.

"Who are they?" she asked, nodding her head in their direction.

"Just a couple cops," Colleen said, choking down a bite of her burger. The grease had congealed and the bun was soggy, but she busied herself chewing.

"They were flirting with you?" Vera asked enviously. "The tall one's kind of cute, don't you think?"

Colleen kept chewing, staring down at her plate as they passed. "Not interested," she said finally.

Vera's eyes followed the two as they pushed the plate-glass door open. "I forgot. You're married to the sweetest guy on earth. Why would you be checking out a couple dudes in a bar?"

"Exactly."

"Maybe you could introduce me," Vera said slyly. "I love a guy in uniform."

It was Friday, and the dentist's office closed at noon. "Want me to give you a ride back to the office?" Vera asked, as they stood by her parked Toyota.

"Thanks, anyway, but I can walk," Colleen said.

"Well, don't have too much fun at that dinner party," Vera said teasingly. "If you get bored, you can always come help me babysit my hellion nephews."

It was the kind of sunshiny late-winter day that made you understand why snowbirds flocked to Florida.

She was in no hurry to get home, so she stopped to window-shop at Maas Brothers, studying the new spring fashions: candy-colored minidresses and cork-soled platform sandals. The dress with the spaghetti straps and yellow daisies? She wondered idly if it would make her hair look too brassy. They were supposed to be on a strict budget, saving to buy their own house. Allen tracked every penny they spent, entering each purchase or bill paid into his ledger. Right now, though, she just wanted a dress that hadn't been sewn by her mom from a Simplicity pattern. Like that darling yellow daisy dress.

Something tickled her neck. She whirled around, startled. He ran the antenna of his police radio down her arm and she shivered.

"Oh hey," she said haltingly, looking to see if his partner was nearby.

"Playing hooky from work?" He playfully slapped his nightstick in his open hand.

"The office closes at noon on Fridays."

"You work for a doctor?"

"Dentist. I'm a dental hygienist."

He nodded. "What happened to your friend?"

"She went home. I decided to walk back to the office. My car's there."

"Maybe I could give you a ride." He gestured toward his cruiser, which was parked at the curb in a no-parking zone.

"Thanks anyway, but I need to walk off that cheeseburger I just ate."

"You look just fine to me." He ran the radio antenna slowly down her cheek. "You look so good, you oughtta be against the law." He moved even closer now. "And I'm the law."

She felt her face, neck and chest flush. She didn't even know his name, for Pete's sake.

"Okay, well, it's good to see you again."

"Jimmy."

"Huh?"

"Jimmy Zilowicz. Everybody calls me Jimmy Zee."

"Right. See you around, Jimmy Zee."

He was still studying her. "How are things at home?"

"Like I said before, everything's fine. Allen really felt terrible, you know, about what happened. He hasn't had a drink since. Not even a beer."

"If he stopped drinking, does that mean he beats you when he's sober too?"

She pulled away from him. "It's not what you think. Anyway, why are you following me? I haven't done anything wrong." She turned to go, but he put his hand on her shoulder.

"Something's been bothering me ever since that night at the Dreamland. You know what that place is, don't you?"

"No. I don't," she said coldly.

"It's a hot sheet joint. A no-tell motel. I bet we get twenty, thirty calls a year to that place. Suspicion of prostitution, drunk and disorderly, like that. So what's a nice young married couple doing shacked up at a place like the Dreamland?"

"None of your business."

"You're pissed at me? He's the one you should be pissed at. Hang on here a minute. Don't make me chase you down, okay?"

Colleen crossed her arms and waited. He reached in the open window of his cruiser and brought out a pad of paper and a pen.

"You're giving me a ticket? For what? This is unbelievable."

He scrawled something on the ticket, tore it off and handed it to her. "Not a ticket. My name and phone number. If he hurts you again? Call me. I guarantee, it'll be the last time the son of a bitch does that."

26

The wind awakened her Sunday morning, howling, whipping palm fronds against the bedroom window screens. Drue jumped from the bed, ran to the living room and threw open the French doors leading to the deck.

She stood on the deck, dressed only in an oversize T-shirt. She tilted her face skyward, letting the wind whip her hair and the rain lash her face, feeling like a wild sea siren.

It was the first storm since she had moved into Coquina Cottage. Dark billowing clouds loomed over the surface of the Gulf, and she could hear waves crashing on the beach. She wrapped her arms around herself for warmth, but let the wind and the rain have its way.

Before, on the east coast, on a day like this, she would have thrown her gear in the Bronco and headed out to the beach for a day of kiteboarding. She'd always had a built-in anemometer to gauge wind speed. Today, she felt sure, it was blowing twelve knots, a rare late-spring event on the west coast of Florida.

When she was thoroughly soaked, she reluctantly went inside and showered. She wrapped her wet hair in a towel and sat at the table in the kitchen, sipping coffee from Papi's mug.

Up until today, she'd deliberately avoided thinking about her old life. But today, with the wind howling, she picked up her phone, and for the first time since moving to St. Pete, logged on to Facebook and the Broward Board Babes page, scrolling through photos of billowing kites, sun-browned women in board shorts and bikini tops, group shots of her friends taken on the beach at Delray or Lighthouse Point.

She stopped scrolling at a photo of a couple, photographed in profile, in a tight embrace, she in a barely there bikini, he, bare-chested, tousle-haired. She recognized Trey instantly but had to enlarge the photo to see that the woman was Chelsee, a much younger woman who'd only joined the group six months earlier. Drue allowed herself a bitter smile. It hadn't taken Trey long at all to find a newer, younger, uninjured version of herself. Drue 2.0.

She closed the app and put her phone down, reaching for her packet of index cards. She read through her notes again, spreading the cards out on the surface of the card table.

There were so many dead ends to the Jazmin Mayes case, she understood now why Zee, the firm's investigator, had declared it a lost cause.

With her phone still in her hand, she reopened the Facebook app and typed Jazmin Mayes's name into the search bar.

Jazmin, she discovered, lived on in the world of social media. Her profile photo showed a laughing young woman, her hair cut short and straightened, grinning flirtatiously into the camera. She had a small cleft in her narrow, pointed chin and wore large gold hoop earrings and a shoulder-baring pink top.

It was the first photo she'd seen of the girl, and noting the resemblance both to Yvonne but more so, Aliyah, Drue felt an overwhelming sense of sadness.

The most recent entry on Jazmin's page was dated April 2018, posted by someone named JeezyD: "R.I.P. Jazmin. We will never forget the good times."

Drue grabbed an index card and jotted down the name. There were several more entries posted on the same date. "Gone, never forgotten." "Heaven has a new angel." "Prayers for your family." She wrote down all the names of the friends who'd posted memorials.

She paused when she came to a photo showing Jazmin and a Hispanic-looking man holding hands and standing in front of a palm tree, with a swimming pool in the background. Could this be the new boyfriend Lutrisha had mentioned?

She shook her head in frustration, but kept scrolling through more posts and photos. There was Aliyah, dressed in a spangly blue and green mermaid costume, posed under a Christmas tree. Jazmin and Aliyah at Halloween, with the girl posed in the same mermaid costume, but this time with a flowing red wig, just like Ariel in the movie.

She paused again when she came to what was obviously a selfie of Jazmin and a friend. Someone had tagged the friend as Neesa Vincent. Score!

Drue tapped Neesa's name to check her other social media posts, but Neesa had a private page. Undeterred, Drue typed out a direct message.

Hi. My name is Drue Campbell, and I am working to help your friend Jazmin's mom get more information about her death. Please contact me.

She typed in her phone number and pressed Send.

The rain slowed but didn't stop. Drue paced in front of the doors to the deck, anxious to be outside, doing something. Anything. She'd never been good at inactivity.

Antsy, Sherri would have called her. Drue opened the guest bedroom door. Her kiteboarding gear took up most of the space in the room. Between her kites, boards, control bar, lines, harness, spreader, bar boots and wet suits, the gear had easily cost her upward of $7,000. Money she'd earned waitressing in crappy beach bars or working in surf shops. She ran her hand over one of her favorite boards, the Slingshot Karenina. Just another dust catcher now, she thought.

Her phone rang and she was surprised to see that the caller was Yvonne Howington.

"Look here, Drue," Yvonne started. "I was thinking about all those questions you were asking me about Jazmin's friends, so I got out the box of cards people sent after her funeral. I'd forgotten how many there were. I guess I didn't know just how many friends that girl had. And I found a little card signed by somebody called Jorge Morales. I'm thinking maybe that was the boy my Jazmin was going out with."

"That's great, Yvonne. I did talk to somebody who knew Jazmin from the hotel and they told me her boyfriend's first name was Jorge, but they didn't know his last name. That gives me something to go on."

"Maybe so," Yvonne said. "Also, Aliyah would like to speak to you."

"Hello?" The little girl's voice was so soft it was nearly inaudible.

"Hi, Aliyah," Drue said.

"I really like my coloring book," Aliyah said. "And the glitter markers."

"You know, I thought maybe you were a fan of Ariel," Drue said.

"Uh-huh. I'm gonna be a mermaid when I grow up," she confided.

"I love that idea," Drue said. "Do you like to swim when you go to the beach?"

"I don't know how to swim," Aliyah said. "Mama said Jorge would teach me, because he had a pool at his apartment, but I haven't seen Jorge in a long time. And Grandmama is afraid of the water."

"Tell you what, Aliyah," Drue said. "Someday soon, I will take you to my friend's pool at Sunset Beach, and I will teach you how to swim, so you can be a mermaid."

"You promise?" the little girl asked.

"I promise," Drue repeated.

She heard Yvonne's voice in the background. "Don't be bothering that lady with stuff like that now."

Then Yvonne was on the phone again. "You'll call me when you find something out, right?"

"I will. And I really would like to teach Aliyah how to swim."

"We'll see," Yvonne said.

After the rain finally subsided, Drue took her beach chair down to the water's edge. Dark clouds lingered, so it was unexpectedly, blessedly cooler. The rain had chased away all but the most dogged beachgoers, so as the sun sank lower in the western sky, she felt she almost had the beach to herself.

After thirty minutes, the clouds miraculously parted, and the sun emerged as a fiery tangerine orb, tingeng the purple-edged clouds with streaks of pink and coral. Twenty yards out, a pair of dolphins dipped and rolled in the surf, so close to shore she heard the snorting sound they made when they breached the water's surface.

Finally, her quarry appeared, picking his way carefully along the water's edge, head lowered, laser-focused on his own fishing expedition. She'd been stalking the blue heron for a week, trying to snap the perfect photo.

The bird wasn't shy, in fact, he seemed oblivious to her presence, but every time she had him perfectly positioned, in silhouette against the setting sun, he always decided to take wing and fly away.

Not today, she vowed. She pulled her cell phone from her

beach bag and stood, careful not to make any sudden movements, which might startle her prey. She crept forward, keeping an eye on the waning sun, estimating she had maybe five minutes.

The heron's stilt-like legs propelled him through the shallow blue-green water. A pair of sandpipers skimmed along behind him, darting in and out of the surf, eventually tiring of the game and moving on.

In the meantime, Drue stood waiting in a half-crouch, her trigger finger poised over the phone's shutter button. "Come on, come on," she whispered.

The bird inched forward at a leisurely pace. Finally, he stopped, directly in front of the setting sun, his head raised, poised in what looked like a deliberate pose. She held her breath and clicked three quick frames, catching the elegant creature in profile against the dying light of the day.

She expected him to fly off then, but the heron turned slightly, then continued on down the beach as the light turned lilac and the sand turned gray.

Drue collapsed back into her chair, pulling up the three photos, silently marveling at the beauty of what she'd just witnessed, at the same time amused at her own ridiculous sense of achievement. God, she scoffed. She'd turned into a total tourist cliché in her own hometown. Soon she'd be clipping coupons and eating dinner at five o'clock.

For now, she settled back in her chair. She was watching for the green flash, the moment just before sunset, but she couldn't stop thinking about Jazmin Mayes and Yvonne. And Aliyah, the mermaid who didn't know how to swim.

27

Breakfast for supper had been a long-standing Sunday-night staple of her childhood years. As an adult, she now realized her mother's menu was dictated by economy—eggs and cereal and toast being much cheaper than chicken or steak. But at the time, Sherri made it seem exotic, as though pancakes, or more often, Pop-Tarts, were a delicacy to be reserved for special occasions. Like Sunday nights. Since she'd moved into Coquina Cottage it was a tradition Drue had unconsciously revived.

She stood at the stove, absentmindedly shaking salt and pepper into a bowl of scrambled eggs before pouring the mixture into her grandmother's cast-iron skillet. The bacon was cooling on folded-up paper towels on the countertop.

Drue stared out the kitchen window, thinking about her last week's dinner with Brice. Had she imagined his startled reaction when she'd brought up the name of Colleen Boardman

Hicks? There had to be a reason her mother had kept that file of clippings about the "missing local beauty." Was there something sinister there? She thought back to what her mother had said about Brice over the years, which really was surprisingly little, now that she thought about it.

Once, shortly after she'd moved back to Lauderdale after that disastrous year with Brice and Joan, she'd worked up the nerve to ask Sherri what had prompted their divorce.

"He's a chaser," Sherri had said in her matter-of-fact way. "Your dad is always looking out for that next best thing—a job, a house, a woman. He'll never be satisfied with what he's got. And that includes a wife. Do yourself a favor, Drue. Don't ever marry a chaser."

Had Colleen Boardman Hicks been one of the women Brice had pursued?

It had started to rain again and she could hear the wind whipping the branches of the Australian pines that separated the cottage from the beach. At least, she thought, the rain would cool things down inside the house.

She turned off the burner and slid the contents of the skillet onto her plate, adding the bacon and two slices of toast.

She sat at the card table and ate, finally pushing her plate aside and picking up the file folder, where she'd shoved her stack of index cards. One of the cards had a single word scrawled across it—BOYFRIEND—followed by a series of question marks.

At least she had a name to search for now, thanks to Yvonne.

Her cell phone rang and she reached for it.

"Dad?"

"Hey kid. How was your weekend?"

Drue was tongue-tied for a moment. Brice wasn't in the habit of making wellness checks on his daughter.

"Okay. Ben and Jonah came over and got my car running again, so that was a win."

"I'm glad," he said. "So, uh, our dinner didn't end so hot the other night, did it?"

"Guess not," Drue said.

He cleared his throat. "I talked to Wendy, and asked her to ease up on you a little bit."

"I'll bet that went over like a lead balloon," Drue said.

"You know, you could try a little harder to get along with her," Brice said. "Like it or not, we're family. And we work together. Okay?"

"Terrific!" Drue said. "We'll all hold hands and sing 'Kumbaya' at the next staff meeting."

Dead silence on the other end of the phone. "Christ!" Brice said. Then he hung up.

28

July 1976

Her orange Camaro was easy to spot in the Boyd Hill Nature Trail parking lot, even though she'd parked at the far end of the lot, under the thick shade of a clump of moss-draped scrub oaks. It was a hot, sticky Monday morning. Not even eight o'clock. He pulled the cruiser nose out next to her car, the one she said her asshole husband had given her for her twenty-first birthday. For her twenty-sixth birthday, which had been six weeks ago, he'd given her a dislocated shoulder.

She lowered her window and looked over. "Thanks for coming. I'm sorry, but I didn't know what else to do."

Brice leaned out to get a better look. She'd gotten good at covering the bruises with makeup, but despite the thick pancake and concealer, he could see her left eye was swollen and bruised. And her lip was cut.

"Damn it, Colleen. Why do you put up with this shit? Say the word, and I'll take care of him. Jimmy and me, we'll hurt him bad. And he'll never see us coming."

She shook her head. She'd fixed her hair so that it fell over the bruised eye. Maybe if you didn't know to look, you might not even notice. "That's sweet. But stupid. You'll just get yourselves into trouble. That's the last thing I want.

"Let's talk about something else," she said.

He got out of the cruiser, walked around and got in the front seat of the Camaro.

She put her arms around his neck and began kissing him. The next thing he knew, she reached down and unzipped his fly.

"Here?" he said, looking around anxiously. "You'll get us both arrested for public indecency."

"I don't care," she said, fondling him.

He pushed her hand away. "Cut it out. We've got guys patrolling this park all the time, looking out for pervs. I could lose my job."

"In the meantime, I'm losing my mind, I'm so hot for you," she whispered, taking his hand and putting it beneath her skirt. "Come on. Just a quickie. Nobody has to see."

Before he could stop her, she'd pulled her top off over her head. Another minute later, she was straddling him.

When they were done, they were both drenched with perspiration and out of breath.

"Jesus," Brice said, tucking his damp uniform shirt into his pants. "How am I gonna explain this to my sergeant?"

Colleen giggled as she searched the floor of the Camaro for the panties that had gone missing in the heat of the moment.

"Tell him you got hot and sweaty chasing pervs at the nature trail," she said, waving the scrap of pink lace under his nose.

"Put those on," he said, batting the panties away. "You act like this is some kind of game."

"It is a game, as far as I'm concerned," she said with a shrug. "Come on. Are you telling me you don't get off on this stuff?"

"It won't be fun if I get fired for conduct unbecoming an officer, and it sure as hell won't be fun for you if your husband figures out what's going on between us."

She got out of the Camaro and using the car door as a shield, stepped into the panties, smoothing her skirt and top before getting back in the driver's seat. Then she pulled down the sun visor and combed her hair back into place and reapplied her lipstick.

"I'm serious, Brice," she said, turning in the seat so that she was facing him again. "If it weren't for times like this, being with you, I think I might go crazy."

"Then leave him," Brice said. "Get a divorce. You're young. You've got a good job. Why do you need that asshole?"

"A good job? My take-home pay is exactly $92.74 a week. You know any divorce lawyers who work for that kind of money? And what if I did leave him? Where would I go? Move in with my mom? Listen to her bitching about what a raw deal she got after my dad left? Thanks but no thanks."

Colleen looked off in the distance, at the playground, with the seesaw and the swings and sliding board. "Anyway, you don't know Allen. He'd never just let me leave. He'd find me. And he'd hurt me even worse."

With his thumb he gently touched the corner of her swollen lip. "I could help you. Let me help you. I want to."

A single tear slid down her cheek. "What? You're going to leave Sherri? For me?"

His face flushed. "Come on. That's not fair. You know how I feel about you."

She leaned in and kissed him. "You're right. I do know how you feel. And I know I can't ask you to leave your wife. I met her, you know."

He drew back, startled. "Sherri? You talked to her? When was this?"

"Don't look at me like that. It was perfectly innocent. I went into that real estate office she works at. Out at the beach. I asked about renting a house this summer. I'm not surprised you fell for her, Brice. She's really cute."

"Jesus!" he exclaimed. "You met Sherri? Why would you do something like that? What if she figured it out?" He slapped the dashboard. "I can't believe you'd do that."

"Why not?" She shrugged. "I didn't tell her my real name. I just, I don't know. I guess I wanted to check out the competition. Is that so wrong? I mean, you met Allen."

"I should have arrested Allen," he said bitterly. "I should have locked his ass up, and then I should have gone home to my wife that night."

"Even if you had arrested him, his dad's lawyer would have gotten him out in a skinny minute."

"So what are you going to do?" Brice asked.

She smoothed the front of his shirt with the flat of her hand. "I . . . I've been working on a plan. It'll sound nuts to you, I know, but it's the only way."

"Tell me," he said.

"I'm going to disappear," she said.

"Huh?"

"I mean it. One day soon, I'll go to work, and I just won't come home."

"Where'll you go?" he asked. "What'll you do for money?"

"I'm thinking maybe Atlanta. A big city, where I can get a job. As for the money? That's the part you might not want to know about. You being a cop and all."

"What? You're gonna rob a bank?"

"No," she said thoughtfully. "I'm going to take what's mine. All of it. Allen and I have been saving up for a house for five years. Since even before we got married. He's such a cheapskate, he keeps me on an allowance, makes me take my lunch to work, sew my own clothes. He's got this little black notebook, and I have to account for every dime I spend. From my own paycheck!"

He shook his head. "If you've got that much money in the bank, why don't you just use it to get a divorce?"

"You don't get it," Colleen said, her voice shrill. "Allen's dad is friends with every lawyer and every judge in this town. A judge is going to say that money is his, not mine."

"How much money is there?" Brice asked.

"A little over seven thousand dollars." Her eyes gleamed with excitement. "I'll have enough to make a new start in a new town."

"What happens if Allen comes after you? Calls the cops and reports that you and his money went missing? Won't he try and track you down?"

"That's where you come in. I need your help."

He exhaled slowly. "What? What do you need?"

She kissed him impulsively. "See? That's why I adore you."

"Nothing illegal, right? I'm a cop, remember?"

"It's nothing, really. Just a fake ID."

He ran his hands through his close-cropped hair. "Just?"

"It can't be that big a deal," she said hurriedly. "All the girls had fake IDs in high school. You know, so we could get into the bars."

"I had a fake ID when I got back from Vietnam, but I don't even think I'd know where to get one now."

She glanced at her watch. "I've got to get to work. When can we meet again?"

"Maybe next week? I'll call you at your office."

"Bring the ID then, okay? I don't know how much more I can take."

After she was gone, he sat in his cruiser for a long time, wondering how he'd gotten himself in so deep, so fast. As he sat, a blue heron emerged from the swampy woods, picking its way delicately through the underbrush. The radio in his unit crackled again, and he started the cruiser and drove away.

29

A huge cardboard file box greeted Drue when she arrived at work on Monday. A yellow sticky note from her father bore the words she dreaded most. "SEE ME." Was she being sent to the woodshed as a result of the previous evening's snarky phone call?

Drue trudged toward Wendy's office, where she found a merry gathering consisting of Brice, Wendy and Jimmy Zee.

She took a half-step backward to beat a retreat, but it was too late.

"Come on in," Brice said, waving her forward.

"You left a file box on my desk?" she said.

"Actually, I left it," Wendy said. She was seated in the wing chair across from Brice, dressed in head-to-toe pastel-print Lilly Pulitzer. "We've got a big med mal case heating up and I need you to go through the client's receipts for the past six years and get everything reconciled. The girls in records are super busy, so while you're off the Justice Line . . ."

"I'm off the Justice Line? Since when?"

"Since I determined generating leads isn't really your strong suit," Wendy said, looking to her husband for backup.

Brice fidgeted with a chain of paper clips on his desktop but said nothing.

"This is bullshit," Drue said angrily. "Why don't you just stick me in the corner of the office and give me a big dunce cap to wear?"

"See what I'm dealing with?" Wendy said, one eyebrow raised.

Zee coughed discreetly. "Ya know, if the kid's got some spare time, I could really use her for this slip-and-fall I'm working on."

Drue shot him a grateful look. Today, like every time she'd glimpsed him, he was dressed all in black—baggy black jeans, black polo shirt with the CCK logo and black motorcycle boots, a pair of mirrored Ray-Bans dangling from a cord around his neck.

Wendy rolled her eyes. "The 7-Eleven case? I thought that was dead. The store has our client and her boyfriend, on video, trying to shoplift a fifth of malt liquor. When the clerk chased him, he dropped the bottle, it smashed and she slipped on that. So her injury arose out of her own criminal act, right?" She glanced at her husband for confirmation.

"Wait a minute," Drue interjected. "That was my case. And it wasn't malt liquor, it was Smirnoff Ice. I talked to that woman two weeks ago, but when I asked her if either she or the boyfriend were arrested, she hung up on me!"

"I guess she called back and spoke to somebody else," Wendy said. She looked over at Brice. "Whose lead was that?"

"Hmm. I think it was Jonah's," Brice said.

"Not that it matters," Wendy said. "I really think—"

"Actually," Brice said, "I kicked it over to Zee. He got a copy of the video from the store which shows that it's the boyfriend doing the theft. The guy's got a long record, but our prospective client is clean. And it now appears she's suffered a traumatic brain injury, not just the broken tailbone she was initially treated for."

"Looking at the police reports, I found a potential witness," Zee said. "It's the old lady who called nine-one-one after our client fell."

He looked over at Drue. "What do you say to a ride-along?"

"This is a waste of time," Wendy objected. "We don't need to invest any more firm resources—"

"Sweetie?" Brice said. "Let's let Zee take one more run at it." He looked over at Drue. "Keep your eyes and ears open and you might learn something today."

A gleaming black Ford F-250 pickup was parked at the curb in front of the law office. Drue hiked herself up and into the passenger seat, and before she'd buckled up, Zee was speeding down the street.

He steered the truck with one hand and reached for a package of Nicorette gum from the seat beside him, tossing the wrapper onto the floor of the truck. He chewed like he drove, rapid-fire.

"Where are we headed?" Drue asked.

"We're gonna go talk to Mrs. Delores Estes."

"She's the witness?"

"Yup," Jimmy Zee said.

He glanced over at her, then returned his eyes to the road. "Wendy's giving you a pretty raw deal, huh?"

"Dad won't let her fire me, so she's trying to force me into quitting," Drue said. "I'm damned if I'll give her the satisfaction."

He switched the gum to the other side of his mouth. "You ever done work like this before?"

"Never."

"That's good," he said. "I won't have to break you of any bad habits."

"Can I ask you something?"

"Depends on what it is," he said.

"What makes you think this case is good? I mean, I thought Dad hated slip-and-falls."

"He does, but this one has a few things going for it. One is the defendant. The owner of that 7-Eleven, who is a franchisee, has excellent liability insurance, which is mandated by corporate. The second is the victim, our client, turns out to have a substantial, provable injury. If we can show that her boyfriend was the thief, and our client was simply an unwitting bystander, that's a win."

She nodded. "That makes sense."

~

Less than a mile away, Zee turned off Fourth Street into a shabby-looking apartment complex called Barcelona Bay. The buildings were two-story affairs, with eight units apiece, tan stucco with pseudo-Spanish-looking rusted wrought-iron balconies.

He cruised slowly, making two quick right turns, then pulled in front of Building 20, Unit 2012.

Zee cut the truck's engine and reached past Drue, popping the catch on the glove box. His hand closed over a small black pistol. He leaned forward in the seat, lifting the back of his polo shirt and tucking the pistol into a holster in the small of his back.

Drue didn't bother to hide her shock.

"A gun? Is that really necessary? To talk to a little old lady?"

He chewed his gum and reached back into the glove box, bringing out a small can of Mace. "Little old ladies who live in Section Eight housing have guns. And they have kids and grandkids and neighbors with guns. I don't ever want to be outgunned. Ya know?"

He handed her the Mace. "That's a present from your uncle Zee. Keep it where you can use it in a hurry if you need to. I'm gonna let you do this interview."

"You are? How come?"

He shook his head. "Again with the questions. Sometimes, little girl, you gotta just trust me and go with the flow, okay? You're gonna talk to her because in my experience, sometimes elderly black ladies don't especially want to open up to white dudes, especially former cops, like me."

She let the "little girl" reference pass. "How did you find Mrs. Estes?" Drue asked.

"Her name was on the police report. She's the one who called the ambulance after our client fell."

"Anything special I should ask her?"

"Ask her what she saw in the 7-Eleven that day. Get everything, down to the tiniest detail. Ask her if it looked like our client was just a law-abiding citizen, minding her own business, when she slipped and hit her head. Ask her why she called nine-one-one. Like that."

"Anything else?" Drue asked.

"Be sympathetic. Win her over to our side. And don't screw it up," Zee said. He opened the truck door and as he got out, carefully pulled his shirt over the holstered gun.

The front door to apartment 8 was open. A television was on inside, and the smell of frying fish wafted into the humid mid-morning heat.

Zee rang the doorbell. Nothing. He pounded on the aluminum frame of the screen door. "Mrs. Estes? Mrs. Estes? Are you home?"

A woman's voice called out from inside. "Who's that?"

Zee nodded at Drue.

"Hi, Mrs. Estes," she called. "Could we please talk to you for a few minutes?"

A heavyset woman walked slowly toward the door. She wore a short-sleeved flowered cotton housecoat, similar to the ones Drue's grandmother once favored, with thick rolls of flesh extending to her hands. Her head was covered with a pink vinyl shower cap, and she wore backless gold bedroom slippers.

Delores Estes peered at the two strangers from behind thick-lensed glasses. She made no move to unfasten the screen door. "What do y'all want?"

Drue cleared her throat. "Uh, well, my name is Drue Campbell, and this is my associate, Mr. Zee. We're here about that accident we believe you witnessed at the 7-Eleven. When that woman slipped and hit her head?"

Mrs. Estes took a step backward. "How'd y'all get my name? Who told you where I stay?"

Drue glanced at Zee, who nodded approvingly.

"The woman who fell that day hired our law firm, Campbell, Coxe and Kramner, to represent her," Drue said. "She was hurt pretty badly, you know. But thank goodness you called nine-one-one and spoke to the police. We got your name from the police report."

"Huh." Delores Estes shifted her weight from one foot to the other. Finally, she unlatched the door. "Come on in, then. I can't be standing here talking to y'all while my fish gets burnt up."

She waddled off in the direction of the kitchen, leaving Drue and Zee standing in the living room of the tiny, stifling apartment.

A moment later she was back, wiping her hands on a dishcloth. "Y'all can sit down over there," she said, gesturing toward a green vinyl-covered sofa.

"I been thinking about that poor lady since all that happened that day," she said. "I asked after her at the store, but

Anna, that's the lady who works there, she told me she don't know nothing about it."

"She has a serious head injury," Drue said. "And a broken tailbone, among other things."

Mrs. Estes dabbed at her perspiring face with the dish towel. "Yes, Jesus. That was really something. She hit her head so hard, I was afraid maybe she was killed or something. And my poor little grand-girl, it scared her so bad, we ain't been back there since."

"Was that the first time you've been to that particular 7-Eleven?" Drue asked.

"Oh no. We used to go there all the time, because that's the closest store to me. Bitty, that's my grand-girl, she stays here with me some days when her daddy is working, she's always begging me to take her up there and buy her a treat. That day, I got my Social check, so we went on up there like we usually do."

"Can you tell me what happened that day? In the store?"

"I got me a Co-Cola from the drink cooler, and Bitty got her a Nutty Buddy. That's a chocolate-covered cone, and it's got nuts all over it. That's her favorite. Anyway, while I was getting my Co-Cola, Bitty unwrapped her Nutty Buddy. We were walking up to the counter so I could pay, and Bitty was licking her ice cream, and the ice cream part, it just slid off the cone and fell on the floor. Then Anna started fussing at her a little bit, because I hadn't paid yet, and that got me mad. That woman knew I was gonna pay! I had the money right there in my hand!"

"What happened next?" Drue asked.

"Bitty got her feelings hurt, and she started crying about

that ice cream, and I told her I'd pay for another one. Right around that time, that white lady and that man came in the store. I wasn't paying much attention to them, because Bitty was really having a fit. So I went over to the ice cream box to get another Nutty Buddy."

"About the clerk, Anna, did she do anything to clean up the ice cream?"

"Uh-uh," Mrs. Estes said. "She stayed right where she was at, behind the counter. I was gonna ask her for a paper towel to wipe up the mess, but before I could, that woman come up front to pay. I believe she had a Slurpee in her hand. And right then, that man she come in with, he started walking real fast up to the front too, acting like he was gonna leave the store. Anna hollered at him, told him he needed to pay, and that's when he kind of took off. He had a bottle stuck down in his pants, and it fell out and smashed on the floor."

"And then what?" Drue prompted.

"All hell broke loose. Bitty was crying, because she was scared and mad at the same time, and Anna, she went chasing after the man, and then that poor lady, her feet come right out from under her and she slammed backwards, hit her head hard on that concrete floor. That Slurpee went flying too. I was afraid to touch her, 'cause she looked bad hurt. That's when I dialed nine-one-one. We stayed right there with that lady until the ambulance and the police came, and then I paid for two ice cream cones for Bitty and we left and we ain't been back."

Drue thought for a moment. "Did the lady fall before or after the man dropped the bottle?"

Mrs. Estes closed her eyes and pondered the question. Finally, she nodded. "Right before."

Drue glanced over at Zee, noticing that he'd quietly placed his phone on his lap and had been recording the interview. He nodded silently.

"Did anybody else come into the store while all that was happening?" Drue asked, hoping she'd tied up all the loose ends in Delores Estes's witness account.

Mrs. Estes dabbed at her neck. "No. It was just me and Bitty until that white lady and the man come in. And Anna, but she works there."

"You didn't see the white lady try to take anything, did you?"

"What? No, I didn't see nuthin' like that. She had a wallet in her hand, I think, getting ready to pay for her drink."

"Fine," Drue said, feeling grateful and encouraged. "That's good to know."

Zee cleared his throat. "If it's all right with you, we're gonna type up our notes about our conversation today. Like an affidavit. Would you be willing to sign that?"

"I reckon so. If it's the truth like I told you."

Drue smiled broadly. "Okay, I think that's all the questions I have for now, Mrs. Estes. I want to thank you so much for talking to us today."

"That's okay. I try to be a good Christian, you know?"

Mrs. Estes pushed the screen door open to let her visitors pass. "Which law firm did y'all say you work for again?"

Zee passed her a business card. The older woman pushed

her glasses down on her nose and studied it. "Oh yes. Campbell, Coxe and Kramner. You told me that earlier. I seen y'all's billboards and television commercials. Let me ask you something. That man on the billboards, Brice Campbell, is he really a lawyer? Or just some actor?"

"He's really a lawyer," Drue assured her.

"Well, he's got some real pretty hair on him," Delores Estes said. "You think that's a wig?"

"It's absolutely a wig," Zee said, his face solemn.

"High five," Zee said, when they were both inside the pickup truck. He held his hand up, palm out, and Drue slapped it.

"The client didn't even slip on the Smirnoff," Drue exclaimed. "It was the ice cream. And the clerk should have cleaned it up. That's negligence, right?"

"Should be," Zee said. "Good work back there. I'd be very surprised if the insurance company doesn't make us a very nice offer once they hear what Delores Estes has to say."

"Really?" Drue's face flushed with excitement. "Wow. I had no idea things could happen so fast. I mean, the Gulf Vista case, it took nearly two years to settle, and in that one the victim was murdered."

Zee frowned. "You're comparing apples to oranges. We had no witnesses to the hotel murder. No evidence that could show the victim wasn't on the clock. This 7-Eleven thing is totally different. We should hear something back today about the client from our neurologist." He picked up his phone and examined it.

"I'm kind of surprised Brice hasn't already texted or called to fill me in."

"You two really work closely together, don't you?"

"We make a damn good team," Zee said. He pulled the pickup into traffic and headed south, toward downtown. "Been like that since before you were born. We went through the police academy together, you know."

"I didn't know that," Drue admitted.

"I was best man when he married your mom. He stood up for me when I got married."

"Was that to . . . ?"

"Frannie," Zee said. His face softened. "She was a piece of work, my Frannie. I used to call her Big Red. She had a temper to go along with the hair."

Drue had foggy memories of a diminutive redhead sitting at the kitchen table with Zee and her parents, doling spaghetti out of an enormous pot. She remembered the table littered with beer bottles and overflowing ashtrays, and the sounds of raucous laughter after she'd been put to bed and the adults started one of their marathon card games.

"I remember Frannie," she said now. "She used to bring me these little Italian cookies with powdered sugar."

"Wedding cookies. They were her specialty."

Drue glanced over at Zee. "I take it you guys split up?"

"Years and years ago. I was too damn dumb to know a good thing when I had it." He ran a hand through his thinning gray hair. "Geez, I haven't thought about Frannie in years. Funny, I just realized, your dad and me, we've been together longer than any of our marriages."

"What's the secret?"

"To the partnership? We don't sleep with each other." He laughed at his own joke. "Your old man knows how to make things happen. Always has. That's the secret to his success."

"And what's the secret to yours?" she asked.

He shrugged. "Always sweat the small shit. The nitpicky details. Ask the extra questions. Make that last phone call. And that's why Brice and me work so well together. He's the big-picture guy. Always had a vision of what success looks like. Like going to law school. He was only a beat cop for maybe five or six years, and he already knew he wanted something bigger. Then he was in a general practice with old man Coxe for a few years, until he figured out personal injury was where the big paydays were. He went looking for those cases, and eventually, when he started getting big settlements, I went ahead and retired from the force and came to work for him as an investigator. That's been, what? Twelve years? I lose track."

Drue studied her father's friend's profile. He was jowly, with ruddy skin that already showed five-o'clock shadow. "Dad said he never made detective when he was on the force. But you did, right?"

"Sure. I retired as a captain."

"Did you ever work on the case involving that missing woman? Colleen Boardman Hicks?"

Zee's jaws worked furiously at the gum but he kept his eyes on the road. "What makes you ask about her? You weren't even born when all that happened."

"When I was moving into the cottage on Sunset Beach, I found some old newspaper clippings about the case, in a box of my mom's things," Drue said, carefully omitting the fact that she'd actually found what looked like the official Colleen Hicks police file.

"It was a big mystery, back in the day," Zee said. "On the news every night."

"Dad told me he went to high school with Colleen Boardman Hicks," Drue said. "Did you know that?"

"Yeah, now that you say it, I do remember they went to school together. But I don't think they were really friends."

"Since you were a detective back then, did you work on the investigation?"

"It wasn't my case, but I did some legwork. That's been more than forty years ago."

"Did you have a theory back then about what happened to Colleen Hicks?"

The truck stopped at a traffic light. Zee turned in his seat and stared.

"Why do you care?"

"I'm not sure," she admitted. "I mean, it's fascinating, isn't it? Colleen Hicks had dinner with a friend one evening, what— less than a mile from where we work? And then she vanished."

The light turned green and they were moving again. "Who knows? At the time, the theory was that she was mixed up in something shady."

"What kind of shady stuff could she have been involved with? She was a dental hygienist, right?"

"Oh, little girl, you don't want to know what all that gal was into. There were drugs missing from that dentist's office she worked at. Maybe she was selling them, but we never could prove it. And we talked to people who said she and the husband were into some kinky stuff. You know what I mean?"

Drue felt herself blushing. "You mean they were swingers?"

"That was the rumor going around. Back then, that kind of stuff wasn't talked about out in the open, like it is now. You couldn't turn on the television and watch ten different porn channels in the privacy of your own home like you can now."

"Do you think there's a chance she's still alive?" Drue asked.

"Maybe. Maybe she's living the good life in Mexico. Don't really care, to tell you the truth."

Zee pulled the pickup alongside the curb outside the green stucco offices of Campbell, Coxe and Kramner. "Okay, kid. End of the line. Good luck with Wendy."

30

July 1976

Sherri Campbell knew Brice was cheating on her again. She always knew, because for a cop, he really wasn't that good at hiding the signs.

Which were the late-night phone calls, supposedly from his partner, Jimmy Zee; the hang-ups; and of course, duh! the nights he came home way after shift, smelling of scotch and the other woman's perfume.

She'd met this particular woman once, when she'd had the nerve to walk into the real estate office where Sherri worked, ostensibly to ask about renting a beach cottage for her family's vacation.

"Two-bedroom, Gulf-front, with a kitchen, because I like to cook, and a pool for the kids," the woman said.

"No pets, right?" Sherri asked, studying the woman, who was Brice's type for sure: petite, blond, big boobs, good legs.

The blond was out of a bottle, but it was a good dye job, probably professional. She wore a lot of makeup, but somehow it didn't make her look cheap. Nice clothes too. And a big, flashy engagement ring.

"No, no pets," the woman assured her, in a baby-doll kind of voice.

Sherri took her time looking through the rental listings, glancing up occasionally to study the woman, who coolly returned her stare.

"How about this one?" Sherri handed over a color brochure for a cottage on Treasure Island. "It's just a couple blocks from John's Pass. Close to restaurants. And it has a patio and grill area."

The woman pretended to study the listing. Sherri looked past her, at the orange Camaro parked outside at the curb.

She'd seen it—how many times? Three or four times, for sure, as it cruised slowly past the house on Brice's bowling night, or afternoons he was out fishing with Jimmy Zee.

And she'd seen the Camaro up close too, the first time she'd followed Brice. She borrowed her cousin's car that night, waited across the street from police headquarters, then followed him to that motel on Thirty-fourth Street North. She'd parked at a coffee shop beside the place and watched while Brice got out of his cruiser, whistling, walked into the office and came back out minutes later with a key, which he used on a unit at the end of the U-shaped complex. Ten minutes later, the orange Camaro pulled in and parked a discreet four cars away. That night, the woman wore spike heels and a short, tight black dress that looked like it had been spray-painted onto her. It was the kind of dress a woman wore when she was fucking another woman's husband in a shitty motel room that rented by the hour. Not that Sherri had any experience in that kind of thing.

"Hmm," the other woman was saying now. "If you don't mind, I'll take this and see what my husband thinks. It looks cute, though."

"It's very cute," Sherri said. "And it's one of our most popular properties. If you think you might be interested, you should really put down a deposit today, Mrs. . . . ?"

"McCarthy," the woman said, after a moment's hesitation. "Karen McCarthy. I'm not ready to commit today, but I'll certainly keep that in mind, and be back in touch if my husband approves."

"Okay," Sherri said. She held out her hand. "By the way, Karen, I'm Sherri Campbell. But you already know that, since you're the woman my husband has been running around with for the past few months."

The blonde's face paled all the way to her roots, but she recovered quickly. Obviously she was way better at lying than Brice was. "You must have me mixed up with somebody else. I don't know what you're talking about."

Sherri pointed out the real estate office's big plate-glass window. "Sure you do. I've seen that Camaro of yours several times driving past our house late at night. What's wrong? Don't you believe him when he tells you he's going bowling with the guys?"

That got her flustered, Sherri noted.

"You're crazy," the woman said, turning to leave, hurrying

toward the door, not bothering to take the brochure she hadn't really wanted anyway.

"Not as crazy as you." Sherri got up from her desk, for some reason grabbing a letter opener from the desktop. It had been a gift from the title insurance company, at their annual Christmas party.

She followed the woman outside to the parking lot, and as she opened the Camaro's door, Sherri grabbed her arm and pressed the letter opener to a spot right between her big, flashy boobs.

"Don't touch me," the woman screeched. "Let me go."

"Brice doesn't care about you. You're just another easy lay as far as he's concerned," Sherri said matter-of-factly. "So if I were you, Karen, or whatever your real name is, I'd drop him. If I were you, I'd stick to my own husband. You know, the one who gave you that nice big diamond you're wearing."

Sherri held up her left hand, flashing the tiny diamond chip on her own engagement ring. "This is the best a cop can afford."

The other woman wrenched her arm away and hopped in the driver's seat, making a show of locking the door. As she pulled out of the parking space, Sherri ran the letter opener along the side of the Camaro, leaving a long, thin scrape in its shiny orange paint job.

31

~~~~~

Ben and Drue were barely settled in their booth at a newly opened Mexican café on newly trendy Central Avenue. It was Tuesday, and the lunch was her payback to Ben for fixing OJ's starter.

"I heard you did a ride-along with Zee yesterday," Ben said. "How was it?"

"Interesting," Drue said. "Once I got past him addressing me as 'little girl' and referring to himself as 'Uncle Zee.'"

The waitress brought a bowl of chips and guacamole and their drinks, a craft beer for Ben and an iced tea for Drue.

"Yeah, Zee's pretty old-school. But I bet it was cool as hell anyway." He gulped his beer and scooped into the guac. "Where did you go?"

"You know that 7-Eleven slip-and-fall you guys told me was bogus? Well, somehow, the prospective client called back, and

Jonah ended up referring the case to Brice, who kicked it over to Zee, who found a witness! It was this old lady who lives over in a pretty sketchy part of town. Long story short, Zee says he thinks Dad can get a fat settlement from the insurance company."

"What was it like, riding shotgun with Jimmy Zee?"

"It was actually kind of amazing. I was scared, but once I got talking to the witness, I just started asking questions and things fell together." She dug in her purse and held up the can of Mace. "Zee gave me this. Did you know he carries a gun in a holster under his shirt?"

"So? His work takes him to some pretty sketchy places. Our clients don't exactly all live in waterfront mansions like your dad's."

"I get that, but it kind of unnerved me."

Drue gingerly returned the Mace to an inside pocket of her purse.

"There's something I wanted to talk to you about."

Ben pointed his finger like a gun. "Shoot."

"Funny. Only not."

She leaned across the table, her voice lowered. "There's something that's been bothering me. About the Jazmin Mayes thing."

He rolled his eyes. "Not that again."

"No. Listen. There's something there, I know there is. And I'm going to get to the bottom of it."

"Oh shit, Drue. Do you realize how crazy all this sounds? I get that you feel sorry for the girl who was murdered, and her family. I get that you want some kind of justice, but you can't just go around sticking your nose in an active police investigation. You're not a cop. You're not even an investigator. You're like me. We're cube rats. We answer the phone and try to get people to hire us to sue somebody. That's it! We don't go poking around the scene of a friggin' murder!"

Drue's shoulders sagged as she felt her mood deflate. "What if I could prove she wasn't working?"

"Okay, don't shoot the messenger, but didn't the hotel video show Jazmin leaving a room like at one-thirty in the morning? And then entering the laundry room—where her body was found? Maybe she didn't routinely work that shift. But that night, she did. She was working, Drue! There's just no way to get around it."

His freckled face showed a mixture of anger and indignation, and his chest rose and fell beneath the faded fabric of his Eagles "Hell Freezes Over" concert tour tee.

"No," she said flatly. "Somebody's lying." She leaned across the table, both hands clenched around her glass. "That's what I really wanted to talk to you about. I'm starting to think that Yvonne Howington was right. Maybe there was a cover-up. Maybe somebody at the law firm is in cahoots with Gulf Vista and its insurance carrier."

Ben removed his glasses, wiped them on the hem of his shirt and replaced them. "Jesus! Are you seriously accusing Brice Campbell, your own father, of taking a payoff?"

"Maybe . . . ?" Her voice trailed off. "I don't know what to think. That's why I wanted to talk this out with you. You've worked for the firm for how long?"

"Two and a half years. But Brice is your father, for God's sake. How can you believe he's capable of something like that?"

"I don't know what he is or isn't capable of," she said calmly.

"In the past, certainly, he's had the morals of an alley cat. He cheated on my mother, he cheated on Joan. It's not that hard to believe he is also ethically challenged. And remember, he hasn't been in my life, not like a real father, since I was fifteen years old. So I don't exactly have him up on your typical father-daughter pedestal."

"Wow." Ben pushed his chair away from the table. "Talk about unresolved issues."

"Yeah. But come on, I'm guessing you know him better than me. Do you think it's even remotely possible that Brice, or somebody else, like maybe even Zee, could have taken a payoff here?"

"No," he said flatly. "Why would they do that? That's some crazy conspiracy theory shit. Your dad and Zee don't need to take payoffs. They're making huge bank as it is. Brice is probably going to ask for a six-figure settlement for this new slip-and-fall case. That's one case out of how many active cases the firm has right now? Three dozen, four dozen? The firm is doing great. He doesn't need to cheat to win."

"Somebody is covering up something at that hotel," Drue said. "Jazmin Mayes was beaten and strangled and her body was dumped in a pile of dirty sheets. I can't get that image out of my mind. I saw the laundry room where she was killed, Ben. I've been to the grandmother's house and I've met Jazmin's daughter. What happened to Jazmin isn't right. And if I can do something to figure out who's responsible for her death, I will."

The waitress paused at their table. "Everything okay here? Anybody need another drink? Or dessert? We've got tres leches cake today."

"I'm good," Ben said.

"Just the check, please," Drue told her. She looked over at her friend. "I guess the rats need to get back to their cubes, right?"

Ben hesitated, then touched her hand. "Are you mad at me?"

"No. Disappointed, that's all. I had to talk to somebody about this thing. And I was hoping that you'd see what I see. And care about it as much as I do."

She opened her purse, took out two twenties and laid them on top of the check the waitress placed discreetly at the edge of the table. "Anyway, thanks for listening."

"Any time," Ben said earnestly.

They stood to go, and saw that the restaurant, which had been half empty when they arrived, was now crowded with the downtown lunch crowd, a line of customers impatiently jostling behind the hostess stand, blocking their way to the door.

Ben lightly placed his hand at the small of Drue's back, guiding her through the crowd. When they emerged from the dim coolness of the restaurant back onto the sidewalk, they both blinked in the bright sunlight and blast-furnace afternoon heat.

"Hey Drue?" he said, as they set out on the five-block walk back to the office.

"Yeah?" She turned to look at him.

"I'm really glad you trusted me enough to talk about this stuff today. But I have to warn you, if you're gonna keep working at CCK, you're going to have to understand that bad shit happens to good people. Not just sometimes, but all the time. You have to stop taking this stuff so personally. Okay?"

"Okay." She smiled. "I'll try."

32

As soon as Drue sat back down at her desk, but before she could don what she thought of as her "office sweater," her phone chirped with an incoming text. It was from Brice.

Drue: See me in Wendy's office. ASAP! Urgent!

"What now?" she mumbled.

"Huh?" Ben rolled his chair backward and poked his head around the corner of the cubicle.

"I've been summoned. To meet with Dad."

"He probably wants to congratulate you on locking down the 7-Eleven thing," Ben said. "Just go."

She trudged toward the office, her curiosity growing with every step.

"Come in," Wendy called, after Drue tapped lightly on her closed office door.

She was surprised to see Wendy and Brice sitting close

together on the leather sofa in Wendy's office, Brice's arm flung casually over his wife's shoulder. His face was flushed; Wendy's was, as usual, inscrutable, at least to Drue.

"Sit down," Brice said, gesturing to the chair near the desk.

Drue did as she was told, crossing her ankles and waiting for the inevitable.

"Go ahead and tell her," Brice said, nudging Wendy, who was dressed in what was, for her, a casual outfit: black linen slacks and an olive green sleeveless silk blouse.

"No, I think this should come from you," Wendy said, a frown creasing her forehead.

"For God's sake, one of you just tell me," Drue said. "If you're going to fire me, let's go ahead and get it over with."

"Fire you?" Brice laughed. "Why would I do that?"

She shrugged. "I don't know. Maybe because double secret probation isn't working out?"

"It's working out fine," Brice assured her. "Don't be so paranoid. Zee tells me you were great interviewing that witness yesterday. But that's not really why we wanted to see you."

He reached behind the sofa cushion and brought out a glittering blue gift bag tied with a bow on the handle. "This is for you," he said, handing it across to her. "Open it, please."

"Oh-kayyy," she said slowly. She untied the satin ribbon and reached into the tissue-filled bag, pulling out a white cotton T-shirt.

"Uh, thanks."

"Read the shirt," Brice said.

She unfolded the shirt and held it up. Printed across the front, in bold blue letters it read I'M THE BIG SISTER!

Drue looked from Brice to Wendy. They were holding hands and grinning like a couple of loons.

"Is this a gag?" she asked, but from the expression on her father's face, she instantly regretted her words.

He looked like he'd been slapped. "A gag? Who jokes about something like that? We thought you'd be happy for us."

Wendy's eyes filled with tears. "I told you she'd be freaked out." She reached over and snatched the gift from Drue's hands. "Never mind. I guess it was too much to expect that you'd be happy about our happiness."

"Wait! No, I'm not freaked out. I'm surprised, that's all. I mean, I had no idea you guys were trying." Drue sat back, trying to gather her thoughts.

"Wow," she said, after a moment. "Really? You're pregnant? Congratulations."

"Thanks," Brice said. He pulled Wendy closer. "Come on, honey, you heard her. She's really happy for us."

He glared at his daughter. "Aren't you?"

"I am," Drue said slowly. "It's just a lot to take in." She held out her hand to Wendy.

"Can I have my gift back, please?"

Wendy tossed the shirt at Drue, who caught it in midair. "So. Tell me all about it. How long have you known? When's the due date?"

"We're due in November," Brice said. "It's not really a surprise. We, uh, had some fertility issues, as you might guess. We started trying as soon as we got married, but it turns out it's not as easy as I assumed it would be."

"Four rounds of in vitro fertilization," Wendy said, sighing and holding her hands protectively across her perfectly flat abdomen. "Fifteen thousand dollars a round, plus hellish amounts of hormones."

"This girl has been a real trooper," Brice said, beaming at his bride. "I would have given up a year ago, but she just wouldn't. It was quite the ordeal for her."

"I'll bet." Drue nodded, although the reality was that she had no idea what was involved with in vitro fertilization. She studied Wendy, who was staring down at her belly.

"Are you feeling okay?" she asked, trying to sound solicitous.

"Still nauseous in the morning, but at least those crazy mood swings from the hormones are pretty much a thing of the past," Wendy said. Her face softened. "I, uh, well, I know I've been pretty bitchy and hard to get along with. But I've been so anxious, worrying that something would happen and I'd lose the baby."

"You're not going to lose the baby," Brice said, squeezing Wendy's shoulders. "The doctor says everything looks great."

"We wanted to wait to tell people until I was well past my first trimester," Wendy said. "You know, just in case. Turns out I'm a high-risk mom. But the doctor says everything is fine, and he's just perfect!"

"He?" Drue looked at her father.

"Didn't we already say that? It's a boy! You're going to have a baby brother."

"You're going to have a son," Wendy said, kissing Brice's cheek.

"I didn't want to say anything to spook Wendy, but I was really crazy nervous waiting on those results," Brice said. "I mean, I'm nearly seventy years old, for Chrissakes! I kept looking stuff up on the internet, trying to reassure myself. My God! A son, at my age!"

"Charlie Chaplin was seventy-three when his last child was born," Wendy said. "Picasso was sixty-eight."

"Same age as me," Brice said. "Mick Jagger was seventy-four when he had a kid, and Ronnie Wood was seventy. And Billy Joel and Elton John were still fathering kids in their sixties," Brice noted.

"Great!" Drue piped up. "Maybe you'll take up the guitar and join a band . . . Just joking, Dad!"

Wendy cleared her throat. "You're the first person we've told, Drue. Because we were hoping, or I was hoping, with the baby coming and all, you and I could bury the hatchet."

Brice looked at her expectantly. "Can you do that? So we can all be a real family?"

Drue's face felt hot. She pasted a smile on her face. "Sure. Of course. A family."

She stood up, went over and kissed her father's cheek. Wendy presented her own cheek, so Drue kissed that too.

"Guess I better get back to work," she said, trying to lighten the mood. "Gotta rustle up some business so we can buy diapers for Baby Boy Campbell!"

Wendy moved over to her desk, smoothing her designer blouse as she took her customary seat. "He'll be William Brice Campbell, Junior, of course. But we'll call him Liam."

"Cute name," Drue said, her hand on the doorknob.

"Wait!" Brice leapt to his feet, holding out the T-shirt. "You didn't even try it on."

He looked so eager, so excited, she didn't have the heart to refuse. Drue pulled the T-shirt on over the navy tank top she'd worn to work that day. It was uncomfortably snug across the chest. Too small, of course.

"I love it!" she exclaimed.

Ben was on the phone when she got back to her cubicle, but she saw him watching as she approached, raising one eyebrow as he regarded her new apparel. She grabbed her sweater and buttoned it.

Five minutes later, as she was explaining to a caller that the firm didn't routinely file lawsuits against a client's parents for breach of promise, she heard the casters of Ben's chair squeaking as he rolled over to her side of the cubicle. She ended the call quickly and reluctantly turned to face him.

"You're the big sister?" he asked. "Whose big sister?"

"William Brice Campbell, Junior," Drue said. "But we're going to call him Liam. You'll have to excuse me now, because I think I just threw up in my mouth."

"She's pregnant?" Ben said, glancing over his shoulder at the door to Wendy's office. "You're kidding, right?"

"Not even a little bit," Drue assured him.

"But your dad is like, what? In his seventies? Is that even possible?"

"He's a robust sixty-eight, and they have assured me that anything is possible, if you have enough insurance. Did you know that Charlie Chaplin's wife had a kid when he was seventy-three?"

"Excuse me, but I find it bizarre that you happen to know that," Ben said.

"What's bizarre?" Jonah stood just behind Drue's chair, his mug clutched in one hand, his coffee pod in the other.

"Drue here is going to have a baby brother," Ben said. "Wendy's got a bun in the oven."

"You guys just figured that out?" Jonah said. He shook his head. "I thought that was old news."

Drue spun around on her chair. "No way you already knew. I was the first person they told."

"I've known it for weeks," Jonah said. "The dark circles under her eyes, and the untucked shirts all of a sudden? But the biggest giveaway was the green tea and soy milk. Most days, Wendy used to drink about a gallon of black coffee, straight up, before noon."

"You're right, damn it," Ben said. "Don't you agree that it's a little much, Brice having another kid at his age?"

"Oh, I don't know. Steve Martin was sixty-seven when he had his first kid." Jonah nodded at his colleagues and sauntered off toward the break room.

Drue waited until Ben got up to join his friend in the break room. She looked around to make sure she wouldn't be overheard, then dialed the number for the Treasure Island Police Department.

"Detective Hernandez, please," she told the operator.

"Which Detective Hernandez?"

She glanced down at the police report half hidden on her desktop. "Uh, Ray Hernandez, please."

"One moment."

The extension number rang twice and a woman answered. "This is Rae Hernandez."

Drue was startled to be speaking to a female detective. "Oh hi. My name is Drue Campbell. I work for the law firm that Yvonne Howington hired to represent her after her daughter was killed two years ago at the Gulf Vista Hotel and Resort."

There was a long silence on the other end of the line.

"Oh yeah. Campbell, Coxe and Kramner," Detective Hernandez drawled. "Brice Campbell, the billboard barrister."

Cute, Drue thought.

"You know, Yvonne Howington's not too crazy about the way you people handled her case," Hernandez said.

"That's why I'm calling," Drue said. "I've obtained some new information about Jazmin's murder, and I'd like to meet up and discuss things with you."

"I'll tell you what I told Yvonne. This is still an open investigation. I'm not at liberty to discuss it with you or your law firm."

"If we could just meet," Drue blurted out. "I think we could help each other help Yvonne get some answers. And some justice."

"I doubt that," Hernandez said.

"Thirty minutes of your time. That's all I ask. I can meet you any place you say, any time you say. I could come in to your office if that's convenient."

"I'm about to clock out. I worked all weekend and I'm off tomorrow, because my son has a baseball tournament down in Sarasota."

"What about tonight?"

"He's got a game tonight."

"I could meet you at the game," Drue said, not caring that she sounded desperate.

"I actually like to watch my son play when I attend one of his games," Hernandez said. "But, tell you what. I'm taking him early, for batting practice, at six. We can talk there. Lake Vista Park. You know where that is? Sixty-second Avenue South? Not far from Lakewood High School."

"I know just where that is," Drue said.

"See you there," Rae Hernandez said. "I'll be the stubby mom with the thick calves, wearing a white ball cap, a Red Wings jersey and a pissed-off expression."

33

Lake Vista Park was teeming with kids and parents. It was still broiling hot under the late-afternoon Florida sun, and the stands of pine trees around the park offered little shade as she walked toward the playing fields from the parking lot. Drue wished she'd asked Rae Hernandez which baseball diamond her son would be playing on, but in the end, she gravitated toward a field where a dozen kids in red jerseys and mud-stained baseball pants were lined up.

She stood at the bottom of the bleachers, gazing up, hoping the detective would spot her, but none of the women fit the description she'd been given. The stands were mostly empty, with only a dozen or so people, mostly moms, with a sprinkling of dads, chatting, idly watching their kids taking batting practice.

There was a concession stand, so she decided to get a cold drink before resuming her search. The woman selling hot dogs and soft drinks was wearing a Red Wings T-shirt. "Do you happen to know Rae Hernandez?" Drue asked.

"Sure," the woman said. "Her son Stephen is on my son's team."

"I'm supposed to meet her here, but I don't actually know what she looks like. Could you maybe point her out to me? Do you know if she's sitting in the bleachers?"

The woman looked amused. She leaned out the window of the stand and pointed toward the outfield, where a lone woman was sitting on a red folding stadium chair.

"That's Rae out there."

The detective had her eyes glued to the field. She had a score-book open on her lap, and as promised, she was wearing a Red Wings jersey and a white baseball cap with her dark hair in a ponytail sticking out of the back.

"Detective Hernandez?" Drue said, as she walked up.

"That's me," Hernandez said. She handed Drue another folding chair. "You can sit here, 'til my husband gets here. He's still at work."

"Thanks for seeing me—" Drue started.

"Hang on." The detective cupped her hands around her mouth as a makeshift megaphone.

"Choke up on the bat, Dez," she yelled. "Come on now. Swing from your hips."

Drue turned and watched as the boy squared himself in front of home plate. He looked smaller than the other players, whom she judged to be maybe ten or eleven. His white pants drooped over the tops of his red-and-white-striped socks, and the batting helmet seemed comically oversized for his head.

The pitcher was a tall, lanky black kid who rifled a fastball at the batter. The kid whiffed at the first pitch.

"That's okay," Rae called. "Wait on it. Just keep your eye on the ball."

The kid whiffed a second time, and his mother groaned. "He's swinging too early," she muttered. "We've told him and told him . . ."

On the third pitch the kid connected, hitting the ball with a resounding *thwack,* sending it spinning toward left field.

"Whoo-hoo!" Rae Hernandez jumped to her feet, pumping her fists in the air. "Way to connect, Dez!" She was, as advertised, short and stocky, her muscled legs tan in contrast to the white shorts and tennis shoes she was wearing.

"Great hit," Drue said. "Your son looks like a real ball-player."

The detective took her seat again. "That idiot coach keeps messing with his swing. It's making us crazy." She turned to Drue, sliding her sunglasses down her nose. "Okay. Talk. You've got twenty minutes before the game begins."

"I really appreciate your seeing me," Drue started.

"You can thank Yvonne. I talked to her today after you called. She seems to think you can help her case against the hotel. Plus you were kind to Aliyah. That's the only reason you're here. That and the fact that you claim to have new information. But before we get started, let me ask you something. Are you like Jimmy Zee's assistant or something?"

"You know Zee?"

"Every cop in town knows him," Hernandez said. "My husband worked with him at the St. Pete PD, before Zee retired."

Drue chose her words carefully. "We work together. He's training me to do investigative work."

She made a sour face. "Just be sure you don't take any ethics lessons from him."

"What's that supposed to mean?" Drue asked.

"Zee has a fast and loose relationship with the finer points of the law," Hernandez said. "But he knows people, so he gets away with stuff."

"I talked to Lutrisha Smallwood," Drue said eagerly.

"The gal who found the body? Not exactly the most helpful witness."

"She was afraid of repercussions from hotel management, I think. She still is. Did you know she'd gone back to work there?"

"That's news," Rae said. "I thought she was working in the bakery at Publix."

"She told me she couldn't get enough hours there," Drue said. "She also said that the hotel manager called all the housekeepers into a meeting not long after Jazmin's murder, to tell them that Yvonne's lawsuit against the hotel could force the hotel into bankruptcy. Which spooked everybody more than they already were."

"Those bastards," Rae said. "They stonewalled our investigation every way they could. I can't prove they destroyed crime scene evidence before we got there, but I've always believed somebody did. What else did Lutrisha tell you?"

"For starters, she admitted that she and Jazmin were closer than she originally let on when she was interviewed by the police."

"Big surprise," Rae said.

"She told me that she'd sometimes cover for Jazmin, when she was going on a date. Instead of going home to shower, she'd shower and change in a vacant room at the hotel, which was a firing offense. She said Jazmin's boyfriend had once worked at the hotel, but left to take a job at another motel. Have you talked to him?"

"Jorge? Yeah. But he had an alibi for the night of the murder. He works at the front desk at the Silver Sands."

"The big motel on St. Pete Beach?"

"Yeah. It's a good twenty minutes south of Sunset Beach. His manager vouched for him, said he's a good guy. And he's got no police record. I interviewed him myself. He was really torn up about his girlfriend's death."

"Does he still work at the Silver Sands?" Drue asked.

"As far as I know, but remember, it's going on two years now since all this happened."

"Did Jorge know anything about a coworker sexually harassing Jazmin?"

Rae shook her head, but her eyes were fixed on the baseball diamond, where her son was now shagging balls in left field.

"No. If some dude was bothering her, she didn't tell him. And before you ask, Gulf Vista's HR woman denied that Jazmin filed any kind of a complaint. But I got the impression that nobody at that hotel filed any complaints. It wasn't that kind of corporate culture, if you get my drift."

"Lutrisha told me that another employee, a guy named Larry Boone, was coming on to her, grabbing her and making lewd comments. She said it ended after she sprayed him in the face with Windex. Did you guys happen to check him out?"

Rae was focused on the baseball field again. "Come on, Dez," she yelled. "Let's see some hustle out there." She turned to Drue. "This is his first game with his new travel team. He needs to make an impression on the coach or else spend the season riding the bench.

"Larry Boone?" she asked, turning back to the subject at hand. "The engineering guy? Yeah, we talked to him. We talked to all the male employees. If I remember right, Boone got off work at eleven that night."

"The same time Jazmin was supposed to get off," Drue said. "What did Boone tell you?"

"He lives way up in Hernando County, so he had about an hour commute to get home."

"Did anybody confirm his whereabouts?"

"At the time, he was separated from his wife, living alone in a double-wide trailer on his brother's property on the river up there."

Drue felt a blip of excitement. "So he didn't have any proof that he was home. He could have been at the hotel."

"But he'd clocked out. And at the time we didn't have a witness who could place him there." A half-smile played across her lips. "That's good info about Boone. We'll definitely take another look at him."

"Lutrisha called him Scary Larry," Drue said. "I looked him up online. He works at an Ace Hardware store up in Brooksville."

Hernandez scribbled something in pencil on the margins of her scorebook.

"You said you talked to all the male employees who were working that night," Drue said. "Did you also interview hotel guests?"

"We interviewed as many as we could round up," Rae said. "It was a real shit show. There'd been a convention of Shriners. Half of 'em were hungover, the other half just wanted to check out and get back to Peoria or wherever the hell they were from. But we never really believed this was a stranger-to-stranger killing anyway."

"Why's that?" Drue asked.

"The nature of the crime," Rae said. "Jazmin wasn't sexually assaulted, but she was badly beaten around the head and face. That's not typically a stranger-to-stranger crime. Somebody had some kind of anger issues with her. And remember, she was strangled. We figure the assailant was a man because there aren't a lot of women who have the strength, or the stomach, to do something that violent."

Drue thought that over. "I read Zee's reports. I thought it was interesting that so many of the employees who worked directly with Jazmin left the hotel not long after she was killed."

"Lot of turnover there," Rae agreed. "Head of housekeeping, engineering, the security guard who was first on scene and called the cops. When I asked the hotel manager about it, he said that's the nature of the hospitality industry."

"And the manager was never a suspect?" Drue asked.

"Gene Wardlaw? No. He wasn't even in town. Ironically enough, it turns out he was interviewing for another job at a hotel in Daytona Beach. Which he subsequently took."

Drue let out a long sigh.

"Yeah. It's frustrating as hell, not being able to find the guy who did this. Yvonne calls me every Sunday night, like clockwork, asking for updates. I tell you, it haunts me sometimes."

"It's haunting me, and I haven't been working it for the past two years," Drue admitted. She glanced at the detective, trying to gauge just how sympathetic she might be to her cause.

"I even went over to the hotel and checked out the laundry room where she was killed," she added.

Rae Hernandez raised a dubious eyebrow. "How'd you get in? Nothing like closing the barn door after the cow got out, but I know they really ramped up security after the murder."

"A friend went with me and we told the security guard at the gate that we were considering the hotel as our wedding venue."

"Ballsy move, but I wouldn't recommend trying that again," Hernandez said. "Technically, they could probably have you arrested for criminal trespass."

"One thing I noticed in that laundry room," Drue continued. "There were mounting brackets on the wall, over the doorway. So, at one time there was a video camera there? Did you guys look into that?"

"We did. Brian Shelnutt, the head of security, said the camera had been broken for 'a while.' He couldn't tell us how long that was. He said it had been removed and another one ordered."

"Convenient," Drue said. "Did you believe him?"

Hernandez removed her sunglasses and polished them on the hem of her shirt before donning them. "I rarely believe anybody. It's an occupational hazard."

"Something I've been wondering about," Drue said, finally getting to the matter she'd wanted to raise since the beginning of this meeting.

"What's that?"

"Wondering if you'd let me see the video from the hotel."

"Oh, hell no," Hernandez started.

Drue plowed ahead. "It's been nearly two years, and you've admitted you don't have any real suspects. What could it hurt, letting me look at the video? Remember, I want the same thing you want—to solve this thing and get a settlement for Yvonne and Aliyah."

Hernandez gazed at her for a moment, her face dispassionate. "You won't like what you see. The video shows Jazmin Mayes was working, way past the time Yvonne insists she wasn't."

"I don't care," Drue said. "I'd really like to see the video."

"I don't want you coming into the station," Hernandez said, choosing her words carefully. "I'll put it on a flash drive. Where do you live?"

"Sunset Beach. Pine Street, I'm just a few blocks away from the Gulf Vista."

"That's convenient. My husband's working tomorrow. Text me the address and I'll have him drop it off to you in the morning on his way to work. But I warn you, there's not much to see. I should know. I've been staring at that damn video for two years."

"Thank you!" Drue said, touching Rae's arm. "I mean it. Thanks."

The detective looked over her shoulder and waved at an approaching man, who wore dress slacks and shoes and a short-sleeved dress shirt. "Here's my husband now. The game's about to begin, so your time is up."

Drue stood and looked toward the field. The stands were filled now, and the opposing team, kids in green jerseys with a yellow Phillies logo across the front, had taken the field for their batting practice.

"Hey, can I ask you one more question?"

Hernandez looked annoyed. "Last one."

"Why are you sitting way out here for your son's ball game? Why aren't you up in the bleachers with the other parents?"

Hernandez shrugged. "I had a run-in with one of the umps last season, after he called Dez out at home. My boy was safe by a mile. The ump had it in for me all season, and Dez, just because I had the nerve to question his strike zone. So I got banned from the stands! Totally unfair. Now I watch the games out here. Which is fine, because I don't have to put up with all those bitchy baseball moms griping about how their precious angel isn't in the starting lineup."

On the way home, Drue replayed her conversation with Rae Hernandez, elated at the possibility that she'd actually get to view the video from the hotel. She pondered something Hernandez had said, as an aside.

"I rarely believe anybody," the detective had told her. Drue wondered what that was like, to never trust anybody. Earlier in the day, she'd admitted to Ben Fentress that she didn't even trust her own father. The question was, who did she trust?

34

July 1976

Jimmy Zee and Brice were walking out to the parking lot at Munch's, their favorite breakfast spot on the south side, when a pale yellow Mustang whipped into the spot beside Brice's cruiser. The teenage driver opened his door, banging it into the side of Brice's unit.

Without missing a beat, Brice reached into the car, grabbed the kid by the neck of his T-shirt and hauled him to the pavement. "Hey, asshole, look what you did!" He pointed at the fresh ding in the cruiser's paint job.

The kid, with long, greasy hair touching his shoulders, squirmed to try to escape. "Fuck off. That was already there."

Brice tightened his choke hold, nearly lifting the kid, who weighed maybe ninety pounds, off the ground. "You just damaged police property, you little turd." He glanced over at Zee. "You saw that too, right, Officer?"

Zee dropped his cigarette butt to the asphalt, crushing it with his heel. "Yeah, man." He glared at the kid. "Don't ever do that again. You understand?"

The kid's face was alarmingly red.

"Come on, Brice," Zee said, putting a hand on Brice's shoulder. "Let him go. We gotta get back to work."

In reply, Brice put his hand on the back of the kid's head and shoved him facedown against the hood of his car. "Hey!" the kid squawked. "Police brutality!"

Brice grabbed a handful of hair and smashed the kid's face down again, hard.

"Come on," Zee said, tugging urgently at Brice's arm. Two women stood just outside the doorway of the restaurant, staring in horror at the unfolding scene. "We gotta roll."

They met up again, by mutual agreement, at the end of their shift, in a back booth at Mastry's.

Zee sipped his beer and studied his oldest friend. "You look like shit," he said.

It was true. Brice's usually immaculate uniform was rumpled. He was pale, with dark circles under his eyes, and he was already on his second scotch and water.

"Fuck you very much," Brice replied, draining his glass and helping himself to one of Zee's Salems.

"What's going on?" Zee asked. "You lost your cool with that kid at Munch's today. You're smoking again and drinking scotch on a weeknight. I've never seen you like this."

Brice blew a long plume of smoke from his nostrils. "Now you sound like my wife. I'm fine, okay?"

"Come on," Zee said. "Don't bullshit me."

Brice rubbed his hand across his face and stubbed out the cigarette.

"I'm screwed," he said wearily. "Got myself into some deep shit, and I don't know how to get out. I'm not sleeping and my gut's on fire." He shook his head. "Christ, what a mess."

"Talk to me," Zee replied.

"Remember that domestic disturbance call we got to the Dreamland back in December?"

The waitress appeared beside their booth and Zee raised his empty beer mug to signal for a refill. "Yeah. What about it?"

"The wife? Her name is Colleen. We went to high school together. After you got the husband out of there that night, I started talking to her, trying to convince her she should leave the guy. She was really rattled, afraid to go home, so I brought her here and we had a few drinks. We kind of connected, you know?"

Zee rolled his eyes. "I think I know where this is going."

"I wish I'd known then where it was going, I'd have minded my own business and gone on home."

Zee gave him a cynical smile. "Not really your style, bro. The husband beat the crap out of her that night. We both know that type. He might have killed her if we hadn't broken it up."

"Allen Hicks is a piece of shit. Violent, controlling and a bad drunk."

"I remember that chick. We ran into her right here, a few months after the thing at the motel. She's good-looking. So what's she doing with a loser like that?"

"The usual. Met him in college, he romanced her and she fell hard. After they'd been married a few months, he began drinking more. Slapping her around."

"Why doesn't she divorce his ass?"

"According to Colleen, the husband controls all the money. She doesn't have the money to hire a lawyer, and even if she did, Hicks's father is a big deal in St. Pete. He's a doctor. Chief of staff at Bayfront. Hell, he's the commodore at the yacht club."

"You're shitting me. That's a real thing?"

Brice propped his elbow on the table. "His picture was in the *St. Pete Times* just this week. Dr. Hicks drinks with every judge in town. She wouldn't get a dime for a divorce settlement."

"Okay, tell her to get a restraining order against Hicks. I mean, we could swear we saw him beat her that night. I'd do it."

"You're not listening," Brice said. "No judge is going to grant her a restraining order. And even if one did, Hicks would come after her anyway. He dislocated her shoulder last month. On her birthday."

Their refills arrived. Brice stared moodily down into the glass, his red-rimmed eyes unfocused.

"You're not the one who's screwed," Zee pointed out. "I mean, it's okay to want to help her out, but in the end, she's the one who married the asshole, and she's the one who decided to stay with him. Not your problem, brother."

"It kinda is," Brice said, looking sheepish. "I've been seeing her. Like a lot."

"What does Sherri think about that?"

"She knows I'm taking night classes, but I told her I'm meeting with a study group on Thursday nights."

Zee chuckled. "But instead you're studying Colleen Hicks?"

"I feel like I'm losing my mind. And she's definitely lost hers. I had no idea just how crazy that girl is. Now she's saying the only way she can leave her husband is if she just disappears."

"Like, *poof,* she's in the wind?"

"That's her plan. And she wants me to help. They've been saving up to buy a house. Her plan is to empty the savings account and hop a Greyhound to Atlanta. She'll assume a new identity and start a new life."

"Where do you fit into this crazy-ass scheme?"

"She wants me to help her disappear, get her a fake ID. She really wants me to go with her too."

"You'd do that?"

"Hell no," Brice said. "Leave Sherri? My job? Give up my plans? If I help her, go with her, I'm a fugitive. What's that do to my plan to go to law school?"

"You think Sherri knows what's going on? She's not stupid."

"I think maybe she suspects. She kicked me out of the house the week before Christmas—that first night I was with Colleen. She only took me back, Christmas morning, after I swore I was through cheating. Now she watches me like a hawk."

Brice shook another cigarette out of the pack of Salems with shaking hands. "I think I'm just gonna do it. Get the fake ID. It's not that hard. Every teenager in town has one."

"I don't like it." Zee shook his head vehemently. "What if her disappearing act blows up? And it comes back on you? The department would can you in a minute. I say you let this chick do what she's gonna do. She can't *make* you help her."

"Colleen already admitted she went and saw Sherri, at the real estate office. Pretending she wanted to rent a house. And I've seen her drive past the house at night a couple times."

Zee didn't say anything. Just shook his head.

"I'm worried that if I don't help her, she'll go to Sherri. Tell her we've been hitting the sheets at the Dreamland every Thursday night . . ."

"The Dreamland? That dump? Are you shitting me?"

"What can I tell you? She gets off on the place."

"Let me get this straight. She's stalking you, stalking Sherri. Making threats?"

Brice leaned back in the booth, avoiding his friend's direct gaze. "Yeah, I know. I feel like I'm living a nightmare I can't wake up from."

"Let me talk to her," Zee said. "Make her see that she just needs to walk away and not look back. Forget she ever met you. No reason to ruin both your lives."

"No. I'm already in over my head. I don't want to get you involved."

"I'm already involved. I was with you the night we broke up that fight at the motel. I went along with not filing a report, remember?"

Brice knocked back the rest of his scotch.

"When are you supposed to see her again?"

"This Thursday night. At the Dreamland. Nine o'clock, after my class gets out."

"How do you usually work it?" Zee asked.

"I know the guy at the desk. He gives me the room, you know, 'cause he likes the idea of a police cruiser on the property. In case there's any trouble."

"Great." Zee rolled his eyes. "Accepting gifts from a citizen in return for protection. You really have lost your mind."

"I know," Brice moaned. "But I can't exactly put it on a credit card. Sherri pays the bills. And I don't have the extra cash."

"Okay, forget it. Is it the same room every time?"

"Yeah. Room eight. The owner's name is Harold. Just go to the desk and tell him I sent you. He's cool."

"Okay. Here's what we're gonna do. You go right home after your class. And I mean right home. Tell Sherri study group was canceled. I'll have a chat with Colleen. Let her know you can't help her anymore. And she should stop calling you and stop riding by your house."

"You don't know her," Brice said. "She's not gonna give up that easy."

"Colleen don't know Zee. But Zee knows lots of crazy girls like Colleen," Zee said. "Don't worry about it, bro. It's handled."

35

When she left Coquina Cottage to go to work Wednesday morning, Drue found a plain white business envelope containing a plastic flash drive on OJ's passenger seat. There was no note, but she was sure it was the video from the security cameras at Gulf Vista, taken the night of Jazmin's murder. "Thanks, Detective Hernandez," she whispered.

But there was no opportunity to watch the video on her computer at work. Another new ad campaign had launched over the weekend, this one aimed at motorists who'd been involved in accidents with long-haul truckers.

The file box of medical receipts had disappeared from her cubicle, and there were no ominous sticky notes, so she gladly donned her headset again.

As she made notes, and between calls, she toyed with the

flash drive, turning it over and over between her fingertips, anxious to view its contents.

Drue finally made a dash to the break room just after noon, with the flash drive stowed in the pocket of her work sweater for safekeeping. She found Jonah at the coffee machine, dressed in his typical pressed khakis, dress shirt and tie, staring morosely down into his blue and orange University of Florida mug with the Gator handle.

"What's wrong?"

"This isn't mine," he said.

"Who else would buy a coffee mug that ugly?"

"No. I mean, it's my mug, but this isn't my Keurig pod. I had a whole stash hidden in my desk drawer, but somebody apparently raided it last night and yoinked all my pods. This is the office sludge."

"Is nothing sacred?" Drue said, her tone mocking. "Shall I call the cops?"

"I don't like the idea of somebody rifling through my stuff, okay? I mean, if you want my coffee, just ask. Don't go stealing."

"It wasn't me," Drue said. "I drink whatever's free and available."

He shook his head, still annoyed. "Are your calls as nutty as mine this morning?"

"Oh yeah. I just had a guy call and claim he was rear-ended by the Oscar Mayer Wienermobile."

"Okay, that could be lucrative," Jonah said. "Or just plain lewd."

"Except that there were no witnesses, he didn't file an accident report and, oh yeah, the guy admits he had his driver's license lifted two years ago for multiple DUIs."

Jonah sighed and dumped the remains of his coffee into the sink. "It must be the full moon. I had a lady who wants to hire Brice to sue FedEx because one of their trucks cut her off in traffic and when she slammed on the brakes her dog got whiplash."

Drue giggled despite herself. "Seriously? What kind of dog?"

"German short-haired pointer. She claims he would have been a best-in-show contender in the Westminster Kennel Club, but since the accident, he refuses to point. Now she says she's missing out on thousands and thousands of dollars' worth of stud fees."

Jonah glanced up at the clock on the break room wall. "Okay, I gotta get back in there." He started toward the door, but then turned and came back.

"Hey, um, are we good?"

"I guess. Even though you apparently found a way to resurrect that slip-and-fall case that should have been mine."

His face flushed. "I told Wendy she should send the client back to you. It was just dumb luck that when she called the second time the call was routed to me."

"Don't sweat it," Drue said lightly. "The way it worked out, Zee asked my dad if I could help interview a witness to that accident. It was a pretty cool experience."

"I'm glad. You know, I hate the way things started out with us. That first night at Sharky's? I swear, Drue, that's not who I am. I know you think I'm your typical horndog, but I'm not." He lowered his voice. "I wish you'd give me a do-over."

"Do-over?"

"Let me take you out. We start from scratch." He stuck out his hand. "'Hi, I'm Jonah. Actually not the random asshole you met at a bar who was trying way too hard to prove to the boss's daughter that he was way cool.'"

He left his hand extended. "This is where you go, 'Hi, I'm Drue. Nice to meet you, Jonah. And yes, I'd love to go out with you for sushi. Or steak. But not shots. Never, ever shots again.'"

He raised an eyebrow. "Helloooo? Drue?"

"Don't rush me," she said. "I'm thinking about it."

The break room door opened and Ben strolled in, clutching his coffee mug. He looked from Drue to Jonah. "What's going on? Am I missing something?"

The mood was broken.

"As a matter of fact, we were just discussing a very serious crime wave," Drue said. "Thinking about getting Zee involved and asking him to launch an in-house investigation."

"Really?" Ben said, pushing his glasses off the end of his nose.

"It's the Keurig heist," she said, gesturing at Jonah's empty mug.

"Thinking it's an inside job," Jonah said. He nodded toward Drue. "Let me know your thoughts, okay?"

Ben watched his coworker exit. "Thoughts on what?"

"Um, nothing, really. We were just comparing notes on all the crazy calls we've gotten this morning. I had a Wienermobile incident, he had a dog whiplash call. How's it going with you?"

"About the same," Ben said. "I fielded about a hundred calls, but nothing that bizarre. How goes it with your investigator training? When do you do another ride-along with Zee?"

"Not sure," Drue said. "Listen, I gotta get back to work before Wendy decides to find some new and different way to torture me."

36

The St. Pete Beach Public Library was quiet. Most of the winter resident snowbirds had fled back north with the coming of warmer weather.

Drue waited at the information desk while a heavy-set librarian with a blue Mohawk and polka-dot bow tie checked out a thick stack of picture books for a harried mom with two preschoolers.

"How can I help?" he asked, approaching Drue.

She held up the flash drive. "I'd like to use a computer to watch this video."

He nodded. "Do you have a library card?"

"No."

"Well, if you have your driver's license, I can get you fixed up with a card and then you'll be free to use materials at any library on the beach."

Drue handed over her license with her old Fort Lauderdale address.

"Oh." He frowned and handed it back. "Actually, you need to be a Pinellas County resident."

"I am," she explained. "But I just moved here a month ago."

He smiled. "When you come back, bring in a piece of mail that shows your current address and we'll get you fixed up."

"I can't get fixed up today?"

"I wish. Sorry, I don't make the rules. What I can do is give you a temporary three-month library card. It'll cost twenty-five dollars."

She sighed, but dug her billfold from her backpack and slid the money across the counter.

With her new library card stashed away, Drue sat down at a computer terminal, logged in with her library card number and plugged the flash drive into the monitor.

She leaned forward, staring intently at the somewhat blurry black-and-white images on the screen.

The first sequence on the video, time-stamped 11:05 P.M., showed a wide angle of the hotel hallway. A petite, slender woman appeared, pushing a cart just like the one Drue had seen in the Gulf Vista laundry room. The housekeeper wore a short-sleeved button-front uniform smock, jeans and tennis shoes, and a baseball cap whose bill partially obscured her face.

The housekeeper paused in front of a doorway and used a key card hanging from a lanyard around her neck to unlock the door.

The door opened and the housekeeper pushed through with the laundry cart. Nearly two and a half hours later, according to the time stamp, the same hotel room door opened and the same housekeeper emerged, pushing the cart.

Drue watched while the woman waited in front of a service elevator. A video camera mounted in the elevator then showed the housekeeper in the elevator, staring down at the cart. The elevator doors opened, and the video went fuzzy. In the next clip, the woman was shown pushing the cart down a walkway that Drue recognized as the service entrance to the Gulf Vista's laundry room. The lighting was much dimmer, but she recognized the laundry room, with its door ajar. The housekeeper pushed the cart through, then closed the door. The computer screen went black.

Drue watched the video clip half a dozen more times, trying to gain some kind of insight into the night of Jazmin's murder.

She pulled her cell phone from her backpack, but another, crew-cut librarian looked over at her from the front desk and pointed to a large ceiling-mounted sign: CELL PHONE USAGE PROHIBITED IN LIBRARY.

Drue nodded, palmed the flash drive and walked outside the library. She got into the Bronco and called Rae Hernandez.

The detective answered after two rings.

"What? I thought I told you my son has a baseball tournament today. I'm busy."

"I know, and I'm sorry to bother you. Please tell your husband I said thanks for dropping off the flash drive."

"What flash drive?"

"Oh. Right. I forgot. An anonymous tipster left an envelope on the front seat of my car this morning. There was a flash drive. It had video clips from the security cameras at the Gulf Vista the night Jazmin was killed."

"Okay, we've established that. Now, what's your point?"

"Is that all you have for the video? I mean, nothing from that hotel room Jazmin entered?"

"Hotels don't have video cameras in people's private rooms. At least, not the legit ones. That's illegal."

"Right. Forget I asked that. Isn't there any other video from that day, something else that shows her?"

"Sure. There's like eight hours of video of her doing her job. There's a video of her clocking in. And buying a Dr Pepper from a vending machine by the pool."

"The hotel has a parking lot reserved for employees, right?"

"Yeah. On the lowest level of the hotel, same level as the loading dock."

"Was there a security camera down there?"

Silence.

"Rae? Detective Hernandez?"

"I'm trying to remember. It's been two years, you know. Lots of cases since then."

"But no other cases where a young single mom is beaten and strangled and tossed in with a load of dirty sheets and towels," Drue said.

"Okay, yeah. There was a security camera in the parking garage. We looked at all the footage. As far as I can remember, there was nothing remarkable, except for some busboys smoking what we assumed was reefer, and a male desk clerk and female housekeeper engaged in what could be called a mutually rewarding act of intimacy."

"They were having sex? Right there in the parking garage?"

"Going at it like it was their job, in the backseat of a Subaru," Hernandez confirmed. "So lots of comings and goings. Literally."

"Ha-ha," Drue said.

"Is that it now?" Hernandez asked. "The Red Wings are at bat. I gotta go."

"Can you get me any more video from that night at the hotel?" Drue asked. "I don't mind watching the boring stuff."

"Don't push your luck, kid," Hernandez said.

Drue sat in the car for a few minutes, trying to decide on her next move. She was now only a few blocks from the Silver Sands Motel, where Jazmin's boyfriend worked. She called the motel and asked for Jorge Morales, but was told his shift didn't start until 8:00 P.M.

"Guess I'll go home and wait," Drue said, starting the Bronco and backing out of the library parking lot.

37

Drue sat in the living room at Coquina Cottage, examining her temporary library card. Had she really been back on the west coast for a month now? Had it been only a month since she'd held her mother's hand and watched as she drifted into unconsciousness?

The cottage was neat as a pin. The floors were swept clean, her refrigerator held neatly organized shelves of perishables, her bed was made and the office she'd set up in the guest bedroom held a desk she'd recently acquired from Craigslist. But the rooms seemed bare and lifeless.

This was not the colorful, joyful home of her grandparents. The cottage lacked soul.

She went into the office and pulled out a box she'd unearthed from the attic but had resisted unpacking until now.

With a smile, she laid the paintings out on the desktop, and then on the floor. These were Papi's masterpieces. A pair of framed paintings of flamingoes. Another pair of red macaws, their bills open, wings extended. There was a large painting of a majestic snowy egret and a pale pink cockatoo perched on a flowering dogwood branch, a blue heron depicted wading in shallow water, much like the heron Drue had stalked at sundown, and another pair of bird paintings, these of roseate spoonbills, returning to roost over a moss-draped swamp. There was even a paint-by-numbers of a dolorous-looking pelican sitting on a piling that reminded her of the pelicans at Merry Pier.

For much of his working life, woodworking had been her grandfather's passion, but after his first heart attack in his early seventies, Nonni had demanded that he find a less active hobby. She'd bought him his first paint-by-numbers kit, a cheesy depiction of *The Last Supper,* and he'd eagerly put down the hammer and picked up the paintbrush.

Drue estimated that her grandfather probably completed at least a hundred paintings before his death, all with his name, Alberto, proudly signed in the bottom right corner. Tropical birds were his favorite subject, but after he'd filled up all the walls in the cottage, he'd moved on to snowy scenes of New England, then sailboats at sunset, followed by exotic depictions of palm trees and grass huts in the South Pacific, woodland scenes of stags and does and elk, then dogs and kittens. He'd crafted his own frames for the paintings, and joyfully gifted them to family and friends, even his cardiologist and the mailman.

She was still filled with remorse at the memory of the paint-by-numbers works Papi had presented to her for her bedroom in Fort Lauderdale: three scenes of ballerinas in pink tutus, which she'd callously replaced with posters of New Kids on the Block. What she wouldn't give to have those long-lost paintings back.

A blank wall in the living room became a gallery wall of Alberto's bird paintings now, and in her bedroom she hung a trio of the Polynesian scenes he'd toiled over for weeks, one of a sarong-clad beauty in front of a grass hut, another of an outrigger canoe at sunset, and the third, her favorite, of a pair of palm trees with a glowing volcano in the background. Now, when she was lying in bed, looking out the window at the dunes and the beach beyond, she could also look at Papi's paintings, and remember the joy his hobby had given him.

Early that evening, she put on her swimsuit and walked out to the beach. She waded into the water and floated on her back for a while, then swam laps, back and forth, parallel to the shore, until the muscles in her arms and legs burned with fatigue. Her legs wobbled as she trod the sand back to the cottage to shower and change.

Standing in the shower, she found herself humming, then singing at the top of her lungs. For the first time since returning to Sunset Beach, she felt whole. She felt alive and glad to be where she was. And she was ready to find the answers to the questions that had been plaguing her since the day Yvonne Howington walked into the reception room at her father's law office.

Drue waited until nine o'clock to present herself at the front desk at the Silver Sands Motel. The place was a throwback to the 1950s, with a low-slung white stucco exterior topped with its exuberantly scripted neon-turquoise Silver Sands sign across the roof, and turquoise-striped awning overhanging the plate-glass doors to the lobby.

The clerk behind the front desk was dressed in a turquoise golf shirt with the hotel logo embroidered over the breast. He was the age Drue thought Jazmin Mayes's boyfriend might be, early to late twenties, with neatly groomed dark hair and mocha-colored skin.

"Hi," he said, looking up from a computer screen. "Welcome. How can I help you on this beautiful evening?"

"Jorge?" she asked.

His smile revealed deep dimples. No wonder Jazmin had fallen hard for this man.

"That's me. Do we know each other?"

She extended her hand. "I'm Drue Campbell. Jazmin Mayes's mother hired our law firm to find out the truth about what happened to Jazmin the night she was killed at the Gulf Vista Hotel and Resort."

The smile faded fast. He shook his head. "I'm sorry. I can't really help you. I left Gulf Vista a couple months before that happened."

"I know that," Drue said. "I've spoken to Detective Hernandez, the investigator from the Treasure Island Police Department. And I've spoken to one of Jazmin's friends who worked with her. They said you and Jazmin were dating pretty seriously."

"We were," he said. He looked around the lobby, which

was deserted. "Look, there isn't much I can tell you. And I'm working, so I can't really talk right now."

"When do you get to take a break?" Drue asked, not ready to give up now that she had Jorge Morales in her sights. "I can wait. Maybe you'd let me buy you a cup of coffee so we can talk?"

"There isn't much I can tell you," he repeated. "I was working here that night."

"I know. I checked. But I need to talk to everybody who knew Jazmin back then, who'd worked at the resort. Did you know that Jazmin's mother tried to sue the hotel for criminal negligence? The hotel claimed she was working that night, so my father had to settle it as a workers' comp case. The money will be in a trust for Aliyah, but it will only be a hundred and thirty-five thousand dollars, which Yvonne can't touch, not even for Aliyah's medical expenses."

"That's all?" Jorge's face registered his disgust. "You know, I tried to get Jaz to quit that place. The management, they didn't care about back-of-house staff. Jaz applied for a job here, but there weren't any openings at the time. And then . . . it was too late."

"That's the kind of thing I want to discuss with you," Drue said. "So, what about it? Can we talk when you take your break?"

"I guess. Can you come back around eleven?"

She winced. Tomorrow was a workday. "No sooner than that?"

He pulled up a screen on his computer and ran a finger

down the listings. "Looks like I only have one late check-in. It's pretty slow tonight." He slid a business card across the Formica countertop to her. "Call me in an hour. If it stays quiet, you can come back and we'll talk. Unless I get a check-in."

Remembering her mother's long-ago advice that it was always better to beg forgiveness than ask for permission, Drue bought two coffees at the Starbucks a few blocks away and arrived back at the Silver Sands thirty minutes later.

She waited while Jorge handed a packet of keys and a hotel brochure to a young couple with a sleeping infant draped over the mother's shoulder. When they'd headed out of the lobby, Drue presented him with the coffee.

"Is now a good time?"

"Okay," he relented. "Those folks were my late check-ins. The phones are quiet." He pointed across the lobby at a pair of armchairs. "We can talk over there."

Drue showed Jorge her cell phone. "I'm going to tape this, if that's okay with you."

"I have no problem with that," Jorge said. "But first, tell me about Aliyah. Is she okay?"

"I guess you know Yvonne is raising her?"

"I figured. You know, I only met Aliyah once or twice, and I never met Jaz's mom. I didn't want us to be a secret, but Jaz said her mom would never accept her dating a Latino." Jorge looked down at his hands. For the first time, Drue noticed he wore a gold wedding band.

He saw what she was looking at. "Yeah. I got married a

couple months ago. I actually met Melissa when she was staying here for her best friend's wedding, and we hit it off. Funny thing, she's got a daughter just about the same age as Aliyah."

"Jazmin would want you to be happy, wouldn't she?" Drue asked. It was a cliché, but she didn't know what else to say. Besides, clichés were usually true, right?

"I think so," he said. "Jaz was great. We had a lot of fun. Not many people knew she had a goofy side to her. She'd been through some rough stuff, you know? But she was smart. She took a couple classes at USF and made good grades. She was a good person."

"So I've heard," Drue said. "Jorge, did she ever tell you somebody at the hotel was sexually harassing her? An older white guy?"

"What? She never said anything about it to me. Where'd you hear that?"

"She told her mom that she'd complained to the management, but they never did anything about it."

"This is the first I'm hearing about it, but yeah, I can totally believe that. The atmosphere over there, it's not professional. At all."

"How do you mean?"

"The men who worked there? They were all the time making dirty comments about the females on the staff and the guests. I'm no prude, but it was pretty disgusting, if you ask me."

"Can you give me some examples?"

"Yeah. Like the head of security? His name is Shelnutt, and he's a piece of crap. He'd have what he called 'porn parties.' He was the one monitoring the security cameras around the property, and he'd make what he called his 'greatest hits' clips—you know, lots of tits and ass: chicks around the pool or on the beach who didn't have their bathing suit tops fastened, people in the hallways who'd come out half dressed, and his favorite, people getting it on in the elevators." He looked away, embarrassed. "I went to one of his parties once, to show I was one of the guys, but it was just gross. I made up some excuse and ducked out after about fifteen minutes and never went back."

"Is that why you left the Gulf Vista?"

"Not really. I was up for a managerial position, but they promoted somebody else, a white guy, who had less seniority and experience, over me. He didn't even have any college. I was fed up. I'd already put in applications at some other hotels out here, and when the Silver Sands called, I went like a shot. You know, if Jaz had left when I did, maybe she'd still be alive. I think about that a lot."

"When was the last time you saw her?"

He sipped his coffee. "Let me think. I know the cops asked me that, but it's been so long. Lots of nights, we'd go out after she got off her shift, if our schedules worked out okay. Sometimes, I'd get us a room here, so we could be together, and then she'd go home, like around two in the morning, because her mom had to get to work, and Jaz was the one to take Aliyah to school."

"According to the hotel, the day she was killed, Jaz's car broke down on the way to work."

He nodded. "Yeah, that Kia was a hunk of junk. But it was all she could afford."

"She called her mom and told her she was going to have the

car towed to a garage, and then she took a cab and got to the hotel more than an hour late."

"I bet Byars reamed her ass out," Jorge said.

"That's the head of housekeeping?"

"That's him. Total jerk. He was always at Shelnutt's little parties."

"Could he have been the one who was coming on to Jazmin?"

"Absolutely. Another piece of crap."

"Did you know Larry Boone? One of the other housekeepers told me he grabbed her and propositioned her more than once."

"Scary Larry, that's what the girls called him," Jorge affirmed. "When Shelnutt wanted to have one of his little parties, Larry Boone, who was head of engineering, would put a room 'out of order' so the front desk wouldn't rent it to guests. That's where the parties would be."

"Back to the night she was killed. Byars told the cops that Jazmin asked to work an additional shift, because she'd gotten to work late. Do you think that's true?"

"I never knew her to work an overnight shift," Jorge said. "She and Aliyah lived with her mom, and the mom had to get to work in the morning. That's why she never stayed overnight with me, and always went home, even though I didn't like her driving home alone late at night like that. That neighborhood she lived in is kinda rough."

"One of the other housekeepers told me that Jaz's best friend was another housekeeper. Neesa? Did you know her?"

"Kinda."

"What's that mean?" Drue asked.

"I know she and Jaz were tight, but I wasn't really a fan."

"Why's that?"

He toyed with the paper band around his coffee cup. "I thought she was a bad influence. This will maybe sound racist, coming from somebody like me, but I can't help it. Neesa was pretty ghetto."

"How so?"

"The way she acted. She was all about the partying. She'd get high at work. Like a lot. And I could never prove anything, but I think maybe she was into some other bad stuff. Jaz mentioned it one time, that Neesa wanted her to get in on something, but Jaz wouldn't. You know Jaz got busted for shoplifting when she was in high school, and she had some weed on her. She told me she got in with the wrong crowd back then, and she wasn't going to make that mistake again. She wanted to be a good mom for Aliyah. That kid was everything to her."

"What kind of stuff do you think Neesa was into?"

He shrugged. "Who knows? She was Jaz's friend, not mine."

"She was working the night Jazmin was killed, according to the police reports. She left the hotel ten days after the murder. I'd really like to talk to Neesa. Do you know where she is?"

He checked his watch. "Right now? Probably doing Jäger-bombs at Mister B's."

"That's a bar?"

"In Seminole. I met her and Jaz there a couple times. Loud country music and kind of a rough crowd."

Drue pulled up the blurry photo of Neesa and Jaz that she'd found on Jazmin's Facebook page. "This is Neesa, right? It's the only photo I could find of her."

"I've got a better one," Jorge said. He scrolled through the photos on his phone, then held it up for Drue to see.

It was a selfie of Jazmin and another young black woman. Their faces were pressed close together, and they were captured mid-laugh. Neesa's complexion was two shades lighter than Jazmin's, and she had a nose with a slight hook. While Jazmin's hair was worn short and natural, Neesa's was an elaborate architectural feat.

"This is her." He tapped the photo. "She's really good with hair, with the braids and whatever you call it."

"Great." Drue handed the phone back. "Now I'll know her when I see her." She handed Jorge her business card. "If you can think of anything else I might need to know about Jazmin, I'd appreciate a call."

"You've got my card too," he reminded her. "Can you let me know what you find out? Like, if the police catch who did that to her? I'm still so sad, you know? Jaz, she was just getting her life together. We had plans . . ."

38

Mister B's was loud and crowded, with men in Wrangler jeans, cowboy boots and ten-gallon hats who outnumbered the women three to one. The hot, damp air smelled overpoweringly like Axe aftershave. Drue elbowed her way through the hordes of boot-scooting boogiers to the bar, which was also stacked two deep.

After five minutes, she was able to inch close enough to catch the attention of a bartender. He was tan and muscled and bare-chested, with a pierced nipple. The bolo tie around his neck was fastened with a chunky turquoise and silver clasp.

"Howdy." He tipped his straw Stetson. "Whatcha drinking tonight? Can I get you started with our drink special? A Mango Tango?"

"God no," she said, shuddering. "Just a vodka tonic. Double lime, please."

While he turned to fix her drink, Drue scanned the length of the bar. A similarly dressed bartender worked the other end. She had long blond braids laced with feathers and beads, and wore a midriff-tied cowboy shirt with jean shorts cut high and tight, exposing an impressive amount of tanned butt cheeks.

Customers had seemingly self-segregated, with the men on the far end, ogling the blonde, and a large number of women clustered at what Drue had already started thinking of as the Roy Rogers end of the bar. If Roy had a pierced nipple and a tattoo of a coiled rattlesnake on his right biceps.

She was surprised at how racially diverse the crowd was. Was country music that universally appealing? Drue wasn't sure.

The bartender was back with her drink. She thanked him and leaned across the bar. "Hey, do you happen to know a woman named Neesa? I think she comes here a lot? Likes Jägerbombs?"

"I don't," he said. "But I just started here this week. Want me to go ask Coco?" He pointed down the bar at the blonde.

She gave him her most dazzling smile. "That'd be awesome."

A moment later, he was back. "That's her," he said, nodding in the direction of a black woman who'd positioned herself on a bar stool at the corner of the bar that angled back toward the bathrooms.

Drue had a five-dollar bill ready, and she pushed it across the bar top toward him.

She sipped her drink and surreptitiously watched the woman, whom she'd never have recognized from the photo Jorge had shown her.

Instead of the elaborate crown of braids and beaded extensions the other Neesa had worn, this one had a chin-length platinum blond pageboy. She wore a low-cut yellow tank top and shoulder-length gold hoop earrings. She was chatting with another woman, but her eyes seemed to constantly scan the crowd. When her head swung in Drue's direction, Drue quickly turned away, leaving her back toward the woman. A moment later, Neesa was engrossed in conversation with a tall Hispanic-looking man, fluttering dramatic false eyelashes and gesturing with long acrylic nails painted neon pink.

The man motioned for the bartender, who brought a new round of drinks. Soon his arm was draped across Neesa's shoulder, his hand resting lightly atop her breast.

Drue nursed her drink slowly. Twenty minutes passed. Roy Rogers returned. "Get you another?" He pointed to Drue's drink, the ice now melted. She didn't want another drink. What she wanted was to talk to Neesa about Jazmin Mayes and then get the hell out of here. She glanced toward the end of the bar. Neesa's new friend was handing her a bottle of Jägermeister, which Neesa upended into her open mouth. The man laughed uproariously, leaned down and stuck his tongue down her throat. Another man approached and tugged at his arm. Neesa's boyfriend tossed some bills on the bar and walked away, leaving Neesa pouting with only an empty liquor bottle for company.

"Maybe just a club soda with double lime?" she told Roy Rogers. She didn't dare order another drink. It was a long drive back to Sunset Beach, and the last thing she needed was to get pulled over for DUI.

She was sipping her drink and plotting her next move when the decision was made for her.

"Hey." Neesa plopped down on the bar stool that had just been vacated. She poked Drue's arm with a long tapered fingernail. "Girl, I seen you staring at me down there. Do we know each other?"

Neesa's eyes were glassy, her words slightly slurred. From her long career working in bars, Drue concluded the girl was, clinically speaking, shit-faced. Drunk and, most likely, high.

"I don't think so," Drue said. "I was fascinated with your hair. It's really pretty. Do you color it yourself?"

Neesa's laugh was a throaty bray. "Nah, girl. This here is a wig." She lifted the bangs away from her forehead, just enough to reveal that her own hair was snugged against her scalp with a tight nylon skullcap.

"Oh wow. I wish I could pull off something like that. My hair is so boring."

Neesa grabbed a strand of Drue's long dark hair and examined it critically. "You got nice hair. Good texture. You could definitely go lighter. But don't be trying none of that stuff out of a box. I could totally take you all the way blond."

"Are you a hairdresser?"

The bartender was back, looking hopeful. "Get you ladies something else?"

"I'll have another," Drue said, seizing the opportunity. "And you can bring my friend here whatever she's drinking."

"Ooh. Thanks," Neesa said. "I'mma change it up and just have a Kahlúa and coffee."

She watched the bartender as he worked at the back bar. "He's so fine," she said, a little too loudly. "I do like a white boy with a good ass. How 'bout you?"

Drue almost choked on her club soda. "Same," she said finally. "So, did you say you're a hairdresser?"

"Cosmetology student," Neesa said. "I been doing hair since I was twelve. Soon as I get my license, I'm gonna open my own salon. Hair, nails, eyelashes, all of it. How 'bout you?"

Drue made a face. "I work for my dad. Nothing very exciting. What'd you do before you started cosmetology school?"

"You know. Whatever. I was working at a dry cleaner's, but me and the owner didn't see eye to eye. Before that, I worked at a hotel, out at Sunset Beach."

"I live at the beach," Drue said. "Which hotel?"

"Gulf Vista. You know the place?"

"It's right down the street from my place," Drue said. She'd been waiting for this moment, hoping for an opening. "Hey, isn't that where that girl was killed a couple years ago?"

Neesa toyed with a tiny gold cross that hung from a thin chain around her neck. "Mmm-hmm. That was my friend. Jazmin. Real sad."

"I'm so sorry," Drue said. "I lost my best friend in April."

Not exactly a lie. Her mother really was her best friend.

"Ooh. I'm sorry. What happened to her?" Neesa asked.

"Hit-and-run accident," Drue lied. "She died on the way to the hospital."

"That's terrible," Neesa said indignantly. "Did they ever catch the guy?"

Drue shook her head sadly, silently begging her mother's forgiveness.

"No. Did they ever find out who killed your friend?"

Neesa stared down into her drink. "No. It was probably some freak. You get a lot of freaks staying in hotels, you know."

"What kind of work did you do at the hotel?" Drue asked.

"I was a housekeeper. Jazmin was too. That's how we met. I miss that girl, you know? I mean, we fussed at each other sometimes, but ain't nobody could stay mad with that girl for long. Jaz, she had a way about her. Always laughing and cutting up."

"She sounds like she was fun," Drue said.

"Mmm-hmm." Neesa tossed back half of her drink, leaving faint traces of the creamy Kahlúa on her vividly painted lips, which she dabbed with her fingertip. "You know, I was working that night."

"The night she was killed?" Drue tried to sound uninterested, but wasn't sure she could pull it off.

"We always took our dinner breaks together, if we could. We met up that night, I guess it was around seven. So hot that night. September, you know? Neither of us felt like eating, so we just got a couple of Dr Peppers from the Coke machine and sat around talking, until it was time to get back to work."

"Was that the last time you saw her alive?"

"Yeah," Neesa said. She drained the rest of her glass, then suddenly stood up, grasping the edge of the bar with both hands to steady herself. "I gotta go. Got class tomorrow morning, and we're doing razor cuts."

She swayed a little, then sat back down abruptly. "Whoa. Cowboy mighta made that last drink a little stout." She dug in her pocketbook and brought out her phone.

"How are you getting home?" Drue asked. "You're not driving, right?"

Neesa looked around the crowded bar. "I thought I had me a ride home, but looks like his friend made him leave already. Guess I'll see about a cab."

"Where do you live?" Drue asked quickly. "I can give you a ride. I was just about to leave, myself."

"Down the road a ways," Neesa said. "You sure you don't mind?"

"Positive."

It had started to rain while they were inside Mister B's. Neesa stood next to Drue with shoulders hunched under the shelter of the club's covered entryway, looking up at the sky. "Girl, I hope the rain don't mess up this wig. I kinda borrowed it from school."

"I'll go get my car and pick you up," Drue said. "Stay here and I'll be right back."

Her bad knee protested as she sprinted through the deepening puddles in the parking lot, but she didn't care. She found OJ, jumped in the driver's seat and pulled out the ashtray, where she carefully positioned her cell phone. Then she drove through the downpour to the club's entry, blinking her headlights to let her passenger know her ride had arrived.

Drue watched while Neesa wobbled toward the Bronco, teetering precariously atop her spike-heeled metal-studded boots. As Neesa approached, Drue tapped the Record button on the phone and slid the ashtray back into the dashboard.

"Where to?" she asked, as they pulled out of the parking lot.

Neesa yawned widely. "Straight down this road for ten miles, then when you get to the Walmart shopping center, take a left at the light. My complex is behind there." She leaned back in the seat, her neck lolling against the headrest.

Drue was afraid the other woman was about to nod off.

"What's it like, working in a big hotel?" she blurted. "Do the guests, like, hit on you? Stuff like that?"

"Sometimes, but really, it's more like the men who work there," Neesa said, her eyes closed. "They're all pigs."

"Like who?"

"The bosses," Neesa said. "Head of housekeeping, head of security, the guys in engineering, you name it, everybody with a dick and a name badge."

"That's awful," Drue said, acting shocked. "Do you think one of them hurt your friend?"

"I don't think it. I know it."

"Did your friend Jazmin—is that her name?—did she tell you that was going on?"

"She didn't have to. I seen it. This one time, I was waiting on the service elevator and the doors opened, and he had Jaz backed into a corner, had his hands down in her pants. As soon as he saw me standing there, he gave me this look and punched the button to close the doors."

"Gross. Who was the guy?"

"Head of housekeeping. His name was Herman. Like Herman Munster, you know? Nasty old piece of shit."

"Oh wow. Did she report him?"

"Jaz? No."

"Did she talk to you about it?"

"Kind of."

"What did she say?"

Neesa yawned again. Her eyes were closed and her breathing had slowed. Drue was afraid she was about to pass out.

"Huh?" Neesa blinked awake. "Who?"

"Your friend. Jazmin. What did she say about the guy who was groping her?"

"Just that he'd been watchin' her, saying things when they were alone, like how nice she looked. And sex stuff. She didn't like it, but what was she supposed to do? He was our boss."

"She never reported him?"

"Hell no. She did what she had to do."

"Which was what?"

Neesa stared and shook her head dismissively. "Forget it. Girl like you? You'd never understand."

"Don't kid yourself," Drue said, with genuine venom in her voice. "I waitressed in beach bars for years. Had bosses peeking at me through cracks in the bathroom door while I was peeing, putting their hands on me while I had a full tray of dishes, sharing all their sex fantasies . . . I felt dirty and disgusted with myself for putting up with it, but like you said, I had bills to pay."

"Huh," Neesa said. "Okay. Maybe you are for real. So yeah. We played the bosses." She affected a flirtatious wink and a breathless voice. "'Oh, you want to feel me up in the elevator when nobody's looking? Okay, but then you better let me off work when I gotta take my sick kid to the doctor.' Or, 'Oh, you want me to come in your office with the door closed and give you a lap dance? All right, but there better be something extra in my paycheck next week.'"

"So, she was, like, blackmailing her boss?"

"That's what you call it. Jaz, she just made sure he treated her right, that's all."

"And she never complained to the hotel manager?"

"I guess she could have, but why wouldn't she tell me? I was her best friend."

"Maybe she didn't want to get you involved?"

Neesa fumbled around in her purse. "You got any smokes?"

"Sorry, I quit."

"Good for you," Neesa said. "Jaz used to *stay* on me about quitting . . ." Her voice trailed off.

"When the cops were investigating your friend's murder, did you tell them about this boss and his arrangement with her?"

"They didn't ask." Neesa nibbled on a bit of ragged cuticle.

"They didn't? For real? How stupid can you be?"

Neesa's eyes were closed again. "Even if they had asked, I wouldn't have told them nothing."

"Why not?"

"I needed that job," Neesa said wearily. "Herman was my boss too. He could hire me, fire me, pay me overtime, give me a better shift, let me clock in whenever I wanted. And if I'd said no, he'd give me a shitty reference so I couldn't get another job."

"That's always the way, right? So, did you have the same kind of arrangement with Herman that your friend had?"

"Not quite." Neesa glanced over at Drue. "I don't know why I'm telling you all this stuff. I don't know you from Jack."

"Who am I gonna tell?" Drue said lightly. "I don't know you either. I don't even know your name. Pretend I'm a shrink."

"True," Neesa said. "This is the first time I've talked about any of this stuff, ever. But what the hell? It all happened a long time ago. Nobody except me even remembers Jazmin's name anymore. You asked if I had the same deal with Herman that Jaz had? The answer is no. My deal was different."

"How so?"

Neesa took a deep breath. "See, I screwed up."

She abruptly dumped the contents of her purse into her lap and pawed through the jumble of detritus. She held up a crumpled pack of Newports. "Damn it. I coulda swore I had one left."

"You want me to stop at a gas station so you can buy some?" Drue asked. She detested smoking, had forbidden Trey and others from lighting up in OJ, but this one time she was willing to make a sacrifice, if it would keep Neesa Vincent talking.

"That's okay. I got a carton at home."

"Thank God for that, right?" Drue said lightly. Her new friend's apartment complex couldn't be that far away. She had to get her back on track again. "So, how'd you screw up at work?"

Neesa toyed with a plastic cigarette lighter, turning it over and over between her long, curving fingernails. "There was an incident, with a guest, and Herman found out about it, and he fixed things. So then I owed him."

Drue looked down at the cell phone, trying to remember how much battery life it had. She prayed it was still recording. "What kind of incident?"

"Some money went missing from a guest's room. There was a car dealers' convention that week, and those men were *all* rolling in money. This one dude, he checked out early, and I was cleaning his room, and I found a wad of bills. Like, hundred-dollar bills, in the pocket of the bathrobe. You know, the ones the hotel puts in guest rooms?"

"So you kept the money. Totally understandable," Drue said.

"Yeah. The dude was drunk when he checked in and he stayed drunk the whole time. And disgusting. You wouldn't believe the things people do in hotel rooms. He messed himself in the sheets, puked in a trash can and left it for me to clean up. And didn't even leave a damn tip. Like, at all. So when I found that money, I tipped myself. Just a hundred-dollar bill. Which I earned, right?"

"Damn straight," Drue agreed. "But what? You got caught?"

"Yeah," Neesa said bitterly. "The guest called the front desk and said he'd left eight hundred dollars in the bathrobe, and he'd better get it back or he'd call the cops. The security chief called Herman in and Herman called his bluff. Said one of the housekeepers had turned in five hundred dollars and the guest must be mistaken, because he was drunk."

Drue couldn't help asking, "What happened to the missing money? Did you get to keep it?"

"I got the hundred bucks and he got the rest. And a couple weeks later, Herman got laid." Neesa stared out the window at the rain streaming down the passenger window. "He has a room at the hotel for when he works late."

"That sucks," Drue said, meaning it. She could see the lights of a shopping center a couple blocks ahead. She needed to cut to the chase before she ran out of time with her edgy passenger. She took a deep breath and just went for it. "Do you think this Herman guy could have been the one who killed Jazmin?"

Neesa suddenly sat up straight, knocking her keys and cell phone in her lap to the floor of the Bronco. "You ask a lot of questions, you know that?"

Drue tried to calm herself in order to calm her passenger, who was now fumbling around, trying to retrieve her belongings.

"Sorry. I guess I sympathize with you and your friend, having to put up with sexual predators like this Herman guy. Men like him, they see girls like us, girls working as housekeepers, waitresses, cashiers, and they don't see us as real people. We're just a piece of meat to them."

"I know that's right," Neesa said, sighing. "We got no power, so what's to stop these dudes from doing whatever they want to us?" She pointed to the fast-approaching shopping center half a block away. "That's the Walmart up ahead. Hang a left there, then make a quick right."

The apartment complex was called Sherlock Forest, but the only trees Drue saw were tall, skinny pines. Neesa directed her to a two-story building with brown cedar siding. "That's me," she said.

Drue pulled up in front of the building.

Neesa plucked the wig from her head, tucked it into her purse, then swung the passenger-side door open. "Thanks for the ride, girl," she said. "And hey, if you do decide to go blond, give me a call. I'll hook you up."

"I'll definitely do that," Drue said. "But how do I find you?"

Neesa reached into her pocketbook. "That's right. I never did tell you my name." She handed Drue a hot-pink business card. "I'm Neesa Vincent. Salon Neesa. That's what my place is gonna be called."

Drue waited while Neesa ran through the rain to the door of a ground-floor apartment, unlocked it and disappeared inside. Then she drove around the corner, put the Bronco in park and reached for her cell phone. Her power level was at five percent. She plugged it into the charger and drove home to Sunset Beach through the rain.

39

When Drue arrived at work on Thursday morning, a yellow Post-it note was attached to the computer screen on her desk: *GEOFF TAKING PERSONAL LEAVE DAY. YOU'RE WORKING RECEPTION THIS MORNING—WENDY.*

"Damn it." She'd deliberately arrived fifteen minutes early, hoping to get time to take another look at the video from the Gulf Vista. But she dutifully donned her office sweater, picked up her headset and went out to the lobby. No sooner was she seated than the front door opened. A tall, imposing black man swept inside.

He was dressed in a vaguely Egyptian-looking ensemble— floor-length gold lamé gown, a homemade cardboard breastplate studded with red bicycle reflectors, and a headpiece made from a woman's striped chiffon scarf wound around his head. The man planted his feet firmly apart, staring at the ceiling and the walls, before finally leveling his gaze toward the woman at the reception desk. He crossed his arms over the breastplate, and she noticed that he had shiny brass serpent-shaped bracelets around his biceps.

"Can I help you?" Drue asked.

His voice was booming. "Brice Campbell. I am here to see Brice Campbell."

"He's not in the office at the moment," Drue said. "Do you have an appointment?"

"Brice Campbell is my attorney," the man said.

Drue smiled nervously, hoping the visitor was harmless.

She placed her fingers on the computer's keyboard. "Are you in our client database?"

"Of course. Brice Campbell is my attorney. My name is Kaa."

She looked up quizzically. "How is that spelled? And is that your first or last name?"

"Kaa. Only Kaa."

"Let me just call Mr. Campbell's assistant to see when he's expected."

She swiveled her chair around, leaving her back to the visitor, and buzzed Wendy's office.

"What is it?"

"Mr. Campbell's client Mr. Kaa is out here in the reception area, and he'd like to see Mr. Campbell."

"Kaa?" Wendy sounded puzzled. "That's not a name I recognize. Get his full name and phone number and ask him what it's in reference to. Tell him we'll get back to him later."

Drue shielded the receiver with one hand and whispered, "He's, uh, dressed as a pharaoh or something."

"Not him again," Wendy said. "Get rid of him."

"How?"

"I don't know. Drive a spike through his heart or something. He's a kook."

"I see that," Drue whispered. "Also, I think that only works on vampires."

"I'm on my way," Wendy snapped.

Kaa had seated himself and was leafing through the latest issue of *Modern Maturity* when the door from the back hallway opened and Wendy entered.

"Mr. Kaa?"

"Yes?" He ripped a page from the magazine, folded it in half and stood up. "When do I see Mr. Campbell? My issue is still unresolved."

"Still? I thought you'd seen a doctor about that problem."

"That doctor was an incompetent quack." Kaa gestured at the front of his robe, where Drue now noticed an impressive bulge. Her lips twitched as she turned away, trying to stifle a giggle.

"I don't know what to tell you," Wendy said, her composure intact. "Your accident was three years ago, as I recall, and your case was settled. We referred you to the best urologist in town."

"And yet this persists." Kaa thrust his pelvis forward and Wendy instinctively jumped backward.

"I see that," Wendy said, quickly losing, then regaining her composure. "I'm sure that must be, uh, socially awkward. I promise I'll have Brice look into the matter and get back with you as soon as possible."

Drue didn't dare look up. She found a tissue in the box and coughed into it.

"I will be back tomorrow. And the day after that too, unless something is done," Kaa said, striding out of the office.

When he'd gone, Wendy looked over at Drue. "He was in a construction accident. Fell two stories from an improperly erected scaffolding, and his fall was broken by a cement mixer. He had broken ribs, broken pelvis and a head injury. Before the accident his name was Grady Lee. Afterwards, he started dressing up like that, and he had his name legally changed to Kaa. Brice sued and got him a decent settlement."

"About that improperly erected thing?" Drue fell into another fit of giggles.

Wendy's placid face crumpled and she began to snigger, which turned into guffaws. "Oh my God," she cried, swiping at the tears running down her face. "I can't even . . ."

"So . . . uh, what causes his condition?" Drue asked, handing Wendy a tissue.

"Damned if I know," Wendy said, sinking down onto an armchair. "He keeps showing up at the urologist's office, with that . . . thing. Last week, their office manager threatened to call the police and have him charged with indecent exposure. He's been back to the neurologist's office too. Same story. Nobody knows what to do about it."

"Find him a concubine?" Drue suggested.

Wendy burst out laughing again, but suddenly stopped. "Oh God," she gasped.

"What?" Drue stood up, alarmed. "Is something wrong?"

"I think I just peed my pants," Wendy said. "And it's your fault."

~

The phones began ringing and didn't stop for the next four hours. It was nearly one when Marianne appeared and announced that she would take over the reception desk for the rest of the day. "Wendy says you should go to lunch," Marianne said.

Ben was sitting at a table in the break room, typing furiously on his laptop, but he stopped abruptly when Drue joined him at the table, and closed the lid.

"You don't have to stop working just because of me," she said, unwrapping her turkey sandwich.

"It's okay. I'm done." He tore open a bag of chips resting alongside his own half-eaten sandwich.

"What are you working on?" she asked. "If it's not top secret."

"Nothing," he said, flushing. "Just a kind of side hustle."

"Lucky you," Drue said. "Wish I had a side hustle."

"I thought you did," Ben said. "The Jazmin Mayes thing? Anything interesting going on with that?"

Drue smiled enigmatically.

"I'll show you mine if you'll show me yours."

Ben raised an eyebrow.

"Get your mind out of the gutter," she said. "I'm talking side hustles."

He hesitated, nervously tapping his fingertips on the lid of the laptop.

"Okay," he relented. "It's a video game. But you've got to swear you won't tell anybody."

"That's it? You're playing video games on your lunch hour? Sorry, but that's not exactly classified information, Ben."

"It's *my* video game," he said, puffing up slightly. "I've been working on it for the past two and a half years and now I'm *this* close to taking it to market."

"Good for you," Drue said. "I hope it sells a million copies."

"It better," he said. "Now it's your turn. Tell me what's happening with your secret project?"

"As a matter of fact, there's a lot going on," Drue said, trying to subdue a yawn. "Last night I tracked down Jazmin's former boyfriend, who had some interesting things to say about some 'porn parties' the hotel's head of security used to throw."

"Gross," Ben said, popping a potato chip in his mouth. "But what's that got to do with Jazmin's murder?"

"I'm getting to that," Drue said. "Did I tell you that I talked to one of the police detectives who's worked on the case since day one?"

"No."

"Yeah. I did. She says that Jazmin's murder wasn't just some random stranger-on-stranger thing. Rae says it was violent and it was personal, and she's sure it was a man. A man who knew Jazmin."

"Rae?"

"Detective Hernandez. She also told me that Gulf Vista's management deliberately obstructed their investigation, right from the start, and maybe even tampered with the murder scene."

"Interesting," Ben acknowledged.

"It gets better. I also managed to track down Jazmin's best friend, another housekeeper who was working with her the night she was killed." She uncapped a bottle of water and drank. "Neesa, that's Jazmin's friend, told me some really nasty stuff was going on with the guy who was head of housekeeping. At first, they put up with his sexual harassment because they couldn't afford to lose their jobs, but eventually, she said, both she and Jazmin traded sexual favors for 'bonuses' and time off."

"So, what? You think this Herman guy maybe killed her? Why? I mean, if she was doing what he wanted, why'd he want to spoil a good thing?"

Ben wiped his fingers on a paper napkin, which he balled up and tossed in the direction of the trash can.

"Swoosh," he said, when he landed the basket. He turned back to Drue. "What's it got to do with the mom's lawsuit? I mean, even if this guy did kill your girl Jazmin, it still doesn't get her mother any more money from the hotel. Right? It happened at work. The hotel has video of her working."

"She's not 'my girl Jazmin,'" Drue said, feeling the blood rise in her cheeks. "She was a person, Ben, and she didn't deserve to die like she did. She was working and taking college classes and trying to be a good mom. And you're right, none of this guarantees more money for Yvonne Howington. But maybe knowing who did it and why is almost as good as money. Maybe it means a sick bastard gets locked up for the rest of his life, and doesn't get to prey on women anymore."

"You know what Brice would say about all this, right?" Ben asked.

"Put up or shut up?"

"That too. But mostly he'd point out that's a lot of 'maybes.'"

The break room door opened and Marianne stuck her head inside. "Drue? Wendy needs you right away."

40

Wendy was lying on the sofa in her office. "Close the door," she told Drue. "Please."

The office manager's face was pale, and she had her legs propped up on a stack of cushions. She wore a chic turquoise A-line dress, the first actual maternity dress Drue had seen her in, but she'd kicked off her spike-heeled Manolo Blahniks.

"Are you all right?" Drue asked.

"Not sure," Wendy said, her voice shaky. "I've started spotting."

Drue sank down onto the floor beside the sofa. "What do you want me to do? Should I call Dad? Or an ambulance?"

"No! Don't call anybody. Your dad is in court, and I don't want him to freak out. And I sure as hell don't want an ambulance. I called my obstetrician's office. The nurse says a little spotting isn't anything to be concerned about."

"What's a little?" Drue asked now, feeling slightly freaked

out herself. Until her mother's illness, she'd never really been around sick people. She'd felt so helpless during Sherri's swift decline, powerless to stop the relentless advance of the cancer. She swallowed back a sudden spasm of anxiety-triggered nausea.

"It's just . . . spots," Wendy said. "The point is, the nurse says I probably need to go home and get some rest. Brice drove us to work this morning, so . . ."

"I'll take you home," Drue said quickly. "Can you walk?"

"Don't be so dramatic. I'm not dying." Wendy swung her feet onto the floor and slipped on her shoes and grabbed her Louis Vuitton tote.

"Let's go," she told Drue. "And not a word about this to the rest of the staff."

As they passed through the reception area, Wendy paused beside the reception desk, waiting while Marianne completed a phone call.

"Drue and I are going out to lunch, and then doing some shopping," she said. "Her phone line will be off-line for the rest of the day. Tell any of my callers that I'll be back in the office in the morning, but do *not* forward any calls to me, unless it's life and death."

Marianne looked astounded. "You're going to lunch, *together*?"

"Girl time," Drue said lightly, tucking her arm through Wendy's.

On the twenty-minute drive out to Brice and Wendy's house at the beach, Drue kept surreptitiously glancing at her passenger.

"Would you quit it?" Wendy said finally. "I told you. I'm fine. I just saw my doctor. I'm not hemorrhaging and I'm not going to have the baby in the front seat of your car."

"Well, that's a relief," Drue said. "I wouldn't want to mar OJ's pristine upholstery or anything."

Wendy looked around the car with obvious distaste, taking in the discarded water bottles and fast-food wrappers on the floor, and the cracked and peeling vinyl dashboard and seats.

"How old is this car anyway?"

"Not all that old," Drue said. "How do you feel?"

"Will you stop?" Wendy said. "I'm only pregnant. I'm not dying."

"Great," Drue said, "because I was just thinking about how Dad will never forgive me and totally blame me for the rest of my life if anything goes wrong with you and this baby."

Wendy gave a weak smile. "Yeah, he is pretty over-the-top about this whole baby thing. I had no idea how emotional he'd get. He's driving me crazy, treating me like I'm some kind of fragile bone-china teacup."

"Well, you are the vessel carrying his son and namesake," Drue pointed out.

"This all must seem pretty absurd to you."

"Doesn't matter what I think," Drue said. "If you two are happy about the baby, I'm glad for you."

"Seriously? You're not jealous? Not even a little bit? I know you and Brice didn't have a very good relationship, back in the day."

Drue shrugged. "It's true we didn't have the typical daddy-daughter relationship. But I wasn't the only kid in the world growing up with divorced parents. And yeah, he wasn't really involved in my life most of the time, but I'm fine with that. I'm not one of these people who want to gaze at my navel and talk about my toxic childhood. Shit happens. You go through it, and then you get over it."

Wendy stared out the window, her long red hair obscuring Drue's view of her face. "Sometimes you don't ever get over stuff. You know, my dad died not long after Brice and I got married. He never forgave me, wouldn't even come to our wedding."

"He didn't approve of the age difference?" Drue asked.

"Among other things," Wendy said. "His loss, not mine." She started to say something, but shook her head.

"What?" Drue asked.

"I guess I've had forgiveness on my mind a lot lately," Wendy said. She looked straight at Drue.

"I've been pretty shitty to you, haven't I?"

"Yeah. You have. We were friends once, until you decided we were frenemies. I was a kid back then, going through a lot of shit, and when you dumped me, it hurt. I was devastated."

"I know," Wendy said softly. "I should have handled it differently. I should have stood up to my dad and admitted that the Disney trip was my idea. I was too chicken."

"He was kind of a bully, your dad, right?" Drue asked.

Wendy's eyes filled with tears. She nodded. "Maybe that's why I fell for Brice all those years later. Because he was the opposite of my dad."

"Daddy complex?" Drue raised one eyebrow.

"No," Wendy said firmly. "Brice is a good guy, Drue. You'll probably never know just how good."

She grimaced slightly and pressed her hands on her abdomen.

"What? What is it?" Drue asked.

"Just a little cramping," Wendy said. "It started when we got in the car. It's probably nothing. Just take me home."

"No way," Drue said. She signaled and made a quick right turn into a shopping center parking lot. "You're either going to your obstetrician's office or the emergency room. Which is it?"

Wendy sighed heavily. "Okay, maybe you're right. Dr. Dillard's office is right next to St. Anthony's."

She closed her eyes and her face contorted again. She took her phone from her purse. "I'll call to let them know I'm coming in. Happy?"

"Delirious," Drue said. She pulled back into traffic. "Can you put the address in your phone so I can get directions? I don't want to get lost."

After several minutes had passed, Drue pulled into the parking lot of the midrise office building that Wendy pointed out. "Her office is on the fourth floor."

Her face contorted again and she gasped and grabbed Drue's arm. "Another cramp."

Drue's heart was pounding in her chest. She couldn't think straight. "What should I do? Can you walk?"

Wendy nodded. "I think so." She clutched Drue's arm tighter. "I'm scared," she whispered.

Drue pulled up to the curb, put the Bronco in park and jumped out. "Me too."

A uniformed security guard marched up, his hand extended

like a stop sign. "Ma'am? Did you see the yellow curb? This is a no-parking zone. You can't—"

"Fuck off," Drue said, opening the passenger door and taking Wendy's hand. "This woman is four months pregnant and she's having contractions. I'm taking her in to Dr. Dillard's office. Unless you want her to bleed to death right here on your yellow curb?"

She dropped the keys into the speechless guard's outstretched hand. "Just park it somewhere, okay?"

Wendy didn't speak again until they were in the elevator. She was still clinging to Drue's arm and leaning heavily against her. "They're probably not contractions and I wasn't going to bleed to death," she said.

"He didn't know that. And neither did I," Drue replied. Her hands were shaking as she watched the lighted numbers on the control panel change during their agonizingly slow ascent. "Who puts an obstetrician's office on the fourth floor?" she demanded. "How many babies have been delivered in this thing?"

Drue had never been good at waiting, especially in spaces that were dubbed waiting rooms, which, for her, had an unfortunate association with all the hours she'd spent in rooms like this one during Sherri's final weeks of illness.

"Hi," she said, approaching the reception desk. "I brought Wendy Campbell in about thirty minutes ago? Can you tell me what's going on?"

The clerk looked up from her computer screen. "Sorry. Patient privacy regulations."

Drue leaned across the high polished wooden countertop. "I'm not some random stranger. Mrs. Campbell is my stepmother, and I'm really concerned about her and the baby. Look, you don't have to say anything. Just nod yes or no. Is she okay?"

The clerk glanced around, then, pursing her lips, gave an almost imperceptible nod.

"Good," Drue said. "Thanks."

Brice rushed into the waiting room fifteen minutes later.

"Dad." Drue jumped up.

"Where is she?" Brice asked. "How is she?"

"In with the doctor. They won't tell me anything."

She'd skimmed the pages of a year's worth of *Parents* magazine and was starting to have strong opinions on co-sleeping, toilet training and caring for cracked nipples when the door to the back office finally opened an hour later and Brice emerged with Wendy on his arm.

"She's fine," Brice said, before Drue had a chance to ask. "The baby's fine too."

Wendy offered her a wan smile. "See? Crisis averted."

"The doctor says it's premature labor," Brice said. "Not that unusual in a higher-risk pregnancy."

"The baby's heartbeat is strong, and he's perfect," Wendy added.

"So what happens now?" Drue asked, following them out

into the hallway. "I mean, how do you stop a baby from coming?"

"Bed rest," Brice said. "I'm taking her home now."

"Do you want me to come too? I could, I don't know, hang out or boil water or whatever."

"No," Wendy and Brice said in unison.

"But thanks," Wendy said, softening. "I'm just going to go to bed and hibernate for a while."

"And I'm going to stick around and watch her for the rest of the day," Brice added. He threw his free arm around his daughter. "Come on now, close it up. Family hugs. Right?"

Wendy nodded and extended her arm to Drue with a questioning look. "Total family hugs," Drue said, closing the circle.

41

Drue was too shaken to return to work after leaving the doctor's office. She called Marianne and told her she intended to take the rest of the day off.

"How's Wendy?" she asked. "Your dad said she's not coming back to work for a while?"

"She and the baby seem to be fine," Drue said. "I'll see you tomorrow."

Drue's cell phone pinged while she was stopped at a light on Central Avenue. The text was from Corey.

How about a swim tonight? Need to check on progress with your knee rehab.

She texted him a thumbs-up emoji. Just before the light changed she glanced to her right. The blocks along that section of Central were lined with antiques and vintage shops, and she loved "window-shopping" during her commute home. Today, on the sidewalk in front of a shop that specialized in mid-century modern, she noticed a glamorous glass-topped rattan dining table with four matching chairs arrayed around it. The seat cushions were covered in a wild jungle-print fabric.

It was love at first sight. The set would be right at home in the dining room at Coquina Cottage. How much? she wondered. The car behind her gave a warning beep and she looked up to see that the light had turned green. Reluctantly, she drove on.

Her plan to finish fixing up and furnishing the cottage had been put on hold for weeks now, due to her growing obsession over the Jazmin Mayes case. In the meantime, the bright blue tarp on her roof had faded and cracked in the relentless May sun, and the water stains on the ceilings were growing by the day. And just that morning, she'd found a legal-looking notice from the city hanging on her front door, warning her that the tarp's continued placement on her roof was a violation of city building code. The notice gave her thirty days to remove the tarp.

She had to at least get the roof patched, if not totally replaced. And oh, how she longed for air-conditioning. Drue had placed box fans on either side of her bedroom and in the kitchen, but mostly they just stirred up the hot, damp air streaming in through her open windows.

Ever since receiving her first CCK paycheck she'd placed herself on a strict budget, but her bank balance was still pathetically lean. Air-conditioning would have to wait, because a patch job on the roof was now priority one.

And that gorgeous rattan dining room set? Just moved to the end of the wish list.

~

Corey was well into his workout by the time she arrived at the Land's End pool. She sat on the side of the pool, dangling her legs in the water, watching, with envy, as his long, lean body cut effortlessly through the turquoise water. He wore swim goggles, and his bald head shone in the late-afternoon sun.

Drue slipped into the water and began the warm-up routine he'd taught her, starting out slowly, clinging to the side of the pool, doing leg stretches, then marching in place, pumping her arms, gradually lifting her knees higher. She walked back and forth across the shallow end, watching Corey's progress to avoid a collision in his lane. Finally, she went back to the side of the pool and did several repetitions of knee lifts, knee-to-chest stretches and flutter kicking.

In between counting her reps, her thoughts strayed back to her conversation with Ben. He was right, of course, to point out that she still hadn't managed to prove that Jazmin Mayes hadn't been killed while on the job. Even if she managed to uncover the truth behind the girl's murder, it wouldn't bring back Aliyah's mother, and might not even give Yvonne Howington a legitimate claim of criminal negligence against Gulf Vista.

She climbed out of the pool and collapsed onto a nearby chaise lounge, and a moment later, Corey joined her.

"How do you feel?" he asked, toweling himself dry.

"Tired," she admitted. "But I think the knee is getting stronger. And I'd forgotten how good it feels to move after a long day spent sitting on my ass in an office."

"Let me see," he said. She extended her leg and he leaned over, gently probing the scar with long, suntanned fingers.

He looked up and smiled. "It's noticeably better." He grabbed his plastic gallon jug of go-juice and took a long drink.

"How are things going at the office?" He offered her the jug, but she made a face and declined.

"Some good, some bad," she replied. "The big news is that Wendy, my stepmother, scared the living shit out of me today by almost going into labor in my car."

"You never told me you were going to be a big sister," he said, raising an eyebrow. "And have you ever referred to Wendy as your stepmother before?"

"Some things take time to get used to," she said tartly, ignoring his taunt. "She's not due until November, but the doctor said she was having premature labor, so she's put her on bed rest."

"How did your chat with that housekeeper from Gulf Vista go?"

"I'm more convinced than ever that somebody covered up something at that hotel," she replied. "I also talked to Jazmin's best friend last night. You wouldn't believe the crap that was going on at Gulf Vista."

She quickly filled him in on what she'd learned about the toxic atmosphere of sexual harassment at the hotel.

"God, men are pigs," Corey said. "How do you women stand it?"

"After a while, you just get numb to it," Drue said. "But not all guys are pigs. I had lunch today with one of my coworkers,

Ben. He's a little nerdy, yeah. I mean, his idea of fun is designing video games. But he and this other guy at work, Jonah, fixed my car, and wouldn't let me pay them. Ben knows I've been digging into the Jazmin Mayes case. He insists that there's nothing sketchy about the way the firm handled Yvonne's case, but at least he listens without staring at my boobs the whole time I'm talking."

"Have you told that police detective about the sexual harassment stuff?" Corey asked.

"I've tried to call her several times today, to tell her about meeting Neesa Vincent last night after I talked to Jaz's boyfriend. I've left a bunch of voice mail messages, but she hasn't returned any of my calls."

Corey pulled on a T-shirt. "What's your next step?"

"I was wondering," she said slowly. "Do you have a laptop? I want to take another look at the video from the hotel's security cameras, but I didn't have a minute to spare at work today."

"Would you like to come up to my place and watch some videos?" Corey asked, waggling his eyebrows.

"Sorry," Drue told him. "You're much too nice a guy to make that sound even remotely smutty."

"Too nice, or too gay?"

She smiled.

Corey's condo was on the second floor, with two sets of French doors that afforded sweeping views of the point where Boca Ciega Bay flowed into the Gulf. A pair of worn tufted-leather Chesterfield sofas separated by a contemporary glass and brass coffee table sat atop an antelope-hide rug. The walls were dotted with framed color photographs of vintage neon signs.

"My ex was a fine art photographer," Corey explained. "I should get rid of these because they remind me of him, but the thing is, I love to look at them."

"He does beautiful work," Drue commented.

"Did. As far as I know, he hasn't picked up a camera in a couple years. His new boo is a rich doctor, so Scott doesn't have a reason to work. He's now a proud member of the idle rich."

Corey gestured toward the open-plan kitchen, which was separated from the living room by a black granite-topped island. "I'm just gonna take a quick shower. If you're thirsty or hungry, help yourself to anything in the fridge."

She walked around the living room for a while, staring at the photos. She recognized a couple of the signs as belonging to local landmarks, including the Sunken Gardens on Fourth Street, the Thunderbird hotel, just down Gulf Boulevard in Treasure Island, and the El Cap, a family-owned bar also on Fourth Street.

After a while, she wandered into the kitchen. The contents of Corey's refrigerator were laughably boring. Four bottles of O'Doul's non-alcoholic beer, a jar of cashew butter, a head of kale, a bunch of carrots and a cellophane bag full of small brown squares that looked like fudge.

She helped herself to one of the squares. It was chewy and tasted vaguely of dried fruits and nuts and unidentifiable herbs, with an unpleasant aftertaste. Drue spat it into the trash and opened an O'Doul's, which didn't taste much better.

Corey emerged from the bedroom area, carrying his laptop. He set it up on the counter and Drue handed him the flash drive.

The screen filled with the black-and-white image of a woman dressed in a uniform smock and jeans, her face partially obscured by the bill of a baseball cap, exiting a room and pushing a laundry cart down the narrow hotel corridor.

"That's her?" Corey asked, leaning in to look. "Jazmin?"

"Yes," Drue said. "The time stamp shows that it's 1:32 A.M. And that's the problem. Despite her mother's insistence that she wasn't working that late, clearly she is working."

"Did the police talk to anybody who saw her working that night?" he asked.

"Don't know," Drue admitted. "Her best friend, Neesa, told me that she and Jazmin took their dinner break together at seven that night and that's the last time she saw Jazmin."

"There's not a lot to see, is there?" he said. "Just hotel corridor, elevator and the walkway to the laundry room. And of course, the housekeeper pushing that cart. You don't even really get a look at the girl's face."

Drue rewound the video and watched it again from the beginning. She pointed at the shot of the woman entering the hotel room at 11:05 P.M. "See? That's her. The video is grainy, but you can see her chin. I saw several photos of Jazmin on her Facebook page. She had a very distinctive chin. Kind of pointy, with a little cleft in it. Come to think of it, Aliyah has the same cleft."

The video progressed, and Drue and Corey watched it two more times. "Something keeps bugging me about this thing, but I can't put my finger on what it is," Drue said. "I really wish I could watch all the video from that day that shows Jazmin."

"You'd watch eight hours of housekeepers walking up and down hallways? It'd be like paint drying," Corey pointed out. "But you know what I notice? Does it strike you as strange that there's nobody else around in this video clip? I mean, when we were there, that hotel was pretty busy."

"May is still their busy season," Drue said. "Jazmin was killed in September. I don't know what September is like over here, but in Fort Lauderdale, things are totally dead that time of year."

"Yeah, maybe you're right," Corey said.

"Although . . . Zee's report said there was a Shriners convention going on then."

"I didn't see any fezzes in that clip, did you?"

"They could have all been at a banquet, or partying down at the pool, or staying in a different part of the property," Drue said. Her stomach rumbled loudly, so she got up and went back to the refrigerator, taking another square from the cellophane bag and popping it into her mouth, grimacing as she chewed.

"What are you eating?" Corey asked.

She shrugged and kept chewing. "Energy bites? You said I could help myself to anything, right?"

Corey fetched the bag and held it up. "These? You ate these? They're Bitzy's protein chews."

Drue paused midchew. "Who's Bitzy?"

"My Pekingese. Well, Scott's. I still dog-sit her sometimes."

She walked into the kitchen, spat out the bite and retrieved another near beer from the fridge. "What do you say we go over to my place?"

"Okay, but why?" Corey asked.

"Because I'm super hungry from my workout and you don't have any food fit for human consumption in your house."

Drue produced a box of chicken burritos from her freezer and placed them on the counter while Corey looked on in horror.

"You're not seriously going to eat that, are you?" he asked.

"Don't be such a food snob. They're very delicious. And the label says they're non-GMO so in my book that's healthy."

She rummaged around in the refrigerator until she found a bottle of spring water, which she handed to her guest.

Corey had seated himself at the kitchen table and was idly leafing through the thick black binder that had taken up permanent residence there. "Hey, what's this?"

"Just another friggin' mystery," Drue said. "I found this in a box of my dad's old law school textbooks, stuck way in the corner of the attic." She gestured upward, then slid Colleen's black-and-white high school graduation photo out of the binder.

"Pretty. Is that your mom?"

"No. Her name was Colleen Boardman Hicks. She went shopping and then to dinner with a friend in downtown St. Pete in 1976 and has never been seen since."

"What's it doing up in the attic of your grandparents' house?"

"That's what's been keeping me awake a lot of nights," Drue said. "I don't know if I told you this, but my dad was a St. Pete cop when my parents were first married, and my grandparents let them live here in the cottage for cheap. They moved into town before I was born, and then, after my dad got out of law school, they split up. That's when my mom and I moved to the east coast. I guess my mom must have stored her stuff here after the divorce. The box I found the binder in had her handwriting on the outside of it."

She put the burritos on a plate and stood in front of the microwave oven, holding the plate aloft. "Last chance. Sure you don't want to get in some of this fiesta of fabulousness?"

Corey made a gagging noise. "I'd rather eat Bitzy's energy bites." He tapped the cover of the binder. "You know, you really should consider getting yourself a hobby."

"You mean an obsession? Like doing an Iron Man?"

"Touché," he said. "So was this one of your father's investigations from when he was a cop?"

"I asked him that, and he said it wasn't, because he was still just a patrol officer. But he did go to high school with Colleen Hicks, although he claims they didn't run around with the same crowd of friends."

Corey still looked puzzled. "Did he have any idea how this file would have ended up here, with a bunch of his stuff?"

Drue placed a plate, napkin and cutlery on the table, carefully pushing aside the binder, and poured herself a glass of wine. "I told him I found a file of old newspaper clippings about the disappearance, in my mom's stuff, but I didn't mention finding this thing." She nodded at the binder.

"Why not?"

She took a sip of wine. "I'm not sure. Maybe because I'm still not a hundred percent sure I trust him. There are just a lot of unanswered questions, you know?"

"Like what?"

The microwave dinged. Drue transferred the hot plate onto the kitchen table. She took a bottle of Cholula sauce from a cabinet and doused the burrito in it.

"To start with, what's the official police file doing in a box in my grandfather's cottage, more than forty years after this woman vanished? Who put it up there? I've read through it. There's no mention of Dad's name in any of the reports."

She tasted a forkful of her dinner, paused, then sprinkled more hot sauce atop her burrito.

"But I'll tell you whose name is in the file—and that's Jimmy Zilowicz, who everybody calls Jimmy Zee and who is not only my dad's oldest friend but a former St. Pete police detective, and currently case investigator at the law firm."

"Coincidence?" Corey asked.

"I asked Zee if he had a theory about the Colleen Hicks case. He said his role was minor, that he just did some leg-work."

"And did he have a theory?"

"He said that Colleen Hicks and her husband were into some kind of kinky stuff. And that right before she vanished, she cleaned out their joint savings account. Allen Hicks, that was the husband, was a control freak, according to Zee. He says she probably disappeared on purpose."

Corey leafed through the binder, pausing at the black-and-white photos in their clear plastic envelopes. "Do you believe him? Do you believe it's possible that she's alive?"

She poked at the burrito with her fork, took a bite, chewed

and swallowed. "If she's still alive, she'd be around my dad's age now. Why would she stay hidden all these years?"

"Suppose she did start a new life? Remarried, maybe had kids, now she'd have grandkids. Whatever happened to her husband?" Corey asked.

Drue reached for her cell phone and typed the name Allen Hicks into the search engine. The search yielded more than three dozen citations. She pulled up the first two and read them.

"Three years after his wife disappeared, Allen Hicks got a Mexican divorce. He remarried, got divorced again and then married a third time." She looked up at Corey. "Clearly the guy wasn't exactly distraught over losing his wife."

She clicked on the next story link and skimmed it quickly. "Allen Hicks retired to North Carolina and died in 2009."

"Which still leaves the question of whatever happened to Colleen," Corey said. "Is she dead or alive?"

"And what, if any, is the connection to my dad?"

"Why don't you just ask him?"

"I did. He denied that there was any real connection."

"Just level with him," Corey said, shaking his head impatiently. "Tell him you found the old police files up in the attic—in a box of his stuff."

"I can't," Drue insisted. "He's not just my dad, he's also my boss. It would be like I was accusing him of something dishonest at best and criminal at worst. I can't say anything to him. Not until I have some kind of proof."

"Proof of what? That he had something to do with this Colleen Hicks person?"

"Both that and whatever was going on at the Gulf Vista," Drue said. "Look, we know that the female housekeepers at that hotel were the victims of sexual harassment. We're pretty sure that whoever killed Jazmin was someone who knew her. If we could just figure out who killed her, then maybe we'd be able to get to the bottom of this whole thing. I can't help but wonder if my dad or somebody at the law firm took a payoff or something."

"And what happens if you discover your dad, and the law firm, is completely innocent? No cover-up, no bribe, but also no money for Jazmin's mom?"

"Then I'll let it go," Drue vowed.

Corey cocked a dubious eyebrow.

"I will. I swear it."

When she was alone again, Drue considered the flip side of the question Corey had asked.

What if she actually uncovered evidence that her father or somebody at the law firm had betrayed their client? Or worse—that Brice was involved in Colleen Hicks's disappearance. What would she do then? How far was she prepared to take this quest for justice? She had no answer.

42

After Corey left, Drue took a glass of wine and walked down to the beach to watch the sunset. The damp sand felt cool beneath her feet, and the breeze off the water ruffled the sea oats on the dune that separated her backyard from the abbreviated seawall. At the last minute, deep-purple-tinged clouds drifted across the horizon, obscuring her view. She glanced up and down the beach, looking for "her" blue heron, but the only birds in sight were a group of sanderlings, skimming in and out of the shallow wavelets lapping at the shore.

She turned around and headed home, for a shower and then bed. All evening she'd kept her cell phone close at hand, hoping for a callback from Rae Hernandez at the sheriff's department, but the only call she got came as a complete surprise.

When UNKNOWN CALLER flashed across the phone's display screen, she didn't pick up, but let it go to voice mail.

"Uh, hey Drue. It's Jonah. From work?"

She grabbed the phone and tapped Connect.

"Hi, Jonah. It's Drue. What's up?"

"I was kind of hoping you wouldn't pick up," he blurted.

"Then why did you call?"

He sighed. "Remember that do-over I asked for? I was thinking maybe we could try it on Saturday night?"

She felt the color rise in her cheeks. He was asking her out. She couldn't remember the last time a man had asked her out on a date. It had to be pre-Trey.

Yes, definitely pre-him. Her six-year off-and-on relationship with Trey had been a long segue from hanging out to living together; now that she thought about it, she realized Trey never had formally asked her out. One night, after a long day of kite-boarding, he'd sat next to her at a bar and bought her drinks. The next night, when their group of friends had drifted off the beach and out to a restaurant, Trey had picked up the dinner check. And the next night, they'd met up at a concert and he'd gone home with her and stayed over for the next week.

"Drue? You there?"

"I'm here. Okay, I'd be up for that," she said cautiously.

"So just to be clear, that's a yes?"

"Yes, Jonah," she said, rolling her eyes. "That is a yes. What did you have in mind?"

"Drinks and dinner? There's a new place downtown, near the Vinoy, that I've heard good stuff about."

"That sounds nice," Drue said. "Tell me the address and I'll meet you there."

"Huh? I mean, I thought I'd pick you up at your place. That's okay, isn't it?"

"Yes. I just wasn't sure if you'd want to drive all the way out to Sunset Beach and back."

He laughed. "God, this is the most incredibly awkward phone call I have ever had with a woman. Does it feel awkward to you too?"

"Incredibly so," she agreed. "Painfully awkward."

"Well, I wouldn't go that far," he said. "But the worst part is over, right? I asked, you said yes. We have a plan. I'll pick you up, we'll have a nice dinner. No stress."

"There's no stress for you, because you're a guy. You don't have to think about what to wear, or what to do with your hair."

His voice softened. "Wear it down, okay, Drue? You have really pretty hair. And if you don't mind my saying so, you look great in jeans."

"I don't mind your saying that at all," Drue said, surprised. "It's actually lovely, hearing a compliment from a man."

"Good. I'll see you tomorrow morning, then. Right?"

"Right."

Once in bed, she fell asleep immediately but awoke after only two hours.

Her dreams were stranger than usual. She dreamed of Jazmin Mayes, staring up from a basket of soiled sheets; of her own mother, Sherri, plucking at the edge of the blanket the hospice worker had tucked around her pale, emaciated body, her eyes clouded by the effects of the drugs in her IV drip. And she dreamed of Colleen Boardman Hicks, and a pile of blood-spattered but neatly folded clothing placed on the bucket seat of an orange Camaro.

Her mind kept drifting back to that binder on the kitchen table, and the mystery of Colleen. Corey was right. She really did need to find herself a hobby.

But in the meantime, she had questions. So many questions.

Exasperated, she sat up in bed and reached for her cell phone, returning to the Google search she'd done earlier in the evening.

She yawned as she skimmed through the first half-dozen articles the search generated, impatient that none of them yielded anything new. But she paused when she came to a 2016 *Tampa Bay Times* article headlined COLLEEN HICKS WITNESS DELVES INTO 40-YEAR-OLD MYSTERY.

> Vera Rennick still remembers the last words Colleen Boardman Hicks, her friend and coworker, said to her on that otherwise unremarkable afternoon on August 20, 1976.
>
> "We'd left work early to do a little shopping. Maas Brothers was having a big summer clearance sale, and afterwards we had dinner at the Suncoast Room. I needed to get home and see about my mother, so Colleen insisted on picking up the check. She stood up and gave me a hug. She told me to make sure to tell my mother hello from her," Mrs. Rennick said. "And then she said, 'See you Monday.'"

But Monday never came. The disappearance of the attractive 26-year-old dental hygienist triggered one of the most intense police investigations in St. Petersburg history. Investigators widened their search to a five-state area, consulted psychics, dragged local ponds and questioned dozens of known sex offenders, but to no avail. The mystery remains unsolved.

Forty years later, Vera Rennick's pale blue eyes still fill with tears at that memory. "And that was the last time anybody ever saw Colleen. Ever. It still haunts me. I wake up so many nights, wondering, Where are you, Colleen? What happened to you? That's why I decided to start my own blog. It's my way of trying to find answers to my questions."

Mrs. Rennick titled her blog *Have You Seen Colleen?* In it, she shares tidbits of information she has personally gleaned over her years of following the case, and invites readers to contribute their own knowledge and theories.

"The police don't care anymore," Mrs. Rennick said. "The fact that it's unsolved is a black eye. They won't even answer my phone calls."

Cassandra Banks, a spokesman for the St. Petersburg Police Department, denied that authorities have given up their investigation. "We welcome any and all information from the public concerning this case, as we would for any still-open investigation."

"People are still fascinated with the case," Vera Rennick said. "And I've received valuable tips. It all happened so long ago that people who might have stayed quiet at the time of Colleen's disappearance have been willing to come forward and share information with me."

She pointed out that Colleen Hicks's husband Allen passed away in 2009, and that the missing woman's parents, Burton and Edith Boardman, died, separately, within *four years* of their daughter's disappearance.

"I'm the keeper of the flame," Mrs. Rennick said. "And I intend to keep asking questions until I find out the truth, or die trying."

"Screw it," Drue whispered aloud, after tossing and turning for another half hour. She found Vera Rennick's blog online, and spent the next hour or so trying to slog through three years' worth of *Have You Seen Colleen?*

The blog was comically amateur, replete with typos, misspellings, blurry photos and stream-of-consciousness posts in which the author posed, then debunked, wildly improbable theories.

One post would examine the possibility that Colleen Hicks was living in a hippie commune in upstate New York, while another would have the missing woman joining a cloistered religious order.

Various "experts" opined that Colleen Hicks had been murdered by a Manson family–inspired cult, by a jilted former boyfriend, even by a disgruntled patient from the dental clinic where Colleen was working at the time of her disappearance.

It was all mildly entertaining, Drue decided, but what she really needed to do was talk to Vera Rennick in person. Just before dropping off to sleep, Drue sent a deliberately vague private message to the blogger.

Hi, Vera. I recently moved home to St. Pete from the east coast, and found a trove of newspaper clippings about the Colleen Hicks case in my late mother's belongings. I'm intrigued and wonder if you'd be willing to talk to me about the case in person? Thanks, Drue Campbell.

43

The woman, Drue concluded, must be a night owl. At 2:15 A.M. she'd responded to Drue's message: *I'd be happy to talk to you about Colleen. I'm free anytime before noon. It's a retirement community on the south side.* She attached the street address.

Still sleepless, Drue checked her phone at seven-fifteen Friday morning and found Vera's response. She typed in her own response immediately. If Vera Rennick agreed, she would visit her today. It would make her late to work, but, she reflected, with Wendy out of the office, there would be no hateful yellow SEE ME notes stuck to her desk when she finally did make it in to work.

I can be there by 9, if that's all right.

Vera's answer came almost immediately. *See you then.*

Drue called Rae Hernandez on the way to meet Vera Rennick. "Call me please, Rae. I have new information about Jazmin Hicks, and it's important that we talk."

Vera Rennick lived in a tidy buff-colored stucco bungalow in the sprawling Sunny Shores retirement community in the Bahama Shores neighborhood on the city's south side.

Before Drue could ring the bell, the door opened. The woman who answered the door wore a floor-length black-and-white floral caftan. She was stoop-shouldered, peering up at her visitor past a fringe of silver bangs, through thick-lensed glasses.

"Drue? How nice to meet you."

She showed Drue into the living room, which, though modestly furnished, boasted a stunning waterfront view.

"Sit here," Vera urged, pointing at an avocado velvet club chair. "It's the best view of Little Bayou." She pointed toward the galley kitchen, visible through the half-wall that separated it from the living room. "Can I get you something to drink? Coffee, maybe?"

"No, thank you," Drue said politely.

Her hostess sat in a worn brown vinyl recliner set between two banks of four-drawer metal filing cabinets. "My research," she said, patting the top of one of the cabinets as though it were a beloved dog.

"All of that?" Drue asked. "All about Colleen Hicks?"

"Most of it. Of course, all my data is also stored in my iCloud, but I guess I'm old-fashioned, because I like to keep hard copies of everything as backup."

"That's very impressive," Drue said. "I had no idea there was that much information available about the Colleen Hicks case."

"Some of my materials are actually about other, possibly related cold cases," Vera said. "You know how it is these days. You do one computer search and pretty soon you fall down that internet rabbit hole and the next thing you know, six or eight hours have flown by. Other bloggers, people in the true-crime community, they share information with me. You'd be surprised how many unsolved cases there are involving missing or murdered women, just in the Southeast."

"It looks like you've become somewhat of an authority on the topic," Drue said. "And your blog is fascinating. I just discovered it last night. I only stopped reading it because I had to get up and go to work this morning."

Vera leaned forward. "Your email said you discovered some old newspaper clippings in your mother's things. But you didn't mention your mother's name. Did she have a connection to Colleen? What did you say her name was?"

Drue hesitated. She really didn't want to divulge anything personal to this stranger. But on the other hand, she couldn't expect to get if she didn't give. Just a little.

"I don't think my mother had a connection to Colleen," she said. "Her maiden name was Sherri Sanchez. She grew up in Tampa, and moved to St. Pete after she married my father. Her parents owned a little house on Sunset Beach, and my parents lived there in the mid-seventies. I recently inherited the cottage, and that's how I came across the folder full of newspaper clippings about the case. It was up in the attic."

"Interesting," Vera said, tilting her head. Her skin was surprisingly smooth and unlined, and her eyes, behind pale blond lashes, were like a pair of large, blue marbles. "Any idea why your mom would have saved those articles?"

"No. But I do know my father went to high school with Colleen Hicks."

"He went to Boca Ciega? What year? Was he in Colleen's class?"

"Um, well, I think maybe he was a year older," Drue said.

Vera propelled herself out of the recliner with a soft grunt. She went to a bookshelf beside the window, pulled out a large leatherette-covered volume and sat back down. "This is the *Treasure Chest* from 1968."

"Excuse me?" Drue asked.

"Her yearbook. This is Colleen's. From her junior year."

"Really? How do you happen to have that?" Drue asked.

"A fan sold it to me," Vera said, her eyes glittering with excitement. "He bought it from a local antique dealer, who bought it along with a box of books at a yard sale after Colleen's parents died, back in early 1980."

She opened the yearbook and began flipping through pages of black-and-white photographs. "What's your father's name, Drue? Is he still living?"

"He's very much alive. His name is Brice Campbell."

Vera looked up sharply. "The lawyer? The man on all the billboards and bus benches?"

Drue winced. "Yes."

Vera began leafing through the yearbook pages, stopping

when she reached the page she was searching for. "Campbell," she said, dragging a finger down the rows of photographs. "Campbell."

She stabbed a photo with her finger. "Here he is," she said triumphantly, holding up the yearbook. "Brice Campbell."

Drue knelt on the floor beside the recliner and stared down at her father's senior class picture. *William "Brice" Campbell. JV baseball, V baseball, wrestling, Key Club,* said the caption under the photo.

The boys of the class of 1968 were mostly a clean-cut group, and Brice was no different. His short blond hair was neatly combed and side-parted, and he was clean-shaven. Like the other boys, he wore a dress shirt, a narrow striped tie and a familiar smirk that suggested he knew more than he should.

The surprise was that her father had signed his class photo, scrawling his name and PIRATES 4EVER across his own face.

"Looks like your father knew Colleen," Vera said. She flipped back toward the front of the yearbook, to signature pages filled with inscriptions of dozens and dozens of Colleen Hicks's classmates.

"He didn't sign anyplace else in the yearbook," Vera commented. "I've cross-referenced all the names of all her friends who wrote inscriptions, and I certainly would have remembered if I'd seen Brice Campbell's name on my list."

"You made a list of everybody who signed her yearbook?" Drue asked, at once fascinated and repelled by the older woman's obsessive knowledge.

"Now you think I'm crazy," Vera said, closing the book and setting it aside.

"Oh no, I don't think that at all."

"Well, everybody else does, including my sister and my nieces," Vera said. "Not that I give a tinker's damn. The fact is, I'm the last known person who saw Colleen Hicks alive. I don't take that responsibility lightly."

"I think that's a good thing," Drue said, choosing her words carefully. "If somebody I cared about disappeared, I'd want somebody to find out the truth. If it were my mother, say, instead of Colleen, I'd make it my business to find out what had happened."

"There you go," Vera said approvingly. "So you do understand."

"I think so," Drue said. "Would you mind talking to me, about Colleen? And about that day she disappeared?"

"It would be my pleasure," Vera said. She heaved herself up from the chair again. "But first, if you don't mind, I'm going to have some coffee. Won't you join me?"

"That's a good idea," Drue said. "I didn't get much sleep last night."

"How do you take yours?"

"Black, one sugar," Drue said.

Vera returned with a small tray holding a pair of bone-china coffee mugs. She handed one to her guest and settled back into her lounge chair. "Now, where were we?"

"You were about to tell me your theory. About what happened to Colleen," Drue said.

"Right. At first, I was convinced she'd run away. I never liked her husband. None of her friends did. He was cold and bossy, you'd call him controlling today. They were total opposites in every way. Colleen was so lively and vivacious. Very popular with the patients. Especially the male patients." She winked at this last statement.

"One of my father's old friends was a detective who worked on the case, just in a marginal way, and he said there were rumors back then that Colleen and Allen were . . . swingers?"

Vera blinked. "That's a new one. I could maybe see Colleen being interested in that. She was . . . frisky, shall we say? But Allen Hicks? No. I just can't imagine him doing anything that unconventional. Colleen told me confidentially that he hit the ceiling one time when she suggested they try something different in the bedroom."

"This retired detective," Drue said. "He also said Colleen might have stolen pills, from the dentist's office."

Vera smiled as she gazed out the window of the bungalow at a white egret picking at something in the grass at the edge of the seawall. "Did he, now?"

"Was that true?"

The older woman shrugged. "Does it surprise you that we experimented with drugs back then? We were young and curious. And it wasn't like we were selling them. Don't tell me you've never tried an occasional controlled substance."

"No, I couldn't say that," Drue admitted.

"I'm curious. What's the name of this detective you've been chatting with?"

"Um, well, I'm not sure he'd want me sharing his name. He sort of told me this in confidence."

"Not fair," Vera said, wagging a finger at Drue. "Here I am, opening up to you, and yet you seem very reluctant to share what you know. I wonder why that is?"

"I'm in an awkward position," Drue said. "I wouldn't want my father or his friend knowing I'm poking around in this old case."

Vera sipped her coffee and her pale blue eyes drilled into Drue over the rim of her mug.

She sighed as she set the mug down. "Then I think we've reached an impasse. Trust goes both ways, you know."

"His name is Jimmy Zilowicz, but everybody calls him Jimmy Zee," Drue said, relenting.

"Don't worry. I'm very discreet about my sources," Vera assured her. "That name vaguely rings a bell. And he was a detective at the time?"

"Not when Colleen first disappeared. I think he was promoted later. At the time, he and my father were patrol officers, and partners."

Vera closed her eyes and pursed her lips. "You know," she said slowly. "Earlier that year, in March, Colleen insisted we have lunch at this seedy bar downtown. Mastry's."

"Mastry's Bar? I've been there," Drue said.

"It was not at all the kind of place we usually went to back then," Vera said primly. "I think we were the only women in there that day. A very blue-collar kind of place, and maybe it was a cop hangout too. I remember, Colleen got up to go to the bathroom, and she stopped to talk to these two young officers who were sitting at the end of the bar. I remember asking her why she didn't introduce me to them. After all, I was single at the time."

"Did she say who they were?"

"I think she said they were just making idle conversation. Sort of hitting on her," Vera said. "It was so long ago. And it was just that one time."

She reached for the yearbook and paged back to the senior class pictures. She tapped a fingertip on Brice Campbell's photo, then looked up at Drue. "I can't swear it was him that day, but I can't swear that it wasn't, either. You don't happen to have a photo of this Jimmy Zee, do you?"

"I'm sorry, I don't."

"No problem." Vera rolled the tray with her laptop over to the lounge chair. "How do you spell that last name?"

"*Z-I-L-O-W-I-C-Z,*" Drue said.

Vera opened the cover and began typing at an impressive clip.

"Ah," she said, a moment later. She swiveled the screen so that Drue could see. It was a photo of a smiling Jimmy Zee, dressed in his characteristic black polo shirt, shaking hands with a white-haired man in a dress shirt.

VETERAN POLICE DETECTIVE RECEIVES AWARD was the caption under the photo.

"That must have been taken when he retired a few years ago," Drue said.

Vera clicked her cursor until she came to a 1978 photo of a much younger version of Jimmy Zee. The black-and-white photo showed him as a stern-faced man, wearing a coat and tie in which he looked supremely uncomfortable. His hair was thick, and his jowls were nonexistent.

"Very Jack Webb," Vera murmured.

"Who?"

Vera smiled. "*Dragnet.* I suppose you weren't even born then."

"Do you think he was one of the cops Colleen talked to that day at Mastry's?" Drue asked.

"I wish I could say," Vera said. She closed the laptop. "Back to your father. Was he by any chance a patient at our office?"

"Um, I don't know," Drue said.

"It doesn't matter," Vera said. "Dr. Garber has been dead a long time now. We girls all thought he was ancient back then, but he was barely fifty. A heart attack took him, poor man."

She leaned back against the recliner's headrest. "The police hounded all of us, for months and months after Colleen disappeared. It affected the dental practice. People were asking questions that we couldn't answer. There was a lot of innuendo. We lost several patients. It was unbelievably upsetting. Particularly for poor Dr. Garber. The police were convinced he was having an affair with her."

"Was he?"

Vera laughed. "He was having an affair, all right, but not with Colleen. He had a young boyfriend, a waiter who worked at Ten Beach Drive, that was a nightclub back in the day. It all came out when the police started digging around. When Dr. Garber's wife found out, she left him and took the girls with her. The poor man was shattered."

"Mrs. Rennick?"

"Vera."

"You said you thought at first that Colleen had run away. Is that still your theory?"

"Haven't you read my blog? I've laid it out very succinctly."

"Forgive me, but I just discovered the blog last night. I only had time to skim."

"I think it was Allen," she said finally.

Drue leaned forward. "But I thought he had an alibi. Wasn't he down in the Keys on a fishing trip?"

"Alibis can be cooked up," Vera said. "And remember, Allen's alibi was his own father. A prominent doctor in town. Chief of staff at Bayfront Medical Center, as it was called back then."

"Why would Allen Hicks kill his wife?"

Vera shrugged. "Lots of reasons. I always suspected there was another woman, a girl who worked in his insurance office. He didn't waste much time marrying her, either. Got himself a quickie divorce in Mexico just three years later."

"Why didn't he just divorce Colleen while she was alive?"

"You don't know very much about men and murder, do you?"

"I guess I don't," Drue admitted.

"Well, I do," Vera said. "There's a name for it, you know. Uxoricide. It means the killing of one's romantic partner. The vast majority of the time a woman is the victim. And the men who kill them are jealous, possessive and controlling. For the man, it's a power thing."

"Makes sense," Drue agreed.

"He beat her, you know."

"Who?"

"Allen. Her husband. The bastard knocked her around. He was abusive. There's been a study done. In England. Did you know that sixty-five percent of men who kill their romantic partners have been physically abusive in the past?"

"Did Colleen tell you he was hitting her?"

"She didn't have to," Vera said. "This one time, I remember, I got to work early and saw Colleen was in one of the examining rooms with Dr. Garber. He was stitching up her lip and she had a tooth knocked out too. She claimed she'd tripped, but that was clearly a lie."

"Did the police know about that?"

"I told one of the detectives at the time, but he didn't believe me," Vera said. "There were no police or hospital records, and Colleen hadn't complained to friends or family that her husband was abusive."

"Probably she was ashamed," Drue said.

"And that wasn't the only time he hit her. She'd come to work with bruises on her arms. It got so that she'd wear long sleeves every day, even in the summer."

"I don't understand. If her husband was beating her, if she maybe suspected he was cheating on her, why wouldn't Colleen leave?"

"People always ask that question," Vera said. "But forty years ago, a girl like Colleen didn't have many options. She didn't really get along with her parents, and Allen controlled all the money. He actually had her on an allowance!"

Drue thought back to the binder on her kitchen table, of the picture of a demurely smiling Colleen on her wedding day.

"Have you talked to the police lately, about your theories about Allen Hicks?"

Vera shook her head. "Not in any official kind of capacity. Everybody's dead now, you know. Colleen most likely, Allen, both their sets of parents, even Dr. Garber. Plus, it's hard to investigate a cold case when you no longer have any of the official investigative file."

Drue feigned surprise. "Really?"

"It's gone. The whole file. It was only discovered missing ten years ago. But it could have been gone much longer than that."

"What happened to it?"

"I wish I knew," Vera said. "I'd give anything to read it. I've put out feelers, on my blog, but it's still missing. Like Colleen, come to think of it."

44

August 1976

She slid the Camaro into a slot around the back of the Dreamland and walked rapidly through the light drizzle that had begun falling at dusk, cinching the raincoat tighter as she walked, her heels clicking against the parking lot pavement.

As she approached the unit, the blonde began unbuttoning the coat. She'd seen his cruiser parked in the usual spot so she knew he was inside, waiting. She'd had to cancel the previous week because it was Allen's mother's birthday, and all day she'd been fantasizing about the coming evening.

Colleen threw the door open and stepped into the darkened room, holding the raincoat open to reveal the outfit she'd spent a week's grocery money on: black lace push-up bra, black lace garter belt, black fishnet hose.

"Surprise!"

He was reclined on the bed, illuminated only by the blue flicker of the television set, wreathed in a cloud of cigarette smoke.

His chuckle was low and throaty and only vaguely familiar.

"Well now, that is a nice surprise." He stubbed out the cigarette in an ashtray resting on his chest.

The blood drained from her face, and her fingers fumbled as she hastily belted and buttoned the raincoat.

"What is this?" she demanded. "Where's Brice?"

Her lover's partner, the cop he called Jimmy Zee, was obviously highly amused. "Brice couldn't make it tonight. He sent me instead. In fact, your boyfriend won't be making it with you ever again. It's over."

"I don't believe you." She glanced around the room, unsure of her next move.

Before she could leave, he made a show of holding up a rectangle of laminated paper. "What? You're going to leave without taking what you came here for?"

She felt herself flush, and she released the doorknob and tightened the raincoat belt. "What I came here for is none of your business," she said haughtily.

Jimmy Zee swung his feet off the bed and laid the rectangle on the nightstand. He reached into the pocket of his sports shirt and produced another rectangle of paper, which he placed beside the first.

"Driver's license. Social Security card."

He studied her face. "You're now officially Donna Woods. You look like a Donna, you know that?"

Colleen edged closer to the bed. She snatched up the documents, then turned on the lamp on the nightstand to get a better look.

"This picture," she said coldly, holding up the driver's license, "looks nothing like me. The hair is the wrong color. The weight? Are you kidding me? I've never weighed one hundred sixty pounds in my life. Ever. This thing is a joke."

Zee was unmoved. "Women change their hair color all the time. They lose weight. That's what Donna Woods did."

"I want to see Brice," Colleen said. "Does he even know you're here?"

"How else would I know to show up to this dump on a Thursday night? He sent me."

"I don't believe you," she said. "Why would he do something like that?"

"Because you and Brice are through, *Donna*. The two of you had some laughs, but that's all it was. He's not leaving his wife for you. And he's not giving up his job and his future to run away with you."

Colleen walked over to the desk on the opposite side of the room and picked up the phone. "We'll see about that."

"What? You're gonna call the house again and hang up when his wife answers? Put the phone down, *Donna*."

Zee's tone was calm. "Like I said, you've got what you need. A new set of ID papers. You can go anyplace you want, be Donna Woods. But you're done threatening Brice Campbell. And you're done driving past his house and harassing his wife."

"I never . . ."

"Shut up," Zee said. "You're done. End of story."

He took a stick of gum and popped it in his mouth, dropping the foil wrapper to the floor.

"And what if that's not what I want?"

"Tough shit. Do you want your husband to find out about your Thursday night action at the Dreamland motel? The same joint where you were screwing his brains out last December? Because I can make that happen. And then what, after he finds out you've been screwing around on him?"

"Allen would kill me," Colleen said, lifting her chin defiantly. "Brice knows that. He wouldn't let you . . ."

"That's why I'm here tonight," Zee said. "Looks to me like you've got two choices. Stay here, let that asshole keep beating on you until he kills or cripples you, or leave. Hit the road and don't come back. Which is it?"

Colleen stared blankly down at the driver's license. "This doesn't seem real," she said, in a very small voice. "I know we talked about it, my just walking away. But I'd be leaving everything behind. My job, my friends, my family . . ."

"Your homicidal husband," Zee added. "Spare me the pity party, okay? You chose the guy. How long were you together before he started hitting you?"

Her hair fell across her face. "He twisted my wrist so hard I got a spiral fracture. The third night of our honeymoon."

"And you stayed," Zee said. "So now, what's your plan?"

Colleen sank down onto the edge of the bed. She closed her eyes as she reviewed the loose plan that had begun forming in her brain.

"Allen and his dad go fishing in the Keys every year. They leave next Thursday afternoon. If I time it right, I can go to work, pick up my last paycheck, get the money out of our savings account and leave that day, after work."

"Leave, how?"

"Just . . . drive away."

"No good," Zee said. "As soon as he gets back and finds you gone he'll call the cops and report you missing. They'll put out an APB. It won't be hard to spot that flashy orange car of yours."

"What do you suggest?"

"Hop a dog," Zee replied. "Go Greyhound and leave the driving to us."

Her upper lip curled in distaste. "You can't be serious."

"Dead serious," Zee said. "Leave the car at work or someplace like that. Then you buy a bus ticket with cash. Get where you're going and then get yourself a new car and a new life. But a quiet one, you know? Change your hair color. Tone down the way you dress."

Colleen got a faraway look in her eye. "Atlanta. That's what I'm thinking. One of my FSU sorority sisters is from there, and it's a great place. There's always something going on there. Not like this place. God's waiting room. I'll have to figure out a new kind of job, but that's cool. I'm sick and tired of scraping crap off people's teeth anyway."

"Good for you." Zee stood up. "Sounds like you've got yourself a plan, so I'm gonna shove off."

He glanced meaningfully back at the bed. "Unless you wanna . . ."

"Dream on," Colleen snapped. "And you can tell Brice Campbell for me that I hope he rots in hell. He could have at least had the decency to show up here tonight in person."

Zee stood very close to her. So close she could smell the cinnamon gum he was chewing.

"Decency? You've been shacking up with a married man at a fleabag hot sheet motel for months. I don't think you get to decide what's decent or not. *Donna*."

She slapped him as hard as she could across the face. He was so startled, he just stood there, stunned, as she swept from the room. Moments later, he heard the screech of tires on the wet pavement, and the Camaro's headlights flashed past the flimsy sheer curtains.

He lit another cigarette. "Bye, Donna," he said.

45

Drue almost felt guilty, sneaking into her cube two hours late after her Friday morning meeting with Vera Rennick. Almost. For once, she thought, Wendy would be none the wiser. But when she turned on her computer she saw a lengthy email from her stepmother, outlining everything she expected Drue to accomplish that day. She would have to skip lunch to catch up.

Jonah paused at her cubicle on his way back to his own desk after lunch. He was freshly shaven and she could detect the faintest hint of aftershave. "How's it going?"

If he was trying to act casual, he'd failed miserably.

"Okay," she said, shrugging. "Wendy might be home on bed rest, but she's still keeping an iron rein. I'm in callback hell, trying to reach out to potential clients who left messages over the past two days. Not a single person I've called has bothered to pick up the phone. I'm starting to get a complex about it."

"You wouldn't want the clients who are picking up when I call," Jonah said. "I just spent twenty minutes listening to a guy who wants to sue Miller Brewing because he insists they secretly increased the alcohol content of Natty Lite, causing him to get drunk and back with his ex-wife after the company picnic."

"What did you tell him?" Drue asked.

"I told him it sounded like a product liability case, which we don't do. And I referred him to an asshole who graduated law school with me who does have that practice."

"A revenge referral? I like it," Drue said.

"Hey Dad," Drue said, poking her head around her father's office door later that afternoon. "How's Wendy feeling?"

"Come on in," Brice said, waving her forward. Jimmy Zee sat in the wing chair opposite the desk. "Oh hey, Jimmy," she said.

Zee nodded hello.

"Wendy's fine," Brice said. "The meds the doctor gave her have stopped the uh, issues. She's sleeping a lot, and bitching at me because she's bored and hates not being in the office, but that's to be expected."

"Glad to hear it," Drue said. "I'm around all weekend, if you need anything."

"Thanks, honey, that's really nice of you," Brice said. "I'll let Wendy know you asked about her. It'll mean a lot."

"Good, well, sorry for the interruption," Drue said, turning to go.

"You're not interrupting. We were just finishing a case conference," Brice said. "Zee's got some video surveillance I need for an auto case, but Mr. Caveman here can't figure out how to transmit it to me."

Zee frowned. "I told you, I tried," he said. "But my phone says the file is too big."

"Just convert it to a download and email it," Brice said impatiently.

"You know me," Jimmy Zee protested. "I don't do all this techno-shit."

"So get Ben to do it for you," Brice said. "But do it right away, because I want to get things squared away before we start discovery on Monday."

Zee followed Drue into the bullpen and stood waiting, impatiently, by Ben's cubicle, frowning down at Ben, who was wearing a rumpled, faded, Mötley Crüe concert tee. As soon as the younger man finished his call, he thrust his phone at Ben. "Here," he said. "I need this converted into a whatever file. Like, now."

"Can I ask what it is?"

"All you need to know is it's video Brice wants sent to him before the end of business today," Zee said. "Just do what you get paid to do, okay?"

"Fine," Ben said, looking down at the phone. "But it would only take a minute to show you—"

"Not interested," Zee said. "In the meantime, I'm gonna step out for a smoke."

He turned and walked away.

"God, what a friggin' dinosaur," Ben muttered, turning to Drue when Zee was out of earshot. "How is he even still working as an investigator? He can't even figure out how to download a file and attach it to an email. I've tried to show him, like, a hundred times."

"At least he treats you like an adult," Drue said. "To him, I'm still a five-year-old."

"Hey," Ben said, standing beside her cubicle. "It's Friday and it's beer-thirty. How about it?"

"No thanks," Drue said, looking up. "I was out of the office all morning. I think I'll hang here for a while and get caught up."

"We'll be at Taco Truck if you change your mind," Ben said, as Jonah walked up and joined him.

It didn't take long for the office to empty out. By six o'clock, she was alone.

Drue went into the break room, got a soft drink, then sat back down and stared again at the video of Jazmin Mayes's last night of work at the Gulf Vista resort.

She watched it, reversed it and then watched it again, hoping in vain that something would jump out at her, some moment that would tell her what had gone so terribly wrong that night.

After another hour of watching, Drue stood, stretched and walked around the empty office. She noticed her colleagues' workspaces. Ben's desktop was clinically neat, devoid of everything but his computer. No photos, kitschy toys, not even a file folder. Out of idle curiosity, she tried the top desk drawer. It was locked, as were the other drawers.

Jonah's desk, on the other hand, resembled a mini-landfill. A stack of empty plastic stadium cups with the orange and blue UF logo sat atop a dog-eared copy of *Sports Illustrated*. A cracked coffee mug held an array of pencils and pens, and a stapler in the shape of an alligator was being used as a paperweight on a stack of computer printouts and file folders. Pushed to the back of the desk was a framed photo of Jonah, posed on the beach between two adorable towheaded preschoolers in swimsuits. She picked up the photo and examined it with interest. Cute kids. She wondered whose they were. Jonah hadn't bothered to lock his desk. The top drawer held a snarl of paper clips, rubber bands, Post-it notes, a half-empty bottle of aspirin and an astonishing number of tubes of lip balm. She counted eleven different brands and flavors before she lost interest and went back to her own desk and the Gulf Vista security video one last time.

Drue's eyes were burning with fatigue as she reached the portion of the video at the 11:05 P.M. point.

Again, she saw the shadowy figure of the housekeeper slowly roll the laundry cart toward a door at the end of a long, narrow hallway. Jazmin's face was obscured by the bill of her baseball cap as she hesitated in front of the door, but when she raised her head to slide her key lanyard from her neck, Drue spotted the girl's distinctive pointed chin. She watched as Jazmin passed the key card over the door lock, then pushed the door open.

At 1:32 A.M. the door to the room opened. The laundry cart

emerged from the room, followed by Jazmin, whose head was bowed as she walked rapidly away from the room.

Drue watched as the girl's figure moved out of camera range. She paused the video, reversed and watched it again. Something was different, she thought. The most obvious thing was the housekeeper's energy level. When the girl approached the room she was trudging, clearly exhausted at the end of a long night. But when she emerged, two and a half hours later, she moved at a near-run.

Drue paused the video again, staring down at the back of the housekeeper's head. Something else was different too. She didn't know what it meant, but she was sure it had to mean something. She reached for her phone and called Rae Hernandez. When the call went straight to voice mail, she left a message: "Rae, call me, please. I think I figured something out."

She went back to work, glancing at her phone every fifteen minutes, until finally it rang, and she saw UNKNOWN CALLER flash across the caller ID screen.

46

She snatched the phone up. "Hey."

"You're starting to get on my nerves with all these phone calls," Rae Hernandez said.

Drue said eagerly, "Look, I've got lots to tell you, which is why I've been trying to reach you."

"So you said. What's up?"

The words came tumbling out, and even to Drue it sounded like she was babbling.

"I went over to the Silver Sands Motel the other night and talked to Jazmin's boyfriend. He told me that when he worked at the Gulf Vista, Shelnutt, the head of security, and some of his cronies there used to get together in a vacant room to watch footage from the security cameras—of half-dressed or nearly naked women at the beach or pool, couples having sex in the elevators. Porn parties, Jorge called them. I also then managed to track down Neesa Vincent, the housekeeper who was Jazmin's best friend. And she admitted to me—"

"What the hell do you think you're doing?" Hernandez demanded. "Who told you to go around interviewing my witnesses?"

"I wasn't really interviewing them, I was just talking, and I think they told me stuff they might not tell a cop . . ."

"Jesus Christ on a crutch." Hernandez moaned. "I knew it was a mistake talking to you. Don't you understand? This is an active investigation. You're putting it and yourself in jeopardy. The last thing I need is some amateur mucking around in things."

"I wasn't mucking," Drue said, refusing to be intimidated. "Do you want me to tell you what I found out? Like how both Jazmin and Neesa were trading sex for favors from Herman Byars, the head of housekeeping? Or do you want to keep bitching me out?"

"What I want to do is go home and have dinner with my family, which I promised my husband I would do tonight," Hernandez groused.

"Okay, fine." Drue disconnected.

Her phone rang again. She waited three beats and picked it up.

"Don't hang up on me again," Hernandez said with a growl. "This isn't some game you're playing."

"I'm well aware of that," Drue said, matching the detective's tone. "Can we meet? Or not?"

"We don't need a coffee klatch. Just tell me everything you learned," Hernandez said.

"I was thinking I could tell you what I know and you could let me see the rest of the video from the hotel."

The sheriff's detective swore softly. "I don't need this shit."

"What kind of pizza do you like?" Drue asked, reaching for her purse and keys.

"What's that got to do with anything?"

"I haven't had dinner and I'm starving. I'll pick us up a pizza on the way to your office."

"Pepperoni. Cheese. No green peppers and no goddamn anchovies."

"Goes without saying," Drue agreed.

Rae Hernandez eyed the grease-spotted pizza box warily. "What took you so long? I'm starving and I almost gave up on you."

"I was all the way in downtown St. Pete," Drue said, as Hernandez led her back to her office, stopping in the break room to buy soft drinks from a vending machine.

Drue put the pizza box on top of a file cabinet, and Hernandez opened a file drawer and pulled out paper plates and napkins. The smell of warm tomato sauce and gooey melted cheese filled the small, cluttered office.

Hernandez rolled her desk chair over to the cabinet and put a slice of pizza on her plate. "Tell me more about these porn parties. It would have been nice if I'd heard about this two years ago."

"Jorge said he only went once," Drue said, putting aside her own slice of pizza. "But he said Shelnutt and his buddies had them all the time. The head of engineering, Larry Boone, would designate a room as 'out of order,' so that the front desk staff wouldn't rent it out."

"And who were the guests at these little soirees?"

Drue ticked off the names she'd been given. "Shelnutt, Herman Byars, Boone for sure."

"How about the hotel manager?" Hernandez asked.

"Jorge didn't mention him."

Hernandez sipped her Diet Coke. "Did Jorge say anything about Jazmin's relationship with those guys?"

"He said she never specifically complained about any of them. But he doesn't have a high opinion of the management staff at his old place of employment."

"That makes two of us," Hernandez said. "How did you manage to track down Neesa? I've been wanting to question her again, but she's been in the wind for nearly two years now."

"Jorge told me she hangs out at Mister B's. The country music club in Seminole. Sure enough, one of the bartenders pointed her out to me, and eventually we got to chatting. She got pretty talkative after I started buying the drinks," Drue said. "And even more so on the drive home."

She placed her cell phone on the desktop and played back her tape of Neesa's conversation.

"Interesting," Hernandez said, when the tape ended. "But totally illegal to tape somebody in this state without their knowledge. Still, you got her to admit to being a petty thief, and whoring herself out to the head of housekeeping to get herself out of trouble."

"So, what do you think?" Drue asked, secretly pleased with her own sleuthing abilities.

The detective shrugged. "I think it's probably time to revisit Herman Byars, and probably Brian Shelnutt too."

"My turn," Drue said. "Can we talk about that video?"

Rae Hernandez stood and closed the door to the office. "I know I'm gonna regret this," she said, as she motioned for Drue to join her in front of the computer monitor on her desktop. "One of our tech guys put this together. It's all footage of Jazmin Mayes on September fifteenth, from the time she arrived at the hotel until the last time she's seen alive."

She tapped some keys, and a grainy black-and-white image of a dimly lit parking lot filled the screen. As Drue watched, a cab pulled into view and a woman dressed in a short-sleeved T-shirt and jeans climbed out of the backseat.

"This is at 2:45 P.M. and shows Jazmin arriving late to work, in a cab," Hernandez commented.

The next sequence, a half hour later, showed Jazmin in what appeared to be a locker room. As she watched, Jazmin spun the dial of a padlock, opened it and placed her pocketbook inside. She donned a uniform smock, then sat on a nearby bench and removed her street shoes before donning a pair of white tennis shoes. As she was finishing up, another woman, dressed in a housekeeping smock, entered the room and began talking to Jazmin. The woman was black, and her hair was worn in a spiraling coronet of cornrows.

Drue squinted at the screen. "Is that Neesa Vincent?"

"Yeah. I thought you just met her."

"Her hair's different now," Drue commented. While the women talked, Jazmin took a cell phone from her pocketbook and stashed it in the pocket of her jeans, then reached inside the locker again and pulled out a white baseball cap.

"Watch this part," Hernandez commented.

Neesa and Jazmin were engaged in a spirited conversation, with Neesa making wild hand gestures, once even grabbing Jazmin by the collar of her smock. Jazmin appeared agitated too, shaking her head emphatically and poking Neesa in the chest with her forefinger.

"Looks like they were having a pretty serious argument," Drue said. "Did you ask Neesa about that when you questioned her?"

"We did," Hernandez said, stopping the video. "She claimed it was just some misunderstanding about scheduling. Said Jazmin had agreed to swap days off with her, and then backed out at the last minute. She also said the two worked things out later that night."

"Did you believe her?" Drue asked.

"At the time, we had no reason not to," Hernandez answered.

The detective restarted the video. Jazmin donned her baseball cap and left the room, pushing a housekeeping cart. Neesa, however, lingered. She pulled out her own phone, pausing to light a cigarette, before tucking the lighter in her pocket. The video showed the housekeeper walking toward the locker room door, opening it and waving the smoke outside.

"Wonder who she was calling?" Drue said.

Hernandez cued up the video and Drue watched for another hour as Gulf Vista's security cameras captured the young housekeeper trundling her cart down narrow hotel hallways, pushing it in and out of rooms, and eventually, at the 7:30 P.M. mark, entering a drab room with vending machines and five or six tables and chairs.

"The break room," Hernandez said. The video showed Jazmin entering, inserting coins into a soft drink machine and retrieving a drink. Then she sat at a table, alone. She removed her cap, talked on her cell phone, then appeared to be typing something into the phone.

"Did you find Jazmin's cell phone after she was killed?" Drue asked.

"No." Hernandez shrugged. "Unfortunately, Jazmin was in the habit of buying cheap burner phones at Walmart, because she couldn't afford a contract. Probably the killer took that phone and destroyed it. We got Yvonne Howington to try calling it, off and on for the next three days, but there was never an answer."

"Do you know who she texted that night?"

"It was a teacher at her daughter's school. Nothing of interest."

"No sign of Neesa," Drue pointed out. "Which means she lied when she told me she and Jazmin got together during their break that night."

The two women continued watching as Jazmin and her cart worked a route through the hotel hallways, each time stopping outside a room and consulting a printed list. Occasionally, Jazmin picked up a small handheld radio and spoke into it.

"Who's she talking to?" Drue asked.

"The front desk. The clerks call housekeepers to determine

whether a room has been cleaned and is ready for check-in, or they'll call up to have more towels or soaps delivered to a room if a guest requests it," Hernandez said.

"She cleaned a total of twelve rooms that night," Hernandez said. "Trust me, there's nothing more worth watching, so I'm gonna speed it up to show you the last room Jazmin cleaned that night, room 133, because I'm tired and I want to go home and see my family and take a bath."

Drue thought better of protesting.

"Here we go," Hernandez said, pausing the video at the 11:05 point.

The video showed a housekeeper in a Gulf Vista smock and baseball cap stopped outside a room. The woman passed her key card over the door's lock and entered. At 1:32, she emerged from the room and set off down the hallway with the cart, getting into the elevator, then walking down the walkway to the laundry room.

"And that's it," Hernandez said. "The last time we have her on camera."

"Can you back that up so I can see it again?" Drue asked.

Hernandez sighed dramatically but did as her guest asked.

Drue leaned in closer, staring at the computer screen. The angle of the security camera showed the housekeeper from above, but her face was obscured by the bill of the baseball cap.

"That last room she cleaned, did you guys find anything there?" Drue asked.

"Nothing. Turns out Jazmin was a really thorough worker," Hernandez said. "We questioned the last guest who'd stayed in the room, but he didn't know anything. He checked out late that afternoon because he had a family emergency. In fact, we checked *all* the rooms in that wing the next morning, and found zip."

"Meaning, you never discovered where she was killed," Drue said.

"It's a big property. Two hundred rooms, guests checking in and out, and hotel staff busy cleaning up what could have been evidence."

Hernandez stood up, stretched and yawned. "Okay, party's over. I'm out, and so are you."

Drue hesitated. "I'd really like to watch that video again. All of it."

"No way," Hernandez retorted. "I'm not hanging around here for another minute. And you're done poking your nose in police business."

"You could just transfer it to a flash drive," Drue suggested. "I'll take it with me and watch it again. Who knows? Maybe a fresh set of eyes will catch something you missed."

Hernandez shook her head again and muttered something under her breath. But ten minutes later Drue was back in the white Bronco, the flash drive tucked securely in her purse.

47

She let herself into the deserted office again, switching on lights as she went. "Next paycheck," she muttered, seating herself at her desk, "I buy myself a laptop. Screw the roof."

The grainy video played out again on her computer screen, and she yawned, wishing for coffee but too tired to trek to the break room to brew a pot. She fast-forwarded the video to the 11:05 mark and watched again as Jazmin Mayes removed her baseball cap, lifted her key card from around her neck and passed it over the door lock, then put the cap in place again before entering the room. She reversed, then froze the frame showing Jazmin's face, tilted for only a moment toward the camera.

"Oh my God," she whispered, reaching for her phone.

~

"Hello?" The childish voice on the other end was breathless.

"Uh, hi," Drue said. "I'm trying to reach Rae Hernandez."

"Who's calling, please?"

"This is Drue Campbell."

"I'm sorry, she can't come to the phone right now."

"Is this her son?" Drue asked. "Because it's really important I speak to your mom."

"I'm not allowed to say," the child replied. "How do you spell Campbell?"

"It's *C-A-M-P-B-E-L-L*. Like the soup." At one point in her childhood, Drue's skate rat pals had actually nicknamed her Soup.

She searched her mind, trying to remember the kid's name. She could picture him, standing at bat, the legs of his baseball pants bagging over the tops of his high red socks. "This is Dez, right? Rae's son?"

"I'm not allowed to say," he repeated.

"Please tell your mom it's really, really important that I speak to her tonight. As soon as possible. Will she be home later?"

"I'm not allowed to say." The boy was definitely his mother's son, as well as a cop's kid.

"Ask her to call me, will you, Dez?"

Drue paced around the office, too keyed up to sit for another minute. Jazmin Mayes had been killed at the Gulf Vista nearly two years ago, and now she was so close to finding the truth about her murder, she had to do something.

She called Corey. The phone rang four times, but finally he answered.

"Hello?" His voice sounded groggy. She glanced up at the clock on the office wall. It was after ten.

"Oh no. Did I wake you up?" she asked.

"Uh, yeah. I've got my Iron Man thing tomorrow. What's up?"

The words poured out in a torrent, tumbling over one another so fast she knew she was barely making sense.

"Corey, I got the unedited security tape from the Gulf Vista. I've been watching it, here at work, all night. And I think I've figured out what happened, but I need to go over to the hotel and get a look at the last room Jazmin cleaned that night."

He yawned loudly. "Okay, but it'll have to wait until Sunday. I've gotta be over in Tampa at six tomorrow morning, and I'll be in no shape to do anything after that."

"Sunday?" She didn't bother trying to hide her disappointment. "I really want to go over there tonight. It won't take that long, I swear. I just need—"

"Honey, I can't," Corey said. "I'm sorry, but I promise, I'll go with you Sunday." He yawned again. "Wish me luck for tomorrow."

"Good luck," she said reluctantly.

She hesitated for a moment, then tried calling Ben. He might disagree with her decision to keep poking around in the investigation, but she felt sure that if she laid out the facts for him, he'd listen to reason.

The call went directly to voice mail. If he and Jonah were still at Taco Truck, he probably couldn't even hear his phone over the noise of the Friday night crowd. Should she leave a message?

"Hey Ben. It's Drue. Listen, I know you told me to leave it alone, but I think I might have uncovered something really big on the Jazmin Mayes case. I want to go out to the Gulf Vista and check out a hunch, and I could really use a wingman if you're available. Call me as soon as you get this, okay?"

Drue considered calling Jonah, but discarded the idea almost immediately. Things were still at the awkward stage between them. That might change after their date Saturday night, but for now, she decided against roping him into her scheme.

She pulled the white Bronco up to the security gate at the Gulf Vista Resort. Two cars were in front of her, and she inched forward, slowly, until she reached the security gate. The guard, a wiry, twenty-something white woman with a clipboard clamped under her arm, greeted her with a businesslike nod. "Welcome to the Gulf Vista. Name and room number?"

"Oh, I'm not a guest," Drue said, offering her a sweet smile. "Just joining friends."

"Did your friends call the gate to get a pass left for you?"

"Well, um, I'm not sure," Drue said.

The guard consulted her clipboard. "Name?"

"Drue. Campbell, like the soup."

"Nope."

"They probably forgot," Drue confided. "It's a bachelorette party, and the maid of honor is a *total* space cadet."

"Not my problem," the guard said. She looked past Drue at a car that had just pulled in behind the Bronco. "Gonna ask you to move along, ma'am."

~

She drove home to Coquina Cottage and paced around the compact living room. Still no callbacks, from either Rae Hernandez or Ben. Drue could hear Sherri's voice in her head, repeating one of her favorite sayings: "If you want something done, do it yourself."

"I will, by God," Drue muttered. "And if I can't get in the front door, Mom, I'll go in the back."

She changed out of her work clothes and into her best beach cover-up, a loud pink and lime-green floral Lilly Pulitzer number she'd picked up at her favorite thrift store back in Fort Lauderdale. She'd never cared for the pom-pom trim, but the top did have deep in-seam pockets, perfect to stash her cell phone, house keys and some folded-up cash money.

Her stomach rumbled as she passed through the kitchen and she realized that she hadn't eaten anything since that slice of pizza earlier. She grabbed a protein bar from her grandmother's cookie jar on the counter and slipped out the sliding-glass doors and onto the deck. The locking mechanism on the doors had rusted in the salt air, and when she was inside, she simply jammed a sawed-off broomstick into the track. Every time she walked out onto the deck she vowed that her next paycheck would go toward installing a new lock. Right after a laptop, but before the new roof.

She was halfway down the beach when she remembered the key card she'd lifted on her last visit to the hotel. She turned around, found the key on top of her dresser and doubled back, headed for the bright lights of the Gulf Vista. As she walked on the uneven sand, her knee twinged, but she kept going until she reached the gate that separated the back of the resort from the public beach.

She looked around, swiped the card and tugged at the gate. It didn't budge. She tried again, then gave up. Maybe the hotel locks had been re-programmed. She didn't have time to wonder. Drue glanced up at the deep blue sky. There was a new moon tonight, mostly obscured by heavy cloud cover. The beach was deserted and cast in darkness, but music wafted from the resort's pool area.

Now or never, she told herself. She placed her left foot on the bottom rail of the gate and swung her right leg up and over in the most awkward vault attempt ever, catching the hem of her top on a gate finial. As she tumbled forward onto the sand on the resort side of the fence, she felt a searing jolt of pain in her bad knee and heard the fabric of her top rip.

Drue sat up, moaning quietly, her leg extended straight out as she kneaded the knee with her fingertips. After a moment, the pain subsided. Maybe, she thought, maybe she hadn't ruptured the joint again.

She stood up slowly, panting from the effort, and brushed the sand from her butt. She gingerly put her right foot down. There was soreness, yes, but nothing like what she'd experienced with her original injury. There was also a jagged rip along the hem of her top, but there was no blood and she could walk, which she did, as quickly as possible, toward the pool and tiki bar area, congratulating herself on her first solo breaking-and-entering effort.

She heard the high-pitched cacophony of women's laughter

as she approached the tiki bar. Sure enough, at least two dozen young women, all dressed in matching pink T-shirts and tiaras, were clustered around the periphery of the bar, drunkenly twerking and bellowing along to the version of "Bootylicious" blaring from a cell phone speaker balanced on a nearby chaise lounge.

Drue edged as close as she could get to the bar, finally managing to edge in between two middle-aged men who were watching the revelry with undisguised appreciation. There had been a time, Drue reflected, when one or both of those men would have struck up a conversation and offered to buy her a drink, but tonight, she was just another face in a crowd of younger talent. It took another ten minutes for the bartender, dressed in a Hawaiian shirt, to work down the bar to her.

"Do you happen to have any bar munchies?" she asked him. He turned, wordlessly, and handed her a bowl of popcorn.

"Great. I'll have a Tito's and tonic, double lime," she said, sliding a ten-dollar bill onto the bar.

He fixed the drink and when he delivered it, added a bowl of mixed nuts to her dinner.

"Thanks!" He nodded and moved away.

She sipped her drink and emptied the popcorn bowl and half the bowl of nuts as conversation swirled around her. After another ten minutes, the balding guy on her left signaled for the bartender to close out his tab, the move she'd been waiting for.

"Put it on my room, please," he told the bartender, signing the bill. "It's Gazaway, Room 325."

"Got it," the bartender replied.

Got it, Drue thought, gulping down the rest of her drink. She skirted the pool area and moved off to the right, looking for the entrance to the north building. She found the door easily, but once again, her key card failed. She tossed it into the nearest trash bin, then hung around for five minutes, planning to slip inside in the wake of a legit guest, but nobody approached the building.

Drue drifted into the hotel lobby and planted herself in front of the reception desk.

The clerk, dressed in the official Gulf Vista Royal Bahamian uniform, looked up as she approached.

"How can I help?" He looked to be around twenty, with a sunburn and a peeling nose.

She patted the pockets of her cover-up. "You're not gonna believe this. I think I misplaced my key."

"No problem," he said gallantly. "What's the name and room number?"

"Gazaway, Room 325."

He turned to his computer monitor, tapped some keys and nodded. "Okay, Ms. Gazaway. Now, do you have some ID?"

She laughed. "That's the problem. I've been down at the tiki bar, and I didn't take my billfold with me, because we were charging our drinks to the room."

"Shouldn't be a problem," he said, nodding. "I just need the address listed on the credit card on your account."

"Oh." She made a pouting face. "The thing is, my cousin booked the room. And I don't actually know her new address, since she got married."

Drue was shocked how easily the lies rolled off her lips.

But the desk clerk was not impressed. "Can you call her?" he asked. "If she comes down to the desk, I can easily get another key made for you."

"Ugh!" Drue exclaimed. "She wandered away with her husband, and she left her phone in the room. Can't you just make me another key without all that rigamarole?"

"Can't," he said, shrugging. "Against hotel policy. Wish I could help."

Drue tried to look helpless. It wasn't working. "Okay," she said, sighing deeply. "Do you have a map of the property?"

He raised an eyebrow. "Yes."

Since helpless wasn't working she held out her hand and tried haughty. "May I have one, please?"

She could sense the clerk watching as she strolled out of the lobby in the direction of the pool. Once outside, she studied the map, trying to get her bearings again.

According to what Hernandez told her, the last room Jazmin cleaned on the night she was murdered was Room 133. Which probably meant the room was on the first floor of the north building.

She followed the stone-paved walkway through the lush junglelike landscaping, flinching once when a tiny green tree frog dropped off an overhanging basket, brushing her arm. The east end of the north building loomed ahead of her. Consulting the map, she was surprised to note that there was a second pool on the property, and that the back of the north building faced it. There was a door here into what looked like the building's elevator tower, but it too was locked. She kept following the path until she could see the shimmering reflection of the pool water bouncing on the back of the building. The sidewalk ended abruptly at a gate in a six-foot-high wooden stockade fence.

Drue held her breath as she hip-checked the gate, which swung open easily. Finally!

A smallish, kidney-shaped pool lay before her. The landscaping here was not nearly as lush or well-maintained as the rest of the property, and indeed, the whole area had the feeling of steerage class on a luxury liner. She gazed up at the building and realized that the architectural style here was also markedly different from the rest of the resort facility. It was a boxy concrete block tower, four floors, with each room outfitted with an abbreviated wrought-iron balcony just large enough for a pair of inexpensive plastic armchairs. This, she thought, was probably the earliest phase of the resort, featuring the most inexpensive rooms, without a beach view.

Lights shone in only a handful of the rooms looking out on the pool. To her disappointment, the first level of balconies was actually elevated about six feet above the pool decking. She stood under the shadow of the balconies and gazed upward, wondering if the theory she'd formed after watching hours of security camera video would hold water.

Would it be possible for someone to access a balcony, and from there, a room, from here? She looked wildly around the deck, searching for something to use as a ladder. Most of the pool furniture looked too flimsy to support her weight.

The most substantial item she spotted was a concrete-encased trash barrel that stood beside an ice maker and a Coke machine. Drue leaned against the barrel and sighed. No way could she move this thing by herself. She was shocked, though, when the barrel seemed to roll out from under her.

She ducked down and saw that the barrel was actually mounted on rollers. Hallelujah!

Drue walked to the far side of the pool area and counted sets of sliding-glass doors. If the rooms on this side of the building were odd-numbered, she calculated that 133 could be the third room from the far end. The room was dark. With any luck, it was also vacant tonight.

Her knee was throbbing badly, but she pushed the trash barrel toward the far end of the building, stopping once or twice to check her progress. Finally, when she had the barrel in position, she ducked down again, and using the flashlight on her cell phone, checked to see if the casters were equipped with some kind of brakes.

Nope. But she spotted a forgotten beach towel slung over the back of a chaise lounge near the pool. She fetched the towel and wrapped it around the casters to immobilize them, then dragged a chair over to the trash barrel. She kicked off her flip-flops. Gritting her teeth, she climbed from the seat of the chair onto the top of the barrel placing her feet on opposite sides of the barrel edges, praying the whole thing wouldn't topple over beneath her weight.

She held her breath, and slowly stood, her calves and thigh muscles screaming in tandem at the unexpected workout.

Drue found herself at eye level with the top of the wrought-iron balcony railing. She swallowed hard and hooked her left leg over the railing, with her right leg in midair. Suddenly a beam of light flashed in her eyes and a man's voice sliced through the darkness.

"Stay right there, ma'am."

Drue froze momentarily, but she didn't dare obey the order, because she simply didn't have the strength to climb down. Instead she propelled herself upward and onto the balcony. The flashlight beam was blinding.

"Ma'am? The police have been called. Now I need you to come back down here, the way you went up."

"I wish I could," she said with a sigh, shielding her eyes with her arm. Her knees and calves were shaking so badly it was all she could do to sink onto the floor of the balcony.

48

August 19, 1976

Colleen sat in the perfect living room of her perfect house. It was just a cracker box, really, the smallest house on the block, and it was only a rental, but it was on Snell Isle, the ritziest neighborhood in St. Pete, and only a few blocks from Allen's parents' waterfront mansion on Brightwaters Boulevard, which was all that mattered to her husband.

A car honked outside, causing her to startle, just a little. Allen emerged from the hallway, loaded down with a suitcase, a tackle box and his deep-sea fishing rod. "That's Dad," he announced, looking out the front picture window.

Colleen stood and walked him to the door. He set the baggage down and pulled her close, tipping her chin up and kissing her. "Be good," he said. He kissed her again, for good measure, thrusting his tongue down her throat, then giving her left nipple a vicious twist.

"You too," she said, forcing a smile and opening the door. It had gotten dark, but she stepped outside and waved at Morton Hicks, who was behind the wheel of his station wagon with his twenty-one-foot Boston Whaler in tow.

"See you Sunday night," Allen called, right before he climbed in the front seat of the Vista Cruiser.

The station wagon pulled away from the curb and she stood, watching, as the distinctive curved taillights receded into the steamy summer night. When she finally saw them make the turn onto Brightwaters Boulevard, she exhaled slowly.

Colleen took the cream-colored Samsonite train case from the top shelf of her closet and set it on the quilted floral-print bedspread. This was her favorite room in the house, and she would miss it. She'd picked out the avocado-green and orange floral bedspread and curtains herself, coordinating them with the thick wall-to-wall carpet she'd badgered their landlord into installing throughout the house.

She didn't plan to take much with her. Just toiletries and cosmetics. Everything else she'd buy new, when she arrived in Atlanta. She had a second thought then, and her lips curved in a dreamy smile.

Colleen reached back into the closet and pulled out the needlepoint racquet cover that had been a birthday gift from her mother-in-law, Rosemary, who was well aware that Colleen despised tennis. She unzipped the case and felt around inside, but the only thing she found was the Wilson Chris Evert racquet. It was in like-new condition, because she'd never used the thing.

She felt goose bumps rise on her arms. The black push-up bra and the black lace garter belt were gone. She'd hidden them there just last Thursday night, away from the prying eyes of Estelle, her once-a-month cleaning lady. But Estelle wasn't due back until next week.

Allen. He'd found her secret hiding place. How many of her other secrets had he uncovered? The realization changed things. She had to get out of this place. Now. Right this minute. She picked up the Princess phone from her nightstand and dialed Brice's house. She didn't care anymore about his friend's threats. She needed to hear Brice's voice, one more time.

The phone rang once, twice, then three times. Someone picked up at the other end.

"Hello?" his wife said. This time, instead of hanging up, for some reason, Colleen didn't end the connection. She breathed softly, listening.

"Hello," Sherri repeated. "Hello?" There was a long, drawn-out pause. "I know it's you," his wife said, her voice hoarse. "I know where you live and I know where you work . . ."

Colleen didn't wait to hear more. She slammed the receiver down, grabbed the train case and fled the perfect house.

Friday morning, at precisely 11:35, she made her way to the teller's cage at the Florida Federal Savings and Loan branch four blocks from her office.

She could forge Allen's signature in her sleep, but just in case, she practiced copying it over and over and over again in her room at the Ramada Inn, where even the pills she'd taken from work didn't help her to sleep at all the night before.

"Hi, Mrs. Hicks." He was the youngest teller on the line, not even twenty-one, with wispy blond hair and a sprinkling of pimples on his cheeks. He was also the only male; the rest of the tellers were a bunch of sour-faced old biddies, who'd probably faint if they ever saw a penis.

Not Christopher, though. She bet he'd seen more than his share of dick in his young days.

"Good morning, Christopher," she said crisply. With her fingertips, she pushed her savings passbook and the withdrawal slip across the scarred marble counter.

His eyes widened when he saw the amount of the withdrawal. "Wow," he said.

"Down payment on our new house," Colleen said.

"Oh, okay. You'll want a cashier's check, right?"

She shook her head. "The seller insists on cash." She leaned in closer and confided, "He's Japanese. They don't do things the same way as us."

"Right." He glanced over his shoulder, looking distinctly uneasy.

"Is there a problem?" She felt like screaming, but forced herself to stay calm.

"Uh, well, a transaction like this, in cash and all, I'd have to get a manager to approve."

"Fine," she said, pointedly looking at her wristwatch. "I can wait."

Colleen felt as though a million ants had taken up residence in her veins. Come on, come on, come on, she wanted to scream.

Five minutes passed. Then ten. Finally, Christopher reappeared, trailing timidly behind a balding middle-aged man in a brown polyester three-piece suit. The buttons on his vest strained, and she could see sweat circles forming on the armpits of his jacket.

"Mrs. Hicks?" The manager extended a hand. "I'm Paul Forkner, assistant branch manager." She took his hand. It was limp and sweaty.

"And I'm Colleen Hicks, and I'm due back at work in five minutes," she replied. "As I told Christopher, we're closing on our new house Monday, and the seller insists on a cash transaction."

Forkner stared down at her passbook, which he was holding in his plump white hands.

"Usually in cases like these, on a withdrawal this size, we require both account holders to sign off," Forkner said. "Perhaps your husband could drop by later—"

"That's impossible," Colleen interrupted. "Allen is on a fishing trip in the Keys, with his father. Dr. Morton Hicks?"

"Um, then maybe Monday?"

"The closing is at eight o'clock Monday morning," Colleen said. She felt the blood rising in her cheeks, the ants stirring just beneath her skin. "Which is why I'm here today. With a withdrawal slip signed by myself and my husband." She leaned across the counter and stared into his pale, bulging eyes. "Mr. Forkner, did you know that my father-in-law is on the board of this bank?"

"Yes, of course. Which is why we need to be certain things are done properly and in compliance with bank policy—"

"I don't give a rat's ass about your policies," Colleen said, so loudly that the prune-faced tellers up and down the line were momentarily frozen in place. "Now, if you would, please instruct Christopher here to complete my withdrawal, exactly as I've requested. Because if he doesn't do that, and I have to tell my husband on Monday morning that we can't close on this house because some bean counter at this branch, where he's banked his whole life, wouldn't release our funds, he is *not* going to be happy. And if you think I'm difficult to deal with, Mr. Forkner? You haven't met my husband. Or his father."

Forkner pursed his lips and examined the passbook again. He handed it back to the clerk, gave a slight nod of his head, then slithered back to his office.

Colleen placed the train case on the counter, popped the lock and gave Christopher a naughty little wink. "Big bills, please."

As he was stacking the paper-banded stacks of bills in the case, she remembered the business envelope she'd stuck in her pocketbook just before leaving the office. She took it out, removed her last paycheck and endorsed the back. "This too, please," she said sweetly.

Vera Cochran was ridiculously pleased when Colleen asked her to go shopping that afternoon. Her coworker was the closest thing she had to a real girlfriend, and Colleen felt almost guilty about making her an unwitting accomplice to her escape plan.

"I'd love to," Vera said, her face flushed with happiness. "But I promised to stay late for one of my regular patients. Can you wait 'til after two?"

"Okay," Colleen said. She had plenty of time until her bus left.

When the office closed, Colleen suggested they drive her car over to Maas Brothers. "It's too hot to walk," Colleen explained. "And anyway, I've had my eye on a new outfit, and I don't want to have to haul it all the way back here."

"Good idea," Vera agreed.

She parked the Camaro on the second level of the parking deck, feeling only slightly anxious about the train case she'd locked in the trunk.

Shopping always relaxed Colleen, especially now that she felt no compunction about actually buying whatever the hell she wanted.

The yellow sundress was on end-of-season clearance sale, and Vera agreed it was a steal. "It fits like a dream," she said, watching enviously as Colleen handed over the pale blue Maas Brothers charge card. They took the escalator down to the first-floor shoe department, where Colleen found a pair of yellow patent leather platform sandals that looked like they'd been designed to go with the sundress, and then, back upstairs to juniors' sportswear, for a pair of Gloria Vanderbilt designer jeans and a slinky print top.

"I'd kill for a pair of those jeans," Vera commented, when Colleen emerged from the dressing room to model her purchases. "Won't Allen blow a gasket when he sees how much you spent today?"

Colleen shrugged. "He'll get over it. Come on, let's go get an early dinner."

Vera grimaced. "I promised my sister I'd babysit tonight."

"It's just now five," Colleen said. "And the store closes at six. Come on, it'll be fun. My treat!"

She hardly had to twist the girl's arm. Vera ordered the club sandwich and Colleen had the chicken salad plate, and at Colleen's insistence, they each had a glass of Chablis.

"This has been so much fun," Vera said, giggling as she gathered her things to leave. "But I really have to scoot now. We should do this more often. Especially the wine part!" She took a five-dollar bill from her billfold, but Colleen waved the money away. "My treat, remember?"

"Okay," Vera said, rising. "Have a great weekend. See you Monday."

Her bus to Atlanta wasn't leaving until seven-thirty. Colleen ordered another glass of Chablis, gulped it down and paid again with her credit card. Then she went into the ladies' room and changed into the tight-fitting new designer jeans and platform heels. She pulled a floppy-brimmed straw hat from her pocketbook and tucked her long hair beneath it. At the last minute, she took off her bra and put it in her pocketbook, enjoying the sensation of the silky fabric against her bare breasts, as well as the thought that Allen would have been apoplectic about her walking around braless in public.

When she got to the orange Camaro she unlocked the trunk and removed the train case, flipping the lid just to make sure her runaway money, as she'd come to think of it, was intact. All was well. She folded the new dress, still in the shopping bag, on top of the cash. She opened the driver's-side door and placed the clothes she'd been wearing, including her bra and pantyhose, carefully folded, on the bucket seat. She tossed the shoes she'd worn onto the floor and thought for a moment. And then she had a flash of genius.

Allen enjoyed inflicting pain, so maybe she'd hurt him a little, as a parting gesture. She took the nail scissors she always carried and carefully punctured the tip of her right index finger, squeezing with her left hand, spattering droplets of blood onto her clothes and the seat, even smearing some on the steering wheel. For good measure, she slashed the pantyhose and bra, smearing blood on them too. All in all, it made for a ghastly little crime scene. It also made her a little light-headed, so she sat in the Camaro for a good ten minutes, waiting to regain her equilibrium.

When she emerged from the parking deck onto Second Avenue, she donned a pair of oversize Jackie O sunglasses and set off down the street, swinging the train case. With each swaggering step she took her mood lightened.

Colleen was standing at the corner, waiting for the light to turn, when a car pulled up to the curb. She heard a voice call her name, and when she glanced over, found she was staring down the barrel of a gun. "Get in," the voice said.

49

The Gulf Vista security guard, who was so young it appeared he might have bought his uniform and badge at Toys "R" Us, had difficulty opening the sliding-glass door in Room 133, outside of which Drue was gloomily perched on a cheap plastic chair.

But after much grunting and sweating, he managed to inch the door open far enough to sternly command her, "Come inside, ma'am."

Drue obliged, stepping into the room. To her delight, the kiddie cop had switched on the overhead light. There wasn't much to see. The room was small, furnished with a queen-size bed, dresser, nightstands and bad art. The carpet was worn and faded and, though it was clean enough, the room smelled faintly of mildew. Any clues to the criminal acts that had led to Jazmin Mayes's death were long gone, she knew.

The door from the hallway swung open and a middle-aged white guy entered. He had wire-rimmed glasses perched atop a beakish nose and was dressed in a white polo shirt, black dress slacks and a black baseball cap with the word SECURITY stitched across the bill.

"Here she is, Mr. Shelnutt," the guard said, gesturing to Drue, who was still trying to take in every detail of the room.

"What do you think you're doing here?" Shelnutt asked, his deep bass voice meant to intimidate.

"Just looking around," Drue said, trying to sound nonchalant.

"Attempted breaking and entering," Shelnutt said. He unclipped a radio from the holster on his belt and spoke into it. "Security one to front gate. A TI police unit should be arriving any minute. Let them in and direct them to Room 133."

The radio crackled but the guard's response was unintelligible.

"Say again?" Shelnutt said.

"Just passed them through," the guard repeated.

Drue slumped down onto the desk chair.

"Who told you to sit down?" Shelnutt barked. "That's hotel property."

She was tired and her knee hurt too much to argue.

"So shoot me."

They heard the soft *ding* from an elevator down the hall and a moment later a uniformed Treasure Island patrol officer entered the room. He was approximately the same age and build as the security guard, although his uniform badge and the service revolver holstered on his hip gave him an air of authority the two rent-a-cops accompanying him lacked, in Drue's opinion.

He looked from Drue to the glowering security chief. "What have we got here?"

"Our security cameras caught her sneaking onto the property from the beach and attempting to break into the north tower," Shelnutt said. "When she couldn't gain access that way, she broke the lock on the back gate here, then climbed onto the balcony outside this room."

"That true?" The cop, whose name badge she couldn't read, didn't seem too worked up about her one-woman crime spree.

"I just wanted to get a look at the rooms here," she protested, extending her arms from her sides. "Look, you can see I didn't take anything, and I certainly didn't damage anything either, except my own knee and my favorite beach cover-up."

"Got some ID?" the cop asked.

"No. I was going for a walk on the beach. If you want to look in my pockets you'll see my phone, my house keys and a couple of bucks," Drue said.

"Name? Address?"

"My name is Drucilla Campbell, and I live at 409 Pine Street, Sunset Beach," Drue said.

"I want her searched," Shelnutt snapped.

The cop looked at Drue and cocked his head.

"Go ahead," she said wearily, raising her arms over her head.

His cheeks glowed crimson as he gingerly patted her down.

"See? No crowbar, no lock picks, no dynamite," Drue said.

"Just a stupid misunderstanding. Can I go now? My knee is killing me and I really need some Advil."

"No way," Shelnutt said. "I want her charged with criminal trespass and breaking and entering."

Drue's heart sank. She'd really thought there was a good chance she could talk her way out of this mess.

"Okay," the cop said, motioning toward the hallway. "Let's go."

"Handcuffs?" Shelnutt said sharply.

"Oh yeah." The cop snapped the cuffs around her wrists and led her out of the building and to his waiting police cruiser, whose flashing blue lights had attracted a small gathering of curious guests.

It was barely a ten-minute drive to the Treasure Island police station. Drue slumped down in the backseat, mortified. At least, she thought, at 2:00 A.M. it was unlikely that anybody she knew would see her riding to jail in the backseat of a cop car.

"Do you happen to know Rae Hernandez?" she asked the officer.

"Detective Hernandez? Yeah, I know her," the cop said.

"Any way I could get you to call her?" Drue asked. "I didn't want to say anything in front of those guys at the hotel, but she's kind of the reason I was there."

"No way," the cop replied. "She's off duty, and I'm not gonna be the one calling her at two in the morning. If you know her, you know what she's like when she's pissed off."

"I do know her, and I promise you she'll be even more

pissed off if you don't let her know I've been arrested for trespassing at the Gulf Vista," Drue said.

"That's a call that's way above my pay grade," the cop said.

After he'd removed her from the cruiser, fingerprinted and booked her, the officer, whose name turned out to be Daniels, handed over her phone.

She stared at it for a moment, trying to think of an alternative, but lacking one, she called her father's cell phone.

It rang four times and went to voice mail, so she disconnected and tried again. This time, to her great regret, Wendy answered.

"Drue? Do you know what time it is?"

"Yes, Wendy, I do. Can I please speak to Dad?"

"He's sleeping. We were both sleeping."

She heard her father's voice in the background, then heard Wendy again. "He wants to know what the problem is."

"The problem is that I've been arrested and charged with trespassing, and I'm at the Treasure Island police station," Drue said.

"Is this some kind of a sick joke?"

Before she could answer, Brice came on the line. "What was that last part? Did you say you were arrested?"

"Yes," she said. "I was arrested at the Gulf Vista. If you'll just come down and get me out of here, I promise I'll tell you everything."

"Unbelievable," he muttered. "I'll be right down. Don't talk to anybody. Tell them your attorney is on the way."

As holding cells went, Drue thought this one wasn't as awful as it could have been. Not that she had much experience with that kind of thing. She'd been a rebellious, pain-in-the-ass teenager, but somehow, she'd always managed to stay out of serious, go-to-jail trouble.

She leaned against a wall, closed her eyes and, despite the fluorescent lights overhead, dozed off.

Thirty minutes later she awoke to see the holding cell door open, with her father on the other side of it. He was dressed like someone who'd just been rudely awakened with the news that his adult daughter had been arrested for a teenager-type crime, in baggy cotton drawstring pajama pants, rumpled T-shirt and leather moccasins. His hair was mussed and he needed a shave.

"Let's go," he said, handing her a plastic bag containing her phone and keys. He kept his hand on her elbow as he steered her out the plate-glass doors and into the parking lot. Just then a silver minivan sped up to the entrance. The driver braked and jumped out.

Rae Hernandez looked just as unhappy as Brice Campbell.

"Drue! What the hell's going on? Daniels just called and said you'd been arrested at the Gulf Vista. Are you out of your mind?"

Brice gripped her arm tighter. "Who's this?"

Hernandez looked him in the eye. "Detective Rae Hernandez. I take it you're this juvenile delinquent's father? I recognize you from your television commercials."

"Brice Campbell," he said. "Nice to meet you, but she doesn't have anything to say to the police."

Drue wrenched her arm away from his. "Actually, Dad, I really, really need to talk to Rae. I've been trying to call her all night." She glared back at the detective. "That's why I went over to the hotel tonight, to see if my theory was right."

"Come on, Drue," Brice said. "As your attorney and your father, I'm telling you this is not the time or place for this discussion."

"Dad, please!" Drue exclaimed. "Rae is the detective working the Jazmin Mayes homicide."

He rubbed the stubble on his cheek. "What's that got to do with you? Yvonne Howington is no longer a client of the law firm."

"You took your legal fee from that crappy settlement you got her," Drue said. "Yvonne deserved better than you gave her. Jazmin deserved better. So yeah, I started poking into it. And I found something. Something you and Rae need to hear about."

"Nobody asked you to go breaking and entering. And trespassing," Hernandez said.

Brice shifted into attorney mode. "From what I've heard she didn't actually break into or enter any premises."

Drue sighed. "Can we just take this someplace else to talk about? Preferably some place with coffee?"

"Waffle House okay?" Brice asked, looking at Rae Hernandez.

She shrugged. "Why not? I'll follow you over there."

50

Brice waited until Drue had worked most of her way through a platter of scattered, covered and smothered hash browns along with a side of bacon.

"I still don't understand what would possess you to break into that hotel. Zee looked into Jazmin's murder very thoroughly. And so did the police. It's tragic, but there was nothing there."

Hernandez set her coffee mug down. "Actually, the hotel employees we talked to at the time were less than forthcoming. Management at Gulf Vista stonewalled our investigation right from the beginning. From what we're now hearing, several male supervisors were sexually harassing and preying on female employees, including Jazmin Mayes."

"Is that true?" Brice asked his daughter. "Where did you hear this?"

"I tracked down two different housekeepers, both of whom were friends of Jazmin's, who, by the way, were never interviewed by Jimmy Zee," Drue said. She couldn't resist getting in a dig about the law firm's investigator.

"I went over Zee's report, he didn't find anything about sexual harassment," Brice protested.

"Maybe that's because he didn't look hard enough," Drue said. "The first time I went to Gulf Vista, I talked to Lutrisha Smallwood, she was the girl who found Jazmin's body in that laundry room. She told me that the head of engineering made a habit of trying to grope her, until she zapped him in the eyes with glass cleaner. And she hinted that another guy, Herman Byars, the head of housekeeping, had a 'thing' with one of the other girls working there."

Rae cleared her throat. "Byars has dropped off the radar. He's not working at the tire store where he was employed when I last spoke to him, and I don't have a current address, but I'm working on that."

Brice nodded and glanced at his daughter, who was mopping up the last of the hash browns with a triangle of rye toast. "You said you talked to two housekeepers. Who was the second?"

"Neesa Vincent. Who was supposedly Jazmin's best friend," Drue said bitterly. "But after looking at the hotel's security video for hours earlier tonight, I'd hate to have a friend like her."

"Why's that?" Brice asked.

"Neesa was in on Jazmin's murder," Drue said. "I'm sure of it."

Brice signaled for the waitress to bring the coffeepot back around and settled into the corner of the booth. "Okay. I'm listening."

Drue filled her father in on how she'd tracked down Jazmin's friend and the revelations she'd made after a night of drinking at Mister B's.

"Neesa admitted to me that she started trading sex for preferential treatment from Byars, after she got caught stealing from a guest," Drue said. "The guest complained to management that he'd left eight hundred dollars in cash in the pocket of a bathrobe. Byars lied for Neesa, turned in five hundred, and said the guest was drunk and mistaken about the amount of cash. Afterwards, he kept two hundred and Neesa got to keep a hundred."

"After you told me that, I pulled up all incident reports mentioning missing or stolen property at that hotel for the past three years," Hernandez volunteered. "Lots of petty theft going on at that place. Jewelry, cell phones, cash. But not a single arrest was made."

"You think the head of security was part of the theft ring?" Brice asked.

"We're looking into that," Hernandez said. She tapped Drue on the arm. "Don't leave us hanging here. Let's hear what you think you figured out from the video."

"It'd be easier if I actually had it in front of me," Drue said.

"Hold that thought," Hernandez said, sliding out from the booth.

A moment later she returned from her minivan with a laptop computer. She pushed away the plates and coffee mugs, raised the lid, tapped some buttons and cued up the video from the hotel's security cameras.

Drue pointed at the screen as Jazmin's cab rolled into view.

"I kept going back to that argument Neesa had with Jazmin in the employee locker room that afternoon," Drue said. "There was a time lag of almost thirty minutes between the time Jazmin arrived at the hotel and when she got to the locker room. Of course, there's no video to prove it, but doesn't it stand to reason she had to report first to Byars, and explain why she was late?"

Hernandez paused the video. "Byars told us that when she got to work that day, Jazmin came to him and asked to work a second shift because she needed the money."

"Yvonne has said from the beginning that Jazmin wouldn't have worked that late because of Aliyah," Drue said. "But what if Byars was lying? What if he told her she'd have to make it up to him later that night for coming to work an hour late?" Drue asked.

"That's just supposition," Brice objected.

"Watch the video," Drue said, turning the laptop so her father could see as the action in the employee locker room unfolded.

"Which one is Neesa?" Brice asked.

"The girl with all the extensions and dreads," Drue said.

They watched in silence. "They're definitely having some kind of spat," Brice commented. He watched while Jazmin left the room and Neesa lit a cigarette and pulled out her phone.

"Any idea what the argument was about?" he asked.

"Rae said that Neesa claimed it was a mix-up over trading days off, but they worked it out," Drue said. "But I think she's lying. Look how agitated she is. And who's she calling?"

"You think it was Byars?" Hernandez asked.

"Definitely," Drue said.

Hernandez started the video again. "You can tell that's Jazmin, mainly because she's wearing that white baseball cap," Drue told Brice, referring to the slender woman shown pushing a cleaning cart down the hotel hallways.

"Yeah, but the bill of the cap hides her face," Brice said.

"Exactly." Drue nodded.

After another five minutes of watching, Brice yawned and looked down at his watch. "My God, it's after three. I'm too old for this crap. Can we just get to the point?"

Now Hernandez was yawning too. "My kid has a baseball tournament in Sarasota starting in exactly five hours, so yeah, Drue, let's wind this up."

"Okay," Drue said reluctantly. "Can you fast-forward it to the last room Jazmin cleaned that night? I think it's around the 11:05 mark."

The detective sped up the video, pausing it at the point Drue requested.

"Now back it up, please, so we see Jazmin approaching the room."

Hernandez did as she was asked.

"Check her body language," Drue said. "She's beat. She's walking slowly, you can tell it's an effort pushing that cart. Her shoulders are slumped, her head is down.

"Pause it again here, Rae," Drue added, as the young housekeeper stopped in front of the hotel room door.

"Now watch, she takes the lanyard with her key card and pulls it over her head. She takes the cap off to do that, and you get a good look at Jazmin's face. Start it again, please, Rae."

As the three watched, the housekeeper did just that. Her chin was sharp and pointed, with the same small cleft that Aliyah had, and her face sagged with fatigue.

"See?" Drue said. "That's Jazmin Mayes. No doubt about it, right?"

"Yeah, that's her. Nobody has claimed otherwise," Rae said.

There was a short gap in the video, then the hotel room door opened and the cleaning cart was pushed from the room.

Brice leaned forward to read the time stamp at the bottom of the video. "There's nearly a two-and-a-half-hour gap. What's up with that?"

"The security cameras in the hotel are motion activated," Rae said. "It was apparently a slow night in that wing of the hotel that night."

"Which is another interesting point," Drue said. "There was a Shriner convention going on in the hotel. People everywhere. Why not in that hallway at that time of night?"

She glanced down at the video. "Pause it here, okay?"

Drue tapped the figure of the housekeeper, suspended in time. "Notice anything about Jazmin?"

"Not really," Brice said. "But from the camera angle, you can only see the back of her head."

Rae leaned forward to get a better look. "Something's different about the hat, right?"

"Bingo." Drue tapped the screen again. "Look how high that cap is sitting up on her head."

"Looks like the cap shrunk," Brice agreed.

"Okay, start the video again," Drue said.

As they watched the video, the housekeeper pushed the cart down the hallway at a breakneck speed.

"Must have chugged a couple of Red Bulls while she was inside that room," Hernandez said. "Or maybe that's not Jazmin anymore. Right?"

Brice shook his head. "What? You're saying it's somebody else? Who? And how did they get in that room?"

Drue exchanged a knowing look with the detective.

"Your daughter is saying that it's not Jazmin pushing that cart. It's Neesa Vincent. Remember all those dreads and braids she was wearing? She had to shove 'em up under that cap so she'd look like Jazmin, at least to the security cameras. And she had to keep moving, and keep her head down."

"That's why I had to get a look at that room tonight," Drue explained. "I watched that video backwards and forwards, and finally I figured it out. Jazmin went in that room at 11:05. But she never came out. Because somebody was waiting for her. Somebody who chose that particular room because it was in the oldest, most isolated part of the hotel, with the crappiest rooms that rarely got rented out."

"Byars?" Hernandez said.

"But how did he get in?" Brice asked. "Unless somebody tampered with that video?"

"I kept wondering if it had been tampered with, but it's

digital," Drue pointed out. "Everything is time- and date-stamped."

"If it was Byars, he got in the room the same way you did, right?" Hernandez asked.

"Through the sliding-glass doors," Drue said, nodding excitedly. "That room's not exactly ground-floor, as I'd hoped, but even somebody with a blown-out knee like me didn't have much trouble climbing up onto the balcony."

"There were no video cameras on the back of that building," Hernandez said. "We checked."

"There are now, though," Drue said dryly. "That's how Shelnutt's security guard saw me climbing up."

"After Jazmin was killed, Gulf Vista's owners took a look at the hotel's security lapses and beefed up everything," Brice said, looking at his daughter. "If I'd known you were going over there tonight I could have saved you from getting arrested."

"No, you would have stopped me from going altogether," Drue said. "But that's not the point, Dad."

"So Byars decides to deal with Jazmin that night, after she gets off shift," Hernandez said slowly. "But not in his office, because that's too public. He uses a room he's probably used before for that kind of thing."

"He was head of housekeeping, so he had plenty of access to stepladders or whatever else he needed," Drue agreed. "And if anybody stopped to ask what he was doing, he could say he was changing a lightbulb or something like that."

Hernandez took a sip of coffee, made a face and pushed it away. "I don't think he planned on killing Jazmin. It was an impulse. Maybe he just intended to have sex with her. She resisted, which either pissed him off or turned him on, or both."

"If I remember correctly," Brice said quietly, "the medical examiner said Jazmin had been beaten and strangled."

"I think she tried to fight him off, and maybe he bashed her with something in the room. Like a lamp or something," Hernandez said. "The medical examiner said she was choked with a ligature. Maybe an electrical cord."

An image of the young mother flashed in Drue's mind, of Jazmin, alone and fighting for her life in that shabby hotel room. She felt queasy.

Drue sipped from her water glass, trying to choke back the nausea.

"I think you're right about it being an impulse killing," she told Hernandez. "Byars was a perv and a predator, until things got out of hand. After he realized what he'd done, he had to act fast."

"Which is when he called his girlfriend, Neesa," Hernandez said.

"I think Byars ordered her to come to that room and climb up onto the balcony. Once she was inside, he had her clean up the room. They loaded the body into the laundry cart, Neesa shoved all those dreads up under Jazmin's cap, and off she went."

"With best friends like that, who needs enemies?" Drue said bleakly.

"He probably planned to move the body off the hotel property, but he didn't get the chance, because there was some kind of screwup, and Lutrisha found it. In the meantime, by the time our officers responded to the Gulf Vista, the murder scene had been cleaned up," Hernandez said.

Brice put out his hand and gently closed the cover of the laptop. He looked at Drue. "You say you've got a copy of this video?"

"On a flash drive. In my purse, at home," Drue said.

"What's your next step?" he asked Hernandez. "You'll re-open the case, right?"

"It was never closed," the detective said. "My next step is to go home, crawl in bed and get a couple hours of sleep. Then I'll try and sweet-talk my husband into skipping golf so he can take Dez to that baseball tournament. Then, I guess I'll go pay a visit to Neesa Vincent."

"I want to come too," Drue said.

"No way. You're not a cop. You're not even a lawyer."

"But I know where she lives, and you don't," Drue pointed out. "And Neesa likes me. You think she'll really talk to a cop? In fact, I've got an idea. A great idea, of how we can get her to talk."

Rae Hernandez pushed herself up from the booth and grabbed her laptop. She fixed Brice Campbell with a malevolent stare.

"She's your kid, all right."

51

"No," Brice said. "Out of the question. At the very least, if you're right, this woman aided and abetted a brutal murder."

"Oh, hell no," Rae Hernandez said.

The three of them were standing in the parking lot of the Waffle House on Gulf Boulevard, clustered around the hood of Hernandez's Honda Odyssey.

"I hate to agree with your father, but that's the dumbest idea I've ever heard of. Neesa Vincent is a wild card," Hernandez said.

"Which is why it makes sense to at least give it a try," Drue urged. "Rae, I honestly think this could work. The night I met her, we clicked. She approached me, not the other way around. And if this doesn't work, you can still do it your way.

"Come on, Rae. Admit it. You never would have figured any of this out without me. I found Neesa and got her to admit to her connection with Byars. You owe me that much. You owe Jazmin."

"No! I absolutely forbid it." Brice slapped the hood of the minivan with his open palm.

"Easy there, Perry Mason," Hernandez said. "Watch the paint job."

"Dad?" Drue spoke up. "No offense, but I'm thirty-six years old. I don't need a signed permission slip for this field trip."

She turned pleading eyes toward Hernandez. "I'll call her later this morning, after we've both gotten some sleep."

"I don't know," Hernandez said uneasily. "Let me think about it. There's no rush, right?"

"We don't know that," Drue said. "I mean, right now, Brian Shelnutt probably has no idea why a woman named Drucilla Campbell was skulking around that room at the Gulf Vista earlier tonight. But if we wait, he might put it all together and realize why I was trying to get into that particular room. We don't know if he's involved in Jazmin's murder or not."

Hernandez ran her hands through her dark hair, still shaking her head, but Drue knew the detective knew she had a point.

"Okay," Hernandez said finally. "But there's gonna be ground rules. And you're gonna do exactly as I say, or the whole thing is off. Understand?"

"Perfectly," Drue agreed.

Brice glared at Hernandez as she got into the minivan. "You better have a backup plan to your backup plan, Hernandez."

~

It was surprisingly easy to convince Neesa Vincent to make a hair-color house call, especially after Drue proved amenable to Neesa's unconventional pricing system.

"Ooh yeah, I remember you," Neesa said, when Drue mentioned how they'd met. "You're the girl I met at Mister B's, with the good hair texture. But now, listen, Saturdays are my busy day. Where'd you say you live?"

"Sunset Beach," Drue said.

"That's right, you did tell me that," Neesa said. "Okay, I think I can move some appointments around, but if I come all the way out there, on short notice, on a Saturday, I'mma have to charge you my surge price."

"That's fine," Drue said. "Just how much is your surge price?"

"Three hundred," Neesa said promptly. "You know, because that's a lot of chemicals to take you from ebony to ivory. And just so you know, I don't take checks or cards. Cash only, okay?"

"I can do that." Drue gave her the address, and they set the time for two o'clock.

Neesa Vincent showed up at two-thirty, at almost the exact moment Drue was about to give up hope.

She bustled into the house carrying a large plastic shopping bag and an open liter bottle of Mountain Dew. The platinum-blond wig was gone today, and her long hair hung straight past her shoulders in ombré shades of lavender to violet.

"Ooh, this is a nice house," she said, fanning herself as she unloaded her supplies onto the tiny kitchen counter. "But how come you don't run the AC up in here?"

"I don't have air-conditioning," Drue said.

"Girl, that's crazy! A house like this, right on the water?"

"I inherited it from my mother. My grandfather built this house back in the 1950s," Drue said. She looked at the line-up of bottles emerging from the plastic bag and felt a new twinge of anxiety. "Wow, that's a lot of chemicals."

"That's why I got to charge you my surge price," Neesa said. "I spent a hundred dollars on supplies at Sally's just now." She turned and took a strand of Drue's hair, rubbing it appreciatively between her fingers. "You got a lotta hair, you know? I bet you got more hair on your bathroom floor than some of these old lady clients I get at cosmetology school put together."

"Thanks," Drue said. "Can I get you something to drink? I've got some beer and some prosecco in the fridge, and I've got a bottle of Tito's too."

"Okay, yeah," the hairdresser said, holding up the Mountain Dew. "You could just pour some of that Tito's right in my soda bottle. My nerves got kinda worked driving over here."

Drue siphoned a good six ounces into the bottle and Neesa took a sip. "That's smooth," she said. She took another sip, and then another, and then snapped her fingers. "Damn. I shoulda told you about the coconut oil."

"What about it?"

"At cosmetology school, we tell our clients to put coconut oil all over their hair the night before and sleep on it like that. You know, to protect the hair from getting damaged by the bleach." She shrugged. "Oh well."

"How badly could it get damaged?" Drue asked nervously.

"I mean, the ends could break off, but then we just trim

it." Neesa took a long gulp from the Mountain Dew bottle and held it out to Drue. "How about you top me off, and then we'll get started?"

Drue did as she asked. "How far along in cosmetology school are you? I mean, you've done platinum-blond before, right?"

"Yeah, well, on a wig, I've done it twice. And my instructor said my toning technique was excellent. Tell you what," Neesa said, handing Drue a small plastic tub of coconut oil. "Why don't we put some of this on your hair now and let it sit for a while? You know, just have a cocktail, and then after an hour, that oughtta be good enough to get started."

"Great idea," Drue said, seizing on any delaying technique available. "Be right back."

She went into her bedroom and shut the door. Rae Hernandez sat on the bed, paging through a magazine, looking bored.

"Are you hearing everything okay?" Drue asked.

"Good thing there's no insulation in this old house. I can hear every word," the detective said. "But if I were you, I wouldn't let that stupid bitch touch my hair."

"That's why I'm stalling," Drue said. She turned to the mirror over her dresser and began lathering coconut oil into her hair.

"Try to get her talking about the Gulf Vista," Hernandez urged. "How much vodka has she had?"

"A lot. Like, half a fifth," Drue said. "If I'd had that much, I'd be on the floor."

Drue went into the bathroom, grabbed a towel and wrapped it around her head, turban-style.

When she returned to the kitchen, she found Neesa mixing

chemicals in a large plastic bowl. The odor of bleach filled the room and stung her nostrils.

"How's it going?" Drue asked.

"Okay," Neesa said. "Lemme see your hair?"

Drue removed the towel and before she had a chance to protest, Neesa grabbed a pair of scissors, flipped up the back of Drue's hair and cut a long strand.

"What the hell!" Drue said, when she saw the hunk of hair Neesa was clutching. "What did you do that for? I didn't want my hair cut."

"This is for the test strand," Neesa explained. She laid the hair on some paper towels, dipped a flat plastic brush into the bleach mixture, then painted it onto the test hair. She turned to Drue. "This way we see how long it takes the bleach to lighten up your hair like we want. You got an oven timer? Let's give it fifteen minutes."

Drue started the timer and noticed that the Mountain Dew bottle was now empty and in the trash, along with the Tito's bottle.

"Did you say you have some wine?" Neesa asked, seating herself at the dinette table.

Drue retrieved the bottle of prosecco she'd bought earlier in the day and held it up.

"Ooh, perfect," Neesa said. "Bubbles."

"Are your nerves getting settled any better?" Drue asked, after Neesa drained her first glass of wine.

"A little," Neesa said. "Being out here, you know, so close

to the hotel where I used to work, it kinda does a number on my head."

"That's right," Drue said innocently. "The Gulf Vista. And you knew the girl who got killed, right?"

"Jaz. My best friend." Neesa looked over at the hair strand. "Me and that girl, we went through some crazy stuff together. I tell you the truth, I ain't been back out here to the beach since I left that place."

"Kinda sucks that they let you go, huh?" Drue said.

Neesa gave her a sharp look. "They didn't fire me. I quit."

"What about your boss? The one you told me about, Herman the Munster?"

Neesa giggled. "Yeah, old Herman the Munster. Now, he did get his ass fired, or so I heard."

"Why did he get fired?"

The hairdresser looked at her over the rim of her wineglass. "How should I know?"

"More wine?" Drue asked.

Neesa nodded and Drue poured.

"You know, it's too bad old Herman did get fired," Neesa said, after a second glass of prosecco. "They shoulda locked his ass up for the way he did me and Jaz."

"Because he was pressuring both of you for sex?" Drue asked.

"That and all the rest of it," Neesa said, gesturing grandly. "Like, if I ever told what all I know? That old perv would prob'ly get the chair or something."

"Instead he just walks away like nothing happened," Drue encouraged her.

"And my poor lil Jaz is dead and her baby ain't never gonna see her mama again." Neesa dabbed at her eyes with the hem of her shirt. She held out her empty glass and Drue refilled it.

Drue looked over at the oven timer, and then at the test strand of her hair, which had already turned an unnatural shade of green with five minutes still left on the timer. If she had any hope of saving her hair, and Hernandez's case, she needed to get Neesa to get to the point before that timer went off.

"So, you think Herman had something to do with Jaz's death?"

Neesa set her glass down on the table, sloshing a little wine over the edge. "Think it? Girlfriend, I know it. Say, you got anything to snack on?"

Drue jumped up and found a box of Cheez-Its in the cabinet.

"That's good," Neesa said, opening the box and shoving a handful of crackers into her mouth. As she chewed, shards of orange crumbs rained down on her shirtfront. She took another swallow of wine.

"Wow," Drue said softly. "So, were you there? I mean, what exactly happened?" She emptied the prosecco bottle into Neesa's glass, silently cursing herself for buying only one bottle.

"I wasn't there when it happened," Neesa said. "I mean, maybe if I had been, I coulda done something to stop him, but prob'ly not. He was hella strong for an old dude. By the time I got there, poor Jaz, she was already dead. Nuthin' I could do about it."

Drue realized she'd been holding her breath. She exhaled slowly and glanced quickly at her cell phone propped up on the windowsill behind a bottle of dish detergent. She hadn't mentioned the phone to Hernandez, who would have objected, but she thought of it as insurance.

"You're saying this Herman guy killed your friend? But why?"

"He *said* she went crazy, soon as she went in that hotel room and saw him standing there. Told me she picked up a lamp and swung it at him, and it was self-defense. I knew that was bullshit. Jaz couldn't have hurt him. She wasn't any bigger than a fly. I think he grabbed her, you know, because he wanted sex, and she said no and probably tried to fight him off."

Neesa shrugged. "She shoulda just kept on letting him do what he wanted to do and kept her mouth shut. Like I did."

"When did Herman tell you all this?" Drue asked. She was pushing things now, she knew, but if she could keep the other woman talking, maybe she'd lay out the whole scheme.

"After he'd done it, he called me on the radio and told me I needed to come to that room right quick. Only, he told me to come the back way, so nobody would see me."

"What was the back way?"

"The balcony," Neesa said. "The rooms in that old wing, the first floor was only a few feet above the ground. There was a stepladder stuck behind the ice machine, so the engineering guys could use it to fix lights and stuff. He told me to climb up that and he'd let me in through the sliding-glass door. So I wouldn't be on the security cameras, 'cause there weren't that many in the old wing."

Gotcha, Drue silently mouthed.

"Huh?" Neesa leaned back in the chair, glassy-eyed, open-mouthed.

"Nothing," Drue said. "Why did Herman call you?"

"To clean up the mess he'd made," Neesa said scornfully. "And help him get the body outta there."

"That's awful," Drue said, meaning it.

"Yeah. You know, it's been two years, and I think maybe I got me some of that, what do they call it, after you been in combat?"

"Post-traumatic stress disorder?"

"That's it," Neesa said. She held both hands in front of her. "See this? My hands are shaking real bad, 'cause we been talking about it."

"How do you hide a body in a hotel room?" Drue asked. She could hear the oven timer ticking away.

"He put her in the big cleaning cart Jaz had brought when she came up to the room. Then, he had me put on this hat she always wore, like, pulled down over my face so couldn't nobody watching the security cameras tell it was me instead of her, then I took it on down to the laundry room. He was supposed to take that cart out of there, and do something, but before he could get there, one of the other girls, Lutrisha, she came in there and started dumping out the dirty sheets, and that's when she found the body."

Neesa picked up the wineglass. It was empty. "And then all hell broke loose," she said.

"I can't believe this creep Byars got away with killing Jazmin," Drue said, her indignation sincere. "Didn't the police or anybody else ask you about any of this stuff? Are they that clueless?"

"I talked to the cops, I didn't tell 'em anything. Some private investigator dude came to the dry cleaners where I was working, asked me a couple questions about Jaz, but hell, I'm not that stupid. After that, I went off the grid, big-time."

She sighed and peered down at the test strip of hair. "Yeah. This looks real good for the first go-round. It ain't all the way platinum, but I think I could come back next week and take it to the next level."

"Next week?" Drue glanced over at the hair on the paper towel. It was a pale orange.

"No charge," Neesa said, pulling on a pair of disposable gloves. "Let's get this party started." She removed the towel from Drue's head and began combing and clipping it into quadrants. She pulled out a long strand of hair and began painting at the hairline.

"Ow!" Drue screeched, feeling the burn of the bleach on her scalp.

"Oh yeah," Neesa mumbled. "I think I was supposed to put some Vaseline on your hairline to keep the chemicals offa you before we started. You got any Vaseline?"

"No!" Drue screeched. "I don't have any damned Vaseline."

The oven timer dinged.

Rae Hernandez walked into the kitchen. "Time's up, Neesa," she said pleasantly. "And you're under arrest."

52

Neesa's jaw dropped open and she struggled to jump up from the chair, but Detective Hernandez easily pushed her back down.

"Stay seated," Hernandez said, her face stern.

"Who's she?" Neesa asked, pointing at the newcomer.

"This is my friend, Detective Rae Hernandez, with the Treasure Island Police Department," Drue said. "She's been listening in the other room."

"Shhhhhiiiiit." Neesa buried her head in both hands. After a moment, she looked up, shoulders slumped in defeat. "Y'all got to know, I didn't have nuthin' to do with what happened to Jaz. That was Byars. He said he'd fuck me up bad if I didn't do what he said."

"Okay," Hernandez said. "Let's talk about what he said and did, and what you said and did."

"What? Aw, hell no. I been running and hiding out from that dude for two years. I can't talk to you. He'll kill me. He told me that night, he would kill my ass if I ever said anything to anybody."

"You already did." Hernandez walked over and picked up the cell phone. She held it up and showed it to the other woman. "And we've got you live and in color."

"That ain't cool," Neesa said angrily. "You can't bug somebody without asking their permission. I know my rights. I ain't saying nuthin' else. I want a lawyer."

"You forget, I was in the next room, listening, and I heard every word you said," Hernandez said.

"Look, Neesa," Drue chimed in. "Aren't you tired of running? Look at it this way. It's him or it's you. I think you should talk to this detective."

"I don't give a shit what you think." Neesa folded her arms defiantly across her chest.

"Okay," Hernandez said. She whipped a set of handcuffs from her belt and snapped them over the girl's wrists. "Neesa Vincent, you're under arrest for murder and accessory to murder. Anything you say can be held against you in a court of law . . ."

"I never killed nobody," Neesa protested.

Hernandez pulled Neesa to a standing position. "Let's continue this at the police station." She gave her a gentle push in the general direction of the front door.

"Don't touch me," Neesa hollered. She turned to Drue. "You saw her. She tried to knock me down. Put that camera back on again. I want this shit recorded."

"Enough chitchat," Hernandez said, putting her hand on the girl's shoulder.

Drue followed the two women outside to where Hernandez had parked her Honda Odyssey across the street.

"Get in," Hernandez said, opening the passenger door.

"What the hell kind of bougie police car is this?" Neesa said. "I bet you're not even really a cop."

"Shut up," Hernandez said, taking a seat behind the steering wheel. She lifted a lock of Neesa's hair and whistled softly. "Girlfriend, I don't think this purple hair of yours is gonna look too good with that orange jumpsuit you're gonna be wearing."

"Hey!" Neesa twisted around in the seat and tried to point at Drue. "Hey. You owe me three hundred dollars. I want my damn money. You can't just call me up and rip me off like this."

"Send me a bill," Drue said. She did a little finger wave as the van pulled away and then she ran inside to wash her hair.

Despite the fact that she was operating on too little sleep, Drue felt oddly energized by the encounter with Neesa. She washed her hair twice, but the front strand stayed stubbornly orange. Maybe she'd start a new fashion trend. Until then, she scrubbed the kitchen of the noxious peroxide odors, then sat down at the kitchen table again with a stack of index cards and made notes about what she'd learned earlier in the day.

She knew that it was Herman Byars who'd beaten and strangled Jazmin, and then enlisted Neesa to masquerade as the dead girl. But how had their scheme gone undetected for so long? Had the hotel's head of security, Brian Shelnutt, conspired with Byars to hide their crime?

Drue thought back to the day that Yvonne Howington had appeared in the law firm's reception area, insisting that Brice had taken a payoff from the hotel. She'd been more than ready, back then, to believe the worst of her father.

But last night, Brice had rushed to her aid after her arrest. And afterward, he'd sat down with her and Rae Hernandez as the two of them outlined how they believed Jazmin's murder had occurred. He'd been skeptical at first, it was true, but he'd listened, and in the end, had agreed that Drue's theory had merit.

Still, she couldn't shake the notion that somebody had turned a blind eye to the sordid goings-on at the Gulf Vista, and probably made a nice fat profit from the deed.

She went into the guest bedroom and found the folder with the printouts she'd made of Jimmy Zee's reports on his investigation.

He'd covered most of the bases with his interviews, she had to admit, but there was something missing. She'd seen, firsthand, how dogged Zee could be once he got his teeth into something. Neesa had said an investigator came to see her, but his report said he hadn't been able to locate her. Which was a lie.

He was thorough and professional when he wanted to be. So what had happened with the Jazmin Mayes investigation? Why had it taken a rookie cube rat like her to figure out what a cesspool the Gulf Vista was?

She made some more notes on index cards, bringing them up to date. There were still plenty of loose ends, she knew. Herman

Byars was still at large. And she hoped Rae Hernandez would follow up and question Brian Shelnutt about his role in the affair.

But she couldn't help feeling jubilant. Neesa Vincent was not just involved in the murder, she was a credible witness. And Neesa's testimony should prove that Herman Byars had killed Jazmin after her shift ended.

Now she had to persuade Brice to renew his efforts for a settlement with the hotel's insurance company. And in the meantime, figure out whether Jimmy Zee had a financial incentive to look the other way when presented with evidence that could have cost the Gulf Vista millions.

And there were still so many unanswered questions about Brice and Jimmy Zee's possible involvement in the forty-year-old disappearance of Colleen Boardman Hicks. Had Brice lied about his connection to the missing woman? Did Zee know more about the case than he'd admitted? Why had her mother collected all those old newspaper clippings about the case? And how had the long-missing police file ended up in a box of her father's belongings right here in the attic of Coquina Cottage?

Drue paced around the kitchen, trying to make sense of things. Finally, she decided to reach out to the one person she thought could.

She called his number and was disappointed when the call went directly to voice mail.

"Hey Ben. Where were you when I needed you last night? Call me, okay? I have big news about the Jazmin Mayes case. There's been an arrest. For real! And I really, really want to talk to you about Jimmy Zee. Okay, bye."

Her cell phone rang five minutes later. It was Ben, and he sounded out of breath.

"Hi," he said. "Sorry I couldn't pick up. I'm actually at a gaming tournament, and we're on a short break. What's the big news?"

"I don't know where to begin," Drue said. "I went to the hotel last night, and figured out that it was Neesa Vincent, not Jaz, on video, working that night, and like I kinda suspected, it was the head of housekeeping who killed her."

"What? How'd you find all this out?"

"It's too long to go into over the phone. But one thing I wanted to tell you. Neesa said she talked to an investigator. But Zee's reports said he couldn't find her. I can't get past the idea that Zee should have figured this whole thing out. Ben, I really think Zee is up to his ears in this thing."

"Are you sure?" Ben asked. "I mean, have you talked to your dad or anybody else about this? That's a pretty radical theory, Drue."

"I know," she admitted. "And I guess I'm kinda keyed up because I haven't had hardly any sleep."

"Okay, well, we should definitely talk before you go accusing Zee of stuff," he said. "Oh shit. I gotta go. My next session is starting. I'll call you as soon as I get out, okay?"

"Talk soon," Drue said.

53

August 20, 1976

Colleen was momentarily paralyzed with fear. The barrel of the revolver was pointed directly at her. She glanced around, frantic for help. A homeless man was slumped over on a nearby bus bench, the pages of a newspaper ruffling gently in the faint breeze while pigeons pecked at potato chips from a spilled bag. A pair of elderly women occupied the next green bench over, their heads bent together, deep in conversation.

She should scream. Or run. Or both. But her feet were rooted to the pavement, her mouth bone dry.

"I said, get in the goddamn car." The driver reached over and wrenched the door handle open. "Now! Or I swear to God, I'll kill you right here."

Colleen obeyed, setting the train case on the floorboards by her feet. With the gun lowered, she could concentrate on the woman's face, and she gasped involuntarily. The driver was Sherri Campbell. Brice's wife.

"Put your hands out in front of you," the woman ordered. Colleen did, and a moment later a pair of handcuffs were snapped across her wrists.

"Why are you doing this?" Colleen's voice was hoarse.

The light changed and the car began moving, picking up speed. "Shut up," Sherri replied. "I don't want to hear a word from you."

Colleen studied her captor's face. The features were regular, but contorted in barely controlled rage.

She began to softly weep, hating herself for being weak and afraid, and as her terror mounted, she was unable to choke back the sobs.

"Stop that!" Sherri backhanded her so hard, Colleen's ears were ringing. A trickle of blood ran down her chin, merging with the unstoppable tears.

"I'm sorry," she whispered, clenching and unclenching her shackled hands. "It's over between us. He said he'd never leave you. That's why I was going away."

Sherri shook her head. "Lying little bitch. I don't believe either of you."

"It's true," Colleen blurted. "I swear. I was headed for the bus station. Look in my purse. I have a ticket. For Atlanta."

"So what? You'd come back. Or he'd go there. To look for you."

"No! That's why I'm going away. Alone. To start over. A new job, new name, new life. Someplace nobody knows me."

"So you can latch onto somebody new, screw some other woman's husband, ruin another woman's life."

"Never. I'm done with that. This was all a horrible mistake. You don't understand. My husband? He beats me. Brice was trying to help me. He wanted to lock Allen up, but I knew it wouldn't do any good. Brice, he's a good guy. We didn't mean to hurt you. Things just . . . happened."

Sherri slapped her again, hard, without warning.

"Do *not* say his name again. I don't want to hear my husband's name come out of your filthy mouth one more time."

Colleen nodded, mutely.

They were leaving downtown, headed west on First Avenue South. She looked out the window, hoping to catch someone's eye, to somehow signal the danger she was in.

But the lights were with Sherri, and against Colleen, and they sailed through every intersection, never slowing, not even when they crossed Tyrone Boulevard and the street doglegged and became Central, and then they were speeding north on Gulf Boulevard.

A cold chill ran down Colleen's spine when she realized where they were heading.

The traffic was unexpectedly light for late on a Friday afternoon. She glanced over at Sherri, whose jaw was clenched, eyes darting back and forth.

"Just let me go," Colleen pleaded. "I'm not a threat to you. I'll leave town." She looked at the train case on the floor. "I have money," she said. "Right here in this case. Everything from my bank account. Seven thousand dollars. You can have all of it. Just let me out of this car."

Sherri laughed. "You think this is about money? Think you can buy your way out of what you've done to me?"

They drove on. The light at the next intersection was yellow as they approached. Colleen swiveled slightly in her seat. If she could get her hands on the door handle, just as they slowed to a stop for the light? Whatever injuries she suffered would surely be better than whatever Sherri had in mind.

The light changed to red. Colleen turned quickly, groping for the handle, but her captor saw the move for what it was and stomped on the gas pedal, hurtling through the light to a cacophony of car horns from narrowly averted cars in the intersection.

Sherri calmly turned and pointed the pistol at her passenger. "Try that again and I'll shoot you right here."

"Go ahead," Colleen blurted. "Kill me. Isn't that what you intend to do anyway?"

"None of your damn business," Sherri snapped. She drove onward, with the gun clutched tightly in her right hand.

Colleen saw a jagged flash of lightning. For the first time she noticed that the sky had darkened, with ominous gray clouds poised just to the west, over the Gulf. Thunder rumbled overhead, and rain began to pelt the car's hood.

It was the kind of typical late-summer Florida thunderstorm that Colleen had always loved. As a child, she would stand transfixed at the front window of her parents' house, staring out at the light show. Now, she gloomily reflected that this storm would probably be her last.

They drove through Madeira Beach, and then Treasure Island, where Sherri made a sudden sharp left turn.

Crushed oyster shells crunched beneath the Chevette's tires as they pulled into the abbreviated driveway of the cottage, which was overshadowed by the shaggy branches of a pair of towering Australian pines.

Colleen, of course, had driven past this house many times, at night, when Brice's cruiser was parked out front. Once, she'd parked in the driveway of a vacant house across the street, watching while all the lights in the house blinked off, wondering if that meant he and his wife were going to bed, imagining what they would do there, torturing herself with all the what-ifs.

"Stay there," Sherri ordered, after she'd cut the engine. She came around to the passenger side of the car and unceremoniously yanked Colleen to her feet. She looked around, cautiously, but the narrow road was empty. Nobody was about. She nudged Colleen forward, through the rain, toward the front door.

"Open it," she ordered, pushing Colleen into the house. Lightning struck then, so close that both women jumped, and the smell of cordite hung in the steamy, ion-charged air around them.

54

Drue was barefoot, dressed in cut-off yoga pants and her fa-vorite raggedy SURF ALASKA T-shirt, when she heard the doorbell ring. She checked the time and frowned. It was five-thirty. Her hair was still wet from the shower, and she was operating on about four hours of sleep and not in the mood for company.

Her mood changed when she opened the front door.

"Ben! I thought you were at a gaming thing."

He stood on the doorstep holding a brown paper bag. "After you called, I decided to sneak out early. I still feel terrible I missed your call last night because I was so wrapped up in that damned tournament. I didn't even notice you'd tried to call until, like, two in the morning."

"Hmm. Two in the morning was about the time I was being hauled to jail by the police," Drue said.

His eyes widened behind the horn-rimmed glasses. "You didn't tell me you got arrested!"

"Come on inside and I'll fill you in on all the sordid details," she said. "And when I tell you what I've been through, you'll see why I look the way I look."

"You look fine to me," he said. "But what's up with the skunk stripe in your hair? Is that a new thing?"

She yawned. "Tell you in a minute. I had a late, late night, and then a crazy, crazy morning. I'm about to fix some coffee. You want coffee, or maybe a beer?"

He held out the paper bag. "I brought you a smoothie from that place up the beach, as a peace offering."

"Kale Yeah? I love that place." She lifted the plastic cup from the bag. A straw poked out from the plastic top. "That's so sweet," she said. "I'll have it later, if that's okay. I gotta get some caffeine in my system before I pass out on my feet."

"I had them put some B_{12} powder in it, for energy," Ben said. "Try that first, and then the coffee."

Drue shrugged. "Okay, sure. Good idea."

He sat down at the kitchen table opposite her. "Okay. Now I want to hear all the gory details. How did you end up in jail?"

She hesitated and then plunged ahead, into the story. "I broke into a room at the Gulf Vista," she said. "Well, I didn't actually manage to break in, but I was about to, when a security guard caught me. They called the cops, and had me arrested for breaking and entering and trespassing, but I'm pretty sure my dad can make them drop the charges. And then I sort of tricked Neesa into coming over here—"

"Slow down," he said. "Tell me everything."

"I know you said this whole thing was a waste of time, but Ben, it really wasn't. After you guys left the office last night, I watched and rewatched the hotel security video from the night Jazmin was killed, and I figured it out."

She took a sip of the smoothie and gave him an apologetic smile. "That's the real reason I didn't go to happy hour with you guys last night. I was afraid if I told you my idea, you'd try to talk me out of it. I had a theory, and the more I watched the video, the more I needed to check it out."

"You should never have gone to that place by yourself," Ben said, shaking his head. "I mean, that's just crazy."

"It's not crazy," she insisted. "And I proved it."

She sipped the smoothie. "I never would have figured it out if I hadn't tracked down Neesa, the housekeeper who was supposedly Jazmin's best friend. It turns out, she was the key to all of it."

"How so?" He sat back in his chair and gave her a quizzical look.

"The night I met her at Mister B's, this honky-tonk out in Seminole, we struck up a conversation. She'd had a lot to drink, and we were just kind of chatting, and I told her that I lived here, in Sunset Beach, and she said she'd worked at the Gulf Vista, which, of course, I already knew. Eventually, she started to talk about Jazmin, and the management at the hotel, and her boss, a guy she called Herman-like-in-the-*Munsters*."

Drue yawned widely. "Sorry. I'm so tired, my mind is kind of foggy right now." It was true. She'd never been much of a napper, but right now, she felt as though she could sleep for a solid week.

"Go on," Ben urged. "Tell me about the *Munsters* guy."

"He's a sexual predator," Drue said. "He pressured Jazmin, and Neesa, for sex. And in return, he gave them better shifts, extra pay, whatever favors he could do."

"Sounds like a pig," Ben said.

"A murderous pig," Drue said. "Jazmin's boyfriend, who used to work at the hotel, said she was trying to get hired at the Silver Sands, down the beach, to get away from this Herman guy. But he wasn't the only perv. The hotel's head of security, even the engineering chief, they were all doing stuff like that. One of the other housekeepers told me . . ."

"Told you what?" Ben asked, leaning forward. "Are you okay?"

"Just super tired," she said. "What was I saying? God, I'm so tired, I'm loopy." She gulped more of the smoothie, hoping the B_{12} powder would energize her. "Anyway, it all came down to Neesa. The night Jazmin was killed, at the end of her shift, Byars got her called up to a room in the oldest wing of the hotel. It's not clear if he tried to rape Jazmin or what, but she fought back, or tried to. So he killed her."

"How do you know any of this?" Ben asked.

"Neesa told me. I tricked her into coming over here earlier today." Drue held up the bleached strand of hair closest to her face. "She was supposed to be dyeing my hair blond, because she's studying to be a hairdresser. Thank God, she won't get that chance. After she had a lot of vodka and a lot of prosecco, she told me everything, but what she didn't know was that there was a detective in the other room."

"Wait. So this Neesa person confessed? You've got me confused."

"Yeah, but of course, she claims Byars threatened to kill her if she didn't help. After he'd killed Jaz, he called her on the walkie-talkie all the housekeepers carry and told her to come to the room. When she got there, he made her help clean it up. He'd already put Jaz's body in the rolling laundry cart."

"Ohhh," Ben said slowly. "But that doesn't make sense. The hotel security cameras showed Jazmin later that night. Working the late shift."

Drue managed a smug smile. "Wasn't Jazmin. It was Neesa. Wearing Jazmin's hat and keeping her head down."

"You said something on the phone about Zee being involved?" he prompted.

"Yeah. Zee, he saw the same videos as me. But he never . . ." She yawned.

"Have you told Brice about any of this?" he asked.

"Hmm?" Her eyelids felt like lead and she was feeling lightheaded and nauseous.

"Does Brice know about any of this?" Ben repeated.

"Not yet. Zee's his friend . . ."

She managed, with difficulty, to stand up. She stumbled slightly as she headed toward her bedroom.

"Are you okay?" Ben asked, scrambling to his feet and following behind.

"Sleep," she mumbled. "I gotta sleep. Call me later. Okay? Bye."

"Yeah, I'll give you a call," Ben said. "Sweet dreams."

Drue heard the front door closing just about the time her stomach began to cramp. She staggered to the bathroom and retched violently.

She was still clinging to the commode, five minutes later, when she heard the front door open and footsteps going down the hall, rapidly, toward the kitchen. She opened her mouth to cry out but she was too weak and too sick. A moment later, she heard the door close again. Her heart pounded in her chest, and her breaths were coming in shallow gasps.

Come back, Ben, she whimpered silently.

What was happening to her? She was cold. So very cold. Her hands felt like ice.

At some point, she either passed out or fell asleep. When she came to, she had no concept of time. Her face was pressed against the cold tile of the bathroom floor. Something was very wrong. She had to get to the phone, had to call for help.

She grasped the edge of the bathtub and tried to pull up to a sitting position. Her arms and legs felt like spaghetti, and her head was throbbing. She sank back onto the floor, sobbing with frustration. Minutes passed, or maybe hours. She wasn't sure.

Her stomach cramped again and she clung to the commode, hanging her head over the side. She reached for a towel and mopped her face with it. She heard the faint ringing of her phone from the other room. Where was it? The kitchen? Living room? Her head was so fuzzy.

She sat up slowly and tried again to pull herself up. This time, she made it, although the stabbing pain in her knee reminded her of the ordeal she'd recently put it through. She clung to the towel bar and lurched forward, grasping the edge of the doorway for stability. Then, slowly, down the narrow hallway, stopping every few inches, until she reached the living room.

By the time she flopped down onto the sofa, the ringing had stopped, and she had no idea where the phone actually was. Her stomach cramped again and she prayed that the feeling would subside, because she had no strength to make it back to the bathroom.

She was lying on the sofa when the doorbell rang. She tried to sit up but was too weak. It rang a second time, and then a third. "Help," she whispered, her breaths coming in short, shallow bursts.

A man's voice called out, impatient. "Drue? You home? Drue? It's Jonah."

"I'm here," she tried to call. But the words came out as little more than a whimper.

"Okay, damn it," he called. "I can take a hint. But you could have at least let me know you changed your mind about going out before I drove out here tonight."

She heard a second voice now, another man.

"Hey Drue?" He knocked on the door. "Hey Drue, it's Corey. You home?" She heard the two men conversing in low tones, but was still too weak to get to the door. She heard the doorknob turn and then rattle. It was locked!

More muffled conversation. And then nothing. Drue rolled onto her side. She couldn't catch her breath, couldn't speak.

And then she heard the sliding-glass door, catching in the track, then slowly, agonizingly slow, someone shoved it open.

"Drue!" Corey and Jonah looked down at her.

"My God, what happened?" Corey asked, kneeling on the floor beside the sofa.

"Sick," she croaked. "Can't . . . can't . . ."

He pressed his fingertips to her neck, near her jaw, then bent his head to her chest and listened. He looked back at Jonah. "Her pulse is weak and her heartbeat is faint and her skin is clammy. If I didn't know better, I'd swear she's overdosed. Call nine-one-one."

She passed out.

"Drue? Drue? Come on, friend. Time to wake up." Hands patted her face.

She opened her eyes slowly. A woman in green surgical scrubs sat on the bed beside her. She was in some sort of curtained-off cubicle, with harsh overhead lighting. An IV tree stood beside her bed and plastic tubing snaked to an IV line attached to her arm.

She blinked and took a breath. She was better. Hell, she was better than better, she was alive.

"You gave us a scare tonight," the woman said. "Do you want to tell me what happened?"

"Happened?"

"You overdosed alone, at your home today," the woman said. "If your friends hadn't gotten there when they did, you would have died."

"Overdosed on what?" Drue asked, confused. "I don't do drugs."

The woman sighed. "Honey, you can lie to your friends and family, but denial doesn't work in here. We found the bottle of pills in your purse."

"I don't know what you're talking about," Drue protested. "I swear, I don't do drugs."

"We found a bottle of OxyContin in your purse," the doctor said. "When your blood work comes back, I'm pretty sure we'll find it was laced with fentanyl. Which could have killed you."

Drue bristled. "Who are you?"

"I'm Judy Trew, and I'm the attending physician here."

"Where's here?" Drue asked.

"You're in the emergency room at St. Anthony's. You're a lucky girl, you know. If that hunky friend of yours hadn't recognized the signs and told the EMTs to administer Narcan when they did, you'd be just another sad opioid statistic."

"Dr. Trew," Drue said, choosing her words slowly. "I did not intentionally take Oxy. You can believe me or not, but I can't take any kind of codeine. I'm deathly allergic. It gives me a horrible reaction."

"Nausea, vomiting, like that?" the doctor asked.

"Exactly. I had knee surgery back in January and the strongest thing I could take was Advil. If you don't believe me, you can check with the surgeon who treated me. Or you can check with the company that drug-tested me when I started my new job last month."

"Okay, calm down," the doctor said. "Morphine allergies are pretty rare, but what you have is called a pseudo-allergy, and the effects are just about the same. In your case, the other reason you're probably alive is because you puked up most of the fentanyl before it could kill you."

"Lucky me," Drue said bitterly.

"I'm going to take this IV out now," Dr. Trew said, donning gloves.

Drue looked away, she felt the tape being ripped from her skin, and a moment later, the deed was done.

"So how did that Oxy get in your system, and where did that bottle of pills come from?" Dr. Trew asked.

"A gift from a friend," Drue said grimly. "Former friend, that is."

55

Drue was perched on the edge of the bed when the curtain of the treatment room parted and Brice Campbell's formidable presence filled the tiny, claustrophobic space.

Wordlessly, he folded her into his arms, crushing her to his chest, stroking her hair, rocking back and forth, crooning something over and over again, but she couldn't quite make out the muffled words. Finally, he held her at arm's length, searching her face for . . . something.

"You're all right," he repeated. "Thank God, you're all right."

She managed a weary smile. "Well, thank God plus Corey and Jonah." Now she was blinking back tears. "Dad, I'm okay. Really. I'm okay."

He let out a long, exasperated sigh, running his hand

through his hair. "Tell me the truth," he said sternly. "Are you just saying that to get me off your back?"

"No!" she exclaimed.

His eyes held hers. "Drue, the doctor told us. You overdosed. On OxyContin. Honey, talk to me. Seriously, I'm not going to judge, but if you have a problem, you need to be honest with me, so I can get you help."

"Dad! I swear. I promise you, I am not a pill head! It was Ben. He tried to kill me."

"Ben? Our Ben? Ben Fentress?" Brice looked stricken. "That's just nuts. It must be the pills talking."

"It is not the damned Oxy!" she cried. "Ben came over this afternoon. He brought me a kale smoothie that he'd spiked with Oxy, which the doctor just told me was itself spiked with fentanyl. Only he didn't know that I'm allergic, sort of, to drugs with codeine. It makes me violently ill. So I puked up most of it—before the fentanyl could kill me."

Brice shook his head sadly. "Why would Ben do something like that? You're friends. You're colleagues, for God's sake!"

Drue slid off the examining table, hurriedly pulling the hospital gown closed. She swayed slightly, grasping the edge of the table for balance.

"I figured it all out today. When Neesa came to my house, she admitted most of what we'd already guessed. That Byars made her help him after he killed Jazmin. And Dad, it was just like what I thought. He called Jazmin, just as she was going off shift, to tell her to come to that room. And when she got there, he was waiting. And there's more—"

"I don't care about that," Brice interrupted. "Talk to me about Ben Fentress and why you think he would try to kill you."

"I am so stupid," Drue said, smacking her forehead. "Such a freakin' idiot. I basically called Ben this afternoon and practically invited him over to try and kill me."

She walked unsteadily over to a narrow locker in the corner of the room.

"What are you doing?"

"Looking for my damned clothes." She flung open the door of the locker and found a large plastic baggie containing her belongings. She opened the bag and fished out her cut-off yoga pants, sliding them up beneath the gown. The T-shirt was next, but it was spattered with still-damp vomit.

"Eew. Gross." She dropped the shirt onto the floor of the locker. When she glanced over at her father, he was staring at her, momentarily speechless.

"Shoes, Dad!" she said, impatiently snapping her fingers. "Where are my shoes?"

"You're not leaving here," Brice said. "The doctor said they'll probably admit you, as soon as a bed opens up."

"Nope." She fished her bra out of the bag, turned her back to her father and proceeded to don it.

"I'm not checking in, I'm checking out," she announced.

"To do what, exactly?" he asked. "You can't even stand up straight. You came here by ambulance, Drue. Five hours ago you were found unconscious in a pool of your own vomit. You practically flat-lined."

"I'm not near death. I'm a little groggy, is all." She pushed past him and poked her head out of the curtain. "I know Corey and Jonah are the ones who found me and called nine-one-one. Where are they?"

"I sent them home," Brice said. "They wanted to stay, but I convinced them to go. Frankly, I think they were relieved because they didn't want to be here when I confronted you about your drug use."

He paused. "They found the pill bottle in your purse, Drue. Your friend Corey went looking, so he could tell the EMTs what you'd overdosed on."

Drue was so angry she was shaking. "Why is it so damned hard for you to believe that I am not a pill freak? I already told you, I don't do drugs. Didn't I pass your stupid drug test? As for that pill bottle, I'm sure Ben planted that in my purse so that when you found my body, you'd come to the conclusion you are so eager to reach."

Brice looked stricken. "I want to believe you, but this story of yours is just not credible. Listen to yourself, Drue. You're telling me that Ben tried to kill you with a smoothie? Where's the smoothie?"

She closed her eyes and tried to find an elusive sense of calm.

"He came back," she said, remembering one of the last moments before she passed out the first time. "I started getting really woozy after I'd drunk about half the smoothie. He didn't have the balls to hang around and watch me die. I'd crawled into the bathroom, and I heard the front door open, and then footsteps. I tried to call out to him for help. I didn't realize he'd deliberately poisoned me. I bet he came back to collect the evidence—the smoothie."

She snapped her fingers again. "My files. The files and all my index cards. I bet he took them too."

"You're still not making sense," Brice repeated. "What does Ben have to do with Neesa Vincent or Jazmin Mayes?"

"He figured it out. All of it. Somehow, he tracked Neesa down after Jimmy Zee couldn't. She claimed she didn't tell him anything, but he figured it out. I think he went to the hotel's insurance company and convinced them to pay him to keep what he knew quiet."

"That doesn't sound like Ben," Brice argued. "He's a computer geek. Not a blackmailer. Certainly not a killer."

"Just get me out of here, okay?" Drue pleaded. "Sign the discharge papers, do whatever it takes, but get me out, and I'll explain everything. And then we've gotta call Rae Hernandez and let her know what happened." She grasped his arm. "Please, Dad? You have to trust me. We can't let Ben get away with this."

Brice nodded reluctantly. "Stay here, okay? I'll see what I can do."

When he'd gone, Drue slumped back down on the examining table. She'd almost dozed off when the curtain parted again.

Brice stepped inside the cubicle and tossed her a set of green surgical scrubs. He set a pair of purple plastic Crocs on the table beside them.

"Okay, you're sprung."

"Sweet. Turn around, will you?"

He did as she asked and she quickly discarded the cut-offs and the hospital gown and dressed in the scrubs, which were two sizes too big.

"All done," she announced. "Let's go."

"Take my arm," he said gruffly, as they moved down the hallway toward the exit. The Crocs squeaked loudly on the linoleum tile with every step she took.

"Where'd you get the clothes and shoes?" she asked, as the automatic doors slid open.

"Money talks," he said. He steered her gently toward the Mercedes, which was parked under the emergency room portico, with the flashers blinking. As they approached, a hospital security guard who'd been lounging nearby stepped closer.

"All set?" he asked.

Brice reached out and shook the guard's hands, obviously passing him some currency.

"All set, thanks."

56

H ey you guys." They turned to see Jonah Kelleher emerge
from the shadows at the edge of the portico. He was still
dressed for the date that Drue had forgotten about, although
his necktie was long gone and his blue dress shirt was stained
and wrinkled.

"Jonah!" Drue exclaimed. "I thought Dad sent you home."

He shrugged. "I couldn't just leave, not knowing if you'd
be okay."

She touched his arm. "That's so sweet. I'm good. Thanks
to you and Corey."

His hazel eyes took in her bedraggled appearance, skunk hair,
oversize scrubs and all. "You don't look so hot."

"Flatterer."

Jonah nodded at Brice. "It's pretty late. If you want, I can
take her home. I mean, we did have a date tonight."

"You did?" Brice looked at Drue. "Really?"

"Really," Drue replied. "But we're not going home. We're going after the guy who did this to me."

"Huh?"

"It's a long story, and I don't have the energy to tell it twice," she said. "You might as well hear it at the same time as Dad."

Brice opened the back door of the Mercedes with a flourish. "Get in, son."

As soon as everybody was in the car, Drue turned to her father and put out her hand. "I need your phone."

He handed it over without comment. She gazed down at it and swore softly. "I don't have Rae's cell number. It's on my phone, which I don't have."

Jonah snaked his hand over the headrests. "Here. I brought it with me."

She turned around and flashed him a grateful smile, then scrolled through the recent calls on her phone until she found the detective's number, grimacing when she noticed the time.

"She's gonna kill me for calling her at one-thirty in the morning."

Drue put the phone on loudspeaker. Rae Hernandez's voice sounded distinctly pissy. "What?"

"Rae?" Drue said meekly. "I'm sorry, but this really is urgent. I'm just leaving the emergency room with my dad. Ben Fentress tried to kill me earlier tonight."

"Wait. Who? Is this connected to the Jazmin Mayes thing?"

"Yes, it's all about Jazmin. Ben works with me, at the law firm, on the Justice Line, but he also does some of the firm's IT work. He somehow saw the security videos from the hotel and figured out what was going on. He tracked Neesa down and somehow, he put it all together. I think he must have gone to the hotel's insurance company and shared what he knew, for a payoff."

"Okay . . ." Hernandez's voice trailed off. "You've lost me now."

"Ben was my friend. I confided in him that I thought there was something shady about the way my dad's law firm handled the case." Her face flushed with embarrassment. "I even told him that at first, I thought my dad had taken a payoff."

Drue shot her father an apologetic look. "Ben knew I was looking into Gulf Vista. I even called him Friday night to tell him I was going over there and needed a wingman. He didn't answer his phone, so I left him a message. And then, after we got the goods on Neesa today, I mean yesterday, I called him again, to tell him about the arrest."

She took a deep breath. "I told him Neesa mentioned that she'd talked to 'some private investigator dude.' I just assumed it was Jimmy Zee, our investigator. The next thing I know, he was standing on my doorstep, with a kale smoothie, pumping me for all the details."

"You say he tried to kill you?" Hernandez said. "With kale?"

"He apparently spiked the smoothie with Oxy, spiked with fentanyl."

"I'm still confused," the detective said. "Why would he try to kill you?"

"For the money," Drue said. "He wanted to keep me from telling my dad that I suspected somebody at the law firm had taken a bribe. I thought it was Jimmy Zee. Turns out it must have been Ben."

"And you're sure it was him? Spell that name for me."

"It's *F-E-N-T-R-E-S-S*. Yes, I'm positive. After you left with Neesa, I was alone all afternoon, until he showed up with that smoothie. He sat there, watching me drink it, until I was so stoned I could barely walk. He left, but then he came back, briefly, I'm assuming to get rid of the smoothie."

Jonah spoke up from the backseat. "Hi. This is another of Drue's colleagues from the law firm. I work with Ben too. We found Drue at seven-thirty tonight. She was barely conscious. Another of her friends, who was with me, recognized the symptoms of an overdose. He's the one who called nine-one-one. While we were waiting for the ambulance, we found a bottle of OxyContin in her purse. But there was no smoothie."

"How about my files? And my notes?" Drue turned to address Jonah. "They were on the kitchen table."

"Nothing like that," Jonah said.

"Okay, I'm gonna take this story of yours at face value," Hernandez said. "Do you have the guy's address?"

"I don't," Drue said.

"I've been to his place," Jonah volunteered. "It's in Wood-lawn."

Brice had been scrolling through the contacts on his cell phone. He spoke up now. "I have it: 1516 Hibiscus Street."

"What kind of vehicle does he drive?" Hernandez asked.

"It's a silver Honda Accord," Drue said. "Late model, and I think it's got, like, a Mötley Crüe decal on the back bumper."

"Do any of you happen to know if this guy has a gun?"

Drue looked at Jonah. "I never heard him talk about owning a gun," Jonah said. "He doesn't seem like the type to me."

"All right," she said, after a long pause. "Woodlawn is out of my jurisdiction. I'm gonna call St. Pete PD and ask them to pay a call on Ben Fentress, and bring him in for questioning. In the meantime, sit tight until you hear from me."

"You'll call us, right?" Brice asked. "As soon as you have him in custody?"

"Yes, Mr. Campbell. I'll be in contact."

Drue disconnected and leaned back on the headrest. "I'm spent."

"*You're* spent?" Brice said in disbelief. "This is the second night in a row I've been up with you at one-thirty in the morning. It reminds me of when you were fifteen, the last summer you lived with me and Joan."

Drue scowled. "Or as I refer to it, my very own bummer summer."

"Under the circumstances," Brice said, "I don't think it's a good idea for me to take you home. You'd better come back to my house."

"Noooo, Dad," Drue protested. "Ben's not coming back to the scene of the crime. He's too smart for that. Just take me home, okay? I haven't slept in nearly twenty-four hours."

"Uh, Brice?" Jonah said quietly. "I caught a ride to the hospital with Corey, so my car's still at Drue's place. If it's okay with both of you, I could hang there, on the sofa, on the off chance Ben does come back."

"Great idea," Brice said.

"Absolutely not," Drue said. "I don't need a babysitter."

"Overruled," Brice said, starting the Mercedes.

Traffic was nonexistent at that hour. Drue had almost dozed off when Brice's voice, low and urgent, startled her awake.

"Will you answer one question? Honestly?"

She knew what the question would be, and was already dreading having to answer. "Yes."

"What makes you think my oldest friend, and your colleague, is capable of blackmail? Of actually being complicit in the cover-up of a murder?"

Drue moaned. "Do we really have to hash this out right now?"

"Yeah. We really do. It's bad enough that you thought I would do something like that. Jimmy's like family, he's like a brother to me."

"Look. It was a mistake, a terrible judgment call on my part. It's just that Zee gives off a weird vibe, you know? Always dressed in black. And he never answers a direct question. After Yvonne Howington walked into the office, I guess I became obsessed with figuring things out. I mean, we're the Justice Line, right? So, where was the justice for Jazmin? And Yvonne and Aliyah?"

"You could have come to me with your suspicions."

"I tried!" Drue said. "You told me bad stuff happens. You told me you'd done your best, but *boom,* case closed, next case."

"And you can't take no for an answer," Brice said, giving her a sideways glance. "Never could."

"And it turns out I was right. There was something there. Just . . . not what I expected. Or who I expected would be behind things."

"But why blame Jimmy? What else did you have against him?"

Drue stared out the window. "It wasn't just the Jazmin Mayes case. There was something else. Colleen Boardman Hicks."

"That again?" Brice's voice was sharp. "The woman's been gone for forty years. What's she got to do with Jimmy? Or me?"

"I don't know, Dad. You tell me. Since we're on the topic of honesty, can you honestly tell me she was 'just a high school classmate'? And there was nothing going on between you? Can you explain why Mom kept a folder full of old newspaper clippings about Colleen Hicks's disappearance all these years? Or why the official case file, which has been missing from the St. Pete Police Department since Jimmy retired, should turn up in the attic of Papi's house?"

Brice turned his head and gave a meaningful glance toward Jonah, who, as it turned out, was out cold, asleep in the backseat.

"Okay," he said finally. "Yeah. You're a smart cookie. Like your mom. I had a thing with Colleen, for, like, six months. But I broke it off with her before she disappeared."

"And Jimmy knew about the affair, didn't he?"

"Yeah," Brice said reluctantly. "He knew. He was there when the nightmare started. But I've got no idea how that police file got in your grandparents' attic. And I don't know, I swear to God, I don't know what happened to Colleen."

Before she could ask any more questions, Jonah yawned, loudly and theatrically, to announce that he was awake.

"We'll talk about this later, okay?" Drue asked.

"Yeah," Brice said wearily. "It's a conversation I can't wait to finish."

~

He rolled to a stop in the driveway at Coquina Cottage. Jonah's shiny black Audi was parked behind Drue's white Bronco. Brice cut the engine and reached under the driver's seat, bringing out a blue steel revolver.

"Here." He turned, holding the gun by the barrel, offering it to the younger man, his voice somber. "You do know how to shoot one of these, right?"

"Dad!" Drue exclaimed, horrified. "What the hell?"

"It's my old service weapon. Smith and Wesson thirty-eight Special," Brice said calmly. "Jonah?"

"Uh, well, not really," Jonah admitted.

"Give me the damn thing," Drue said impatiently, holding out her hand. "I guess you've forgotten that you used to drag me out to practice at the pistol range for hours on end that last summer."

"That's right," Brice said. "Father-daughter bonding time. I had forgotten. So, you remember how to use it?"

Without a word, she broke down the gun to show him her competency.

"I hated every minute of that time, and at the time, I hated you too. I still hate guns," she said. "But I guess maybe I've gotten used to you."

He nodded. "Okay, kiddo. Same here. Lock all your doors, okay? And let me know the minute you hear from Hernandez that they have Ben in custody."

Jonah scrambled out of the backseat and opened the passenger door for Drue. He leaned inside. "Hey, Brice. I'm no good with a gun, but if Ben shows up here again? He's going down."

57

August 20, 1976

"Sit there," Sherri said, pointing to a chair in the living room. "And don't you move. You hear?"

Colleen did as she was told, a nice girl, sitting with her shackled hands folded in her lap, her feet crossed at the ankles.

The heat in the room was oppressive. She could already feel the sweat pooling between her shoulders, running down her neck.

Sherri went into the kitchen. Her guest heard the sound of an ice tray cracking, of cubes tinkling into a glass. Liquid poured.

A minute later, her captor was back, holding a tumbler of amber liquid in her right hand and a fifth of Jack Daniel's in her right. Colleen's hopes soared and then died when she saw the revolver tucked into the waistband of Sherri's jeans.

With nothing better to do, Colleen appraised the room.

There was a bamboo-looking sofa, hideous oversize lamps with gold-fringed shades and ugly harvest-gold carpet. The drapes were floral swagged satin. It was an old person's room. Brice didn't like talking about his home life, but he had mentioned, once, that the house belonged to his wife's parents.

Sherri went to the sliding-glass doors, pulled the drapes apart and opened the doors to the deck beyond. A strong gust of wind billowed the drapes and the rain pounded against the wooden deck.

"Where's your husband tonight?" Colleen asked, being careful not to use his name.

Sherri took a long slug of whiskey. "None of your business." And then she smirked. "I'll tell you where he isn't. And that's the Dreamland motel with some cheap whore."

"So what's the plan, Sherri?" Colleen asked. "You gonna keep me here, handcuffed, until he gets home?"

Sherri gulped some more whiskey. "By the time he gets home, it'll all be over. You, me, all of it. And he can clean up the goddamn mess he made of our life."

A cold shiver traveled down Colleen's spine. Stay calm, she told herself. Don't panic.

"You know," she said, her tone conversational, "it doesn't have to end like this. You could let me go. Take my money, leave his ass. I mean, he cheated on you, right? You're the injured party. Do what I did. Take the money and run."

Sherri ignored Colleen's advice. "We had a good marriage. Not great. But it worked. Until you came along and ruined everything."

Colleen's lip curled in contempt. "Keep telling yourself that,

Sherri. If it was so good, how come he happily hopped in bed with me the first chance he got?"

"You mean that night back before Christmas?"

Colleen didn't bother to try to hide her surprise. "You knew?"

"I always knew when he was screwing around. He was like a little boy, thought he had to be naughty to get my attention. I kicked him out that night, but it was Christmas, you know? And like he always did, he promised it was over, and like I always did, I believed him."

Sherri emptied her glass and poured herself another healthy tot.

Colleen crossed and recrossed her ankles, carefully working her feet loose in the cumbersome platform sandals.

"You know, it's really kind of rude of you to drink in front of me and not offer me one. If you're gonna kill me anyway, the least you could do is fix me a drink."

Sherri laughed. "Ooh. Where are my manners?" She picked up the bottle and gestured toward the kitchen. "You go first."

Colleen stood but didn't move, waiting until the other woman, annoyed, moved closer to give her a push.

At that instant, Colleen swung her shackled hands and knocked the glass from the startled woman's hands, and before Sherri could react, raised her arms and gave a mighty slicing backswing, bashing Sherri in the face with the full weight of the handcuffs, knocking her to the floor.

Colleen kicked off the shoes and ran, out the sliding-glass doors and onto the deck. She slipped and went sprawling on the rain-slicked boards. She scrabbled around, terrified, finally managing to get back on her feet.

She ran toward the beach, looking back only once, to see Sherri silhouetted in the doorway, the gun raised, clutched between both hands. She fired and Colleen screamed as the bullet ripped through her shoulder, knocking her down again.

The wounded woman lay still for a moment, hearing the panting of her own breath as blood oozed from the wound. But the adrenaline still pumped through her veins and she got back up again. This time she ran without looking back, blindly heading for the cover of the stand of Australian pines and what she knew was the beach, just beyond.

She was still running when she hit the shallow seawall of broken concrete riprap. Colleen could see the waves crashing ashore and heat lightning dancing on the gold-tinged horizon. A squadron of pelicans cruised past, their shapes silhouetted against the dark clouds. But she didn't see the carpet of slimy moss and seaweed clinging to the rocks. When her foot slipped and she fell, the pelicans were the very last thing she saw.

58

~

"Sit," Drue said, gesturing toward the sofa. She went into her bedroom and found an extra pillow and a lightweight blanket.

"Here," she said, tossing them to her guest. "But you really don't have to do this."

"I want to," Jonah said, stretching out on the sofa with the pillow beneath his head. "Get some sleep, okay? I'll hang out here. I'm too wired to sleep."

"The first thing I'm getting is a shower and my own clothes," Drue said.

When she emerged from the shower fifteen minutes later, her hair hung damply on the shoulders of her clean cotton T-shirt, and she was dressed in drawstring pajama pants. Jonah's head was tilted back and he was snoring, openmouthed.

She went to the sliding-glass doors and opened them, and he sat upright, giving her a sheepish grin. "Some bodyguard I turned out to be. I'm here fifteen minutes and I fall asleep on the job."

"It's okay," she reassured him. "There is zero chance Ben is coming back here."

Jonah thought about it for a moment. "I still don't get it. Any of it. I know you say he probably got a payoff from the insurance people, but it's not like Ben ever cared about money. I mean, did you ever see the place where he lives?"

"No," Drue said. "I got the feeling he was a little embarrassed by it."

"He lives like a damned hobo," Jonah said. "I mean, the dude makes decent money. But he rents a room from this little old lady in Woodlawn. He doesn't even have his own kitchen. And he buys most of his clothes at Goodwill and brown-bags his lunch most of the time."

"Did he ever tell you about the video game he was working on?" she asked. "His side hustle?"

"*Insect Assassin?* Yeah. He actually had me play it a couple times. Like as a beta tester. I'm not that into gaming. I had an Xbox, and I played some in undergrad school, but I kind of outgrew it, I guess. Anyway, it was more than a side hustle. He really believed *Insect Assassin* would make him rich. And it was a pretty cool game, I'll admit. But the graphics were lame. He had some famous artist chick in Korea he wanted to work with, to design the graphics, but he said she was crazy expensive."

"And that's why he did what he did. To get the money to take his game to market," Drue said.

Jonah nodded in agreement. "Where do you think he is now?"

"In hell, I hope. It's what? Nearly two-thirty?" She picked up her cell phone and frowned. "Hernandez hasn't called yet. You'd think by now they would have picked him up."

"You know what?" Jonah slapped his knee. "Ben told me he was playing in a gaming tournament this weekend."

"You're right. That's where he was the first time I tried to call him Friday night, and where he called me from yesterday," Drue said. "But that wouldn't still be going on now, right?"

"Maybe. These tournaments? I went to one with him once, to watch him play *Madden NFL*. Which he sucked at, by the way. These guys, they play around the clock, they only stop for pee breaks."

"Do you know where this tournament is?"

"Probably at the same place I went to. It was this grungy former multiplex over near Central Plaza."

"I know where that is," Drue said. "I'm gonna call Hernandez and tell her to check that out."

Rae Hernandez picked up after the first ring. "No, we haven't located Ben Fentress yet. And yes, we are actively looking. I met a St. Pete patrol unit at his address. He wasn't there, but his car was. We even woke up his landlady, but she said she doesn't keep tabs on him."

"We think we know where he might be," Drue said excitedly. She looked over at Jonah, who'd looked up the tournament information on his phone.

"It's at that same place I went to," Jonah confirmed. "It's called Central Gaming."

"Oh God," Hernandez moaned. "My kid made me take him

to one of those tournaments. Once and only once. A huge room full of testosterone-challenged dudes pretending to do battle with cartoon monsters and extraterrestrials. Kill me now."

"So you'll call me once you find him, right?" Drue repeated anxiously.

"I'll call you, and then I'll call your dad, who I just got off the phone with," the detective promised and disconnected the call.

"I can't sleep," Drue told Jonah. "I'm dead on my feet, but I know I can't sleep."

"Me neither. You wanna watch some television?"

"Great idea, except I haven't gotten around to having cable hooked up." She pointed out the door. "We could take a walk on the beach."

"I like it." He picked up the revolver from the end table where she'd placed it. "We should take this, right?"

"What for? You don't do guns, and I don't have any pockets in these pants."

He looked down at her. "Are those pajamas?"

"Who wants to know?"

"Okay, I'll put it in my pocket." He thrust it into his hip pocket, where it stuck out comically.

"No. You'll probably shoot yourself in the nuts, like that guy in the Walmart." Drue laughed. She knew she was punchy, but she didn't care. "Leave it here."

She went to her purse and dug out the can of Mace, which she promptly stuck in her bra.

"Where'd you get that?" he asked.

She rolled her eyes. "A gift from my 'uncle Zee,' as he put it. Let's go."

They kicked off their shoes and left them on the edge of the deck. When they got down to the water, they both rolled up their pant legs and walked companionably along, letting the warm water lap at their ankles.

At one point, Jonah stopped and pointed at the lights of Sharky's. "Look," he said, a devilish glint in his eye. "Someday, we'll tell our kids that's where we met. And had our first kiss."

She shook her head and kept walking, smiling despite herself. She stopped, a couple hundred yards farther, and pointed to the dune line. "If I remember correctly, that's actually where the first kiss occurred."

He caught her hand in his and laughed. "And things went downhill from there, in a hurry."

"I thought I told you none of that ever happened," she said, giving him a stern look.

"How could I forget those golden hours in your arms?" Jonah teased.

"And how could I forget the sight of you doing the walk of shame the next morning," she retorted.

They walked on and paused again, when they saw the mass of the Gulf Vista up ahead.

Drue shuddered involuntarily, thinking of Jazmin Mayes's sad fate there.

"You know," Jonah said, "I saw an article in the business section of the *Tampa Bay Times* this week. It said they're going to rebrand the place, and knock down the original part of the hotel that dates from the 1970s. They're going to build a fancy state-of-the-art spa and fitness center in its place."

"That explains why that wing was almost totally vacant Friday night," Drue said thoughtfully. "I guess it's a good sign that they've got the money to expand. Hopefully, Dad is going to sue the living daylights out of them on behalf of Jazmin's mom, now that we know the truth about how and when she was killed."

He put his arm around her shoulders. "Did I tell you yet that I think it's pretty cool what you did? Figuring everything out? Maybe you should think about going to law school and following in your old man's footsteps."

"Never," she said quickly. "The thought of three more years of school is more than I can bear. Sitting at a desk all day? Like I do in that damned cubicle of mine? No thanks."

"What about becoming an investigator? Like Zee. You never see him sitting at a desk."

"It's crossed my mind," she admitted. "I always liked puzzles. And mysteries."

"That's how you got so wrapped up in that missing woman thing?"

"You heard?"

"Yeah. I only pretended to be asleep, to save Brice's pride. But you don't actually still believe that Zee or your dad had anything to do with that, right? I mean, Brice flat-out denied it."

"And I want to believe him. I really do. But he lied to me about it from the beginning, and so did Zee. And the other thing is, which I didn't bring up with my dad tonight, I actually went and talked to the last woman who ever saw Colleen Boardman Hicks. Her name is Vera Rennick. She worked at a dentist's office with her. On the day Colleen disappeared, back in 1976, they went shopping and had dinner together. Colleen told her, 'I'll see you Monday.' And then she vanished."

"Doesn't mean your dad killed her," Jonah objected. "Just because they had an affair."

"Vera Rennick has this true-crime blog now," Drue said. "I found it online. When I went to see her, she told me that a few months before Colleen disappeared, she insisted they go to Mastry's. For lunch. A place women just didn't go back then. While they were there, Colleen stopped to talk to two uniformed St. Pete police officers, who were sort of flirting with her."

"And you think it was Brice. And who? Zee?"

"Maybe. I showed her a photo of them. She wasn't sure. But Dad and Jimmy Zee were best friends even back then. They were in the Marine Corps together in Vietnam, and when they got home, they went through the police academy together," Drue said. She shook her head, as though trying to shake off the disturbing images that had taken up residence there.

"Maybe you should straight-up ask Zee about it," Jonah suggested. "Get it all out in the open."

"Maybe, once all this stuff with Ben is over, I will," Drue said lightly. "I'm only one woman, you know. I can only solve one mystery at a time."

They'd turned around at the Gulf Vista, and wandered slowly back in the direction of Coquina Cottage. They paused and Drue frowned at the sight of the blue tarp draped over the roof.

"I'm gonna break down and get a new roof," she said with a sigh. "I got a notice from the city last week. I'm in violation of some stupid building code."

"The joys of home ownership," Jonah said. He reached out and turned her toward him. "You know, we were supposed to have a do-over tonight. I had dinner reservations at a fancy restaurant near the Vinoy, and big plans for us."

"And I'm sorry about that," she said earnestly. "How can I ever make it up to you?"

He kissed her lightly, and she leaned in and wound her arms around his neck, and the kiss deepened. When they finally parted, she sighed again.

"What's that?" he asked, looking concerned. "Regret?"

"A little," she said. "Not about this, just about the way things started with us. And about the time I've wasted since then, hating your guts."

"But lately, my irresistible charm has grown on you, hasn't it?"

"Don't push your luck," she told him.

"Maybe we could continue this conversation inside?" he asked. "Since we're both too tired to sleep, possibly we could find some other distraction?"

"You're relentless. You know that?"

"So I've been told."

They picked up their shoes on the edge of the deck and went into the darkened house.

"Hey there." They heard the click of a light switch, the lamp on the table beside the sofa.

Ben sat in the armchair. He had the revolver, and it was pointed at Drue. "Welcome back."

He wore a baseball cap with a backward bill and a blue and white polyester bicycle racing jersey, with the words TEAM DANGERBOY written in script across it.

Drue took a step backward and her breath caught in her chest.

"What do you want?" Jonah asked, his voice menacing.

"Just thought I'd drop by to check in on Drue."

"To make sure she was dead?" Jonah asked. "You're a sick bastard, you know that?"

"Aren't we all sick bastards, deep down inside?" Ben giggled a little at his own joke.

"The thing is, I was just about to leave the tournament. In fact, I was standing outside, about to head home on the Vespa, when I saw half a dozen cop cars roll up. And I said to myself, 'Dude, this is not good.' So instead of going home, I thought I'd come out here and pay Drue a visit. And maybe borrow her car. I think that's fair, don't you? Since I'm the one that got it running again?"

Drue stared. "Are you high?"

"Just a little bit," he said, giggling again. "I'd offer you some of mine, Drue, but we both know it doesn't agree with you."

"So take the car and go," Jonah said. "You got your money from the insurance people, right? I'm sure you weren't planning on sticking around, especially now. So just go."

"See, the money thing is off," Ben said, his mood turning angry. "Everything was all set, until Drue decided to stick her nose where it didn't belong and fuck me over."

He waved the revolver from Jonah to Drue, then back to Drue. "Rookie move, Drue. Leaving a gun in an unlocked house. Whose gun is it, just out of curiosity?"

"It's my dad's," Drue said. "You hurt me, Ben, and he's coming after you. And he'll never stop until he's caught you and locked you up."

"No doubt," Ben said. "But I'll be long gone by the time he figures it out."

He smiled at his former colleague. "Hey, my man. You don't mind if I borrow that sweet Audi of yours, instead of that crappy car of hers? I mean, making a getaway in a white Ford Bronco, it didn't work out so good for the last guy, did it?" Ben snapped his fingers and held out his hand, palm up.

"Fuck off," Jonah said. "This ain't *Grand Theft Auto*."

Ben pointed the revolver at a spot directly over Drue's head and fired. She jumped reflexively, the shot ringing in her ears.

"The next shot I fire will be in her head," Ben said calmly. "Now give me the fucking keys."

"Okay," Drue said, her voice shaking. "Jonah doesn't have the keys. I've got them."

"In your pajama pants?" Ben's voice mocked.

She reached into her bra. "No. They're right here." Her hand closed over the can of Mace and she took a step toward him.

"Hand 'em over," he repeated.

Her hand trembled, but she fixed her thumb over the nozzle, extended her arm and emptied the can of Mace directly into his eyes.

He screamed and managed to get off one wild shot in the air, just before Jonah charged him, head-butting him to the floor and cold-cocking him into unconsciousness.

She stood there, stunned, gazing down at the two men sprawled across her living room floor. The next thing she knew, her front door was being broken down.

Jimmy Zee charged into the room, his weapon drawn. He looked from her to Ben, whose bloody jaw was now arranged in a new and unnatural way, to Jonah, who'd seated himself atop the unmoving man's chest.

"Oh, little girl," he said, shaking his head and looking at Drue. "What have you gone and done?"

59

August 20, 1976

The storm raged on. Thunder boomed overhead and lightning sizzled on the deep blue horizon. Inside the cottage, the lights flickered and then the house went completely dark.

The rain was so loud, she felt rather than heard his footsteps on the deckboards. But she didn't look up until he put his hand on her shoulder.

She was huddled at the edge of the deck, her arms wrapped tightly around her folded knees, looking like a drowned kitten. An empty bottle of Jack Daniel's sat beside her.

"She's out there," Sherri said, looking up with swollen, red-rimmed eyes. She pointed toward the fringe of Australian pines.

"Okay." He tramped off, his sneakers sinking into the wet sand. He wore a black windbreaker and his usual dark sunglasses, despite the deepening twilight. He was back moments later.

"Is she . . . ?"

He chewed his gum, switching it from one side of his mouth to the other. "Yeah. Do you have a tarp or something like that?"

"A tarp? What good's that going to do if she's dead?"

"I've got to move her, Sherri," he said patiently. "Before somebody comes along and finds the body."

"There might be a painter's drop cloth in Papi's shed."

"I'll get it," he said. "Go inside and dry off. And no more of that," he said, pointing at the empty bottle.

"That's all there was in the house," she said sadly. "Or I would have drunk that too."

He sat down beside her on the edge of the deck, oblivious to the rain, their bodies close but not touching. "You want to kill yourself?"

"That was the plan," she said. "Her, and then me. But I'm such a chickenshit, I can't seem to do it." She lifted the revolver, dangling it from her middle finger.

"Brice's service revolver? Christ, Sherri!" He took it from her. "That's what you shot her with?"

"What else? You know I don't like guns."

He stood up and pulled her to her feet, then stuck the gun in the waistband of his jeans.

"Go on, now. I'll deal with this. How soon do you think Brice will be back?"

"Around nine? The class he just started taking this quarter only meets at the USF campus in Tampa. Or it might be later. He won't drive across the Howard Frankland Bridge in a storm like this. You know how he is about that bridge."

"Right."

~

Thirty minutes later, he knocked on the glass of the doors. He was soaked, and rain dripped from his nose. "Do you happen to have the keys to the handcuffs?"

Her reactions were still dulled from the shock and the whiskey. "They're in the cigar box where he keeps the cuffs."

"Get them, please."

She looked over his shoulder and shuddered at the sight of the rolled-up lumpy form resting at the edge of the deck where they'd just been sitting.

When she came back with the keys he took them and knelt down beside the lifeless form.

"Here." He handed her the handcuffs and the keys. "Get a towel and wipe them off good, then put them back in the exact same place you found them."

"Okay."

He handed her the revolver, and she took it, reluctantly.

"Do you know how to clean one of these?" he asked.

"Yeah. Brice showed me when he taught me how to use it."

"Good. Clean it like he showed you, then take a towel and wipe it down completely and put it back where he always keeps it."

"What about you? Where are you going?"

"Like I said, I'm going to take care of that." He jerked his head in the direction of the corpse.

"Is there anything else?" he asked. "Any other sign that she was ever here? Think, Sherri. This is important."

"I'm trying, Jimmy," she said plaintively. "But my mind's not right. Everything's all mixed up. Oh, wait. She left her train case on the floor of the front seat of my car. She said it's full of money."

"I'll deal with that too."

The lights flickered back on again, revealing an upended chair, a broken glass and a wet spot on the wall-to-wall carpet.

"You need to get the place straightened up," he said.

"I will. I'm sorry, Jimmy, that I got you mixed up in this. I didn't know what else to do."

"It's okay. That's what friends are for, right?" He touched her face, and she flinched. There was a nasty gash across her nose. She had a black eye and a huge bruise on her right cheek.

She caught his hand in hers and released it a second later. "What am I going to tell Brice about my face when he asks?"

He thought about it. "I know. There's a big tree limb out front that must have snapped off one of the pine trees in the storm. Tell him you went outside to roll up the windows of the car and the branch hit you as it was coming down."

"Good thinking. You're a smart guy, Jimmy. You know that?"

"You're smart too. Just do what I told you. And then forget any of this happened."

She had her arms wrapped tightly around her torso, chilled from the dampness. "How do I do that? I killed her. How do I live with that?"

"You'll figure it out. Anyway, you didn't kill her. The bullet barely grazed her shoulder. That riprap out there is covered in slimy seaweed. When she fell, she hit her head on one of those rocks and cracked her skull. That's what killed her. Not you."

"But what will you do with the body?" she asked. "What if you get caught with it?"

"I'm not gonna get caught," he repeated. "I'm a smart guy, remember?"

60

I'm gonna call your dad and let him know you're okay," Zee told Drue, holding up his cell phone. "And then, I guess we'd better buzz your pal Rae Hernandez, so she can call out the cavalry for this piece of shit."

He poked Ben in the side with the toe of his black motorcycle boot, then looked up expectantly at Drue. "You got any coffee?"

"If you'll show me where the coffeemaker is, I'll make it," Jonah offered.

"In the kitchen," Drue said. "Come on. I'll help."

"We can all go," Zee said. He prodded Ben's ribs again with his boot. "This asshole isn't going anywhere." He gave Jonah an admiring salute. "Good work, my man. I think you managed to break his jaw. But you're probably going to need some ice on that hand of yours."

"What about me?" Drue demanded. "I'm the one who sprayed him with the Mace."

"Which I gave you," Zee reminded her. "Like they say, teamwork makes the dream work."

They were sitting on the deck at dawn, sipping their coffee, when they heard the police sirens approach.

"How did you even know Ben was here?" Drue asked Zee, who'd just returned from walking out to look at the water.

"Your dad called and woke me up when he couldn't reach you," Zee said. "Which reminds me. You need to recharge your phone. He asked me to do a drive-by, just to make sure things were okay here."

"Why didn't he just come himself?" Drue asked.

"He couldn't leave Wendy, because she was spotting again. He said she was having a rough night."

"*She* had a rough night!" Drue exclaimed, rolling her eyes. "In the past forty-eight hours I've been arrested, interrogated, poisoned and shot at."

Zee punched her shoulder lightly. "You're a tough kid. I mean, woman. Like your mom."

Before she could ask him what he meant by that, they heard cars pulling up at the front of the house.

It was after eight Sunday morning by the time Brice met them at the Treasure Island police station, with three Mocha Grandes and three toasted bagels. Drue and Jonah sipped coffee and devoured the bagels while they waited for Hernandez to join them in the cramped conference room.

"Okay," she said, bustling in and closing the door behind them. "Just so you know, Ben Fentress was admitted to St. Anthony's. He's having surgery to wire his jaw back together, which is kind of a shame, but while he was waiting in a treatment room he declined to chat with me without counsel present anyway, so it's kind of a moot point."

Hernandez was dressed in mom jeans and a Red Wings baseball jersey, with a blue blazer thrown on top of it.

"Has he been charged?" Brice asked, his yellow legal pad at the ready.

"Yes. Two counts of attempted murder, two counts aggravated assault and . . ." She opened a steno notebook and flipped through the scribbled pages. "Trespassing."

She sat down at the table. "Sorry you had to wait, but I wanted to be able to tell you what we discovered after we got the warrant to search his apartment in Woodlawn. The main thing is his laptop. And a bunch of files. And of course, we've got his cell phone.

"For an IT guy," she said, looking directly at Brice, "he was surprisingly careless. There was a yellow index card, taped to the inside cover of his MacBook, with all his passwords on it. I think my ten-year-old son could hack that thing. Hell, my seventy-five-year-old mom could hack it, and she still uses AOL."

She paused momentarily. "And one more thing. When we were searching Fentress's apartment, we found his passport and some travel documents indicating he was planning on moving to the Cayman Islands. Were you aware of that, Mr. Campbell?"

"News to me," Brice said, grim-faced.

"He'd even set up a bank account there. Looks like he was anticipating a big payday."

Jonah insisted on driving her home. It was almost ten o'clock, and the sun was already blazing hot when he pulled into the driveway. "Do you want to come in?" she asked, feeling suddenly shy.

"I do. But I think you could probably use some rest," he said.

"I really, really do need to sleep. Like, for days, but I'd settle for a good four or five hours," she said, leaning over to kiss him lightly.

"Call me, please? As soon as you wake up. In fact, FaceTime me."

"Okay, but why?"

"So I can hear you, and see what you look like, when you first wake up."

She looked at him dubiously.

"Oh please. That's a line from an old chick flick, isn't it?"

"Possibly. But it's still one hundred percent true."

Jonah said, "I'm serious, Drue. Call me."

She kissed him again. "You know, for a fratty Mcfrat boy, you're kind of cute. And sweet."

He rested his forehead against hers. "And you are a total badass. I think maybe I'm developing a thing for badass chicks."

She chuckled as she opened the door and looked back at him over her shoulder. "We'll see about that."

61

The next time she looked at the clock on her nightstand it said six o'clock, but it was still dark outside her bedroom. Drue sat up and grabbed her phone and looked at the calendar.

Six o'clock. Monday morning. Somehow, she'd managed to sleep for eighteen hours straight. Remembering the last conversation she had with Jonah, she scrolled through her contacts, found his name and before she lost her nerve, tapped the icon for FaceTime.

The phone made that weird *boop-boop-boop-boop* noise, and then Jonah's face—and water-beaded bare chest—filled the screen of her phone.

"Good morning," she said, yawning.

"And to you. Did you forget to call me last night?"

"You won't believe it. I went to bed and just now woke up. I slept like the dead. How about you?"

"I'm ashamed to admit that after I left your place, I went to the gym, worked out, did laundry, and went home and watched television until I fell asleep at eight."

"I love that you're such a girly man," Drue said, laughing. "Tell me you watched HGTV and I'll be yours forever."

"Close. It was *Masterpiece Theatre,* but you've got to swear not to tell a soul."

"I'll take it to my grave," she said, crossing her heart.

He leaned closer in to the screen. "Say, what's that you're wearing? Is that, like, what? A camisole? I like it!"

"We are *not* doing this," Drue said. "It's way too early in the morning. I'll see you at the office."

"Wear that to work," he urged.

"I'm hanging up now."

Drue walked through the reception area and Geoff stood up, grabbed her and hugged her. "Ohmygod!" he said breathlessly. "I just heard about Ben. I can't believe he actually tried to kill you. I mean, I'm stunned. To my core."

"How did you hear already?" she asked, extricating herself from his clutches.

"Brice sent out a firm-wide memo first thing this morning," he said and grimaced. "And since Mr. Fentress is no longer with the firm, Wendy emailed and says I'm on the Justice Line, at least until we hire somebody new."

She patted his arm. "You'll be great."

The bullpen seemed oddly quiet. Ben's desktop was as clean as he'd left it at quitting time Friday, which seemed like years ago, although his computer was gone and the desk drawers were open and empty. She looked over at Jonah, who was on the phone, and nodded at him.

Her heart sank when she saw the yellow note stuck to her computer monitor.

SEE ME. It was Brice's handwriting.

She found her father seated at his desk, a plastic cape around his neck, with paper towels tucked in a protective ring around the collar of his blue dress shirt. Marianne the paralegal was applying pancake makeup to his face. She turned and nodded at Drue, then went back to her handiwork.

Drue's eyes widened, and Brice gave her a broad wink. He was clearly having the time of his life.

"Dad? What's all this?"

"Just a little proactive public relations," her father said. He looked up at Marianne, who was brandishing a tube of Chanel mascara.

"Did you confirm with Rae Hernandez at Treasure Island?" he asked. "The producer from the CBS affiliate told me it's a no-go without the detective who cracked the case."

"She's not wild about a press conference," Marianne replied. "Hold still and look up, please." She brushed his lashes with three coats of Chanel ultra-black. "So I called back and spoke to the police chief, and she looooves the idea."

"Of course she does," Brice said. "How often does a department that small crack a two-year-old cold-case homicide? With good old-fashioned shoe-leather detective work? Of course, we're the ones whose shoes did the work, but it won't hurt to let them take most of the credit."

"Does that mean what I think it does?" Drue asked.

"Herman Byars was arrested without incident yesterday. He was actually mowing his lawn when the police pulled up to his house. Hernandez is pretty close-mouthed, but when I called her last night, she said they were confident they have a water-tight case."

"How about Neesa? Is she talking to them?"

"Hernandez says she's cooperating, so I'm assuming so."

"What about Ben?" Drue asked.

"Not as cooperative. But I don't think it's going to matter that much. I fired off a letter to counsel for the hotel's insurance company first thing this morning. This matter is a huge black eye to them. There should be serious criminal implications for whomever Ben was dealing with there."

"Isn't it a major black eye for Campbell, Coxe and Kramner too? Since Ben worked for us and extorted the insurance company?" Drue asked.

"That part isn't so great," Brice admitted. "I've already retained counsel for us. Frankly, the whole thing is a shit show all the way around. But the bottom line is, eventually, there will be a settlement for Jazmin's family."

"And how long will all that take?" Drue asked.

"It takes as long as it takes, Drue. The wheels of justice grind slowly sometimes."

"If at all," she said. "Was that what you wanted to talk to me about? I guess I better get out there to the phones."

"Don't worry about the phones," Brice said. "Just finish up whatever you were working on and ship it over to Wendy. She's set up a command post in our bedroom. For today, we're routing calls over to the offsite call center, and in the meantime, Wendy has posted openings for two positions online."

"Two?" Drue said.

"That's what I wanted to discuss with you," Brice said. "Jimmy's been talking about slowing down for a while now, and after yesterday, he came over and we had a couple of drinks and talked about a succession plan."

She let the phrase sink in. "Does that mean what I think it means?"

"If you want it to," Brice said. "I admit I had my doubts about it, but Jimmy insists you're more than capable. You've got good people skills—he claims yours are much better than his, by the way—a strong work ethic and, the most important thing, at least according to him, killer instincts. What do you say?"

She looked up at the ceiling and down at her hands, then across the desk at him. "Let me think about it, okay?" she said.

Her reply obviously took him by surprise. "What's to think about?"

"Well, I'd like a job description, for one. And I'll need to know about the compensation and benefits package."

His face began to redden beneath the pancake and he began to sputter.

She balled up a piece of paper and tossed it at him. "Just

kidding, Dad. Yeah. I'll take the job. But it does come with a raise, right? I really have to do something about my roof."

"Did I not mention your signing bonus?" Brice asked. "How does twenty-five thousand sound? That should buy a roof and replacement doors for the cottage, right?"

Drue found herself grinning despite herself. "A roof, and maybe even central air." She stood up and stuck out her hand.

Brice laughed, shook her hand and went to give her a hug.

"Brice, please," Marianne protested. "Your shirt! You'll get it wrinkled and then it'll look like you slept in it."

After Brice left for his press conference, Drue went back to her cubicle. She had paperwork to finish up, and calls to field from the firm's newest television ad campaign. At one point, she looked up and saw Zee walking through the bullpen. She reached out and snagged him by the fabric of his shirt.

"Dad told me about the new succession plan," she said. "Can I take you to lunch today? There's some stuff I need to ask you about."

"Can't. Brice wants me to do follow-up interviews with some of those other current and former housekeepers at the Gulf Vista. He thinks there's a potential for a class-action lawsuit against the hotel for sexual harassment. That place is the gift that keeps on giving."

"Okay. Then how about a drink? After work tonight?"

"Maybe. Text me when you leave here and let me know where you want to meet."

~

Drue stopped at Target on her way home from work and picked out several more coloring books and a Little Mermaid bathing suit and beach towel.

When she got to Yvonne Howington's house, she saw the Plymouth parked in the driveway. The hood was open and the vehicle, which was missing two tires, was raised up on concrete blocks. Drue got a very intense sense of déjà vu.

"Come on in," Yvonne said, after Drue knocked on the screen door.

"What's wrong with your car?" Drue asked, following Yvonne into the living room.

"What's not wrong with it?" Yvonne said, seating herself in the recliner. "Needs new tires, new battery, new everything. My nephew's supposed to start working on it, when he gets the time."

"How do you get to work?" Drue asked.

"Sometimes I get a ride from somebody, but mostly I just take cabs," Yvonne said resignedly.

Drue handed her the Target bag. "This is for Aliyah. How's she doing?"

Yvonne accepted the bag without comment. "You want to see her? She's in the bedroom coloring in that book you brought her. She's about wore out those glitter markers."

"I do want to see her, but in the meantime, have you seen the news?"

"No. Cable's out." Yvonne leaned forward, a glimmer of hope in her dark eyes. "You got news for me? About my case?"

"I do," Drue said. "There's been an arrest."

"Praise Jesus." Yvonne raised her hands. "He is good all the time."

She quickly filled the older woman in on the latest developments, leaving out the more sordid details of Jazmin's uneasy arrangement with her killer.

"I knew it," Yvonne said, nodding vigorously. "Jazmin was afraid of that man."

"Jazmin's friend Neesa was also arrested," Drue said quietly.

"That nice girl? I can't believe she would do that."

"Herman Byars bullied her into it," Drue said. "She was just as afraid of him as Jazmin was, but she helped him conceal the crime and lied to the police, so I'm afraid she's in real trouble."

"I'll have to pray for her," Yvonne said. "But now, what does that mean for my case against the hotel?"

"That's the other thing I need to discuss with you. First off, we've discovered a lot of new information, including the fact that Jazmin should have been off work at the time she was killed." She paused, as she considered how to put a good face on Ben Fentress's betrayal of their client and his employers.

"We also just learned this weekend that one of my colleagues at the law firm knew that Neesa and Herman Byars staged it to look like Jazmin was working that late shift, when in reality, she was already dead," Drue said. "He went to the hotel's insurance company and demanded a payoff to keep quiet about it."

"That dirty, dirty dog," Yvonne said indignantly. "I hope your daddy fired that bad man."

"He did. And Ben's in jail. I don't think he'll be getting out anytime soon," Drue said.

"Now that we know that Jazmin had finished her shift when

she was murdered, we can pursue a third-party wrongful death claim against the hotel. So, I need to ask you, first, if you'd like us to continue to represent you. And I also have to warn you that the process is going to take time. It's a whole lot more likely to get a bigger settlement for you, but it won't happen overnight."

"Did your daddy send you over here to talk to me today?" Yvonne asked.

"No, ma'am," Drue said. "I just wanted you to hear the facts from me, instead of from the television or newspaper."

"Mmm-hmm," Yvonne said, her lips pursed. "To tell you the truth, Miss Drue, I'm not sure I trust your daddy no more. I did, but then look how he did me. My sister said that man is too pretty to be real. She says get you an ugly lawyer."

Drue laughed, thinking about her father's morning camera-ready makeup session. "To tell you the truth, I felt the same way about my dad when I first went to work for him. But I've come around now."

"And what changed your mind?" Yvonne asked.

"I realized I was judging him by what kind of a father he was to me, which probably isn't really fair. He'd be the first to tell you, now, that he was a lousy father. He's not perfect, but he's not a crook. He really cares about clients like you, and he wants to win for them," Drue said.

Yvonne gave her a world-weary side-eye. "You ever meet a perfect man?"

"Nope," Drue said. "There are a lot of dogs out there, and I think I've known or dated most of them. But there's this guy I know. Let's just say, I think he might have potential."

"Can't ask for more than that," Yvonne said.

"Grandmama?" Aliyah stood in the doorway.

"Look who came to see you today, Aliyah," Yvonne said. "Miss Drue brought you a present."

The little girl ran over to Drue, her eyes sparkling. "Are we going swimming today, Miss Drue?"

"Not today, I'm afraid," Drue said. "But soon. And this is for you for when we start our mermaid lessons."

Aliyah tore the bag open and held out the swimsuit. "Look, Grandmama. That's Ariel. I'm gonna be just like her."

"What do you say to Miss Drue?" Yvonne said.

Aliyah beamed. "Thank you."

Yvonne walked Drue to the front door. "Tell your daddy I said I'm still his client," Yvonne said. "And about that man with the potential? You tell him for me that I said he needs to step up and do right by a nice girl like you, got a good job and a car of her own and a pretty daddy."

62

Drue was sitting in a back booth at Mastry's Bar when Zee walked up. He slid onto the bench opposite hers, already looking distinctly uncomfortable. She'd ordered a chardonnay for herself and a beer for him.

He took a long pull on the beer. "Brice tells me you've agreed to the new job. That's good news for both of us, right?"

"It is," Drue said. "Thanks for the recommendation."

She hefted a cardboard box onto the tabletop and pushed it toward him. "I brought you something."

"You didn't have to do that . . ." He opened the box, and lifted out the black binder. He rifled through the pages, nodding. "Where'd you find it?"

"In a crate of Dad's stuff, up in the attic at the cottage," Drue said. "I think I know why you took it, but I can't figure out how it ended up there."

"I put it there, and then I completely forgot about it."

"When?"

He scratched his chin as he pondered the question. "It was the year after I retired, while I was living there."

"You lived in my cottage?" she said, taken aback.

"Technically, it was still your mom's cottage back then. I was, as you might say, between relationships at the time, so I rented it for six months, before I bought my condo at Bayfront Towers."

"I had no idea," Drue said. "Dad never said anything, and Mom sure didn't. But then, there was a whole lot she never told me."

Zee took off his sunglasses and swung them by the earpiece. He settled back in the booth. "Brice told me you had a lot of questions about Colleen Hicks. So that's what this meeting is about?"

Before she could answer, a hand gripped her shoulder. Brice stood there. "Mind if I join you?"

The waiter appeared and Brice ordered a double martini.

When they were alone again, Zee opened the box and showed his friend the contents.

"Son of a bitch," Brice said.

"Yeah," Zee agreed. "She found it in the attic at the cottage."

"So you did take it," Brice said, nodding. "I wondered."

"I've read most of the file," Drue said. "And I talked to Vera Rennick, who has her own theories, but I'd appreciate it if you two would just please tell me the truth."

"You might not like it," Zee warned.

"I'm a big girl. I think I can handle it," Drue countered.

Zee sipped his beer. "Yeah, you keep telling me that."

"I told Drue I was having a thing with Colleen," Brice said. "She'd already guessed that much."

"Vera told me Colleen's husband was abusive," Drue said.

"That's putting it mildly. Allen Hicks was a sadistic drunk," Brice said.

"Piece of shit dirtbag," Zee put in. "You know what our big mistake was? We should have taken him out and dumped him in Lake Maggiore that first night at the Dreamland. Let the gators take care of him."

Brice filled his daughter in on the domestic call the two partners had responded to at the motel, the week before Christmas in 1975.

"There was nothing about that in the file," Drue said.

The former cops exchanged a meaningful look.

"Colleen refused to press charges," Brice said. "We never even called it in to dispatch, so there wouldn't be any paper trail."

"It started that night," Brice said, looking miserable. "I thought I was being so damn clever. I told Sherri I had a study group on Thursday nights, but she eventually caught on."

"And you knew Dad was having an affair with Colleen?" Drue asked Zee.

"It didn't take a genius."

"Things ramped up with her so fast, I didn't realize, until it was too late, that Colleen had emotional problems," Brice said.

"Total head case," Zee agreed, swirling his finger beside his face.

"I guess it was in July when she really started talking crazy. Allen beat her up pretty bad. I kept telling her she should leave him, get a divorce. I offered to help her, but I was very clear that I was never going to leave Sherri."

"You'd screw around on Mom, but you didn't want a divorce?" Drue asked, her voice dripping scorn.

"Believe it or not, I loved your mom. Through everything, God help me, I loved her. When things got really crazy with Colleen, I realized, too late, that I wanted to make my marriage work. Your mom and I had a life together. We had plans. I was going to go to law school, we were gonna have kids." He sighed and fished the olive out of his martini.

"And what did Colleen want?" Drue asked.

"She wanted to run away, assume a new identity, a new life. When I told her there was no way I'd leave, things got ugly. She got hysterical, made threats. She was stalking me, driving past the house. She even went to the office where your mom worked, to check her out! I didn't find out 'til later that Sherri knew exactly who Colleen was."

"What happened next?"

"She was calling me all the time, driving past the house, acting so crazy, I thought I'd lose my mind," Brice said. "I couldn't sleep. I got ulcers." He looked over at his former partner.

"I told Jimmy what was going on with Colleen, all the wild threats. He told me he'd handle it."

"And I did," Zee said. "I made her understand that if she was going to go, she was going to go alone. We got her a fake driver's license and a new Social Security card. It wasn't that hard back then, before everything was computerized. She told me she was going to withdraw all the money from her and Allen's savings account, hop a bus to Atlanta and start a new life."

"Is that what she did?" Drue asked.

"As far as I knew, it was," Brice said. "When she disappeared like she did, I thought that was a sign. That Sherri and I were getting a chance to start over. That I could make things right with her."

Zee was staring toward the door, watching people drift into the bar.

"Jimmy?" Drue asked. "Colleen never did get on that bus, did she?"

"No," Zee said. "She never did."

He took a long swallow of beer and recounted the night, decades earlier, when Sherri, hysterical and already half drunk, had called him at home to say that she'd killed her husband's lover, and was about to kill herself.

Brice stared, silent and uncomprehending, as his oldest friend told the story.

Zee sipped his beer and put the sunglasses on again.

Drue buried her head against her father's chest and sobbed. When she finally regained her composure, Brice handed her a paper napkin from the dispenser on the table, and she blew her nose.

"You told me you could handle the truth," Zee said apologetically.

"Because I thought, at first, Dad killed her. Then, I was sure it was you. I never dreamed Mom"—she said, sniffling—"Mom was capable of something like that." She fixed her father with an accusing stare. "And you never suspected Colleen was dead? At all?"

"I didn't want to know," he admitted. "For years, I never stopped looking over my shoulder, wondering if one day, Colleen would just show up, and destroy my life for good. She was . . . unbalanced. It's no excuse for what happened, or how I let her down, but looking back, I think now, maybe, she'd be diagnosed as bipolar."

"And that whole big police investigation, where they dragged lakes and consulted psychics and questioned sex offenders, all those years, nobody ever connected the two of you to the disappearance?" Drue asked.

"No," Zee said, shrugging. "Nobody ever even came close. Until you found those newspaper clippings of your mom's. And then the file."

"And what would you have done? If the cops had arrested somebody? An innocent man? What would you have done then?"

"It never came to that," Zee said. "That's why I waited so long to retire. I figured, if I was still a detective, I could do something, if there was eventually a real suspect. And it's why I took the file, when I did leave. I probably should have burned it." He pulled the box closer. "And now I will. Tonight. As soon as I get home. And the whole thing will be done. For good."

"Do you really believe that?" Drue asked. "Have you seen Vera Rennick's blog? It's called *Have You Seen Colleen?* She's determined to solve the case. And she's got a huge following of amateur cold-case detectives."

"Oh God, her," Brice muttered. "That damned woman, stirring things up."

"She can stir things all she wants," Zee said defiantly. "There's no trail. No file. Nothing to connect either of us to Colleen Hicks."

Brice raised his head and stared at his best friend. "Unless they find the body."

"They won't," Zee said. "It's been forty-two years."

Brice clutched his forehead with both hands. "Jesus. I thought this nightmare was over. Honest to God. When I got together with Wendy, I figured, finally. This is happy. No more chasing, no more crazy. I built the law firm, tried to do good, to help people. I'm sixty-eight and we're having a baby. And now this?"

Zee grabbed Brice's elbow. "Calm down, okay? If it ever came to that, you've got a legit alibi. You were nowhere near Sunset Beach that night. You were clear across the bay taking a class in Tampa. Remember?"

"Doesn't matter," Brice said. "I know I didn't kill her, but I look guilty, even to me."

"You're not," Zee said firmly. "Nobody's guilty. Not you, or me or Sherri. It was an accident. She fell and hit her head, and if it ever came to that, which it won't, then I'm the one taking the heat, not you."

Brice's shirt pocket lit up, then buzzed. He took out his phone and read the incoming text. "I gotta go," he announced. "Wendy wants me to pick up Chinese on the way home."

"Go," Zee said, making a shooing motion. "Go take care of your wife and baby. I'll hang here with Drue for a while."

~

Drue gulped her glass of wine and when the waiter came back, ordered another round for both of them.

"So," Zee said. "I can tell, we're not through with the questions, are we?"

"Sorry," she said, but she wasn't, and he knew it too.

"Since we're laying everything on the table tonight, tell me, Jimmy. You and Mom?" She swallowed more wine, for courage. "Did you two get together?"

He avoided looking at her, gazing around the room, up at the huge mounted tarpon on the wall.

"You know, Big Jim, one of the guys who started this bar? He was a helluva fisherman. He took me out tarpon fishing one time, back in the day. Too much like work for me, you know? You can't even eat the damn things."

"About Mom," Drue said gently.

"I'm getting to that," Zee said. "Yeah, I'm not proud of it, but we did have a thing. Your dad was in law school at Stetson, and when he wasn't studying, he was working nights as a security guard for concerts at the Bayfront Center and the Curtis Hixson, over in Tampa. The marriage was in trouble. And by then, Frannie and I were divorced. Sherri was lonely, and I was a shoulder to cry on. We had that shared secret, you know? It only lasted a short while."

"Do you think Dad knows?"

"No," Zee said firmly. "Never. It was over, almost as soon as it started. Your mom got pregnant, and it was the happiest I'd ever seen her."

Drue's eyes widened to the size of saucers. "Hold on. Are you telling me . . . ?"

"No!" he exclaimed. "God no. I swear it. I'll admit, there was a moment there, when she told me, I guess I kind of secretly thought, maybe? But Sherri set me straight. The timing was off. And when you were born, and I saw you? Lucky for you, you're Brice's kid, no ifs, ands or buts."

"No offense, but I'm really glad," Drue said. "I think I've had enough shock for one week."

"None taken," Zee said. He toyed with his sunglasses again. "Hey, did you know I was at the hospital when you were born? In fact, I'm the one who took your mom to the hospital."

"I never knew that."

He placed his hand over his heart. "True story. Brice was in a hearing at the courthouse up in Clearwater, and your mom was at Publix, when her water broke. Your dad had a beeper, but we didn't have cell phones back then. Sherri went to the customer service booth and had them call the station. I'd made detective by then. Dispatch radioed me, and I hauled ass across town with flashers and sirens. Never so scared in my life, that she'd have that baby in the back of my Crown Vic. But we made it to St. Anthony's, and by the time they wheeled her into the delivery room, your dad was right there with her."

Drue smiled. "That's a nice story, Jimmy. I wish I'd known it before."

He started to say something, but shook his head.

"What?" Drue asked. "What else aren't you telling me?"

"It's nothing," Zee said.

"Please tell me," she begged.

He put the sunglasses on again. They were, she realized, his personal invisibility cloak.

"Did you find anything else up in that attic at the cottage?"

"Not really. An old sewing machine, some boxes of baby clothes, my grandmother's photo albums. Mom wasn't really a saver."

"See any luggage up there?" he asked casually.

"As a matter of fact, yeah. I think I did see some old suitcases. Why do you ask?"

He reached into his pocket and placed a crisp fifty-dollar bill on the tabletop. Then he stood up, the cardboard box tucked under one arm.

"You're the detective now," he said. "Check it out. Understand?"

"No," she said. "I don't understand at all."

"You will."

When she got home, she stripped down to her camisole and a pair of shorts and climbed up into the attic. The heat was palpable. She'd brought a flashlight, but there was still enough sun shining in through the west-facing attic window that she easily spotted the stack of luggage.

Nothing interesting, she thought. A graduated set of blue Samsonite suitcases, the heavy old kind nobody wanted anymore because they didn't have wheels. She pulled each case out, snapped the latch and looked inside. Nothing except for satin lining and some dried-up silverfish carcasses. It wasn't until she'd pulled out the biggest suitcase that she spotted it—a cream-colored train case, shoved all the way back into the eaves and covered with a thick coat of dust.

Sweat poured off her face and down her arms. She grabbed the suitcase, sat cross-legged on the rough floorboards and opened the lid. The top was mirrored, and when she saw what was reflected inside, it took her breath away.

Stacks and stacks of banded bills. She lifted a bundle out and saw that there were more bundles beneath. She remembered the yellowing newspaper clippings her mother had squirreled away all those years ago.

Jimmy Zee was wrong. It didn't take a detective to figure this out. She was looking down at the money Colleen Hicks had withdrawn from the bank on the last day of her life. Her running-away money. She rifled the bills, twenties, fifties and hundreds.

"Now what?" she wondered out loud. "What the hell do I do with all this money?"

63

Drue called Jonah from the attic. "I know this sounds crazy, but is there any way you could come out to my house tonight? I promise there won't be any more armed maniacs skulking in the bushes. Oh, and bring your laptop."

"Sure," he said. "I'm leaving right now."

True to his word, the Audi pulled into the drive at Coquina Cottage not quite an hour later.

"Word at the office is that you got a big promotion today," Jonah said. They sat comfortably side by side on the living room sofa.

"Thanks, Geoff," Drue said sarcastically. "I guess Wendy must have assigned him to deal with applicants applying to the online job posting."

"Are you excited about the prospect?" he asked.

"I sort of am," she said. "Scared and nervous, but thrilled that I'll be escaping from that damned cubicle."

"Looks like I might be escaping soon too," he said casually.

"What does that mean?"

"I've had a job offer. Contingent on passing the Florida bar exam later this month. Second time's the charm, right?"

"From who?" she demanded. "I mean, Dad's offered you a job, right?"

"Brice and I have talked," he said. "But there's another offer on the table."

"Tell me it's not those shysters at Secrest, Fuller, Post," Drue said. "I heard they have a mobile legal unit in a converted school bus that actually chases ambulances. You wouldn't go to work for the competition, right?"

"I can neither confirm nor deny," Jonah said. "So let's change the subject. What's this legal matter you can't discuss with your own father?"

"It's complicated. And I don't want to put Dad in a compromising position."

"I, on the other hand, would love to have you put me in a compromising position," he said.

"Maybe later." She removed his hand from her knee, went into her bedroom and brought out the train case, setting it on the coffee table in front of him.

"Open it," she said.

He did as directed, staring down at the stacks of currency. "Is this your way of telling me that your side hustle is drug dealing? Or money laundering?"

"I found this up in the attic," she said, ignoring his attempt at a joke. "It's been hidden up there since 1976. And I'm not sure what to do with it."

He picked up a stack of bills, riffling them like so much Monopoly money. "After eavesdropping on that conversation with your dad the other night, I took the liberty of reading that *Have You Seen Colleen?* blog. I read up on the case too. I have a pretty good idea of where this money might have come from. Does this mean you know what happened to her?"

Drue gulped and nodded. "Yes."

Jonah stood up and walked around the living room. "I respect that Brice is your dad, but Drue, if he killed her . . ."

"He didn't," she said quickly. "And neither did Zee. All I can tell you is that I found this money."

"Let me guess. There's seven thousand dollars."

"Yes. More or less."

"Now I see why you can't talk to Brice about this."

"Colleen has no family left, just in case you were going to suggest that. Her parents died in 1980. She was an only child, and she and her husband never had children. Allen Hicks remarried two more times, and he never had children either. Besides," she said. "Everyone who ever knew Allen Hicks agrees that he was a bad, evil person."

Jonah riffled the bills again. "I'd say this money would be evidence in a criminal matter."

"Which means, if I turned it in to the police, they'd ask me a lot of questions about how it got up there in my attic. They might even come over here and dig up my yard or something."

"That's a possibility," Jonah agreed.

"If I give this money to the police, they'll keep it," Drue said.

"Yes. I think that's true. It would probably go into their general fund," Jonah said.

He gave her a curious look. "You're not thinking of keeping it or spending it, right?"

"No. But what if I wanted to give it away?"

"Like, to a charity?"

"In a manner of speaking, yes. But this charity isn't an organization. It's just a needy, deserving individual. And I would do it anonymously."

He nodded. "I guess that would work."

"I'd need some technical assistance," she said.

"Is that why you asked me to bring my laptop?"

"Yeah. Do you mind?"

They spent the rest of the evening poring over online listings. Jonah checked Blue Book values and Drue emailed potential sellers.

Drue poked the train case with her bare toe. "Do you think the cash will be a problem?"

He picked up a banded stack of cash. "These aren't new bills, and as far as I can tell from what I've read about the case, the bank didn't keep records of the circulation numbers of the cash Colleen withdrew. All the sellers I contacted are more than happy to accept cash."

"Good." She leaned over and closed the lid of his computer. "We missed the sunset. But do you feel like a walk on the beach anyway?"

"Only if you promise to let me carry the Mace this time," he said.

~

They strolled down to the water's edge and Jonah slipped his arm around her shoulder.

"This view never gets old," Drue told him, kicking at a wavelet with her pointed toes. "And you know the funny thing? When I was kiteboarding, I never really paid attention to it. I loved being on the water, and I really, really loved doing tricks and flying, but the water and the wind? They were just there. Part of the equipment, like my board and my harness and my kite. Being grounded with this stinking knee injury has made me really stop and appreciate all of this."

"Do you miss it?" he asked.

"Yeah. Sometimes. It was my passion for so long, from the time I was fourteen and started working at a skateboard shop and then a surf shop on weekends to get money for lessons, right up until my accident. I built my life around kiteboarding. And it never occurred to me that it could be taken away from me in a split second."

"If your knee gets rehabbed, would you go back to that life?"

"Right now? I'm not sure. I still have nightmares, sometimes, where I'm falling, and I can't release my harness, and the kite is dragging me through the water and I'm drowning."

"Really? I can't imagine a badass like you being afraid of anything. Especially not after the way you got the jump on Ben two nights ago."

"I'm afraid of lots of things," Drue admitted. "I just hide it better than most people."

"Like what?"

"Spiders. Fire. Anchovies." Her tone turned unexpectedly serious and she reached for his hand. "Dying alone, like my mom."

"You weren't with her when she died?"

Drue shrugged. "Physically, yeah I was right there in the room with her. But my mom wasn't your typical mother. I always knew she loved me, but she was very closed-off, emotionally. She had boyfriends, over the years, after she and my dad split, but nothing was permanent. I think that was by design."

A breeze kicked up then, ruffling her hair, and she felt goose bumps raise on her arms.

"Let's walk," she said.

He took her hand and they strolled past the lights of Sharky's and the Gulf Vista, without comment.

They were almost back to the cottage, and Jonah stopped, taking in the view of it from the beach. They'd left the lights on inside.

"It looks so peaceful from here, it's weird to think about everything that happened here two nights ago," Jonah said.

He kissed the top of her head. "I'm guessing you must have had that talk with your dad? About Colleen?"

"Yeah. I met him and Zee for drinks at Mastry's, after work."

"How'd it go? Pretty awkward?"

"Very awkward. And painful." She swallowed the unexpected lump that rose in her throat.

"If you ever want to talk about it, I'm willing to listen," he told her.

"I know you are," Drue said gratefully. "I don't want to be like my mom," Drue said, looking directly at him. "Or my dad, when it comes to that. Okay?"

"Okay," he said. "Understood."

Jonah insisted on entering the cottage ahead of her, to, as he put it, "run reconnaissance."

"No bad guys," he reported, after searching all the rooms, including both closets.

He gathered up his laptop and headed for the door.

"Where do you think you're going?" Drue asked, hands on hips.

"Home?"

"What about that do-over you promised me?" she asked.

He raised one eyebrow. "On a school night? You are a naughty girl."

Later, naked and tangled up in sweat-dampened sheets, Jonah got out of bed and propped the fan up on the dresser.

"My apartment is tiny and crappy and the only view is of the next-door neighbor's roof," he said, spooning his body next to hers, "and I never thought I'd say this, but I also never thought I'd miss air-conditioning as much as I do right now."

"You get used to it," Drue said.

He kissed her bare shoulder.

"I certainly hope to."

64

On the next sunny Saturday morning, Rae Hernandez stood on her doorstep, her hand resting lightly on Aliyah Mayes's shoulder. The girl was dressed in a purple print two-piece swimsuit, staring up at her through a pair of neon-green swim goggles.

"Surprise!" the detective said.

"Um, hi," Drue said. She leaned down and smiled at Aliyah. "Hi, Aliyah. What's going on?"

Aliyah beamed. "Miss Rae bought me swimming glasses."

Drue looked up at Hernandez. "Seriously, what is going on?"

"You promised to teach her how to swim so she could be a mermaid, right?"

"Is this a joke?" Drue opened the door wider. "Come on in,

honey," she said cheerfully. "Why don't you go sit down in the living room while I have a word with Miss Rae."

Aliyah looked up at the detective, seeking her approval.

"Go ahead," Hernandez told the child. "It's all right. I checked. Miss Drue doesn't have a criminal record."

Drue waited until the girl was out of earshot. "Are you serious? I have plans for today. You can't just drop a kid off like this. Does Yvonne know you're doing this?"

"It was Yvonne's idea," Hernandez said. "She got called in to work at the hospital today, so I said I'd help out. Aliyah has been driving her crazy, asking when she was going to have her swim lesson. Today seemed like as good a day as any."

"You couldn't call first and check with me? What if I had company? What if I hadn't been home? Would you just leave her on my doorstep?"

"Of course not," Hernandez said. "I didn't call first because I figured if I did, you'd find an excuse to be someplace else. And I knew you were home, because I had one of our patrol officers drive by fifteen minutes ago."

"No," Drue said. "Today is absolutely not a good day. I said I would teach her to swim, and I will, but . . ."

"No buts," Hernandez said cheerfully. "I've got some paperwork to do at the office, so I'll check back with you in, what—two hours? That's enough time for a first swim lesson, right?"

"Don't do this to me, Hernandez, please?" Drue said, looking over her shoulder into the living room, where Aliyah sat patiently on the sofa, staring out at the beach. "I don't know anything about kids. Or teaching. Or teaching kids to swim. What if something happens to her?"

"You'll be fine," Hernandez said. "Just don't let her drown, okay?"

"Okay," Drue said. She'd changed into her swimsuit. Now they stood at the water's edge, Aliyah's hand clutched tightly in hers. "Let's do this! Let's wade into the water."

The girl looked up with saucer-size eyes. "You won't let go?"

"No," Drue said solemnly. "I will not let go."

When the child was ankle-deep in the water she looked up at Drue.

"I don't like it."

Drue sat down in the sand, letting the gentle waves wash over her. "What don't you like, sweetie? The water's nice and warm. Here, sit down beside me. I'll hold your hand. Okay?"

"It's touching me!" Aliyah screeched. "Something touched my foot!" She wrenched her hand from Drue's and ran all the way to the safety of the dunes.

Drue filled the bathtub with warm water and coaxed Aliyah to climb in. "See? There's nothing in the bathtub. No shells, no minnows, no seaweed. It's just like your bathtub at home."

"My bathtub's white," Aliyah said.

"But pink is even nicer, right? Okay, put your goggles on again. And then, I want you to stretch out on your tummy. Can you do that?"

The girl nodded and looked up. "Now what do I do?"

Drue was wondering the same thing. She couldn't remember a time when she didn't know how to swim. After puzzling over it for a moment, she decided to plunge ahead.

"I want you to take a deep breath. And then, I want you to put your face in the water, and blow bubbles. Can you do that? Like this?"

"*Bbbbbb,*" Drue said, pursing her lips and blowing out. "Like that."

Aliyah obediently ducked her head underwater, but came up seconds later, sputtering and gasping.

"No, no, don't suck the water in," Drue said, laughing. "Blow it out. Like I showed you. Big breath in, then put your face in the water and blow out. *Bbbbbb.* This time, I'm going to count to five. When I say five, lift up your head and take a breath."

After five more minutes of bubble blowing, Aliyah looked up expectantly. "Now what?"

Drue was ready. "Now we float! Like a jellyfish! I want you to let your arms and legs just relax in the water. Can you put your face down and do that? Let everything relax? And remember, blow your bubbles while you're doing that, to the count of five."

Without further prompting, the little girl did as instructed. Drue counted down, and Aliyah raised her head triumphantly, water streaming from her face. "I did it! I floated like a jellyfish!"

"You are the best jellyfish ever," Drue assured her.

"When do I get to be a mermaid?"

"Very soon. Next, I want you to fly in the water," Drue said.

"I never saw mermaids fly," Aliyah said.

"It's just an expression. So, I want you to scooch all the way down to the other end of the tub, and this time, when you're doing your jellyfish, I want you to use your feet to push off from the end of that tub, and fly to the other end of the tub. Can you do that? Remember, face in water, blow bubbles, let your arms and legs relax, and then *jet* to the end."

Aliyah jetted back and forth for the next ten minutes, giggling hysterically as she sent great waves of bathwater sloshing over the edge of the tub.

"Okay, I think you've got bubbles and floating and jetting down pat," Drue said, drying her off with a beach towel.

"What next?"

Drue stood up and winced as her bad knee protested.

"We really have to get you in deeper water to get you swimming," she said. "Do you feel like going back down to the beach again?"

Tears brimmed in the child's big dark eyes. "Do I have to? I'm afraid."

Drue sat down on the edge of the tub and hugged the child against her. "No. You absolutely don't have to. But you know, mermaids are rarely found in bathtubs. Even pink tubs like mine. Mermaids swim in the ocean, right?"

Aliyah nodded solemnly.

"For your next lesson, I'll show you how to stroke with your arms, and kick with your feet," Drue said. "But in deeper water. Okay?"

"How much deeper?"

"It won't matter how deep," Drue said. "Because your body just naturally floats. It's okay to be afraid at first, but then, after a little bit, I'll let go of your hand, and the next thing you know, you'll be in the water and you'll be swimming like a mermaid."

"Okay," Aliyah said.

"Are you hungry?" Drue asked. "Do you happen to like peanut butter and jelly sandwiches as much as I do?"

"I only like strawberry jelly," Aliyah said. "And chunky peanut butter."

"Me too!" Drue exclaimed. "Let's eat!"

They had lunch on the deck, eating off paper plates and enjoying the stiff breeze coming off the beach.

"Look!" Aliyah said, pointing at a billowing orange and green kite floating through the sky just past the treeline. "What's that?"

"Let's go see," Drue said.

They walked hand in hand down to the beach. A sun-browned teenage girl stood with her back to the wind, both hands grasping the control bar of a trainer kite. Her long blond hair streamed out behind her as she walked down the beach, and the kite swooped and dipped and fluttered at a forty-five-degree angle over the waves as the girl expertly turned the bar.

Except for the girl's blond hair, Drue thought, that could have been her, twenty years ago.

"What's she doing?" Aliyah asked.

"She's learning how to fly with that kite. And she's pretty good already."

Aliyah looked up at her. "Do you know how to fly like that?"

"I used to," Drue said. "A long time ago."

"Why did you stop?"

Drue gazed down at her knee. There was no swelling today, and the incision was no longer an angry red.

"I hurt myself, and then I was too afraid."

"Are you still afraid?" Aliyah asked.

Drue thought about the spare bedroom in the cottage, and the door she thought she had so firmly closed on her past.

"A little bit," she said. "But I think I'm getting over it."

65

She'd called ahead to tell Yvonne that a courier from the law firm would be dropping off some legal papers on Saturday morning. "Will you be home then?" Drue asked.

"Ain't got no place else to be," Yvonne said.

Drue followed Jonah to Yvonne's house in his Audi, and he was at the wheel of the ten-year-old Acura, which they'd washed and vacuumed and waxed until it sparkled like it was new.

She waited in the Audi while Jonah got out and knocked on Yvonne's screened door.

The rusted-out Plymouth was in the same place it had been on her last visit. The hood was still raised, and the same two tires were still missing.

When the grandmother appeared in the doorway, Drue sank as far down in the seat as she could. After a moment's discussion, Yvonne came out onto the front stoop. Jonah handed her the keys, then pointed at the gleaming silver Acura.

Yvonne's hands flew up to her face and she screeched something unintelligible. Then the screen door flew open. Aliyah walked slowly over to the car, her face enveloped in a wide, blissful smile, followed by her grandmother.

Yvonne ran her hands over the hood and and then the doors and the trunk of the car, exclaiming so loudly that the neighbors across the street emerged from their homes to see what all the fuss was about.

Jonah made a dash for the Audi, and before Yvonne had time to react or ask questions, Drue had already driven away and was halfway down the block.

"That was fun," Jonah said. "We should give away cars bought with ill-gotten gains every week."

"What was Yvonne hollering?" Drue asked. "She was so excited, I couldn't quite make it out."

"'God is good,'" Jonah said. "I bet she said that a dozen times."

After they got back to the cottage, Jonah suggested lunch at Sharky's.

"Really?" Drue wrinkled her nose. "The food's not even that good."

"That's not the point," he said. "Sharky's is our place now. The place where it all began. Just humor me, okay?"

They ate mediocre grouper sandwiches and were about to

walk back to the cottage when they noticed a crowd gathering a few hundred yards up the beach at the Gulf Vista.

"Wonder what's going on?" Drue asked.

"I know," Jonah said. "Today's the day they start demolition of the original wing of the hotel, to make way for the new spa. Let's go watch."

"Why?"

"It's the little kid in me," Jonah said. "I love that stuff. Dump trucks and backhoes and excavators." He tugged at her hand. "Come on."

She reluctantly followed him up to the point where the beach ended and the resort's property line began. The crowd had swelled to nearly a hundred people, and the gate had temporarily been replaced with orange plastic construction netting and DANGER—KEEP OFF signs.

The glass in all the windows of the now-vacant building had already been knocked out, leaving gaping holes in the façade that resembled rotted-out teeth. A backhoe's claw chewed into the top of the concrete structure and the roof collapsed inward.

"Cool," Jonah said, awestruck.

Another backhoe on the south side of the building was busily ripping into the concrete foundation of what had been a three-story parking garage. With each bite into the building, the claw swivelled around and deposited a load of debris into the bed of one of a line of half a dozen dump trucks.

"Why are they digging a hole there?" Drue asked.

"I saw a rendering of the plans for the new spa in the paper," Jonah said. "I think there's going to be a new indoor pool there that'll be connected by a wall of glass to a pool on the other side."

His eyes were glued to the proceedings. "I always thought if I couldn't be a lawyer, I would love to be a heavy equipment operator," he said. "I don't care what you say, that's artistry, when you operate a machine like that."

"Bulldozer ballet," she muttered.

"Exactly."

The sun beat down on her neck, and she was growing bored with the proceedings. "Can we go now?" she asked.

"In another minute," he said, still mesmerized. As they watched, the backhoe clawed deep into the growing pit. A hard-hatted construction foreman in a yellow safety vest blew a whistle and at his direction, the driver of the first dump truck drove away.

The second dump truck driver pulled forward, but before he'd moved into position, the backhoe operator miscalculated and prematurely released the claw. Debris rained down over the bed of the dump truck and onto the ground.

The construction foreman stepped forward, looked at something on the ground and blew his whistle, wildly signaling for the backhoe driver to stop. The foreman blew the whistle again and again. The backhoe operator clambered down out of his cab, and joined the foreman at the bed of the dump truck.

"What's going on?" Drue asked. "What are they looking at?"

"Let's see," Jonah said, shouldering through the crowd of rubberneckers, who were also moving closer.

A woman screamed then, and pointed at the ground, where

a human skull balanced daintily atop a pile of jagged concrete and rebar.

Drue clutched Jonah's hand. "You've been following all the stories about this new spa. Did you read anything about when the first phase of the hotel was built?"

"It wasn't originally called the Gulf Vista. When it was built in seventy-six, it was called something else. Maybe the Treasure Chest? Why?"

She turned and walked as fast as she could, away from the construction site.

"What is it?" Jonah asked, catching up. "What's wrong?"

"I think," she said, "we've just seen Colleen."

Epilogue

April 2019

The late-afternoon sun hung low on the horizon above the sparkling expanse of blue-green sea. Drue sat beneath the shade of the beach tent the men had set up earlier in the day, watching the breeze ruffle the tent canopy.

"Miss Drue, Miss Drue," Aliyah called, racing up to Drue's chair.

"Shhh," Drue cautioned, nodding at the infant carrier where her baby brother slumbered. "You'll wake up Liam."

Aliyah bent down and studied the drowsing child, who sucked contentedly on a Tiffany mother-of-pearl and silver-tipped pacifier, his perfect rosebud lips curved upward.

"He's smiling," she reported, looking up at the baby's mother. "How come he's smiling like that when he's asleep?"

"He's a happy little guy," Wendy explained. "He usually only cries when he's wet or hungry. And he always smiles like that when he's asleep. I think it means he's dreaming about something nice."

"Like ice cream," Aliyah said.

"Or a big juicy steak," Corey suggested.

"Or puppies," Jonah added, as he joined the group gathered under the shade of the tent.

"Or seven-figure insurance settlements," Brice said. He plopped down onto the chair beside Wendy's and handed her a cold drink.

"Eight-figure," Wendy corrected him. "We've got college to fund now, remember?"

"Miss Drue," Aliyah said in a stage whisper. "I want to show you something I can do."

"All right," Drue said, holding out a hand to Jonah, who helped her to her feet.

"But I need Mr. Jonah too," Aliyah said. She reached into a beach bag and brought out her neon-green swim goggles, fastening them over her new eyeglasses.

The three of them trooped down to the water's edge and Aliyah waded in without hesitation.

"Watch this," she said, turning her back to an incoming wave, then diving headfirst into the crest and allowing the wave to carry her into the shallow water.

"You're body surfing," Drue said. "That's great. Pretty soon we'll have to get you a wakeboard."

"Okay, but I really want one of those," Aliyah said, turning to point at the same teenage kiteboarder who'd seemingly staked out this part of the beach over the past year. As they watched, the kite soared into the air, and she and her board skimmed over the surface of the water, the girl's face etched with glee.

"Soon," Drue promised. "First, why don't you show me your new trick?"

Aliyah turned and pointed at Jonah. "Okay, but I need a diving platform."

Jonah groaned good-naturedly and sank down into the water to allow the girl to clamber onto his back, and then stand on his shoulders.

He raised his hands and Aliyah clutched them in hers, one foot on each of his broad shoulders.

"Ready?" he asked.

"Ready!"

"One, two, three!" Jonah called, and Aliyah pointed her toes and gracefully dove, her body slicing into the water with an almost imperceptible splash.

"Amazing," Drue cried, clapping her hands in approval when the girl resurfaced a few yards away.

"I can hold my breath for a really long time now," Aliyah bragged. "And when I'm under the water, I open my eyes and I look at the little fish, and I'm not one bit afraid."

"Just like a mermaid," Drue said. "But with goggles."

Aliyah paddled back to where Jonah stood in the waist-deep water.

"Again?" He rolled his eyes and let his body sag in feigned exhaustion.

"Again! But this time let's do the really cool new trick you showed me."

Aliyah climbed onto Jonah's shoulders and stood, perfectly balanced, her arms wide-stretched.

"Ready?" Jonah called.

"Ready!"

He grasped each of her feet with his hands and pushed her off, launching her high into the air as Aliyah screamed with pure joy.

She swam back and looked up at Jonah, water streaming from her face.

"Again?" she said hopefully.

"Again," Jonah said.

The aroma of charcoal smoke and roasting meat wafted down from the direction of the deck. Corey walked down to the seaweed line, cupped his hands and yelled.

"Come on, you two. Steaks are almost ready."

"Ten more minutes," Drue called back. "Tell Wendy I'll toss the salad when I come up."

The tent and the rest of the beach gear and the still-slumbering baby had been packed and hauled back to the cottage. All that was left were the two folding beach chairs Drue had excavated so many months ago from Papi's shed.

Drue walked down to the edge of the water, where Jonah was waiting, cell phone in hand.

The sun hovered inches from the horizon, a fiery orange orb in the deepening violet sky.

She shaded her eyes with her hands, anxiously looking up the beach.

"He might not show up tonight," she fretted. "I think some people up the beach are feeding him."

Jonah put his arm around her waist and kissed her neck. "If he doesn't show up tonight, no worries. There'll be lots of other sunsets." He kissed her again, and she sagged comfortably against him. "Hundreds and hundreds of gorgeous sunsets. And we'll watch them together. Right here."

A V-shaped formation of pelicans flew past then, their dark shapes silhouetted against the dusky sky.

Jonah raised the phone and clicked off a series of photos.

"You know? I think we might see the green flash tonight," Drue said. The sun had dipped so low on the horizon the only thing still visible was a faint orange streak.

"Hey, look." Jonah turned and pointed. He handed the phone to her. The blue-gray bird approached, neck outstretched, eyes trained down on the water, balancing delicately on sticklike legs.

Drue held her breath, waiting, as the heron finally stood poised in front of her. The bird lifted his head, turned and seemed to be staring directly into her camera. She clicked the shutter only once, and put the phone down.

A brilliant phosphorescent burst of green slashed across the horizon and was gone. "There it is," Jonah said. "A perfect sunset."

"The first of thousands. Tens of thousands of sunsets," Drue murmured. The heron startled, unfolded his wings and flew off.

"They'll all be perfect to me," Jonah said.

Drue swung around and faced Coquina Cottage, lit up against the night sky. "Let's go home," she said.

Read on for an excerpt from

HELLO, SUMMER

by Mary Kay Andrews

1

1

I hate these things," Conley Hawkins said, gazing toward the newsroom's glass-encased conference room, where the rest of the staff were gathering. "Stale sheet cake, lukewarm champagne, and tepid farewells. It's such a farce. At least a third of the people in that room don't even like me. I've said goodbye to the people I care about. Can't we just leave it at that?"

She'd almost succeeded in making a clean break, only feet away from the elevator, when Butch caught her trying to sneak out. "You can't skip your own going-away party," he'd said. "Everybody's waiting. You'll look like an ingrate if you try to duck out."

Before she could argue, he'd deftly taken the cardboard box she'd just finished packing and placed it on her desktop.

Her *former* desk in the fourth-floor newsroom at *The Atlanta Journal-Constitution,* her home away from home for the past four years.

"It's actually more like two-thirds of the people in the room who detest you," Butch pointed out, steering her toward the conference room. "Nothing personal. Call it professional jealousy. Well, except for Rattigan. Nothing professional about his feelings, right?"

Butch Culpepper wasn't just some dude who'd sat at the desk right next to hers for the past three years. He was her social conscience and self-appointed office husband and, therefore, privy to most of her secrets.

She winced at the mention of Kevin Rattigan. "Don't."

He raised an eyebrow. "Too soon?"

"I really didn't think he'd take it so personally," she protested. "We weren't even all that serious."

"You were living together," Butch pointed out. "Most women I know would call that serious."

"It was only for six weeks, and I only let him move in because he couldn't afford a two-bedroom after his roommate got transferred to Miami."

By now, they were standing right outside the open doorway of the conference room, and Roger Sistrunk, her assignment editor, was waving her inside.

"Hawkins! Get your ass in here! You might not have anything better to do, but some of us still have a paper to get out today."

"Oh God," she mumbled.

And then the champagne corks were popping, and she was being presented with the signed caricature from the paper's political cartoonist, and Roger was making a well-meaning speech about how much she'd be missed, using a rolled-up copy of the Metro section as a makeshift megaphone.

"Attention! Attention, please," he called. "Okay, well, somehow, our esteemed colleague Conley Hawkins managed to scam these pinheads in D.C. into offering her a job making twice as much money for half as much work," Sistrunk began. His bald head gleamed under the fluorescent lights.

Light laughter and a few catcalls. She smiled weakly, and despite herself, her eyes sought out Kevin, who was standing, stony-faced, in a far corner of the room. His wheat-colored bangs flopped over his glasses, and her fingers itched to push the hair back, clean the smudges from the glasses, and whisper a smutty joke in his ear, just to watch the bright pink flush spread over his pale freckled face. He caught her staring and quickly looked away.

Butch pressed a paper cup into her hand, and she drained the champagne in two gulps.

She didn't catch the rest of what Roger was saying. Tiana Baggett approached and flung an arm over her shoulder and leaned her head against Conley's. "Gonna miss you, girlfriend," she said, sniffling loudly. "I can't believe you're really gonna go and leave me behind. Who's gonna watch scary slasher movies with me now? Who's gonna rewrite my ledes?"

Aside from Butch, Tiana, the Metro section's police beat reporter, was her best friend on staff.

"Come on, Tia. Don't do this to me," Conley begged. "Look, you know as soon as I hear about an opening up there, I'll put your name in the hat."

Tiana sniffed again, extended her arm, and attempted to take a selfie with her smartphone. "Aw, damn," she said, shaking it. "I've got no juice. Gimme your phone."

Conley pulled her phone from her pocket, extended her arm,

and clicked off three quick frames. As she was shoving it back in the pocket of her jeans, she heard the distinctive bicycle bell ringtone alerting her to an incoming text message.

Tiana looked down. "Who's the text from? Kevin?" She looked hopefully across the room. She was the one who'd set them up and who'd accused Conley, more than once, of being heartless since the breakup.

"No." Conley shook her head. "He won't even look me in the eye. It's actually from my sister."

"Grayson? The one you think can't stand you?"

"I don't think it, I know it. Wonder where she got my phone number?" The text had a link to a Bloomberg wire story. She tapped the link and read the first paragraph.

Intelligentsia, the trailblazing online investigative news service, announced today that it will suspend publication immediately, citing the failure of a recent round of venture capital financing.

Conley stared down at the sentence, her brain and tongue temporarily frozen. Beads of sweat popped out on her forehead.

"What's wrong? Did somebody die?"

Conley handed her the phone.

"Jesus Hopscotching Christ," Tiana muttered. "Is this your sister's idea of a joke?"

"Grayson is incapable of joking," Conley said. "She lacks a humor chromosome."

"You think it's true?" Tiana asked. "About *Intelligentsia*? I mean, if it were true, you would have heard something, right? Maybe it's just a rumor."

"Maybe."

"You should call that guy, the editor, what's his name?"

"Fred Ward." She pulled up the list of recent callers, but there was nothing from Fred Ward, nor were there any calls with a D.C. prefix.

"Conley! You need to cut the damn cake!" called one of the sportswriters.

"Yeah," another voice chimed in. "Let's get this party started. I got a story to file."

She looked up. So many faces watching hers. She swallowed hard, fighting back against a wave of nausea swelling up from her gut, the champagne sour in her mouth.

"Just do it," Tiana whispered.

Roger was holding out the pica pole, which was tied with a faded red ribbon. The pica pole was a quaint relic from another era, from the Marietta Street days, back when newspapers were physically laid out on drafting tables in the downtown composing room, instead of digitally designed in this gleaming smoked-glass box in a suburban office park.

Conley took the stiff aluminum ruler and made a horizontal slash through the gooey white frosting, then another vertical slash, dividing the cake into quadrants. She handed the pole back to her editor. "You do the rest," she said, forcing a smile. "I can't eat cake. I'm gluten-free."

His dark eyes studied her. "Since when?"

"Give me a break," she said quietly. "Something's come up. Please?"

"Okay, but see me before you take off. And I mean it."

While the staff clustered around the table, helping themselves to slices of cake and more champagne, she walked down to the ladies' room on the third floor. She locked herself into a stall and reread the story. *Suspended publication.* What did that mean?

She found Fred Ward's name in her list of contacts and tapped his number.

The phone rang once before clicking over to his voice mail. His deep, sonorous voice oozed from the phone like an amber stream of cane syrup. "This is Fred Ward, managing editor at *Intelligentsia.* I can't come to the phone right now cuz I'm fixin' to put the paper to bed. Leave me a message, and I'll eventually get back to you."

"Fred?" She tried not to sound too panicky. "Hey. It's Conley Hawkins down in Atlanta." She gave a shaky laugh. "I just saw the craziest item on the Bloomberg wire, saying you guys are shutting down. Call me, okay?"

She disconnected and waited five minutes. She walked slowly up the stairs to her now-stripped cubicle. The space, in the back row of the newsroom, facing a bank of windows looking out on the continually under-construction interstate, had been home for the past four and a half years. Now, though, her stuff—the books, clip files, the stained coffee mug, even the dozens of lanyards with laminated press credentials from events she'd covered over the years . . . in short, the detritus of a career—was all packed in cardboard cartons stacked in the backseat of her Subaru.

This day, the one she'd been anticipating since the thrilling

email from Fred Ward—subject line: "When can you start?"—
had finally arrived. Sarah Conley Hawkins was ready to leave
The AJC and Atlanta in the rearview mirror. The question was,
where would she be going?

"Hawkins?"

Roger sat down in Butch's vacant chair. He frowned, his
rubbery face arranged in jowly folds, speckled with the gray of
his five-o'clock shadow. "What's up?"

"Nothing." She shrugged. "I suck at goodbyes. Guess I'm
gonna miss all you assholes after all."

"Try again."

She sighed and showed him the text message from her sister.

He looked up, his wire-rimmed bifocals sliding to the end
of his nose. "I take it this is the first you've heard?"

Conley nodded.

He reread the text message. "This is your sister who runs
your family's newspaper? Back in Florida? I take it the two of
you have some issues?"

"We've got more issues than *The New Yorker*," she said, sighing. "This is Grayson's way of saying, 'Nonny nonny boo boo.'"

"And you've called that character who hired you away? Fred
Ward?"

"The call went directly to voice mail."

He swiveled around and typed his password into Butch's
computer. He found the Web browser, typed in "Intelligentsia," and a moment later, he was shaking his head.

"According to *The Wall Street Journal,* it's a done deal. Their
lead investor was some hedge fund genius who decided new
media was too risky." He grimaced. "The publisher pulled the

plug last night. A hundred twenty people showed up for work in Bethesda this morning and found the place shuttered."

Conley stared out the window, past the construction cranes and high-rises. Traffic was already backed up on I-285. It was four o'clock. She'd planned to be on the road by now. Headed for D.C.

"Hawkins?" His hand, surprisingly small and delicate for such a burly, bearlike man, rested gently on her forearm. "I'm sorry." He pushed the glasses back up his nose. "You know I'd do anything for you. I fought like hell to try to match their offer, but the money's just not there. You know what our budget's like."

She nodded. "And you've already hired my replacement. I know that, Roger."

"I could make some phone calls. Since you won the Polk Award, your name's a commodity. Epstein's at the *LA Times* now. He's not a bad guy, and he owes me big-time. Charlene's kicking ass in Miami, and she always liked you. I bet she could put in a good word."

"Yeah," Conley said, pushing herself up from the desk. She grabbed the last cardboard box. "That would be great, thanks."

They both knew the reality. The world of print journalism was shrinking. Every newspaper in the country was cutting back, laying off reporters, tightening belts. Once-thriving major metro papers were either shutting down or going to digital only. Epstein was lucky to have a job in LA, and Charlene had gone from assistant managing editor at *The AJC* to beat reporter in Miami with zero say in new hires.

"What are your plans?" Roger asked. "You got a place to land while you figure things out?"

"Oh yeah," she lied. "My lease isn't up until the end of the month."

"Good," he said, relieved. "That's good. I'll walk you out, okay?"

"Not necessary. But could you do me a favor?"

"Anything."

"Just, uh, keep the *Intelligentsia* thing to yourself, for now. I mean, people are gonna find out, but I'd just as soon not be the object of pity until I'm actually out of the building."

"You got it."

She was standing in front of the elevator when he hurried over.

"Hey, uh, I almost forgot. HR sent me a memo reminding me that you're supposed to turn in your ID badge."

The lie rolled easily off her tongue. "I don't have it, Roger. I think I packed it yesterday."

"How'd you get in the building this morning?"

"Butch and I met for breakfast before work. He badged me in. I'll mail it back to you. Okay?"

"Whatever."

It looked as though he was going to hug her. Mercifully, the elevator doors slid open, and she hopped inside, punched the down button, and nodded goodbye.

She'd just merged onto I-85 southbound when her phone rang. She could see the caller ID screen. Butch. He'd keep calling until she answered.

"Sneaky bitch," he said. "I thought we had a dinner date."

"Roger found the *Wall Street Journal* story online. It's all true. Sorry. I had to get out of there before word started to spread."

"Where are you now?"

"Headed home."

"I thought Kevin took over the Seventh Street lease. Isn't that going to be awkward?"

"Not home to Midtown. Home, home."

"You mean, like, Lickskillet, Florida?"

"It's Silver Bay. Sweet Home, Florida."

"Seriously? Is that really necessary?"

"Afraid so," she said. "Where else could I go? Tiana's place is the size of a shoebox, and anyway, I'm allergic to her cats."

"I have a perfectly nice sofa, no cats, and premium cable," he said.

"You also have a brand-new boyfriend," Conley said.

"So that's it? You're disappearing, just like that?"

"Strictly temporary. Roger promised to make some calls for me, and in the meantime, I'll start sending out my résumé and clips. I'll be fine, I promise."

"I guess Florida is better than camping out in a van down by the river," he said, sounding unconvinced.

"Lots better. I'll stay with my grandmother. Her house is a God-honest mansion. She's been begging me to come home for months now."

"You'd better call me as soon as you get there," he said. "What's the name of that town again?"

"Silver Bay."

He sniffed. "Never heard of it."